HEMINGWAY'S
GOBLET

To Sheena

HEMINGWAY'S GOBLET

A NOVEL

DERMOT ROSS

To James

with very best wishes

Dermot

MARY EGAN
PUBLISHING

Published by Mary Egan Publishing
www.maryegan.co.nz

This edition published 2024

© Dermot Ross 2024

The right of Dermot Ross to be identified
as the author of this work in terms of section 96 of the
Copyright Act 1994 is hereby asserted.

Designed, typeset and produced by Mary Egan Publishing
Cover designed by Anna Egan-Reid
Printed in China

ISBN 978-1-7386176-0-9

1

Nick Harrieson had an almost mystical regard for Hampstead Heath. It was his special place, where he would go to be alone to assess major looming decisions, to reflect on life, or just to clear his head. The forest, the lakes and the wide paths that wound through the trees and around the water areas offered a haven, a place of detachment and withdrawal from his daily urban existence. The presence of joggers and picnickers, of noisy children and shuffling pensioners heightened his feeling that the heath was unique, an island *in* London but not *of* London.

Emerging from the Tube station into the late afternoon, early summer sunshine, with the mellow sounds of the Cure filling his ears from his iPod earphones, Nick reflected that it had been years since his last visit to the heath. Almost ten years, to be precise.

Laura, his wife, had greeted him one day after he came home from work and said she wanted him to leave home. The children were staying with Laura's sister's family that night. She had insisted he sit down in the drawing room, then made her announcement, adding, 'I'm sorry, Nick, but I've had enough. I can't put up with it, or with you, these days. You've gone cold, you've withdrawn from me, and from the family too. You hardly show me affection anymore, you rarely want to make love to me, and when you do it's not like before. You're often out late boozing with your law friends, leaving me with the children. You've lost your spark. It's as though you've been punishing me for some reason. The kids notice it,' she said, her voice breaking. 'They've mentioned it a few times.'

Nick was bewildered. 'I'm gobsmacked. I had no idea you think those things of me, that you feel so ... miserable.' When Laura looked away, he added, 'I know you've said some of those things before, but I didn't know it had come to this.'

Laura regarded him with an icy expression. 'I've told you many times, but you just don't listen. You'd rather walk the dog than cuddle up next to me on a Sunday morning. And when did you last buy me flowers or give me a gift out of the blue? I can't even remember when that happened. And before you say it, setting the table and mowing the lawn every week or two aren't enough.'

Nick threw up his hands. 'But, darling, I don't want to leave, and I'm hurt that you want me to.' He paused, then said with determination, 'I'll try harder.'

She had accepted his promises, and he did try harder. But not sufficiently hard, and after a few weeks she again insisted that he leave the home. This time, most reluctantly, he agreed.

The day after he told Laura he would move out he went to Hampstead Heath, to try to make sense of what had happened.

It had been a miserable wintry day, the icy wind lancing at his face as he braced himself behind the heath's hills and hedgerows. He'd brought Fifi with him, the poodle loved by everyone in the family. Faithful Fifi ignored the cold and ran off in all directions, kept warm by her tartan coat.

Nick could find no fault with Laura and couldn't blame her – she was loyal and loving, a perfect mother, intelligent and well-informed, a devoted and understanding wife, a wonderful hostess and dinner companion. They presented to the world as a model couple, shining examples of happiness and success. And yet – the biggest 'yet' of all – he admitted that the romance and passion had gone from them, after drifting away bit by bit each year. The heady emotions of their early years, the gloriously frequent sex and the impecunious dates, the thrill of setting up house together, the chaos and joy of raising children – these were all now consigned to memory. Happy memories. Wasn't it said that all marriages turned out like theirs, with romance turning to contented companionship?

The truth, which Nick had acknowledged on the heath that day, was that he was no longer in love with his wife. He respected her, admired her, liked her company and was grateful to her for running the family and the household with assurance and harmony. Yes, he loved her still, yet he couldn't say he was still in love with her.

As he had stood high on Hampstead Heath looking south towards central London he had realised that Laura had been right. He had withdrawn from her. Happy to be married and to be a father, yes, but he hadn't been able – or, more troublingly, willing – to make the effort to ensure that Laura's needs were met. He felt sadness and guilt.

Nick hadn't felt good about the results of his self-analysis, but at least he had known how he felt, and being on the heath had given him a platform to think it all through clearly and with a jarring clarity. Two weeks later he moved into a small flat in Kensington Park Road in Notting Hill, and a few months after that he fell into the seductive arms of Kathy Mulligan.

He climbed to the top of Parliament Hill, his eyes squinting against the sun as he surveyed the couples and families lying on the grass. Boisterous kids were trying to fly kites on the hill.

That all seemed so recent, and yet many years had passed. Thankfully, Laura had made the separation and divorce as amicable and as stress-free as any break-up he had ever seen. She had been, and continued to be, in his eyes admirable in every respect.

Nick was not always inclined to rigorous self-examination

but today some was called for. He didn't feel the need to spend hours with a therapist in an effort to unlock the deficiencies in his emotional make-up. That was all too American for his liking. Now, for the third or fourth time in less than ten years, and twice in the last month, he found himself accused of having some reprehensible qualities, accused by women of high intelligence and integrity – less of the latter in Kathy's case, in his opinion. There was a common core to what these women said about him: he was superficial, unable to commit emotionally, insensitive, self-centred, old-fashioned. Admittedly, they would agree for the most part that he was good company, humorous, often charming, with a healthy interest in sex (although late-stage Laura would disagree with that judgement), and generous financially. But he knew that that wasn't enough. Modern women were entitled to more, it seemed.

Nick had enjoyed reading years ago about women being fundamentally different from men. Venus and Mars, as it was claimed. This was simplistic and populist, but many of his friends, of both sexes, agreed that there was some truth in it. Nick knew of so many women in their thirties and forties, now single but survivors of failed relationships and marriages, who lamented the dire lack of decent men, men who could commit to an equal, monogamous and stimulating relationship. Nick wondered if it was true that all men were genetically wired and as flawed as that. But after further consideration he figured that that was nonsense. Millions of couples had marriages that lasted for life. Tellingly though, most would no doubt agree that one of the secrets of a marriage's success was that you needed to work at it.

Today, having contemplated all this, he felt bruised and despondent, and the sunshine and the calmness of the heath didn't seem to help. He had been dumped two weeks before by a woman who possessed all the qualities Nick was drawn to and admired. He knew now that his lover had been hurt beyond repair. Only the day before she had texted to confirm that there was no hope of reconciliation.

And he'd had a dalliance, an infatuation, with a younger woman with whom he'd had a complex friendship for nearly two years, but on their last day together she too had delivered him a few uncomfortable truths. Nick was distraught, angry at himself and his weakness.

Today, as he strolled on Hampstead Heath's walkways, they were not providing him with the clarity of thought he'd experienced on previous occasions. He couldn't see a way through his glumness and self-loathing. It didn't help to know he couldn't blame anyone but himself.

He walked down Parliament Hill, appreciating the lengthening shadows and the contrasts of the light, and set off for a walk through the nearby woods. From a distance he admired two tall young blonde women who were jogging in front of him. He stopped to watch a French juggler in a striped sailor T-shirt entertain a group of kids and their mothers and au pairs, taking in the innocent, engaging banality of the scene.

He noticed that the juggler had in his bag a French translation of Hemingway's *The Old Man and the Sea*. Ha! thought Nick, you just couldn't get away from the great man. He reached into his pocket and put a five-pound note into the juggler's beret as it was passed around.

He turned away, and after a few minutes' walking, he decided to widen the focus of his thoughts. It wasn't right or fair just to look at his shortcomings; a broader stock-take was in order. He made a mental note of what he called a Life Scorecard, a template of which he had provided on occasion to young students who he mentored as part of the University's staff/student mentoring scheme. He would write down a few headings down the side of a piece of A4 paper: Health, Family Relationships, Academic Progress, Residential Situation, Income, Social Life, Financial Stability, Mental Wellbeing, Hobbies and Relaxation. Sometimes there were other categories of particular relevance to the mentee. He would ask the student to fill out the paper, giving marks out of ten to assess the importance to them of the particular heading and, more importantly, how they saw their score at the moment.

The students told him they found the exercise helpful, and also confronting. More often than not some relevant personal information would be revealed which transformed the subject matter and direction of the mentoring sessions. One student from Yorkshire revealed that he was being bullied by his flatmates because of his accent. Another student told Nick that she worked weekends as an escort to finance her studies and living costs. When the mentoring sessions had run their course all of the students would tell Nick how much they appreciated the exercise.

He'd never applied the scorecard to himself, and in his mind he went through it as he walked through the heath's woods. On the easily measurable things he gave himself high marks – a conservative eight for health, job success, social life, income and financial security, and for his living arrangements. For family life, he gave himself a five. Relations with Laura were still amicable, but he wished he featured more in his children's lives. For his love life he gave himself a zero, conceding that only a couple of weeks earlier he would have awarded himself a nine. For general well-being he thought five would be fitting.

All in all it wasn't a bad tally. Life did have its blips, and they could be buried away for a while in compartments, opened only in times of need. Until recently the last few months had been ones of revelation and pleasure, and there was no reason to believe that the future didn't hold some promise. As a matter of fact there were some potentially very exciting things to look forward to in the coming months.

He walked back toward the village and the Tube station. Dusk was setting in now, and the day's visitors were heading back to their homes. Hampstead Heath hadn't let Nick down after all. He felt upbeat, his gloom of a few hours before forgotten. His ability to isolate the bad from the good was serving him well. *Win some, lose some.* It was time to move on, with optimism. There was no point in indulging in self-pity. He wasn't a bad man. Weak at times, yes, but not dull.

And he wondered about his paternal grandfather, whose life Nick had been delving into. Would he have had marital problems had he survived? His grandfather William had died in World War Two, at an age younger than Nick was now. There could be no answer. No one else could ever know what went on in a couple's relationship.

Nick took his seat on the train, watching other passengers read their Evening Standards. He shifted his thoughts to the issues of the wider world. He despaired over the incompetence and hypocrisy over Brexit from the MPs on both sides of the House. And as for Trump, the so-called leader of the free world, he was a cartoon character of narcissistic malevolence. Things hadn't changed much in those respects over the last year and a half. In fact, it was a little over a year after Trump won the election that his own life had taken a drastic twist. He smiled as he recalled the unexpected visit Peter Hargreaves, his Dean, had made to Nick's office that December evening, and how his life had been turned upside down as a result.

2

'I'm sorry, Nick, but I have to tell you straight up. A complaint has come in that you have sexually harassed one of your students. I have no idea if the claim has any substance, I sincerely hope not, but the University's response is mandatory. You must be stood down for a month while the matter is investigated.'

Nick struggled to take it all in. He had no idea what Dean Hargreaves was talking about. Harassment? He couldn't recall a single incident.

'There must be some mistake,' he said at last. 'I pride myself on treating all my students with respect, and appropriately, without favour. Who doesn't? I'm certain my conduct has been without reproach. You know that as well as I do.' He rubbed his forehead. 'Please tell me who the victim of my harassment is.' His voice was now sarcastic.

'Yes, of course, you've always acted properly. At least to my knowledge,' Peter added. 'But this is different. There are witnesses. The student's name is Adrienne Kim, one of your Master's students.'

'Adrienne? You must be mistaken. I get on very well with her. I'd say she and I have a very … amicable relationship. But definitely a professional one. And what, pray, am I alleged to have done?'

'According to the complaint, at the Faculty / Master's students function last week you made a comment to her – in front of two witnesses – to the effect that you would give her a better mark for her thesis if she'd sleep with you. The witnesses have confirmed the conversation.'

Nick leaned back in his chair. He pressed his hands together on his chest, fingers entwined, and rested his chin on his knuckles. He fixed his gaze on the textbooks in the bookcase opposite his desk, behind where the Dean was standing.

'This is ludicrous. It must be a case of mistaken identity. I know that sounds stupid, but I simply have no recollection of saying anything like that.'

Peter Hargreaves shuffled through some papers he had in a manilla folder. A clump of his grey hair fell over his glasses, which he brushed away. 'Ah, there it is. You said, or at least you are alleged to have said, to Miss Kim in response to a comment from her that she was hoping to get an A for her Master's thesis, "Well, you will have to be extra specially nice to me then".'

The Dean paused. 'You may lose your job over this. It's out of my hands now. The University disciplinary committee will consider the complaint. You will have an opportunity to defend yourself, but if it's upheld then I'm afraid that will be curtains for you.'

Nick had stopped listening. All he could think of was the cocktail function last week. Of course he remembered talking to Adrienne, among others. He had been in top form. Quite witty, with lots of talk of Brexit and Theresa May, and how embarrassing it felt to be British.

Slowly the conversation came back to him. Yes, he had said something like that, but it was a joke, a private one between Adrienne and him.

Now he remembered the two others who were in the same conversation, one on either side of him. A bearded, intense student called Paul Singh, and Kathy Mulligan.

Nick looked up at Peter. 'Do sit down, old man. I realise

this isn't an easy conversation for you. And I know you're just the messenger.' Peter looked relieved but said he would rather stand.

Nick slumped further back in his chair. 'I take it that Kathy was one of these two witnesses?'

'Yes, she was.' Nick knew that the Dean was not enamoured of her either. 'And I know too that she might be said to have her own agenda. But the other witness, Singh, has corroborated the complaint. So I'm afraid that you can't blame Kathy for this. It doesn't look good, Nick.'

No, it didn't look good. There was a simple explanation, but this wasn't the time to mention it. Why would Adrienne want to jeopardise his career over such a casual comment? A joke, even. She liked him, he knew. He liked her too, but he had always made sure that he didn't overstep any mark of propriety.

Silence descended. Peter Hargreaves seemed lost in his own thoughts. Then Nick wearily said that he remained mystified.

'So am I. The funny thing is, the complaint hasn't been made by the girl.' Peter had the habit, now voiced only in private conversations with Nick and a handful of other male lecturers, of referring to women under the age of about forty as girls. 'No, the complaint was made by Kathy Mulligan, and corroborated by Paul Singh. It seems that Miss Kim may have been, shall we say, *encouraged* to join in the complaint. I'm afraid I know little more than that.'

Nick straightened up. He could see it all. This was an opportunistic payback for Kathy, who lectured in family law. Kathy often accused Nick and other male lecturers in the faculty of being sexist and biased, of having had easy rides up the ladder which she, as a woman, had had to work doubly hard for and for only half the rewards and recognition. Everyone agreed she possessed a very sharp intelligence, evidenced by an ability to analyse case judgments and statutes to a forensic degree that was the envy of her colleagues. She had three or four articles published every year in the legal journals, including one the year before in the prestigious *Modern Law Review*, whereas Nick would publish only one every two years or so. He had been made a full professor at thirty-three while Kathy was still only an associate professor at forty-five.

Nick knew she resented him, his popularity and what he thought of as his easy, likeable manner. In a moment of intimacy, almost ten years ago when they had been lovers, she had described him as a rare combination of being a man's man and a woman's man. He wasn't sure it was meant as a compliment, although he took it as one. Nick had reversed the comment, and Kathy had had trouble pigeonholing herself as a man's woman or a woman's one. Truth be told, she was neither. She was not unattractive to men; in addition to her fine brain she had a quick and earthy sense of humour, was tall and shapely, with a symmetrical but angled face and a magnificent head of deep red hair. But there was a hardness to her, a lack of femininity, that it was said a succession of lovers and suitors found unappealing after a while.

Early on, circumstances combined to put a strain on their burgeoning relationship. It came time for the Dean to select which lecturer would take charge of the next academic year's Legal System lectures. This was a year-long course for first-year students, designed to introduce them to many different facets of the law and the judicial system and, also, to encourage them to continue their pursuit of law degrees. All the academic staff knew it was important that the classes were given by lecturers who would engage their students' attention. Lecturers were encouraged to apply to Dean John Maurice-Allen, Peter Hargreaves' predecessor. Nick was busy enough with other subjects, but Maurice-Allen, aware of Nick's reputation with successive cohorts of students, pressured him to apply. Kathy made no secret of her wish to lead the Legal System classes. One or two others applied for the position too.

In the end Nick was chosen, in the opaque way of these things in university circles, and Kathy took it badly. She said she was happy for Nick but complained to him and others that the process had been rigged, that it was jobs for the boys again, and that the faculty was not doing enough to promote women lecturers to the students, the majority of whom were now female. Nick agreed she had a point, but he declined to join her in her protestations to the Dean. While they never discussed it again, Nick always thought that Kathy felt, if not betrayed, let down by his unwillingness to decline the role or at least to add his weight to her complaints to the Dean. In the end Nick made a big success of his Legal System lectures, kick-started by his lecture at the beginning of the course, and the law faculty roll increased over the years. While Nick made a point of offering Kathy a number of guest lectures each year – an offer not accepted again once their affair ended – he sensed that she saw it was only meagre atonement.

Peter jolted him out of his reverie. 'There is a process to be had, Nick, and we are naturally following it. There are several things which I'm obliged to tell you.' He looked again at his papers. 'I've already said that you'll be stood down until the complaints committee has ruled on the matter. That will ordinarily happen within twenty-five or thirty working days. By early-to-mid February, by my calculation. If the University's general counsel believes that there is a case to answer – and I'm afraid there is, no matter how innocent your intentions may have been – then the complaints committee will hold a hearing. You will be given every opportunity to put your case forward, and you have the right to be legally represented. I'd urge you to take legal advice straight away. And don't be the proverbial fool of a client. Get outside advice.'

Peter sighed. 'I've arranged for Darren Tobias to take over your Law of War lectures, starting tomorrow morning. He'll contact you this evening to discuss that. He'll also take over supervising the young woman's thesis. I'll assume your Torts lectures, although I'm a bit out of touch and I hardly need the extra responsibilities. I'll email all faculty staff tonight to say that you're taking a month's leave for personal reasons. Luckily Christmas is almost upon us and people will be rushing around anyway.'

It was now the Dean's turn to look tired. He was a kindly man, Nick knew, whose benevolent face and solicitous manner hid a streak of toughness. Many saw his geniality and low-key personality as weaknesses. Kathy, for one, often criticised him. He was in his mid-sixties, easing his way into a retirement spent gardening in Cornwall. He didn't want anything to upset his life, and Nick knew Peter had to play this situation by the book. A very recently adopted book, which the women on the council had insisted be adopted after the humiliating publicity of a lecturer in the engineering faculty being accused of rape by one of his male students. The lecturer was now in Wormwood Scrubs.

Nick remembered the framed citation on Peter's office wall, partially hidden behind the door. In among the degree awards, and the photos of a fresh-faced and long-haired Peter Hargreaves with Lord Denning (Peter had been a clerk for the great judge in Denning's later years) and Margaret Thatcher, was a framed citation, on Royal Navy parchment, of Peter Hargreaves' bravery in the defence of the Falkland Islands in May 1982. It was signed by the Secretary of State for Defence. Peter always refused to talk about it. 'It was nothing,' he would say, as if it were a commendation for picking up rubbish off the street. All agreed it was hard to equate the mild-mannered Dean of the law faculty with the naval war hero of his youth.

'This hasn't been easy for me, Nick,' he said now. 'I'm sure you'll appreciate that.'

Nick nodded.

'But I'm sure, or at least I hope, there's a simple explanation, and that in a month's time you can bat it away and resume your position. But if you can't ...' Peter Hargreaves paused, and Nick could see sadness creasing his face. 'But if you can't, Nick, then I'm afraid there will likely be no way back, at least at London King's University. Not even your fine career and unblemished reputation will save you then. I am sorry, Crosser, you may be our best lecturer, certainly our best known, but that's how it is.'

Crosser. Crosser Harrieson, he was known as. The nickname had come early in his career. At Cambridge he had tried the *Times* cryptic crossword and occasionally managed to complete it. For several years afterwards, until he decided doing crosswords was a waste of time, he would look forward to testing his mental agility by doing the daily puzzle. When Peter Hargreaves persuaded him to leave his City law-firm job and become a junior lecturer at London King's he decided to spice things up for the students by constructing an elaborate crossword, using legal words and expressions from his lecture and, by means of an overhead projector, beaming the results on to the whiteboard at the front of the class.

He remembered his first lecture, when he was just twenty-seven. The lecture was to second-year law students, and the course was the Law of Contracts. He had been nervous beforehand, but had prepared well, and felt that he won over the students. Two or three of his jokes drew widespread laughter, and he could see the students (especially the girls, he thought) smiling at him. Every two or three minutes he would write another word or two into the crossword.

As each word was added he could sense the increasing expectation of the students. About two minutes before the bell the crossword had about twenty interlocking legal words (judges' names, case names, fields of law). But he had one last contribution to make. As he finished his summary of one of the leading cases of the last 150 years he wrote the defendant's name into the crossword.

While adding the words 'carbolic', 'smoke', 'ball' and 'company' he heard murmurs and laughs of recognition. A burly young man at the front stood and yelled 'Bravo' and started clapping. And then all two hundred students were standing and clapping. Nick, blushing but happy, bowed. Within a week his lectures had swelled to three hundred students, and his name was assured. The law faculty student newsletter did a profile on him, called him Nick 'Crossword' Harrieson, and described him as dashing, witty and having a common touch. The Crosser name followed soon after.

But now, twenty-two years later, none of this was any consolation. Others would be keen to let him fall by the wayside. It would serve him right for courting publicity, for showing off so brazenly every year (he did the crossword gimmick only at the first lecture of every year now).

'It's over to you,' Peter said. 'I sincerely hope you can clear your name, but I can't imagine that Kathy will let it go easily. Two other things to be aware of. You mustn't contact the girl under any circumstances while the matter is being investigated. And you're banned from the University premises too. Sorry, but my hands are tied. So tidy up your office tonight and take with you all your personal belongings. Good night, Nick. And happy Christmas too.' Peter offered Nick a formal but firm handshake. He saw himself out.

Nick sat in his office chair and looked out the window into the wintry night. Everything seemed bleak and depressing. In the distance he could see the top half of the dome of St Paul's Cathedral, just visible through the gloom. He would miss that view, and the interactions with the students too. He decided to pack his things up once Darren Tobias had gone.

Just two minutes after the Dean had left, Tobias poked his head around the door, wearing an embarrassed smile. 'I'm so sorry, old chap. There but for the grace of God and all that.'

Nick explained where he was up to in his Law of War lectures and gave Tobias a few folders and notebooks. Tobias scurried out of the office after a minute or two.

Nick picked up the photos of his children and put them in his bag. How would he be able to explain this to them? They were far more socially aware as teenagers than he had been at their age, perhaps even more aware than he was now. They would be appalled and embarrassed.

He saw them once a week at most, often only once a fortnight. They were both well settled living with their mother in Shepherds Bush. They were good kids, and level-headed, especially Emily. Only seventeen, and in her last year at school, she thought Jeremy Corbyn was the most enlightened politician in Britain: her judgement would be harsh, he knew. George was nineteen and at a tech college, and would likely be unconcerned. His main fields of interest were video games and Chelsea Football Club.

He didn't fear Laura's reaction as much as he feared Emily's. He and Laura had divorced eight or nine years ago but remained on good terms. Even as the divorce papers were finalised Laura said that she couldn't understand why they were separating for good, even though she had initiated it. But Nick, having made up his mind on Hampstead Heath, pushed it through. He had the feeling, as he approached forty, that there was more to life than a sedate, no-longer-exciting marriage, and he felt (selfishly, he admitted) that he wanted to be on his own, even if it meant sacrificing custody of the children.

Laura never criticised him in front of the children, for which he was grateful, although occasional comments would filter back from family and mutual friends that she had been angry at him for his self-centredness and confused by his behaviour. Still, she encouraged him to take part in the children's lives and he was a frequent visitor for dinner. Weekends for the children at Daddy's apartment proved boring for the children and fizzled out after a couple of years. The routine of their own bedrooms and the company of Laura suited them better. They preferred Nick to visit for dinner or to call.

Nick decided that he would not tell Laura and the children until he had to, a month or so hence, after the complaints committee had handed down its verdict and punishment. There was no point in diminishing himself in their eyes unless and until it was inevitable. Ignorance is bliss, he reminded himself. He knew it would be difficult, close to dishonest, to keep the news to himself when he visited Laura's apartment for Sunday dinner at the end of the coming week. He decided to tell Laura he had a pressing work requirement which meant he couldn't join them for the dinner.

3

Nick was exhausted. After depersonalising and tidying his office he'd rung Laura to postpone dinner. It was tempting too to ring Adrienne, to ask her motivation for potentially ruining his career, but he decided against it.

He took a cab home, as he didn't fancy getting the Tube. His flat in Kensington Park Road in Notting Hill Gate was dark and cold. After turning all the heaters on he opened a bottle of sauvignon blanc and poured himself a big glass, which he downed in little more than a minute. He poured another.

He sat in his armchair, perplexed at what had happened. His comment to Adrienne at the party had been innocuous, and he was certain that she had smiled – conspiratorially, too – when he said it. Kathy, ever alert for Nick to slip up, had subsequently seized on the remark and turned it against him. But why would Adrienne agree to the complaint being made? *We're friends, aren't we?*

Adrienne and Nick had met about fifteen months before, shortly after the beginning of the 2016/2017 university year. He was teaching a course on the Law of War, a subject which he, like virtually everyone else, was surprised even existed. It featured things like the Geneva Convention on the treatment of prisoners of war and the legality of killing someone in wartime. Nick had always had an interest in military matters, notably the two world wars, and was keen to expand his knowledge of the legal aspects by volunteering to take the first semester.

After his second lecture a tallish Asian student came up to the front of the class and introduced herself. She was clutching her satchel, so Nick didn't offer her his hand. He had noticed her in class. She sat by herself, tapping notes into her laptop. She had black hair to her shoulders, and high cheekbones in a broad and smiling face. Her brown eyes contributed to an impression of beauty.

'Hi, I'm Adrienne Kim,' she said, looking at him with a confident smile. She had a soft accent – was it an American one? 'I'm liking your lectures very much.'

'Why thank you, ma'am. I hope you're not the only one.'

'Oh no,' she said, looking serious. 'Lots of other students have told me they're keen to come to your classes. Especially after that crossword in the first lecture. We were all very impressed that you managed to get Austerlitz, Passchendaele and la Résistance into it.' She continued to smile at him.

Is she flirting? Nick wondered, his senses on alert. 'Well, why use short words when you can use long ones, eh?' She smiled at his little joke.

He looked at her again. She was older than most of the students, perhaps thirty. She had fine teeth, and he once more regretted being born a decade or so too late for orthodontic treatment as a rite of teenage passage.

No, he decided, she was just being polite. 'And what can I do for you, Adrienne? I imagine you're not here because you're a crossword enthusiast.'

She laughed. 'No, I just wanted to say that I'm thinking of doing my Master's thesis on an aspect of the law of war, and I wondered if I could talk to you about it. If you have time, that is.'

Nick knew that he would always have time for Adrienne. She latched her gaze onto his eyes. 'Are you free for a coffee now?' he asked.

They walked across the main courtyard to the Chancery, the law faculty café. She ordered a hot chocolate with a marshmallow, he a green tea – not his usual drink.

'I have a sweet tooth,' she said, looking sheepish as she bit into her marshmallow.

'Tell me more,' he said after they had found a table. 'The fields of Mars are an unusual place from which to reap a Master's topic.' Nick chuckled at his own metaphor.

'Well,' she said, pulling a lock of hair from her right eye, 'you mentioned the Death Railway in your lecture last week. I thought there may be a topic there. I have a personal interest in the Thai-Burma Railway because my great-grandfather served in Thailand during the war. In fact he died in one of the camps.'

'Please excuse my ignorant prying, but what nationality was your great-grandfather? I assume from your surname he was Korean.' Nick felt he was on dangerous ground here.

'Yes,' she said, to Nick's relief.

He was not an expert on the Railway, but he knew enough from the famous movie and from his reading that Koreans had not been prisoners in Thailand. They had been guards, notoriously savage in their treatment of the prisoners.

'My parents don't know much about his war, except that he was shipped out to Thailand via Indonesia in 1941 or 1942 to be a guard, leaving a young family behind in Busan. He never returned. Do you think there's a topic here which I could write a thesis on? I was thinking of an investigation of how the Japanese treated the prisoners. Were they really POWs for the purposes of the Geneva Convention? Did the Japanese deliberately ignore it? Was the inhumane treatment of prisoners simply a matter of the individual beliefs or prejudices of the camp commandants? If there was culpability, how far up the chain of command should it have rested?'

'Good questions.' Nick thought for a while. 'Yes, I think there is a topic there. The 1929 Convention was a worthy effort to deal with the experiences' – he had to stop himself from saying the 'learnings' – 'of World War One. I know there's a lot of contemporary material from the prisoners, and I think from the Japanese side too. I'm afraid I know nothing about the Korean literature. I tell you what, why don't you write a synopsis, no more than a page and a half, of what your thesis would cover? We can meet next week to discuss it.'

She nodded, giving Nick a broad smile. He knew how hard it was to pick a suitable topic for a thesis. Some topics were too narrow and didn't warrant such a detailed and lengthy treatment. Others were too big, and students would despair at the size of the task ahead.

And so their friendship began. They tended to meet once or twice a fortnight, for coffees and a discussion of progress on her thesis (he felt honoured to be asked to supervise it). They would meet in the Chancery after his lectures, and after a while he suggested that they try other cafés a few hundred yards away.

Gradually Adrienne's background emerged. She said she had just turned thirty-four – she looked pleased when he said she looked ten years younger – and had been born in Busan. Her father had been posted to London in the late 1990s to work in the city branch of one of the leading Korean banks, and the family moved to a semi-detached house in Wimbledon. Adrienne struggled to learn English from a very low base, but with hard work and strong parental discipline she found that she could compete with her schoolmates and soon became fluent. She played piano and violin to high levels ('just like all Asian immigrant kids,' she said) and excelled at her classes.

She attended Bristol University ('Oxbridge wasn't for me, although my parents wanted that. Besides, my grades were probably not good enough'), where she gained a BSc in maths, accounting and finance. She admitted that she was one of the two top maths graduates in her year at Bristol. She seemed pleased when Nick complimented her on her achievement.

Starting as an auditor ('God it was boring'), Adrienne then worked as an accountant at Ernst Young in London, before moving into corporate finance and transaction management at EY. The highlight was a secondment to Paris for a year, which helped improve her schoolgirl French.

The hours were long, and she was always tired, and so she quit EY to take a place in a chamber music group, which gave recitals in churches and stately homes around the South-East. It was great fun, she said, but it was not for her, as she found her fellow musicians to be dull and obsessive and uninterested in the wider world. So, at a crossroads in her life, with her savings running out and having just turned thirty ('and unmarried too, but most of the guys I've met are dropkicks – we Koreans call them *sae-ggi* – who do little but play video games'), Adrienne decided a career change was in order. She had always liked police and courtroom books and TV shows and decided that the law was her next challenge. She enrolled to do a three-year Bachelor of Laws course at London King's.

Nick said he hadn't seen her in his undergraduate classes. She laughed at that: 'I was in your torts class two years ago, for a semester. One of about three hundred students, so I'm sure you wouldn't have seen me. It was virtually standing room only that year after your opening lecture.' Nick was warming to Adrienne.

She liked the law so much, she said, that she decided to stay on to do a one-year Master's. Her interest in criminal law had been superseded to an extent by a curiosity about the role of law in places other than the courtroom. She enrolled in the Law of War classes.

'Well, I'm very glad you decided to do that.' Nick wanted to say how much he looked forward to seeing her, how he wanted to learn more about her background and her views, how he admired her achievements and, he had to admit, how attractive he found her. All these things he couldn't mention. Personal relationships with students were problematic at best and job-threatening at worst. He had to keep a distance, and he was happy simply to enjoy the company of an intelligent and engaging woman fifteen years his junior.

For some reason Adrienne seemed to like Nick. She would often text him at all hours about her thesis or having a catch-up, and even started recommending books and TV programmes to him. He always tried to be humorous and sophisticated in his interactions with her and liked to think that he had both of those characteristics. He accompanied her ('as my plus one') on two occasions to the University's monthly French-speaking club soirée, which gave him the opportunity to prove that he could converse in passable French.

But that was then and this was now. Nick gulped, finishing the bottle of Oyster Bay. He asked himself how it had come to this. Especially after their wonderful evening together only two nights before the faculty / staff party. He was tempted to text 'WTF?' to Adrienne, but thought better of it and went to bed instead.

4

'It's good to see you again, Nick. Perhaps not in these particular circumstances, but it's always a pleasure.' Nick gave Sadie a peck on her made-up cheek. She beckoned him into a meeting room off the reception area.

Sadie was one of Nick's favourite people. They had been at Cambridge together, and he had been entranced the moment he set eyes on her; she was so blonde and pretty and worldly. She had a figure that he thought of as Monroe-esque and talked with a ra-ra accent that he would have tended to dislike in anyone else. Within only a few weeks of arriving at university she had been able to bat off with aplomb all the Sadie the Cleaning Lady jokes, and her friends rarely referred to the song again. She had what his mother would have called a potty mouth and a deep, naughty laugh. Nick could so easily have fallen in love with her if he'd had half a chance, but that was never a realistic possibility, as she was taken already by the suave banker she would shortly move in with. He would become the first of her three husbands. The third had reportedly left the matrimonial home, unwillingly, only a few months ago.

Nick had called Sadie the morning after Peter Hargreaves had visited him to inform him of the complaint. Nick knew hundreds of lawyers in London but didn't know who would be the most suitable to represent him in this embarrassing little matter. He asked Sadie for a recommendation of a name or two, and was a bit surprised when she assured him that she was well qualified and would be happy to take on his case.

'Well, my dear Nick, tell me all about it.' Sadie's pen hovered over a yellow legal pad.

She let him speak without interruption. After he had finished, she put the pen down, put her hands together as if praying and said gently but with a warmth he could feel, 'You're in a pretty pickle, aren't you? My initial reaction is that it doesn't look good. I accept that your comment was meant to be humorous, and that you weren't propositioning or flirting with her. But before I talk about what you said to Miss Kim, or rather what you are *alleged* to have said, do you mind if I offer two little observations?'

Nick waved his hand to signify assent. 'The first is that this complaint is extremely serious for you. There's every chance you'll lose your job if the case can be proven. Your career will be jeopardised, perhaps fatally. You may become unemployable in the British education sector. Who will want to hire a known harasser?' She paused, as if to let her words register with Nick.

'And the other observation?'

'Please forgive me for raising it, Nick, but I do so as your long-standing friend. What on earth were you thinking, meeting a student under your direct supervision at cafés and venues off-campus and then going to the movies with her? There are boundaries, especially in the teacher/student area, and you've gone way beyond them into dangerous places. It's 2017, don't you realise, not 1917? You have to be so careful not to overstep the mark these days. Surely you must realise that?'

Nick studied his hands, clasped around his teacup. 'Well, I suppose if you put it like that I did act, er, foolishly. But it was all innocent and well meaning. I had no intention whatsoever in pursuing any kind of relationship with Adrienne.'

'I know you didn't. But you're being naïve, Nick. I have to

say that. To a great degree it's the perception that matters. And the perception is terrible. Am I right that Master's dissertations at London King's are marked by the supervisor and not sent off to an independent marker from a different university?' Nick nodded.

'Well then, if you give her a Distinction for her thesis, then people will say an A for a lay. If you give her a Fail, she might say that you were being vindictive because she wouldn't sleep with you. She might even claim that you tried to rape her after going to the movies. All lies, but you can't disprove any of it.'

She paused, the teacher having finished lecturing her pupil. Nick grimaced and raised his head a degree or two.

Sadie smiled. 'That's enough venting from me. I won't mention it again, but I think there are a few things there for you to chew on. To masticate, as it were.' She was laughing again. 'That's why we have to win this case. We fucking well have to, a lot's riding on it. Now, we were talking about the words you said to Miss Kim. Those words are quite clear. You've admitted you said the words complained of. You will have great trouble denying them, as Miss Kim and the two witnesses have all sworn that you did say them. The words look awful in the context of a relationship between a male teacher and a female student. A student of his.'

Sadie looked towards the far corner of the meeting room. '"Extra specially nice to me"? A student being merely nice to her teacher might get him a cup of tea, I suppose, or bake him a cake. And if she was being specially nice then at a pinch you might get away with her wearing a mini skirt or letting him look down her cleavage. But *extra specially* nice?'

Nick leaned forward with mounting anxiety.

'That can only mean one of two things, and probably both.' She paused, noticeably enjoying the theatre of the moment. 'Shagging him senseless or giving him a blowjob.' Sadie threw her head back and burst into laughter. 'You look so miserable,

Nick. I do exaggerate, but only a little, and we will have to assume that the Council's complaints committee has as lurid an imagination as I do. Let me think about our strategy for a few days. I'll call the University's legal department and have copies of the complaint and witness statements emailed to me. Undoubtedly the complaint will go before the disciplinary committee. We can then meet to discuss how we should defend the claim. And I'll need the names of two character witnesses who will be willing to testify about your previously unblemished behaviour and your strong moral compass.'

Nick wasn't sure if she was being sarcastic.

'My initial thinking is that we'll have to go on the attack. It's most odd that the femme fatale was not the one who complained. As I understand it, she has simply confirmed what you said. I may have to submit her to my famously rigorous cross-examination. I won't let her get away with letting my old mucker Crosser come a cropper.' She looked at Nick with a cheerful smile, no doubt relishing the lawyer's delight in his or her own voice and vocabulary.

'I'd prefer it strongly if you don't do that, Sadie. Even though she's a mature student she's been manipulated here by that … by Kathy.' Nick was beginning to get angry now. 'Hell hath no fury, et cetera. She has it in for me, simple as that.'

'No, Nick. Forget about going after Kathy. She's not the one on trial. You'll have seen all the publicity in America and here about the MeToo hashtag in the last two months. But that's only the new public face of it. A lot has been going on in the last few years below the radar. Predatory men are getting their comeuppance in all spheres of life and business. And that includes the universities. The early word on the street from the 1752 Group is that they are finding dozens or even hundreds of cases of sexual harassment in Britain's tertiary education sector, with only a tiny number leading to the disciplining or sacking of the male perpetrators. Their report is due out in the first half of 2018, and my university contacts tell me that the councils and boards of governors are bracing for some highly awkward publicity.

'Even if your alleged offence is relatively minor – you didn't rape her or put your hand up her skirt – London King's will be keen to throw the book at you. More to the point, they'll need to be *seen* to be throwing the book at you. They'll feel they need to hang you from the rooftops, so to speak. Our only course of action will be to fight hard and dirty.'

Sadie ushered him to the lift. 'There's little for you to do now. Leave things to me. I'll do my best for you, old sport. After all, we go back thirty years, to when you were a shy and spotty boy. And when it's over, we'll go out to dinner. Hopefully to celebrate.' The lift door opened. 'It'll be my shout.'

5

'Welcome, Nicko. It's great to see you.' Nick returned his sister's hug. 'But you look like shit. What's up?'

Nick sat down by the fire in the tiny living room, and after accepting a welcome glass of Beck's told Jo of his visit from the Dean the previous night and his meeting with Sadie that morning. As she listened she offered occasional words of sympathy.

'I'm likely to lose my job. There could also be a wave of publicity for a few days, or even weeks. It's not looking promising, despite the brave face Sadie tried to put on it today.'

'Yes, you're in an awkward position. I can see how your comment at the cocktail function has been taken as it has, but you're the last person to say anything deliberately offensive. Still, it's a very serious matter, and you have to treat it like that. You definitely don't want to be fired or have to resign your professorship. But I don't think any the worse of you if that helps.'

How blessed he was to have Jo in his life. Even when he was a toddler she had been a kind and reassuring presence, mindful of his safety and comfort before her own, and things hadn't changed over the years. They now saw each other only once or twice a month, but it was always affectionate.

Nick looked around the room as Jo prepared the dinner. On

the mantelpiece were some silver candlesticks and a goblet. The walls were covered with paintings and photos, all higgledy-piggledy, with a print of Monet haystacks next to a family photo of Jo and Nick, aged six and three respectively, sitting on their parents' laps. It had been taken in a photographer's studio in Aylesbury and was dated 1971. The colours were fading. Jo had had a shock of bright-white curly hair then, like a blonder Shirley Temple, but now her hair was dyed a bohemian orange.

Nick was sad that Jo had never married. There had been a few boyfriends over the years, including two live-in relationships. She was just one of those many good women – women of integrity, intelligence, achievement, culture, empathy and attractiveness – who for whatever reason had trouble attracting a worthy man. For every available good man, he figured, there must be a hundred good women.

As they tucked into the lasagne, Jo asked about the background to the remark that was giving her brother so much grief.

'There's really not much to it. Two Tuesdays ago, I went to see a French film with Adrienne, the student the subject of the complaint. It was her idea. She and I both speak okay French, and she had heard that a film at the Ciné Lumière in Kensington was hilarious. It wasn't a date at all, more of a companionship thing.'

Jo looked at him but said nothing.

'Anyhow, it was a love story between two thirty-somethings, set in Provence somewhere, and their conversation was sparkling and increasingly sexy. And then at dinner, he was stroking the back of her hand, and he said, I'm quoting from the subtitles here, "I would like to do something nice to you." And she looked at him in a way that could only be said to be erotically charged. "And I would like to do something especially nice to you." It was up to our imagination what these nice things were, but in the next scene they were naked and in bed. Adrienne burst out laughing at their exchange of endearments, cackling in a way which is unique to her, and I laughed too. We both liked the movie and went our separate ways in good spirits. A fun night, no more, no less. The next time I saw her was at the law faculty drinks evening.'

Jo frowned. 'I'm not sure that helps your case. For one, a lecturer and a student were on a date, no matter how you downplay it. And second, those two phrases speak of nothing but sex, sex, sex. There's no doubt about that.'

Jo always saw things with a clarity Nick envied, although he protested on this occasion. 'But don't you see, my comment to Adrienne at the party was just a private joke, a little reminder that she and I had had an enjoyable – and entirely innocent – evening together two days before? Nothing more than that. And now I'm being treated as a lecherous predator. It's grossly unfair.'

'No, it's not. Life can be a bitch, as we both know. I suggest you leave things in Sadie's capable hands. And let's talk about something more positive, shall we?' She squeezed his shoulder as she took the dinner plates to the kitchen.

After they had stacked the dishwasher and tidied up, Nick took his glass of port and went over to the mantelpiece. His eye caught the silver goblet there, which he remembered from his childhood used to sit in one of his mother's dining room cabinets. A faded brown-grey sheen covered its graceful shape, about six inches high. It had a short stem and could hold a decent glass of wine if needed. On the cup was an inscription:

To Don G. You were damned right. Everyone does behave badly. Especially me. Don E. July 1925.

Nick asked Jo what the inscription meant. 'No idea. Nor did Dad. You'll recall he left it to me in his will.' Nick dimly remembered. 'It came from Dad's father, old William Harrieson who died in World War Two, and so we never knew him. Apparently he left a note to Grandma Cecilia, written when the Japanese invaded Malaya, that the goblet was to be given to Dad, and that when Dad died he was to give it to the 'most literary' of his children. That was me, haha.' Nick nodded as he surveyed the bookcases in the library which ran off one end of the sitting room.

'Apparently the goblet had some significance to Grandpa, God knows what. It looks vaguely south European, Italian or Spanish, perhaps. It has a medieval shape, but there's a mark on the inner of the stand which has a date stamp of 1923. And the inscription? It reads like an apology of sorts, but from whom and to whom is a mystery.' Jo poured herself a glass of port. 'I've had an idea. You have a few weeks of downtime ahead of you, so why don't you do a bit of research about Grandpa's life? By all accounts he was quite a character, a man of many interests and a few adventures. It would be a nice thing for your kids – and for us – to know about one of our recent ancestors. You may even be able to dig up something about the goblet.'

'That's not a bad idea. I'll need something to distract me from this other business. Remind me what you know about Grandpa William.'

'It's all very sketchy. He was brought up in Aylesbury, must have been born in 1900 or so. He went to Oxford, then joined the Colonial Service. He was a district officer or similar in East Africa for many years, and then in Malaya. He was captured by the Japanese, put in Changi in Singapore, and later shipped by train up to work on the Burma Railway. He died there, as so many others did. He was buried in a Thai cemetery. He left behind his widow, Cecilia, and two children, Dad and Aunt Mary. You might want to start with Aunt Mary.'

Back at his flat Nick decided he needed to talk to Adrienne, despite Peter Hargreaves' injunction. It had been just over twenty-four hours since Peter had given him the bombshell news, and since then Nick had had no contact with her. Come to think of it, he had had no word from her since the fateful drinks party, now six days ago.

It was too late for a phone call, so he sent her a text:

Please tell me what's going on. I'm devastated.

The reply was swift:

im sorry its out of my hands now

She had the practice – or was it an affectation? – of rarely using punctuation when texting. At first it had irritated him, but after a while he had concluded that her messages were clear and that apostrophes and capital letters were in fact redundant.

What do you mean out of your hands? You've made the complaint. You know my comment was harmless.

She responded quickly:

no i don't know that Kathy and Paul were adamant u were propositioning me

Nick replied:

Don't you see you're being manipulated? Kathy's using you to get at me. Can we meet for a coffee to talk about it? Tomorrow morning?

im not allowed to talk to you please dont mssge me again it is what it is

Nick wondered what she meant. Was she saying the complaint wasn't one she was actively involved in? He changed tack.

You must realise I may lose my job and possibly my career because of this.

He got no response. He sent a follow-up:

Adrienne, I thought we were friends.

The reply was as damning and final as it was immediate:

no we arent friends you are or were my teacher good night o-o

Nick switched off his phone and threw it onto the couch. He felt alone. Only later would he realise that the final 'o-o' from Adrienne was the equivalent of the middle finger being thrown at him.

6

Nick woke with a purpose. The whole day stretched emptily ahead of him with no lectures or appointments, and he wryly noted the pleasure of not having to set his alarm for six a.m. to ensure he was in good time for the first lecture of the day.

He knew only a little about the Burma Railway, including how terrible it had been for the prisoners of war who built it. He went online to Wikipedia and other sites and began to appreciate the enormity and folly of the Japanese plan to build a railway all the way from Bangkok in the south to Rangoon in the north, thereby opening up supply and troop routes from Singapore to India. The railway was to be constructed in some of the most inhospitable terrain on the planet, through mountain ranges and over rivers and swamps, through the tropical jungle, in fetid and humid heat, with daily risks of dying from exhausting tropical diseases like cholera and dengue fever, or from sunstroke, or from drowning in monsoon-swollen torrents. Not to mention the snakebites or starvation, or beatings from the Japanese and Korean guards. It was hell on earth, of that there could be no doubt, and Nick knew he was not going to like what he would learn about his grandfather's time in the war.

YouTube was full of grainy black-and-white videos of the camps, of emaciated men in knee-length shorts or loincloths staring into the distance behind the camera. There were reminiscences from survivors, and even interviews with Japanese camp commandants years after the war.

Nick wasn't the most adept searcher on the internet, but it didn't take him long to establish from Colonial Service records that his grandfather, William Forbes Harrieson, had been a lieutenant in the Federated Malay States Volunteer Forces, which was a collection of men living in what was then the Federated Malay States. They had formed in 1940 and 1941 as volunteers to prepare to defend the country against a possible Japanese invasion. They were teachers, shippers, rubber planters, engineers and civil servants, among other occupations.

William's address was listed as The Residence, Ipoh. Nick found that Ipoh was a pleasant town in the centre of the Malay Peninsula, not too far from the highlands or from the coastal settlements with their white beaches, palm trees and turquoise waters. It must have been an unchallenging appointment for an officer in the Colonial Service.

William had been captured in Singapore in February 1942 and incarcerated in Changi, the huge prison camp made famous to the next two generations in films such as *The Bridge on the River Kwai* and *King Rat*. He had been transported by train and cattle truck to Bangkok in September. There the trail went dead. Nick spent hours on the website of COFEPOW, a British-based group called the Children of the Far East Prisoners of War, but was able to establish only that there had been a man called Harrieson at the Tamuang camp at some stage in 1943. Nick would later corroborate this while skim-reading the detailed, matter-of-fact diaries of the Australian medic Weary Dunlop, which made a passing reference to a man called Harrieson. Nick felt confident, without knowing, that this particular Harrieson was William.

After a day and a half of morbidly fascinating but never dull research, Nick decided to go to the British Library in Euston Road to see if there was anything there that might help him.

He spent the afternoon leafing through memoirs and diaries of POWs, but not finding any mention of his grandfather. He was just about to go home and resume the next day when he caught sight of a face he recognised sitting twenty yards away and intently reading what appeared to be a typed manuscript. He could not mistake that shiny black hair resting on her shoulders.

He was debating whether he should acknowledge her presence when she raised her head and looked straight at him. She seemed surprised, startled even, but then gave him that familiar broad grin and he went over to her.

'Hello, Adrienne. I didn't expect to see you here.'

'My own thoughts exactly,' she whispered, seemingly anxious not to disturb the others in the reading room. 'I don't think we should be talking to each other. We'll both get into trouble.'

'Don't you worry. No one will see us.' He looked Adrienne in the eye. 'I hope you don't hate me now.'

'You're not a bad man, just a dinosaur from a different generation.'

Nick was shocked. Had she always thought that of him? Surely not. Otherwise, why would she have sought out his company so often and, especially, suggested a movie date? He felt sure that Kathy had influenced her thinking.

'Well, perhaps we shouldn't talk about that. I'm not meant to be speaking to you. The reason I'm here is that I've just found out that my father's father was also working on the Burma Railway, so I'm here to see if I can find out anything about his war.' He glanced at the books on the table in front of her. 'I see you're doing the same, except it's your great-grandfather.'

She explained that she was in the library principally to research her thesis, and also to find out something about her great-grandfather's time on the Railway. She had found Korean archive material online which revealed he had sailed from Busan to Sumatra in mid-1942, and from there to Singapore. He was then sent up the peninsula to one of the Thai railway camps.

Nick mentioned the little information he had found about William and expressed his frustration at his lack of online searching skills.

'How about I do a few hours' searching for you, to show you that I'm not completely hostile? If I dig anything useful up I'll let you know, okay?' She smiled at him, that wide, lovely smile. It was as though her coldness of the evening before, and even her comments a few minutes ago, belonged to a different person. 'And if I do find anything then *you* will have to be especially nice to *me*.' With that she turned, with a flourish of her hair, and swanned out of the reading room, her hips swaying. Nick stared at her as she went through the revolving door.

Nick's phone rang later that night, just before eleven. *Who has the nerve to call me at this hour?*

'Brace yourself, Nick,' came the familiar sound of Adrienne's voice. He could feel the excitement in her voice.

'I've found out your grandfather died in Tamuang camp in October 1943. The same month the Railway was completed. No cause of death is specified. He's buried in Kanchanaburi, in Row K of Plot Eight.'

'Good work, Adrienne. Thanks so much. That's definitely helpful.'

'*Dak-cho*! Shut up! I haven't even started yet. I located online a copy of the diary of a doctor called Flaws. He also died in Thailand, but his diary was somehow preserved. I'll quote a paragraph in full. Are you sitting down?' She didn't wait for him to reply. 'The entry is dated 24 February 1943. Here goes. *It was another backbreaking day for the men today. On the road by seven a.m., with only the most minuscule of rations, and they did not return until sundown. They were absolutely exhausted. But after tenko this evening a few of us sat outside our barracks, talking about various experiences before the war. One of my companions, a Colonial Service man called Harrieson, a lovely chap, told a pip of a story. He in fact*

37

told many stories of colonial life, of trout fishing in East Africa and travelling in the American Midwest. But the one that I must record is that he says that in the mid-1920s, somewhere in Spain, he had a fist-fight with no less a figure than Ernest Hemingway. Fancy that. It seemed a bit far-fetched, but he is a level-headed fellow and he gave no indication that he was making it up.'

Adrienne stopped. 'You've got to be joking! That's amazing.' Nick was stunned. Could this be true? Hemingway was a renowned boxer, often picking fights with friends and strangers alike. But with his grandfather? How on earth did they meet?

For several minutes the harassment complaint was forgotten as they talked animatedly about this new information. 'I don't know much about Hemingway. He's so last-century. But I'm a Google-fiend. I can research online for you to see if your grandfather gets a mention in any Hemingway materials. Only if you want me to ...'

'That's very kind of you. I'm pretty hopeless with a computer, as you know, but all the same I think I'll do it myself.' He added, with more malice than he intended, 'After all, I have nothing better to do these days.'

'No worries. Besides, I have to do more work on my thesis. I've promised Darren Tobias a first draft by next week.'

Touché, thought Nick.

7

The next day was fruitless. Nick spent all morning at his computer, reading articles about Hemingway in Spain in the 1920s and making a list of biographies that covered him in those years. There were no mentions of William online. He spent an unproductive afternoon in the British Library and at Foyles, and again there was no reference to his grandfather in any of the Hemingway materials. Nor was there any sign of Adrienne in the library which, to his mild surprise, added to his disappointment.

That evening he received a phone call from Peter Hargreaves, who said that Kathy had informed him that Nick had been seen chatting with the 'Korean girl' yesterday, at the British Library. 'I told you to stay away from her. She's bad news for you. It's a clear breach of our rules and processes in a situation like this and exposes you to the additional charge of trying to intimidate a witness. This makes it look worse, Nick. You have to cease all communication with her. That's an order.'

Nick sighed. London now seemed small, full of improbable coincidences, and life was very wearisome. 'I met her only by chance, and we didn't talk about the complaint.'

'That may be so, but I'm not sure the complaints committee will be as easy to convince as I am. I will do what I can to dissuade the fearsome Kathy from taking things further, but I can't guarantee I'll succeed. Good night.'

Nick felt he had to get out of London for a while, away from the gloom of the looming disciplinary hearing, and on a whim he decided to visit his aunt in Auckland. New Zealand was as far as possible from London, and several days away from the winter would do him the world of good. Nick was hardly the impulsive type, but a despond had settled on him over the Christmas period and a bit of a damn-the-torpedoes feeling came over him.

Mary, when he rang, seemed unsurprised that he should want to visit. She sounded as if he was a neighbour wanting to drop in. 'I'll aim to be there in three days,' said Nick. 'I'll let you know my flight details and will call from the airport when I arrive.' He booked his air tickets, excited by the idea of travelling to the other side of the planet just for a few days.

That afternoon he decided to take advantage of all the spare time his fall from grace allowed by taking a leisurely walk through Hyde Park to Oxford Street to buy a cabin bag for his trip. Emerging from the park near Speakers' Corner he was surprised to see a familiar face walking towards him, speaking animatedly on her phone. It was Emily. London was getting smaller by the day.

Nick's first instinct was to veer away, to pretend that he hadn't seen her, but he quickly abandoned the idea. She had spotted him and was waving to him. She finished her call and gave Nick a bear hug, as she always did when they met.

Emily stood back, her blonde fringe almost covering the tops of her eyes and her hair resting on the shoulder of her school blazer. She looked him up and down, evidently noting that Nick was in a pair of dirty jeans and hadn't shaved for a day or two. 'Do tell, Dad. How come you're not at work? You're looking decidedly boho.'

Nick could feel embarrassment colouring his face. He had no wish to tell his daughter about why he wasn't at work, but he knew that lying about it wasn't a good idea either. He asked her if she had time for a coffee or a cuppa. She nodded.

As they walked into Oxford Street she explained that her class had been let out early and she had come into the West End to do a bit of shopping. As they sat down in the café after ordering their peppermint teas, Emily looked at Nick, no doubt waiting for him to explain the situation. She had always been intellectually and emotionally ahead of her age, and she had a moral compass and sense of right and wrong which he found both admirable and fearsome over the years. He remembered her disgust when he came home one evening, about six or seven years ago when Emily was aged ten or eleven, very much the worse for wear after a boozy lunch with some old university friends. Laura had not been pleased, but Emily was shocked to the core. She started crying and refused to accept a hug from Nick. She ran off to her bedroom and sulked for two days. Laura later explained that Emily was now convinced that Nick was an alcoholic and potentially violent, wondering whether it was still safe to have him in the same house as the rest of the family.

Now Nick knew that he was about to receive another moral judgement from Emily. He played the situation down, saying that his absence from the office was more of an administrative measure as a result of a misunderstanding in the law faculty, but he could see that Emily was not accepting that. He could also see sadness and disappointment in her eyes. He told her the bare outline of the complaint.

'But how could you have suggested something so bad, so *gross*, to one of your students? At your age, too. And you said she's Asian? You're lucky you're not being accused of racial prejudice as well.'

Nick didn't have the will to argue. Instead, he took Emily's hands in his and agreed he had made a mistake, an error of judgement, and he was now having to face the consequences. It wasn't the end of the world, he said. 'No one has died or been to hospital or anything like that. I hope I'll be vindicated by the University committee in a few weeks and I can then resume my job. But if not … Well, I have a good name, and I'm sure I can get a senior position at another university.'

'Yes, Dad, I'm sure you're right. But it's not just about you. Think of the poor woman. She must be traumatised, and subject to harassment by a man she trusted, a man in a position of power and influence.'

Nick took his hands away. *Trust her to pick the side of the underdog.* Emily had always done that, being vocal about injured sparrows in the garden, and particularly seeing homeless men on the street or starving Africans on the television news.

'You needn't worry about her. She's fine. At most she's confused, but definitely not traumatised. By all accounts,' he added, not wishing to admit he had seen Adrienne as recently as yesterday.

Emily insisted on knowing all about her: her age, her looks ('I suppose you could say she was attractive,' said Nick), her name and even the subject of her Master's thesis, and what lecture courses she was taking. He was uncomfortable with Emily's questions, ruefully reflecting that several times he'd told his children to get a full understanding of the facts before forming an opinion (and especially an unfavourable one) about someone.

For years Nick had encouraged Emily to study law. She was undecided about what bachelor's degree she would take (she was inclining towards majoring in history or political science) or where she would study. She said she didn't want to go to Oxbridge ('too elitist for the twenty-first century, Dad') even though her grades were good enough, and said she wanted to go to London King's. It had a good reputation and was regarded as progressive and liberal, which suited her set of values. Plus, it was in central London, and not in a provincial city.

Occasionally she had sat in on Nick's lectures during school holidays, and she had said how impressed she was by his knowledge and speaking ability and particularly liked his 'crossword' lectures. By fourteen she was already as tall as a lot of the students and didn't look out of place in the lecture theatres.

'Oh my God. I've just realised. If you get kicked out of London King's in disgrace, I'll never be able to study there. I'll be known as the daughter of old Crosser, the creepy lecturer. The one who tried to proposition his students. Eek!' She made a face.

'Don't you worry, darling. It'll blow over soon. I'll be vindicated and back at work before you know it.'

'Mum will be devastated. She doesn't know, does she?' Nick shook his head. 'Do you want to tell her, or should I?'

'Why don't you tell her, darling? I think it may be better coming from you.' Nick knew that, for all her censoriousness, Emily would be fair in what she said to Laura.

He remembered a phone conversation he had had with Laura a year or so ago. She had rung to say that she thought he should be aware that on a few recent occasions Emily, then sixteen, had brought boys home for the night – decent boys, not lowlifes. Laura had apparently told Emily that she was too young and that there would be time at university and beyond for falling in love. Nick had laughed out loud at the last part.

But Emily had insisted. 'Sorry, Mum, either they stay with me or I stay the night at their houses. Besides, it's my body, not yours.' Laura had given in quickly and assured Nick that birth and STD control measures were in place and that Emily was safe. Nick surprised himself by accepting the news calmly. His principal reaction was to marvel at how mature his daughter had become. He never had any fears that Emily would succeed in life.

Their teas long finished, Emily gave her father another bear hug as they bade farewell on the pavement. 'It'll be all right, Dad. Hang in there. I'm sure you'll be back at work soon.' Nick could see the love, and the pain, in her eyes. She turned, and her tall, graceful frame strode purposefully away up towards Oxford Circus.

Laura rang within the hour, as he knew she would. Emily would have telephoned her as soon as she was out of sight. Laura was surprisingly sympathetic and said that it was much ado about nothing, and she was sure that everything would be fine.

He thanked her for her understanding, hoping she was right. After she hung up he rationalised that Laura would have been upset and critical about his conduct and the whole situation, but she was decent enough not to add to his woes by telling him what she thought.

All in all, Nick felt he had got off pretty lightly in his conversations with Emily and Laura. It put him in a good frame of mind as he packed for his trip to New Zealand, flying out the next morning. He liked long-distance air travel. He liked the solitude, and being forced to sit for twelve or thirteen hours at a time was not a huge imposition. It gave him time to think about things, about the state of his life and the people in it.

As he flew over Germany he felt depressed and anxious about the ordeal ahead before the disciplinary committee. By Azerbaijan, fortified by three glasses of merlot, he felt better. It was not the end of the world, after all, and if there was publicity it would last only the figurative fifteen minutes. His reputation was good enough to get another lecturing position (perhaps something better paid overseas?), and it may even be a good excuse for a career change.

By the time the aircraft was over China, Nick was in an ebullient mood. His thoughts had moved to Hemingway and William (what on earth was that all about?), and to the women in his life. To his ex-wife and daughter, how he missed them, and the satisfying comfort of a family routine. To Jo, his sister, what a good and reliable presence she was. To Kathy, a thorn in his side, bitter, angry, resentful that their affair had gone nowhere and her career had only spluttered forward. To Sadie, so direct and smart and impressive. And to Adrienne, the maddening and beautiful Adrienne. Her complexity and their differences drew him to her, but her age and unpredictability were like big warning signs on the edge of a cliff.

He knew very little about her life. Did she live alone, or with flatmates? Or even with a boyfriend? He presumed not, as she never mentioned one and she was unlikely to want to see a movie with Nick if she was living with someone.

She had been in environments like university and EY where life was social and there were many opportunities, and there was the internet too. Nick had studiously avoided enquiring about her personal life. The HR people at London King's frequently reminded the teaching staff of the section in the University's code of behaviour advising that it was *'inappropriate, intrusive and possibly legally actionable'* to get too personal with students. Nick used to think that was all balderdash.

Nick arrived bleary-eyed into a bright summer's morning in Auckland. He was struck by the large expanse of blue sea and the number of islands surrounding the city as the plane made its landing approach, a veritable South Seas paradise, and by the miles and miles of suburban homes in all directions, each with a small garden. It looked to be a green and pleasant land. He felt a bit silly for never having visited New Zealand before.

Aunt Mary greeted him at her villa in Remuera, a leafy suburb, with the warmest of hugs. It had been over twenty years since they had last met. She was in her early eighties, sprightly for her age. Her hair was thick and white, and her red face was dominated by a prominent nose, which did not detract from the benevolent aura she presented.

Nick looked around the immaculate sitting room as Mary made morning tea and buttered some fresh scones. He noted the framed degree certificate on the wall from the University of Reading, a Bachelor of Arts awarded to Mary Hadley Harrieson in 1957, shortly before she married a New Zealand former serviceman and headed to the southern hemisphere for a life as the wife of a schoolteacher. They had never had children.

Nick explained that he was on a 'leave of absence of sorts' from his university job and was using the time to research the life of Mary's father.

'Well as you'd expect I hardly knew him. I was born in Kuala Lumpur, in what was then the Federated Malay States. We didn't live in KL. The family lived in Ipoh, two or three hours north. I was only a small child, but I remember the big house and running on the verandas, and our devoted amahs Ah Lin and Ah Ying, and days spent on holidays at the beach, paddling in the warm sea and collecting shells. Your grandfather was a wonderful father. When he was there. He often had to travel around the district. He used to read to me in bed at night, and he always had a homily or quotation for every situation. He loved quoting from the Bible or Shakespeare. To this day I can't think of 'waste not, want not' or 'do unto others as you would wish them to do unto you' without thinking of him. He was a dear man, and it was terrible what happened to him.

'And then he shipped us all off to England, in May 1939. My mother, your father and me. I was only four. He said things could get dangerous in the FMS, and he wanted us to be safe. As it turned out, we had to avoid the bombing in England during the war. But we never saw him again. He wrote lots of letters for a couple of years, and how we all treasured them, but then he was captured and sent to work on that horrid railway, and the letters stopped. One or two postcards, but that was it. I will never forgive the Japanese.'

Mary's eyes were now glistening. Nick was moved too, and wondered how it would feel to lose your father at such a young age.

'All we knew was that he had been put in Changi. We hoped he would survive the war there, but about September 1945 Mum got a letter to say he'd died two years earlier, on the Railway. So, so sad. We all cried for weeks, and Mum never got over it. To this day I don't know what he died of.'

Then another thought appeared to come to her. 'Mind you, I was born when Dad was away on a fishing trip in America. Mum wasn't too pleased about that, as she would often say in her later years. It wouldn't have been easy being left alone in the tropics for two months at the end of a pregnancy.'

Nick reflected that his own issues were of no significance. His aunt had had to deal with a whole lifetime of what-ifs and regrets.

He turned down the offer of a second scone. 'Did you ever inherit any papers from your parents? As far as I can tell Dad didn't receive any family papers after Grandma died.'

Mary's face brightened and she smiled. He realised – remembered – that in her younger years she had been something of a beauty. 'Yes, I did. There's a box or two of papers in my garage. I haven't looked inside them for thirty years or more but I remember a few letters and things. Mum gave them to me before she died. Come with me, I'll show you where they are.'

She raised herself unsteadily from the armchair. Nick offered her a helping hand, which she brushed away. In the garage there was no car, but a jumble of bookcases, lawnmowers, garden implements and cardboard boxes. Everything was covered with dust and cobwebs.

'Over there,' she said, pointing through the dusty light at a carved, wooden box in the corner. It was made of teak, perhaps a souvenir of life in Malaya. Nick clambered over to it and removed two cardboard boxes from the top. 'Bring them into the kitchen. You can look through them at your leisure there.'

For the next few hours, Nick sifted through the contents of the boxes as he sat at the kitchen table. There must have been fifty or so letters, dated from 1939 to 1941, sent to Cecilia and her children in England. Nick skim-read them all, but there was nothing in them to advance his quest. They all followed a similar pattern: a

47

summary of day-to-day goings on in Ipoh or surrounding areas, amid mounting concern about the possibility of a Japanese invasion and an anxious sentiment that William hoped they were safe and coping well in England. One letter, however, was about twenty pages long, so Nick saved that for later.

In a small envelope was a faded brown postcard, presumably sent from Changi. The Japanese command allowed all prisoners to send a postcard to their loved ones after their capture. Fifteen words was said to be the maximum permitted. Including anything controversial, such as the location of the prison camp, meant that the card would be confiscated and destroyed.

William's card was addressed to Cecilia in England, and read simply:

20 March 1942
I AM A PRISONER OF WAR. I AM IN GOOD SHAPE.
MISSING YOU ALL.
FIGHT THE GOOD FIGHT.
LOVE, WILLIAM

And then there was his war diary. Starting from February 1942, a few days after he was captured, and finishing on 5 January 1943, it was written in tiny print first on the back of a book of unused invoices for the Selangor Timber Company, and then for three months on toilet paper. Nick knew that keeping a diary in captivity was forbidden, and the diarists risked execution if the journals were found. Most Railway diaries tended to be pedestrian and factual, rather than opinionated and political, recording the rudiments of daily life. William's was no exception. Many of the pages were faded and torn. Two typical entries read:

4 November 1942
Another dull day. Tenko at 9 a.m. had to be repeated at 10 a.m. and

11 a.m. because of miscounting. No breakfast. A chicken wing and a ball of rice for lunch – a luxury! Bible class and PE in late afternoon. Stinking hot. Rice stew for dinner.

12 December 1942
Torrential rain all night. Hardly slept. Tenko at 7 a.m. Holmes fell sick in night, and two of us carried him to the hospital. Muddy and hard work all day, trying to put in foundations for bridge over river. Badly bruised my hands. Exhausted by trek through mud back to the camp. Teeth sore and wobbly in mouth. Dreamed last night of roast beef and Yorkshire pudding.

The final entry was dated less than a month later:

Last entry. No more paper. God bless us all.

Nick marvelled at the stoicism and the humour. He thought again of the photos of some surviving prisoners that he had seen during his recent research, with their skeletal physiques and gaunt, haunted faces, photographs that could have been taken at Belsen. His grandfather must have looked like that too.

There was nothing in the diary about Hemingway or Spain.

The final item in the box was a letter to William's widow Cecilia. Typed on the letterhead of the Royal Military College, it was dated 5 September 1945, and addressed to Mrs W.F. Harrieson, The Elms, Old Stoke Road, Aylesbury.

Dear Mrs Harrieson,
I understand that you have recently been informed of the tragic loss of your husband Lt. William Forbes Harrieson in the service of his country.
He was under my command in Thailand for the six months prior to his passing, and it is my privilege and duty to write to you.
Your husband was a fine man and soldier. He never shirked

responsibility, and always placed the welfare of his comrades ahead of his own. He never flinched in the face of adversity, and his spirit and patriotism did not waver despite deprivations that no human should have to endure. He spoke often and warmly of how he missed you and the children, and of the support and companionship that you and your children gave him.

He was a wonderful and erudite companion. He was famous among our cohort of prisoners for peppering his conversation with proverbs or quotations. For example, he would offer 'Neither a borrower nor a lender be' when another prisoner wanted to borrow a pencil – but would lend it to him anyway!

Another memorable expression was 'Send not to know for whom the bell tolls. It tolls for thee,' which discomfited some in the camp. He would say that directly to the camp guards, who fortunately did not understand English. Once he said he had given the latter quote to Ernest Hemingway, the American novelist, as a suggested title for his recent novel, but none of us believed him.

When he was at Changi he gave a series of well-received lectures on the modern American novel, so I dare say he was well informed about Hemingway anyway.

William was much respected by his peers. He died in terrible and tragic circumstances, a brave and proud Englishman, comrade and soldier to the end. I sincerely hope you can take some solace from my words.

I enclose the diary which William kept during the first part of his captivity. One of our men retrieved it and kept it hidden for the last two years.

I remain,
Yours sincerely
(Capt.) J.O. Dineen

Nick showed the letter to Mary. She read it in silence. When she had finished she raised her gaze to the window, as if she were staring into a bygone age. 'I haven't looked at this for thirty years. It's so terribly sad. What a waste, but at least he made a positive contribution for his country.'

'He most certainly did. You should be so proud of him.'

Nick sensed that Mary needed his company. They spent the rest of the day and all evening reminiscing about the greater family, and about Malaya and New Zealand and post-war England. Mary said the decisions to marry Bert and move to New Zealand were the best she ever made, and what a fine country it had been to her as an immigrant sixty years ago.

That night, in the spare bedroom's creaky single bed, Nick read the letter and its attachment that he had saved when rummaging through the boxes. It was written in William's neat and disciplined hand. It took half an hour. When he had finished he was excited beyond measure. Here was the proof of the Hemingway connection, and it left a hundred questions up in the air. How he wished to share his discovery with Adrienne. He sent photos of the first two pages to her SMS and resolved to call her in the morning.

8

Nick eased back in his seat and reflected on his forty-eight hours in Auckland. Tiring, yes, but successful beyond expectation. His excitement levels remained high. He had found something of major family significance and possibly of literary historical value too.

Adrienne had shared his elation when he rang her. It was almost midnight in London when he called, but she answered straight away and they chatted for half an hour, zipping from one topic to the other. He never mentioned – in fact, he now realised, he never even thought about – the harassment complaint. She said that she had printed the letter when he emailed a copy to her and had made about twenty notes for further enquiry.

The black beaches of the west coast near Auckland had long receded from view as Nick pulled out the letter again. It was well preserved, considering it was dated 3 May 1941.

The Residence,
Ipoh, F.M.S.

Mrs W.F. Harrieson
The Elms
The Old Stoke Road
Aylesbury, Bucks.

My darling Cecilia

This will not be my usual weekly letter. I am writing to send you a record, for your and my benefit and possibly that of the literary world, of a most remarkable encounter I had with Ernest Hemingway in Hong Kong last month.

First, I must enjoin you to secrecy about the contents of the attached monograph. In the wrong hands it would cause the Great Man unwanted attention and not inconsiderable embarrassment. You must promise that no one else will see it until at least five years have passed since EH has died. And if, heaven forbid, I do not emerge alive from the Japanese war that will start soon then I ask you to bequeath the monograph in a sealed envelope to Mary, with the instruction that she not open it until she is at least 21 years of age, if that is still relevant. So – Mum's the word.

Enough of the preliminaries. You will recall that I travelled to Hong Kong in late April to be briefed, along with representatives of other volunteer defence forces from the region, by some Royal Military College officers on various strategies and procedures should a Japanese invasion be imminent. I am afraid that I am sworn to secrecy about that.

Shortly after I arrived I noticed a small item in the South China Morning Post *to announce that the eminent American writer Ernest Hemingway and his new wife Martha Gellhorn had been in Hong Kong, although she had just left to return to the US. He was staying at the Peninsula Hotel – where else, you will be entitled to ask, would one of the most famous novelists of the times stay when visiting Hong Kong? I thought that enough time had elapsed since the trip to Spain in 1925 that there would be no lingering resentment (and after all he did send me that nice present afterwards) so I sent a note to the hotel, suggesting that we dine together the following evening. The reply came back within hours: 'All right. 8 pm at the hotel. EH.'*

I have attached my summary of my visit to Ernest. In it I use quotation marks as though these are word-for-word recordings of our conversation. No one's recall is perfect, but I have complete confidence in the substantial accuracy of the recorded conversation. When I returned to my hotel following my visit to the Peninsula, I spent several hours recording the details in my diary. I did so in a state of some excitement, as I knew already that what I would record has considerable value to literature scholars and possibly even to others.

I want you to keep this letter in a safe place. It properly belongs with my memoir of the trip to Spain in 1925. I do hope that old Beryl is looking after that memoir, because I don't have a copy, and I am determined on my next visit to England – which I pray will be soon – to retrieve it.

I will write again of more mundane matters tomorrow or the next day.

Your loving husband,
William

MONOGRAPH

A note of an encounter with Ernest Hemingway, the eminent American writer, on 30 April 1941 at the Peninsula Hotel, Kowloon, Hong Kong.

I presented myself at the Peninsula a little before 8 p.m. I strolled through those arched doors at the entrance and marvelled at the huge vaults that the lobby restaurant fills. The tall straight pillars made the scene even more magnificent than when Cecilia and I had that pleasant lunch there in 1937. Both sides of the restaurant were packed with noisy diners, with what seemed like hundreds of waiters scurrying around in their pressed black-and-white uniforms. The Grande Dame had never looked grander.

The man at reception told me that Mr H would see me in his room, and I was escorted up the grand central staircase, down some long corridors and up some more stairs. I knocked on the door, and EH greeted me with a grim face and beckoned me into the biggest hotel suite I have ever seen. The sitting room must have been 20 yards long, and the mahogany furniture was tasteful and expensive. Trust Ernie to travel in style.

He looked older than his 41 or 42 years. He had a thick bushy moustache, just like in the photographs in the newspaper, and his face was red and puffy. He wore rimless spectacles, and he was beginning to go grey at the temples. His chin looked as though he had not shaved for a day or two. He was also quite rotund, but still had that huge physical presence that I remembered so well. He was wearing a blue and gold silk dressing-gown, which led me to think that he may have forgotten about dinner. I could smell whisky on his breath.

He handed me a stiff glass of Scotch, and said, 'It must be 15 years, Limey?'

'Yes, almost 16. It's very good to see you again, Ernest.'

He smiled at me. 'You don't have to say that. My behaviour then was – how do you English say it? – beneath me, unbecoming. I'm sorry for what I did. I can blame only part of it on the drink. I've whacked and fought many men over the years. Most were blowhards or jerks, but you were one of the good guys. Took me a few weeks to figure that out, though.'

He chuckled and downed his drink in two or three gulps. I assured him that I bore him no ill will. I mentioned the line in Jane Eyre about life appearing too short to be spent in nursing animosity or registering wrongs. He liked that, he said, and complimented me on my ability to remember quotes.

I told him why I was in Hong Kong, and he agreed with me that war with Japan is inevitable. He had just been in China ('a godawful primitive place, worse than Kansas'), and said they too expect Japan to do something major in military terms within the next few months. He spoke knowledgeably about the political and military situation, and had met many of the leaders of the various factions in China.

I congratulated him on his recent wedding and said I hoped he had been having a happy honeymoon. He looked long and hard at me and said, 'No, we argue all the time. She's a tough broad and takes no crap from me or anyone else. We had far more fun before we got married.'

I said that I had followed his career closely over the intervening years and had read all of his books.

'I'm sorry to hear that,' he laughed. 'Most of them are not worth touching. Only two or three have any lasting quality. Sun, A Farewell to Arms *and* Death in the Afternoon. *Particularly* Death. *All of the rest are junk, no better than the rubbish produced by other quote, well-known writers, unquote.* I was described last week in the New York Times *as the best-known writer of the age. Shows you how little they know. But everyone concentrates on the headlines – the marriages, the fights, the life and not on what I write. The critics are stupid. Failed writers themselves, most of them, with batting averages of less than 100, and they wouldn't know a decent piece of work even if I threw it at them. Which I'd like to do.' He laughed at his own joke.*

I told him that I was honoured that he saw fit to base a character on me in The Sun Also Rises, *and said he had been rather easy on me.*

'Harris? Yes, I could've gone to town on you, a jumped-up Limey know-it-all smarmy prick, and I was in fact going to do that but Hadley persuaded me not to. She said that you were – her words – a good man and didn't deserve being pilloried. I wasn't so sure about that at the time, but she brought me around.'

I told him that we English didn't mind being lampooned, and that we rather encouraged it.

As he was filling up his third glass of whisky – and I assume he'd had at least one or two before I arrived – I asked him why he'd left Hadley out of the book.

'Ha,' he said, 'I knew you'd ask me that. I began to realise during the 1925 fiesta that I didn't love her anymore, and I don't think she loved me either. She was jealous of me talking to other women, especially Duff. I know you were aware of that.' I nodded in agreement. 'In your private conversations with Hadley she must have told you what a drunken, violent bastard I was and that she would leave me?'

'Not at all. On the contrary. She said how much she loved you and how much you needed her. For what it's worth, I agreed that you needed someone like Hadley to love you and look after you. She struck me as very loyal to you.'

EH stared at me. 'Do you think so? Perhaps I was too hard on her. I was only 25 or 26 at the time. Still a pup.' He paused. 'Did you stay in touch with Hadley after those two days in Pamplona?'

His question unnerved me a bit, as it betrayed some concerns or even suspicions on his part. I said no. I did not tell him that Cecilia and I had thought Hadley was such a pretty girl's name that we had given it to our daughter.

'Hadley and I were never the same after that trip to Burguete and Pamplona. We were happy together before we got to Spain, but in Pamplona and after we argued all the time, and I poured all my energies into writing Sun and drinking wine and whisky. I wanted to blame you for coming between us, but after a while I was intelligent enough, and I know that's hard to credit, to realise that the fault was mine. All of it. Hadley was a good woman, a fine wife and mother. Still is, I believe. In fact I met her in Wyoming a year and a half ago. She was with her husband Paul, a solid sort of guy. She – they – seemed content enough. I got the feeling she was relieved she didn't have to put up with me anymore.' Ernest laughed out loud, and I detected a hint of sadness and wistfulness in his expression.

'I think you'd have to say that she was a bit too sensible for me, more of a mother than a wife. Pauline was too, although she had a swell sense of fun. I should never have allowed Pauline to inveigle the happy life Hadley and I had in Paris. And Martha! Well, you haven't met her either, but she's a real ballbuster. I often think I'd be happier having lots of mistresses and keeping holy matrimony out of punching range.' He emptied his glass.

He seemed lost in reverie for a minute, perhaps contemplating the life of a bachelor. He then fetched another glass of whisky for each of us. 'You know, I never f—ed Duff. I nearly did. When she wanted me to yence her, I said no, and later she turned me down a few times. Hadley always thought we'd f—ed, and never believed my denials. I wished I had. She was a swell girl too, but difficult.'

I can guess what 'yence' means.

'It was fun in Burguete in 1925,' I offered. 'The company was great, and Donald and Bill were cracking jokes all the time. Pity the fishing wasn't the best. I assume that you based the fishing stories on your visits to the Irati area the year before.'

Ernest seemed to be thinking of other things. After a few seconds he said, 'It was hardly fun for me. I made an ass of myself with that

57

girl – a would-be nun, for Christ's sake. You saved my bacon that night. Hadley was giving me a hard time already – you wouldn't have seen that – and threatened to kick me out when she managed to get from me what had happened. And my, er, condition made walking difficult.' He chuckled. 'God knows why I asked you to help me out there. And the fishing was lousy. Still, you put me on to Africa, and I love that darby place, where the animals run free and there are fish in the mountain streams and the people are honest and no one stabs you in the back.'

As he was speaking, I thought of the green hills of Africa, and Ernest jotting down notes as we sat around the dining table drinking and talking late into the night at the Burguete Hotel. So many of my phrases and quotations ended up in his works, but my sense of diplomacy prevented me from reminding him of that. He seemed to be aware of my thought processes. I wonder if the reviewers would say such reverential things about Ernest if they knew that some of his key phrases and titles had been suggested by me.

'You know what, Guillermo? And this is something I have never told anyone. But it was you who gave me the idea to write Sun. *When we went to Pamplona, I wanted to research what would be the definitive book on bullfighting. Non-fiction, no bull's-milk. I'd been thinking for a year or two about writing a novel, even started one or two. But nothing stuck. Then you persuaded me, without any effort, that there was sufficient material within our group of friends to write a novel. What was it you said? Truth is stranger than fiction? Whatever, you saw that there was a work of fiction among those layabouts and losers and bums, not to mention saucy old Duff, and all the arguments and the tension and the sensuality and the bullfighting and the drinking and the fighting. Your comment hit me like a sucker punch right on the jaw. I looked at everyone differently from that moment on.'*

Ernest looked at me, almost like a father to a son, even though we are roughly the same age. I could see the gratitude in his face. 'Funnily enough, Donald made a similar suggestion a day or two after you. He too could see a novel there in Pamplona, although he suggested that a satire or a comic take on everyone might be the path to pursue. Anyhow, writing the book was the making of me. I wrote it in six weeks' flat. So, I owe you.' He raised his whisky glass in an exaggerated manner and emptied it in one gulp. 'Mind you, at the time I wanted to kick your f—ing ass all the way back to London town. You're lucky I didn't kill you on that last night before you left.'

We both laughed at that. I'm sure he was joking when he said those things, but you never know with him.

'You probably don't know this,' he said, 'but the very next night I nearly got into a fight with Loeb. I would've knocked his head off. Can't remember why. Hadley gave me such a hard time over that.'

I said that I hadn't been aware of the fight with Harold, and then conversation moved to other things. He made no mention of dinner, and it occurred to me he may already have eaten. We talked about relations between China and Japan, the bleak state of the war in Europe and how he hoped that the US would join the Allied side.

He even said that he was being trailed by Russian spies who wanted him to spy for the Soviet Union! I found this hard to believe, but he seemed very earnest (pun intended) about it, and asked me if I had seen them sitting in the hotel lobby earlier. Two shifty-looking men with moustaches and long coats, apparently. I said I would look for them on my departure. (I forgot to do that.)

After about an hour of chatting – and I must say we were getting on pretty well – the most extraordinary thing happened. There was a loud knock on the door, and when Ernest opened it in walked three beautiful Chinese girls. They were aged about 20, I guessed, wearing long traditional dresses of varying hues and bright-red lipstick. They were quite obviously 'ladies of the night'.

EH seemed surprised but delighted. One of them had a card hung around her neck, with the inscription "Love from CW" on it. Ernest roared with laughter when she handed him the card, saying to me that CW was one of his wealthy Cantonese friends in Hong Kong.

The young women chattered away in Chinese – I don't think they spoke a word of English – and draped themselves over him. One started stroking his moustache, pretending that it was a demonstration of virility. The two others slipped their hands inside Ernest's kimono and started stroking his chest. Throughout EH was whooping and clapping.

One of the girls started trying to kiss him, but he pushed her away and beckoned me over. 'Help me, Guillermo. I don't think I can cope with three of them at once.'

I politely declined, and I remonstrated when one of them walked towards me to lead me over to the others.

'Trust me,' he said, 'Asian girls are the best. They'll do anything for you. I had one in Hong Kong a few weeks back when Martha was interviewing local politicians. I had the best time.' Ernest was prone to exaggeration and bravado, but all I could do was stare and take it in.

Ernest ignored the young women, removing the hand of one from this thigh. 'Did you know that they say there are about 50,000 prostitutes in Hong Kong at the moment? 50,000!'

I didn't know what to say, so I said nothing. Ernest was warming to his subject.

'I've been told that these rich Red Chinese scour the villages all over China and send the prettiest of them to Hong Kong as working girls. The hotel bars are full of them. They sure are swell to look at, but conversation is difficult.' He let out a loud belly laugh.

He pushed the girls away and stood up. 'I'm going to have a shower with my new friends. That will help me get to know them better.' He pulled one of them towards the bathroom, and the others followed, giggling while they waddled across the carpet to the bathroom at the far right of the lounge. It was like a scene from the Mikado. 'You're welcome to take one and stay around for some action later.'

I stood and said that I ought to be heading back to my own hotel on the island. He looked rather patronisingly at me, as though I was a spoilsport for not wanting to join him, but I would never have joined him in that in a million years. He didn't try to stop me. We shook hands, and he looked me in the eye and said, 'Real life? Fiction? They're the same thing, Limey. Look me up after the war. I'll likely be in Cuba. We can go marlin fishing.' And on that odd note I made my way to the door, while the girls, by now wearing only towels to cover *their modesty, dramatically pretended that they were grief-stricken by my departure.*

Well, one can imagine what a strange evening it was, from start to finish. I never got to eat dinner with Ernest and never saw him again during my remaining days in Hong Kong, but I did get a card from him the next day, which said in his elegant handwriting: 'To Don G. Your loss. Simply the best. Don E.'

I laughed long and hard when I received the card. I like to think he was referring to the quality of my company and conversation, but I rather suspect not ... Unfortunately, I failed to keep his note where I would find it later, and I couldn't find it when I checked out of the hotel.

Wm Forbes Harrieson
The Residence
Ipoh
Federated Malay States
4 May, 1941

9

Nick had planned a two-day stopover in Bangkok on his way back to London. He thought about cancelling it and flying straight through, as he was keen to sit down with Adrienne to discuss William's letter and monograph, but in the end he decided he would break the journey in Thailand after all. He had never been there before, and there was a purpose.

The next day Nick stood in his shorts and T-shirt, sweating heavily despite it being the cool season, in front of William's grave at the Kanchanaburi War Cemetery. He had taken a day tour from Bangkok, which included an early pick-up from his hotel. Thailand was a festival of noise and colour. He marvelled at the incessant traffic in Bangkok and on the road west, the honking of horns, the people everywhere on the sides of the road with their stalls of produce or trinkets, chattering away. Motorcycles, scooters and bicycles slowed the traffic down to a crawl for much of the journey, but Nick didn't mind. He was entranced by this engaging land, where people smiled and treated everyone with courtesy and respect.

The cemetery was not hard to find. It was a key part of the tourist trail centred on the Death Railway, and when he arrived Nick knew exactly where he would find the grave. Lot 8 was on the left of the entrance, about a hundred yards away, and he quickly left his tour companions and headed in that direction, past hundreds of identical-looking gravestones, each represented by an angled charcoal-grey metal plaque mounted on a concrete block about seven to ten inches high. On the left of William's plaque was a large, simple cross, and to the right, under the crest of what Nick took to be the FMSVF, were the simple words:

1812489 LIEUTENANT W.F. HARRIESON
Federated Malay States Volunteer Forces
2nd OCTOBER 1943 AGE 44

AT THE SINKING OF THE SUN AND IN THE MORNING
WE SHALL REMEMBER THEM

Nick felt a well of emotion as he stood before the grave. His grandfather died young, only a few years younger than himself. How could a starving forty-something do a twelve-hour day of heavy labour, seven days a week, in appalling conditions? And what did poor William die of? Was it cholera or measles? Was it starvation? Executed by the Japanese? A work accident? Suicide, even?

Tears flowed down Nick's face. Here was the grave of a good volunteer soldier, a loyal servant of his country, a devoted family man, an expert of sorts on modern US fiction and no doubt many other subjects, and dead after almost two years of captivity and soul-destroying labour in pursuit of a mad plan to build a railway through the jungle. It was only a small consolation that his name and legacy were still remembered, seventy-five years later.

He was tempted to glue a paper onto the plaque, with a further inscription:

FRIEND OF ERNEST HEMINGWAY

Now *that* would set William apart from the thousands of other servicemen and prisoners who were buried in Kanchanaburi.

Late that afternoon, back in his Bangkok hotel, Nick felt lonely and sad. He was mourning the loss of a relative, someone whom he was getting to know, and despairing of the futility of William's death. He needed to talk to someone. He considered ringing Jo, or Adrienne, but decided instead to call Aunt Mary. Even though it was late in New Zealand he knew that she liked to stay up almost to midnight most nights. She answered on the second ring.

'Hello, Mary. Nick here, from Bangkok. I've been to see Grandpa's grave.'

'Oh, I'm so pleased. I feared that you might not be able to find it. Please tell me everything you saw.'

Nick told her of the cemetery, the rows of immaculately tended graves, the inscription on the headstone. He talked of the pride he felt, and of the futility of the last two years of William's life.

'Yes, you're right. The Japanese have so much to answer for. But he gave his life willingly, for king and country, and for the protection of his family.' Nick thought he could hear a stifled sob.

'He was a dear man, much loved by us all. God, how we all wept when we knew at last that he would never be coming home.' She was crying now, and Nick felt for his aunt, all alone with her sad memories.

'Well, I was there honouring him today. For you, and Dad, and Jo, and for Grandma. He lies in peace, honoured by a beautifully maintained headstone and lawn, and side by side with his fellow prisoners and servicemen. He is in the best hands, Mary.'

'Yes, I know, Nick. And thank you, from the bottom of my heart.'

'You can also draw comfort from the fact that his life was

64

a full and rich one. He lived in far-flung places, he knew some famous people, and he was knowledgeable in so many fields. He had a fine family whom he loved.'

'Yes, that's very true. Do find out more about his life if you can. I'd love to learn more. I must sleep now. Good night, Nick. Your visit has brought me much joy.'

Nick put the phone down, feeling tired as well as emotionally wrung out. Within a minute he fell asleep.

Not long after his plane took off from Bangkok airport the next morning, Nick retrieved a copy of *The Sun Also Rises* from his bag. He had bought it at a marvellous little bookshop in Auckland's CBD. Remarkably it was still in print. This particular edition had been reprinted fifteen times since 2000. He had never read it before. At school he had read *The Old Man and the Sea*, and at university he went through a minor Hemingway phase and had read and been impressed by *A Farewell to Arms* and *For Whom the Bell Tolls*, and some of his short stories. He settled down to read.

10

Nick and Adrienne were both ten minutes early for their 10 a.m. rendezvous. She jumped up and, to his considerable surprise, hugged him as soon as he walked into the Ladbroke Grove café he had chosen as being sufficiently out of the way that they wouldn't be spotted.

She was fizzing with energy and excitement about William Harrieson's 1941 letter. Nick had brought along a copy of the letter and the monograph with him. 'Nick, what you've found is so exciting. But first of all, how do you know they're genuine?'

'It's definitely William's handwriting. My aunt confirmed that when I showed her the letter a few days ago. I think we need to do some research to find out whether Hemingway was in Hong Kong in April 1941. It does seem late in a historical perspective, bearing in mind that Europe had been at war for eighteen months by then.'

'Yes. What's more, Hemingway does come across as a bit of a jerk. What we call a *sae-ggi*. And you have to admit those stories about the prostitutes and the Russian spies seem fanciful. Since I got your email I've been so busy on my thesis that I've had hardly any time to Google everything about Hemingway. I know he was obviously quite a guy, who knew heaps of famous people and had lots of success with his books, and I'm going to read everything I can about him when I get the time. One thing

I have learned is that Hem was a great exaggerator, and invented stories about himself and his exploits, and perhaps the spies bit may fall into that category. But the Chinese hookers? We have your grandfather's word for it, not Hem's, and that must be worth something.'

'Yes, I'm sure you're right. William was by all accounts a sensible and moral man and civil servant. It would be unthinkable for him to invent such a story. And the fact that he asked my grandmother not to publish the monograph for a long time supports that too.'

Adrienne nodded. 'I'll do some research online to see if Hem was in fact in Hong Kong then, and if there's anything written about the prostitutes or the Russian spies.'

'Thanks, but I think in many ways the Hong Kong aspects are of lesser importance.'

Adrienne frowned.

'Sorry, I don't want to deter you from doing that research. On the contrary. But to me the major revelation is that William seems to have been with Hem, as you call him, in Pamplona in 1925 and that the character Harris in *The Sun Also Rises* is based on William. I'm sure that's news to the literary world. Have you read the book?'

Adrienne shook her head.

'I think you should. Read my copy.' He handed her the book he had bought in Auckland. 'In it there is a rather colourless character called Harris – not a million miles from Harrieson. They meet while on fishing trips in a town called Burguete, which is near Pamplona. Burguete gets a mention in William's monograph. But Harris doesn't appear in the main part of the novel, in Pamplona. I have no idea why.'

'Yes, I need to read it *tout de suite.*'

Nick smiled. Her use of French phrases in her conversations with him suggested a bond between them, almost a conspiracy. And then he remembered the harassment complaint. *What a bizarre situation he was in.* 'Yes, you must,' he said.

'There are so many mysterious references in the monograph. William saving Hemingway's bacon over a girl – can't wait to find out more about that. And William seems to imply that Hem used a lot of your grandpa's expressions and quotations in his books, as if Hemingway was a bit of a copycat. And that discussion about Hem's wife Hadley struck me as weird. I take it that a character based on Hadley is *not* in *The Sun Also Rises*?'

Nick nodded.

'Perhaps the Hemingway marriage was falling apart in 1925. I think he got together with Pauline Pfeiffer in 1926, according to Wikipedia, possibly even in late 1925, didn't he?'

'I believe so.' Nick paused to collect his thoughts. 'The answers to all those questions – and we haven't even talked about the reference you found about William and Hem having had a fight and Hem's apparent apology about that – must lie in the memoir William mentioned of his trip to Spain in 1925. How exciting it would be if we could track it down.' Nick was startled that he had used the word 'we' without thinking.

'Absolutely,' said Adrienne. 'That's the key. And luckily we have a big clue. 'Old Beryl', whoever she may be. Does that name ring any *cloches* for you?'

Nick gave her a broad grin. 'Not at this stage, I'm afraid. I've been racking my brains about it for the last three or four days. I mentioned it to my Aunt Mary before I left Auckland. The name meant nothing to her. I also emailed my sister. Jo had no recollection of the name either. She wondered whether Beryl might have been a neighbour, or possibly a family friend of my grandparents.'

'Well, it seems that finding Beryl may be the key. And if Beryl was 'old Beryl' in the early 1940s then she would have died over fifty years ago. Even seventy years ago. I'm not sure where you'd begin to look for her.'

Nick nodded his acknowledgement of the apparent

impossibility of the task. 'And even if we could find Beryl's descendants, the chances of the memoir being in existence must be pretty slim.'

'Cheer up, Nick. You can't be defeated so early. With your trusted and talented research assistant to help, nothing is impossible.'

All Nick could say was a limp 'Thank you.'

'I'm afraid I can't help much over the next few days. I have two blogs to write by the end of tomorrow, and I have to work on my thesis too. I've dug up some interesting stuff about the Koreans' role on the Death Railway, and I need to check a few more references. Plus I have to read *Sun*. There's no rest for the wicked.'

'Blogs? What blogs do you write?'

'I thought I'd told you. A few years ago I started a website for Korean foodies visiting London. It's all in Korean. I visit lots of restaurants – most will give me a free meal in exchange for a mention on the website. I don't do it for the money, but I ask visitors to the site to transfer a bit of money to my Paypal account if they find my blogs and recommendations helpful. I get about five hundred pounds a year.'

'I had no idea,' said Nick. 'You're clearly multi-talented. A top musician in two instruments, proficient in at least three languages, a foodie, a blogger, an internet entrepreneur, with several university degrees under your belt.'

'And the rest. Don't stop there. But all of it doesn't help me find a good man who wants to marry me and give me babies.'

This was a new side to Adrienne. He wondered whether she was being flippant, and decided she wasn't. He now saw her vulnerability, the first suggestion that despite her outward confidence and drive she may be insecure. He felt compassion and smiled at her with empathy.

She giggled. 'Just joking. I said that for a laugh.'

They agreed to meet in a week's time, at the same place, but promised they would be in contact if one of them made any significant discovery.

Just as they were about to part, Nick sat up with a start, admonished himself and put a hand on Adrienne's arm to stop her from leaving. 'Silly me. I've just realised that I forgot to tell you one of the main things I discovered after reading the book.' He told her about the goblet his sister possessed, and its mysterious inscription. 'In *Sun,* the lead character, Jake, makes a comment that everyone behaves badly. That matches almost exactly the wording on the goblet. So there's a clear connection. And who is Don E? I think that must be E for Ernest, and Don as you know is a Spanish honorific of some description. And Don G? Well, G may be short for Guillermo, which is the Spanish equivalent of William. And—'

'Hem called him Guillermo in the monograph. The goblet must have been given by Hem to your granddad as a peace offering. Well done, Nick. You're obviously much smarter than you look.'

He laughed. 'Yes, and it all fits in with the apology Hemingway gave William. Now all we have to do is find out what he was saying sorry for. Without doubt it was for behaving badly. The plot has thickened.'

'It certainly has.' Adrienne rose to her feet, clutching her tote bag under her arm. 'I have to go. *Au revoir.*' She smiled and made her way out into the wintry gloom.

That night Nick called Aunt Mary in Auckland to update her on his investigations into William and Hemingway. Again she answered on the second ring. He wondered whether she spent all day and night beside the phone. After swapping pleasantries about his trip back to London, Nick mentioned he'd now read *The Sun Also Rises.* 'A few things in the Hong Kong letter now fall into place. Most important, the character Harris in the book does seem to be based on Grandpa, although the character is nondescript and unimportant to the plot.'

'Well, my father was a relatively modest and unassuming man, according to my mother, so that's really no surprise.'

'That may be so, but Grandpa was clearly in Spain when Hemingway was there in 1925. Something must have happened between the two for which Ernest apologised to Grandpa in Hong Kong. And there is some corroborating evidence too.' Nick described the inscription on Jo's goblet and the reference in the book to everyone behaving badly.

'Yes, the goblet. I remember it now. Mum used to keep it in a cabinet in the sitting room in Aylesbury. Your father and I had no idea what the inscription meant. Mum always said she didn't know, but perhaps she did, after all. How interesting.'

'It certainly is. The key thing now is to try to find the memoir that Grandpa apparently wrote after his trip to Spain. That will mean we need to find out who 'old Beryl' is. Any further thoughts on who that might be?'

'I'm sorry, Nick. I've tried as hard as I can over the last few days to remember who Beryl was. I can vaguely remember Mum mentioning the name once or twice. But I can't remember the context. It would have been sixty or seventy years ago. My memory isn't what it used to be.'

'Whose is? It's a very long shot, I know.'

'But if I do remember you'll be the first to know. Anyway, I'm still coming to terms with the fact that my father knew Ernest Hemingway. I feel so proud of him. He did get about a bit and met lots of people through his work on his travels. So perhaps it's not such a big surprise. But still …' Mary's voice tailed off.

'Well, we'll certainly stay in touch on this. You never know what might turn up.'

'Oh, one more thing. Any family correspondence or memoirs you dig up, including the 1941 letter about Hong Kong, treat them as yours and Jo's. They're no use to me now. Do with them what you wish.'

11

Nick emerged from the staircase of the Brompton Road Tube station. It was fitting that Sadie's office was less than a hundred yards from Harrods. He could see her buying her lunch at the food hall or buying a new dress for an important dinner.

Sadie was wearing a stylish, knee-length bright-yellow dress and navy high heels. She welcomed Nick with a broad smile and a kiss on the cheek. She closed the door and they sat down in the meeting room.

'Thanks for coming in,' she said. 'I think it's important that we discuss the next steps and how I see things playing out. I take it you've read the complaint from Kathy Mulligan, and the witness statements from Miss Kim and Mr Singh?'

Nick nodded. 'Yes, as quickly as I could. I couldn't believe how they've all distorted what was a friendly conversation, just banter.'

'Well, there's banter and there's banter. And I'm afraid we're having to deal with the other type of banter. Plus, there's more. I've received a letter from the University's lawyers, no doubt written at the behest of Ms Mulligan. They express, I quote, "deep concern" that you were seen talking to the witness Miss Kim at the British Library about ten days ago.'

Nick admitted talking to Adrienne, but said they'd run into each other by accident. They had not talked about the complaint, he said.

'That makes no difference, I'm afraid. They describe it as an attempt by you to pervert the course of justice, which I think is overstating things, and they also say that if you make contact with Miss Kim again before the hearing they'll report you to the Law Society. If the Law Society wants to investigate, you could end up losing your practising certificate. And without your practising certificate you won't be able to continue to eke out a bit of extra income by writing opinions to practising lawyers on obscure legal points. What's more, your ability to move into private practice in the future will be jeopardised. So you definitely do *not* want the Law Society getting involved. I'm afraid they have grounds for complaint about your contact with Miss Kim. University policy, which you have agreed to abide by under your employment contract, is crystal clear that in these circumstances as a staff member accused of harassment you are not permitted any contact with a complainant or a witness.'

'Yes, I know, but the contact complained of was accidental.'

Nick could see straight away that Sadie's finely honed instinct as an experienced cross-examiner picked up on his choice of words. 'And have there been other contacts?' Her face was impassive.

Nick thought for a few seconds. 'Well, yes, actually. We both have an interest in an item of, er, historical research. We don't talk about the case.'

Sadie smiled. 'And why am I not surprised, Crosser? You know the University rules, and you know my advice on the subject.' Now it was her turn to pause. 'But if you do feel you have to contact Miss Kim on this other, undoubtedly vitally important matter of historical research' – the sarcasm was heavy, as if a steaming pile of horse manure had been deposited on the meeting room table – 'then make sure you're not seen by anyone, and nothing in writing, please. And that includes emails and texts.'

'Thank you, Sadie. You're most understanding.' He smiled at her.

'Now, Nick, these witness statements. One thing that struck me, and I would like your view, is that all three statements look as if they've been written by the same person. The language used is similar, and they all recall identically the same words that you are alleged to have said. Witnesses, in my experience, rarely have identical recall, even minutes after the event.'

Nick seized on this. 'Yes, my thoughts exactly. Certain words are classic Kathy: "sleazeball", "leering", "patriarchy".'

'Quite. I allowed myself to smile when I read the word "patriarchy".'

Sadie was regarded as a role model for young women in the legal profession, but Nick knew she regarded herself as a feminist with a lower-case 'f'. She had written and lectured often on the desirability and need for women lawyers to be promoted and rewarded in law firms and universities to the same degree as men were, but her words were never polemical or hostile to men. The simple fact was that she liked men despite their many faults and, Nick thought, in many ways because of the faults.

'So let us assume Kathy wrote these. Then there's a good chance that Miss Kim and Mr Singh may not feel as strongly, and may not recall as lucidly, as she does. So I think we need to attack those two, in cross-examination. I'll need to be particularly firm with Miss Kim.'

'Do you have to? Apart from this wretched complaint, I like her very much.'

'I'm sorry, Nick. You're facing career ruin here. Publication of your name in the national press, opinion pieces in the *Guardian*, the whole women's lobby attacking you from every angle. The Twittersphere will go ballistic with trolls and abuse from mindless idiots. I suspect you don't follow its workings, but the women and equalities subcommittee of the House of Commons has just announced an enquiry into sexual harassment at work. They're bound to look at the universities. The PM herself is reportedly very supportive of the committee's work. We have to fight this and fight it hard. And we must do it at the hearing. If we lose there may be no grounds for appeal.'

Nick felt troubled. He wanted to save his job and his reputation, but not if it meant destroying the good, decent and vulnerable Adrienne. He suppressed a thought that he should tip her off.

'We have to attack her testimony,' Sadie said. 'That means that your friendship with her will be aired before the committee, but at most I think that will be only slightly embarrassing for you.' She paused. 'I promise I'll be as gentle on her as possible. I'll call her testimony only after I've given Mr Singh and, I hope, Ms Mulligan a good working over. Deal?'

'Yes, we have a deal,' said Nick, but without conviction.

Nick took the Tube up to Islington to have lunch with his sister. Jo owned a bookshop in Canonbury. It was small, but whenever he visited there were at least a dozen customers browsing through the shelves. The shop was always a riot of colour, famous for the range of books displayed in the shop window, a display which changed once a week. Beside a book of glossy Helmut Newton photographs would be one on French nineteenth-century philosophers, a photographic survey of dress hemlines, the latest Wisden cricket almanac, a new biography of Vivien Leigh, or a history of West African gay literature.

Nick always liked visiting the shop, staffed as it was by earnest and well-read English Lit graduates, invariably women, who appeared to have total knowledge of all of the books in the shop. Rarely did Nick buy one without the assistant congratulating him on his choice.

Even though he was dismayed by his meeting with Sadie, he was looking forward to seeing Jo. He had reported to her on his visits to Mary in Auckland and to William's grave and had emailed her a copy of the Hong Kong letter and monograph.

When he had figured out the quote on the goblet sitting on her mantelpiece, he had rushed to call her again. She had joined him in his excitement, delighted that the goblet had such a provenance. 'Let's have lunch tomorrow. There are a couple of books in my shop which will interest you. Come any time after noon.'

When Nick stepped into the shop Jo waved him over to the extensive Biography section. She pulled out two books for him, a paperback and a hardback. 'You'll need these, and they're both fascinating.'

Nick was drawn to the title of the paperback. He gave a 'Ha!' of recognition. It was *Everyone Behaves Badly* by Lesley M. M. Blume. Below the title was the famous black-and-white photograph of Ernest and his merry band (Hadley, Duff Twysden, Harold Loeb, Pat Guthrie, Donald Ogden Stewart and Bill Smith) at the Café Iruña in Pamplona in 1925.

'This is essential reading for you. It gives a wonderful portrait of Hemingway's life in Paris and, even better, a detailed description of his visit to Spain in 1925. I haven't read it, but Chloe' – she pointed to a young woman with red curls and tattooed arms – 'tells me it's brilliant and full of fun stories. I'm afraid Grandpa's name isn't in the index.'

Nick felt his heart rate increase. There would be so much information there.

'The other book is fascinating too.' She handed him *The Hemingway Log*. 'It's by Brewster Chamberlin, an American academic. It sets out exactly where Hemingway was every day of his life, or nearly every day.'

Nick bought both books and an extra copy of *Everyone Behaves Badly*.

At the restaurant Jo ordered a Thai beef salad, and Nick had a Provençal-style trout with aubergines and asparagus. They chatted easily.

'You'll love those books,' Jo said. 'Chloe said that the thing she took from *Everyone Behaves Badly* is that you have to pick your holiday companions very carefully. I think you'll see what she means when you read it. Who did you buy the second copy for?'

Nick stumbled over his reply. 'Oh, a friend at London King's who's been helping me with research on Grandpa.' Jo raised her eyebrows. 'No one important,' he added.

Jo moved on. 'The other book is remarkable in its own way. It confirms for me what a vast Hemingway industry there is out there. You would think that no one, especially not a frontline publisher, would be interested in the daily location of a novelist who died almost sixty years ago. But the opposite is true. Apparently on average five significant biographical works on Hemingway are published every year. There are Hemingway societies and online user groups, many of them very active. He's still studied at universities across America. Multi-day symposia on him are held frequently, and they are well attended. And his novels still sell. I read somewhere that over three hundred thousand copies of *The Sun Also Rises* are sold every year, even now. That figure seems far-fetched to me, although in my little shop we would sell four or five copies a year. The book comes out of copyright in 2022, I believe, which will mean further editions will be published.'

Nick listened intently. 'And you know what's bizarre about all that?' Jo's question was rhetorical. 'The funny thing is that Hemingway, in 2018, is regarded by everyone with a brain, and by virtually all women, as mysogynistic, violent, unhealthy, gun-nut, animal-hating boozer. A caricature. Almost,' she finished with a flourish, 'the stereotype of a Trump supporter.'

'Yes,' agreed Nick. 'Except for his left-wing sympathies. No doubt the reason he remains in the public eye is because of the things you mention, not despite them. In a world of celebrity he's head and shoulders above what passes for fame these days. Just think of all those footballers, reality-show stars, television presenters and the like who fill up the MailOnline. And what's there not to be fascinated by? A legendary womaniser – four wives, for God's sake. Big-game hunter. Marlin fisherman. Expert on bullfighting. Writer of best-sellers and winner of the Nobel prize. Famous war correspondent. Fights and feuds with all and sundry. And then he blew his own head off with a shotgun.'

Jo smiled. 'Yes, all of that and more. How amazing that our grandfather was a friend of his. I do hope you get to the bottom of it. There's a story there.'

Yes, but Nick didn't have any confidence that he would be able to find out much more unless he could identify 'old Beryl'.

They talked more about their grandfather's account of his visit to the Peninsula Hotel. 'That sure was a surreal visit, if ever there was one,' said Jo. 'Those prostitutes, all that whisky drinking, all those cryptic references to their previous experiences in Spain. One thing that struck me about the monograph is how frank he was in recording the events and conversations. I would have thought that the code of the day would have meant that a well-educated man didn't write such things to his wife, presumably sitting chastely at home looking after the kids.'

'Yes, I noted that too. Perhaps our grandparents had a modern-type relationship? That Cecilia's ears and eyes didn't need protecting? Apart from those silly little gaps in the naughty words …'

Nick smiled. 'I'm sure you're right. I'm impressed too that Grandpa had sufficient recall of his visit to Ernest to put all the conversations in speech marks.'

'Mmm. I remember Dad saying once that he was assiduous about writing up his daily diary, often staying up late to record the day's events. So he would've had the best source material for his recollections.'

'Certainly would have. And didn't Dad also say that a year or two after the war Cecilia threw out all of Grandpa's diaries and journals? Apparently because they took up too much space in their little house in Aylesbury. But you do wonder …' Nick paused. 'What a shame the diaries don't exist. I imagine they told a much fuller story than we'll ever know.'

'Yes, the more we find out about Grandpa the more we realise we don't know.'

By the time Nick's train had reached Notting Hill Gate he had ascertained that the great American novelist had been in Hong Kong at various times between February and May 1941, staying part of the time at the Peninsula Hotel. There was even a footnote in *The Hemingway Log* to the effect that three prostitutes may have visited Hemingway at the hotel. Nick knew then that William's account of his Hong Kong visit was authentic. And it would be of huge interest to Hemingway scholars and possibly of greater public interest too.

12

By two in the morning Nick had finished *Everyone Behaves Badly*. There was no mention of his grandfather, but the stories of Pamplona and the bulls, and the drinking and the fighting and the sexual tensions, were hugely entertaining.

He resolved to visit Pamplona. He knew that the annual San Fermin *fiesta* was held every year in July, and this year he would go. Not to run with the bulls – he was too sensible to do that – but to get a feel for the place.

When he woke there was a text from Adrienne on his phone, sent at one o'clock:

We need to talk. C u at 11?

Adrienne was in the 'less is more' camp of texters, and Nick had no idea what she wanted to talk about. He arrived late at the café, cursing himself for deciding to take the Tube when it would have been quicker to walk to Ladbroke Grove, even if it would have meant more time outside in the freezing late January air. Adrienne had her back to the door. Her hair was tied up, her neck long and refined. He thought of Audrey Hepburn.

Adrienne seemed startled to see him when he sat down, but gave him a pinched-looking smile as she turned off her phone and removed her earphones. 'Sorry,' she said. 'I was miles away. I've been listening to all these true crime podcasts, and I just can't get enough of them. They're beginning to distract me from my thesis. This one is particularly gripping. Ted Bundy, you know?' She paused and looked down at the table between them.

'I think you have something you want to say, Adrienne. Do tell. You'll feel better for having done so.'

Adrienne lowered her head even further.

'I'm afraid I can't go on meeting you or helping you with your research. I got such a threatening email from Kathy Mulligan last week when she found out that we'd been seen together at the British Library. She said such mean things to me.' She looked stressed.

Nick reached out and pushed away a few strands of her hair that had fallen in front of her eyes. She didn't seem to mind, or perhaps she didn't notice.

'Kathy's a bitch,' he said. 'She gave me a bollocking too. Isn't it silly that we're both terrified of her?' Adrienne gave him the faintest of smiles. 'But I'm afraid she has a point. The hearing is less than a week away, and we're taking awful risks by staying in touch like this.'

He leaned across the table and took her hands in his. She didn't resist. 'I feel conflicted. I think you're wonderful, for so many reasons.'

She smiled, appearing grateful for the compliment.

'How it has come to this ghastly hearing is a mystery to me. And I think it's even a mystery for you too.' She nodded. 'But that's where we are. I have no idea what will happen at the hearing. I'll try to defend myself, as I don't want to lose my job, or my good name. I'm not looking forward to it, obviously.'

Adrienne looked unhappy, her eyes glazed. 'Yes, it'll be awful. I can hardly sleep worrying about it. We Koreans have a word for it. *Joj-dwaesseo*. It means I'm fucked, whatever happens.' Nick empathised with her anguish, but said nothing.

'I know you're not a bad man. You do have, ah, redeeming features. But you shouldn't have said what you said at the party, at least not in front of other people. That was humiliating for me.' Nick let go of her hands. How soft her skin had felt.

Nick paused for a second, remembering how she had smiled for a brief moment when he had said the words at the cocktail function, and also how she had taunted him with the same expression at the British Library a few weeks back. 'Yes, I accept what you say. I can understand it, too.' There was so much more to say. Instead he stood up. 'I should go. Whatever happens, I wish you well, and I do hope you get a Distinction for your thesis. I'll carry on the research on my own, and I'm more than grateful for your contributions.'

He cursed himself for the formal way he often spoke when he felt threatened. He was just about to depart when he realised that he had brought his second copy of *Everyone Behaves Badly* for Adrienne. He reached into his bag and handed it to her. 'Here. I got this for you. It's well worth a read, even if you won't be working on the Hemingway connection anymore.' She tried to decline the gift, but he insisted. He moved to the counter to pay for their teas and left the café without looking back.

13

The next few days passed slowly. Nick's thoughts were dominated by the upcoming disciplinary committee hearing, now less than a week away. He began browsing through industry periodicals and websites to see what vacancies there might be for a law professor in other English universities. He flirted with the possibility of taking a job abroad – perhaps in America or Canada, parts of the world he didn't know well.

He wondered about chucking teaching in. Why not sell his flat and go to live in Crete or the Algarve, open or buy a café or a seaside bar, and live a lotus-eating existence? He could call it Sloppy Joe's and serve Hemingway Daiquiris as the signature cocktail. But then, a ghastly thought, if and when Brexit occurred, he might not be able to live and work in Europe.

Two days before the hearing he took the underground to meet with Sadie. He wore a bright-red shirt in a vain effort to lift his spirits. He felt like a prisoner facing the gallows. Sadie had insisted that he prepare fully for the hearing. She coached him on his answers to the questions she would ask him, and also to those she expected from the University's barrister. She briefed him on his manner in the hearing. On no account could he be arrogant or dismissive of the process or the disciplinary committee, and under pain of death he was not to betray any sense that he was the victim of a personal vendetta or a feminist conspiracy. The only possibility of a successful outcome would depend upon attacking the sincerity of Adrienne's statement and the supporting testimony of the student Singh.

Nick urged her to take it easy on Adrienne.

'Yes, I hear you. But don't forget she has submitted an affidavit which, if accepted at face value by the disciplinary committee, will mean that you lose your job. You will receive unwelcome publicity in the media if Fleet Street picks it up, and that's a real possibility.' Nick's heart missed a beat at the thought. 'I'll be firm with her, professional, and persistent in getting her to answer my questions, but I won't be scathing or aggressive. Okay?'

Nick nodded, with a slight grimace.

'And just to remind you, once the University has put its case I'll be responding with evidence from you about your friendship with Miss Kim and the positive, nurturing and' – she appeared to be searching for the right word – 'wholesome lecturer/ student relationship you and she had prior to the, ah, incident. The risk is that the University tries to bring up any evidence or questions about you and Miss Kim being in touch – including the accidental meeting at the British Library – since the incident.'

Nick wished she didn't keep referring to it as 'the incident', as though he had physically groped or lunged at Adrienne.

'If they do that,' Sadie looked Nick in the eye, 'they will try to portray you as a predatory or controlling Svengali.'

When he left Sadie's office Nick was in a state of semi-automatism, feeling defeated and pilloried already. That evening, in his flat in Kensington Park Road, he drank a whole bottle of sauvignon blanc and was tempted to open another after reading a text from Kathy Mulligan:

Bet you're looking forward to the hearing on Friday. I am, big time!!!

Five minutes later, as Nick was considering whether and how he should respond, he received a follow-up text:

I can recommend people who are expert at cleaning out offices at short notice! Haha.

Nick decided another glass of wine was justified. He decided not to reply – if it ever became relevant he would pretend not to have received the texts – and instead allowed his mind to reflect on a previous text Kathy had sent him. It was over nine years ago, after the two of them had returned from a weekend in Whitstable in Kent. It was only a month after their relationship had become a sexual one, and it was their first holiday together. Nick was keen to visit Whitstable to see if he could recognise any of the locations he remembered from reading *Cakes and Ale* and *Of Human Bondage* in his student days.

The weekend had been an unqualified success. The town was attractive, more or less as described by Maugham ninety years or so before, the oysters were fresh and the beer crisp, and the sex had been varied and exciting. Kathy had been enthusiastic and high-spirited and altogether the best companion. Not long after they returned to their respective abodes on Sunday night she had sent him a text. Even now, after all the years and everything that had happened, he could recall the message word-for-word:

You beautiful man. Thank you for the most memorable, loving and sexy weekend I have ever spent. I have never known a man with your intelligence and generosity of spirit (not to mention stamina!!!) xxx

Kathy had always liked using exclamation marks in her texts. Now, Nick struggled to find any generosity of spirit towards her. There was none that he could see in her make-up anymore. He was glad that their relationship had not continued for long. It was fortunate that they had kept it quiet, as they had not wanted to alienate colleagues in the law faculty nor give any ammunition to Nick's wife during the divorce negotiations.

Nick sat in his armchair, pondering the vicissitudes of his current situation, when his phone beeped again. *Not another text from Kathy, surely?* But no, it was from Adrienne. He had not expected to hear from her.

have found out something terrible about your granddad will explain it face to face also have decided that i wont offer any evidence at the hearing ive asked that my affidavit and the complaint be withdrawn.

Nick was astonished and confused. Would this mean the hearing itself would be discontinued? Would the university's lawyers proceed anyway? It was too late to call Sadie, and he resolved to do so early in the morning. He replied to Adrienne:

Thanks, I'm very grateful. I am sorry things have come as far as this. I want you to know I never meant anything hurtful or objectionable.

Adrienne shot back:

Well why not arent i attractive enough for you or too old or too young haha

Nick was puzzled. She seemed drunk, or drugged, and unstable. He tried again:

You misunderstand me.

Her reply came within seconds:

dont think so haha night xx

Nick stared at his phone and wondered at this turn of events. What on earth had got Adrienne into this state of mind? Then he remembered her comment about William in her first text, a few minutes ago. What were the terrible things she had discovered, and why did she have to tell him in person?

He sat back in his armchair, not knowing whether his ordeal was over. He would find out soon enough. He hoped Adrienne was okay. He realised now that this whole, abject thing had been an ordeal for her too, pressured and bullied to make a complaint against a lecturer she liked, obliged to have a different supervisor for her thesis, facing an unpleasant and potentially hostile cross-examination at the hearing and, he figured, fearing being responsible for Nick losing his job and derailing his career. Little blame could be attributed to Adrienne. She had been a pawn in the game. No, the real villains were himself and Kathy Mulligan.

14

Nick awoke early, a little tense as he wondered what the day would bring. He didn't have to wait long. Just before nine, as he was dressing after his shower, Sadie rang him on his mobile. She didn't even bother to say hello.

'It's all over, Nick. The complaint has been withdrawn, the hearing tomorrow won't take place, and that'll be the end of the matter. The University's barrister emailed me first thing. She's very pissed off. She was looking forward to putting you through the mincer.'

Nick looked upwards. 'Thank God for that. I was very worried about the hearing.'

'You were right to be. It could have been very nasty for you. Apparently Miss Kim withdrew her statement yesterday and has refused to testify. God knows why. Perhaps she was terrified of the grilling she was going to get from me.'

'Yes, I'm sure that was the reason. She texted me last night to say she was withdrawing.'

'Really? I suspect that I know only a quarter of the story of you and the mysterious Miss Kim, but at last she's come to her senses. Your ordeal is over, Nick. One thing to be aware of, though. Complaints laid against the teaching staff which are withdrawn before a hearing can't be reinstated in the future or form the basis of a further complaint by the same complainant.

But here the complainant was Kathy Mulligan, not Miss Kim. So in theory the young lady could lay her own complaint about the same incident, and the rules would not prevent her doing that. It's hardly likely to happen, but she has eighteen months from the original incident to do something about it. That would make it mid-June 2019. It's worth keeping at the back of your mind. Have a good day, Nick. All that remains is for me to send you a fat bill for all my efforts.' She laughed and hung up.

Nick had little time to process what Sadie had said before his phone rang again.

'Nick? It's Peter here. What wonderful news. I've just been told by the University's general counsel. Apparently the girl realised the folly of her actions and withdrew her complaint. If you ask me, she should never have complained in the first place. I always thought the complaint was wholly without merit.'

Nick whistled to himself. *That's not what you said originally.*

'Are you still there? Yes, good. The important things are that there will be no mention of this sad episode on your University record, and you can come back to lecturing and teaching straight away. Your enforced holiday is over, Nick, starting Monday at 10 a.m. with Torts 101.'

'Great. I'm champing at the bit to get back into the lecture theatre. It's been a most uncomfortable month.'

'Yes, I can imagine. It hasn't been all that easy for me, either, you know. I've just had Kathy in my office. She was apoplectic about the situation. She was railing at you, but then she turned on me, accusing me of not having supported her over this. I told her to pull her head in. I'm afraid there'll be some bad blood to deal with there when you get back to the common room. She may even try to call you herself. She said she was going to.'

Nick slumped. He had no wish to speak to Kathy ever again but knew he would have to.

'Oh, one final thing. Miss Kim's thesis. I don't think it would be right for you to resume supervision. It could be upsetting for her, don't you think? I'll tell Darren to continue.'

'Yes. I hadn't given it any thought, but it would be a bit awkward.'

'I'll be glad to have you back. It's all been most unpleasant. I'll see you on Monday morning.'

Nick skipped into the kitchen for his ritual vegetable and fruit smoothie. Like drinking green tea instead of coffees, and walking the three or four miles to work on occasion, Nick had made a number of concessions to the twenty-first century, designed to make himself healthy and live a longer life. He had shifted only half of the spinach and kale into the Nutri-Bullet cup when his phone rang for the third time that day. And still not yet nine-fifteen. He saw who it was, paused, shrugged and picked up the phone.

'Kathy, good morning. What a—'

'Don't you good morning me. You nobbled Adrienne, didn't you? You've breached every ethical and procedural rule. You should be ashamed of yourself.'

'My conscience is clear. Miss Kim made the decision entirely of her own volition. It's nothing to do with me. Truth be told, I think she always thought it was your complaint, not hers.'

'Don't give me that shit, you fucking sleazeball. You think you're God's gift, with your tawdry crossword showing-off and your urbane manner, but you're just another weak, out-of-touch male, hostile to women and stuck in a time warp.'

'On the contrary, my dear. I'm not hostile to women, as I think you once saw first-hand.' He could hear her suck in her breath. 'See you on Monday,' he said and hung up before she could reply.

She rang back immediately, but he didn't answer. She didn't leave a message. He would give her time to calm down, to move on to a different cause or project. They couldn't avoid each other at work, and starting next week he would try to patch things up so that at the very least they could be civil.

He smiled as he remembered the famous Kathy Mulligan temper. He had experienced it on half a dozen occasions over the years, including once in a faculty staff meeting when she took on the Dean, in front of all the lecturers and tutors, about his unwillingness to allow student representatives to have a say on the faculty's timetabling committee, which scheduled not just the year's lectures and tutorials but decided what courses would be offered.

But it was the first time that Nick felt the ferocity of Kathy's temper that he remembered most. They had been secret lovers for about nine months, still delighting in the excitement of their relationship. One Saturday morning as they lay in bed Kathy mentioned that she had received a job offer and wanted his views on what she should do. The job was at Edinburgh University, as a senior lecturer (she was still a mere lecturer at London King's), with an immediate pay rise of almost £5000 and a clear path through to a professorship and tenure in four or five years.

'Wow,' Nick had said. 'That's amazing. Long overdue recognition for your skills, darling. What an opportunity for you. And Edinburgh's a city that everyone adores. I'll be so happy to visit you. Especially at Festival time.' As soon as he said it he knew it was a gaffe.

'At Festival time, Nick? Is that all you can say? If I take the job, what does it mean for us?' She sat up on her elbow, looking at him. Her jaw seemed more prominent; her red hair hung loosely over one eye.

'Us? Well, I suppose it would be more of the same. We can visit each other as often as we can, talk every day on the phone, regular weekends together, holidays, that sort of thing.'

'That sort of thing! It doesn't work like that. Long-distance relationships don't work out. Everyone knows that. You'd meet someone, or things would just fizzle out.'

'It doesn't have to be like that.'

She glared at him, so he tried a different tack. He knew that this was a once-in-a-career chance for her and that she wanted the job. 'You're entitled to put your career first. This is an amazing opportunity.'

She was not persuaded. 'I'll turn it down if you want me to stay in London with you.'

Nick could see now that he was being worked into a corner from which there would be no honourable escape. If he agreed, she might always blame him for holding back her career advancement. And if he said, 'Don't turn it down for my sake,' she would seize on that as a clear indication that she did not figure in Nick's long-term plans. Instead, he said nothing, which didn't help either. He reached out to cuddle her, but she pushed his arm away.

Kathy sat up, cross-legged on her haunches. She was naked, as Nick was, her thick hair hanging over her breasts. She spoke quietly now, but hesitantly. 'How about you come to Edinburgh with me? With your reputation I'm sure they'd be chomping at the bit to hire you.'

Nick looked away. He could never leave London. His impending divorce notwithstanding, his life was here. His children, his friends, his successful career at London King's. He didn't want to give that up, and he realised that he didn't want to give it up for Kathy.

'I'd love to, darling, but I can't leave my children at the moment. The separation has been hard for them and they need to know I'm nearby. The deal with Laura is that I have them every weekend. It wouldn't work commuting to and from Edinburgh.'

Kathy exploded with a fury that Nick had never seen before. 'Of course you wouldn't put yourself out for me. You're a fucking selfish prick. You've treated me like shit. We get together only when it suits you, you cancel get-togethers at the last minute so you can see your precious children. I haven't even *met* your kids, for God's sake. You're not willing to let the world know that you and I are together because it would upset your divorce negotiations. Everything's on your terms. And *I'm* the one who's had to make all the adjustments, all the sacrifices. You're weak and pathetic, Nick. You're half the man you think you are. It's now crystal clear that you have no long-term interest in me. You don't care at all about my feelings, my aspirations. I'm just someone you fuck twice a week.'

She burst into tears. She turned away from him and covered herself with the sheet, heaving with sobs. Nick moved to soothe her, saying things were not as she said. He put his arms around her, and to his relief she didn't push him away.

Things were never the same again between them. Nick saw something in Kathy that day that frightened him, and while he knew that her accusations were valid, to a large degree, he was not willing to change his life for her, and definitely not to commit to their relationship. He saw too that she had realised he was not for her. The relationship carried on for several more weeks, in an awkward and tense way. And while there was some passionate sex, the romance was no longer there. When Kathy put an end to it Nick didn't protest.

She turned down the Edinburgh job. She told Nick and fellow lecturers that she wasn't willing to forego her life in London. Nick always suspected that she blamed him for that missed opportunity, and for her continued limited progress up the London King's law faculty ladder. She became bitter as the years passed, quick to criticise the sexism she saw all around her in the law faculty.

Nick, buoyed and elated by the unexpected withdrawal of the complaint against him, opened his laptop and researched his trip to Pamplona. The annual San Fermin festival was due to start on Friday 6 July. He wanted to be there in time for the official *chupinazo* opening on that day, when a rocket would be fired at noon from outside Pamplona's city hall and hundreds of thousands of tightly packed revellers would then go crazy for the next week or so.

He booked an eight-day trip. Three days in San Sebastian in a spacious Airbnb apartment near one of the city beaches. Then he would hire a car to take him to Burguete, in the lower Pyrenees, where Jake and his cronies went fishing in *The Sun Also Rises*. He booked a room in the Burguete Hostel, where (when it was known as the Burguete Hotel) Hemingway had stayed on more than one occasion en route to or from the annual *fiesta* in Pamplona.

Accommodation for the festival was almost booked out. The Hotel Tres Reyes had a room available for the first four nights at the eye-watering cost of £440 a night. Nick never begrudged anybody from gouging tourists, but this time he was tempted to make an exception.

He was able to rent spaces on balconies in the central city for the opening ceremony and for one morning of bull-running, and also tickets to the bullring for the madcap *encierro* after the running of the bulls and to one bullfight on his final evening in Pamplona. On an impulse he decided to buy two tickets to each event. He might have a girlfriend by then. Failing that he could always invite Jo, although he knew she would be horrified by the crowds and, even more, by the brutality of the treatment of the bulls.

The day had gone well. Nick decided to visit his local for a pub lunch. The Sun in Splendour was only a hundred yards from his flat, tucked away at the entrance to Portobello Road. He ordered a pint of IPA and some nachos. He was still in the dark about what Adrienne had learned about William, so he texted her.

Thanks so much again for your brave actions yesterday. I'm very grateful, and I restart at the University on Monday. Keen to catch up for a drink or a coffee and hear what you found out about William.

Four hours later she replied:

still upset exhausted leave me alone

Nick was surprised but not offended. He sensed her vulnerability, and possibly her loneliness. He had never seen her in the company of others, which was perhaps to be expected as she was a decade or so older than most of her Master's cohort at London King's. She had much on her plate and didn't need the extra stress of reliving the harassment complaint by seeing him again. He decided to leave her alone.

For the next three months he concentrated on his job and was soon into the satisfying routine of preparing for lectures and tutorials and then delivering them. He was pleased that hardly any of his colleagues or students knew, or at least let on that they knew, he had been the subject of a sexual harassment complaint.

On his second day back at work, he walked into Kathy's office and sat down in front of her desk, not waiting to be invited to do so. She gave a pinched smile. 'Well, well, the golden boy is back, his reputation intact. You were a bit lucky there, don't you think?'

Nick nodded. 'Yes, I was fortunate. My lawyer said the complaint was unlikely to stick—'

'Hardly. It was a slam dunk, and you know it.'

'But I'm not here to debate that. Let's say I made a mistake and leave it at that. I'd like to call a truce. I think it demeans us both the way we talk to each other. I have no animus against you, and I do still remember some wonderful times we had all those years ago.'

Kathy had been looking at him with wide eyes and a mock po-face as he spoke. She grinned when he finished, her fine white teeth shining. 'Fair enough, Nick. I have no need to waste my energies on you. But on one condition, I need your support at the faculty meeting on Friday when I put my name forward as convenor of the staff hiring committee.'

Nick realised he quite liked Kathy still. 'I'd be delighted to, my friend. We have a deal.'

Suzanne from Durham University, who he'd met at a two-day law conference in Croydon a few months back, came down to stay for two weekends. She was a sparky young lecturer with whom he had shared a panel discussion at the conference. Suzanne, about ten years younger than Nick, had made all the running by handing him a little note with her room number and the message "See you after dinner". They had spent a happy night together.

Nick enjoyed accompanying her to concerts and the theatre, and even managed to persuade her to join him at an Arsenal game at Emirates Stadium. He was pleased to wake up next to her naked body in his bed. She said she would be keen to see more of him, in London and elsewhere, but he parried the idea by indicating that he wasn't in the market for a serious or long-term relationship. 'I'm afraid I'm a bit set in my ways,' he explained.

In his spare time Nick read a slew of Hemingway biographies, which Jo sourced for him. He marvelled at the rich material of Hemingway's life, character, friends and works that biographers could draw on. Many concentrated on the Paris years and the lost generation, others on the wives; one had Hemingway's boat *Pilar* as the centrepiece. He concentrated on the years 1925 and 1926. He read an academic dissection of *The Sun Also Rises*. Nick had thought, after one reading, the novel was merely a tightly written, spare story of some disparate and mostly obnoxious individuals carousing in Paris and holidaying in Spain. Scholars saw much more – they identified religious, historical and literary references and allusions on nearly every page, many of them obscure and, in Nick's eyes, debatable. He liked the idea that Hemingway had been a great writer because of the simplicity and tautness of the language used and was dismayed to think that his works were considered by the cognoscenti to be full of hidden references and subtexts.

15

Out of the blue, in mid-May Nick received a text from Adrienne. She said that she had finished her thesis and that she was leaving London in seven weeks. She would like to see him before she left.

He was pleased to hear from her. He had thought of her often over the past few months, though less frequently as time passed. Occasionally he would ask Darren Tobias how her thesis was progressing. Tobias, a man of few words who imparted information as though it was on a need-to-know basis, would reply 'Good', 'Haven't seen her for a few weeks' or, on one mysterious occasion, 'She's dug up some dark material'.

Nick always thought of Adrienne with fondness. He had warmed to her resourcefulness and intelligence, and her openness, and had always looked forward to spending time with her. He respected her drive and her success at reinventing herself in several guises over her adult life, although the up-and-down nature of her moods had unnerved him at times.

Nick suggested a drink after work in a couple of days at their usual spot in Ladbroke Grove because, their recent truce notwithstanding, he didn't want Kathy or her putative spy network to see them together.

Do also email through your thesis. I'd love to read it.

She emailed the Word file of the thesis. Her covering message said that there was a brief reference to Nick's grandfather in Chapter Seven. That chapter was headed 'Atrocities by Japanese and Korean Guards'.

Nick could find only one reference to William, in a footnote. The main text included a sentence to the effect that it was indisputable from first-hand accounts that Korean guards on the Railway had been frequently brutal and sadistic in their treatment of prisoners. The footnote read:

See, for example, The Railway Man *by Eric Lomax; the descriptions of the deaths of Cpl. Desmond Kember and Lt. William Harrieson in* The Tamuang Diaries, *by Colonel Ian McDougall at pp 112–115; and multiple references in* War Diaries *by E.B. ('Weary') Dunlop.*

Nick hadn't come across *The Tamuang Diaries* in his research, nor had he heard of Colonel McDougall. A quick Google search left him none the wiser.

He was on edge when he sat at the bar of the café at the appointed time. His anxiety was in fact two-fold. He was bracing to learn the truth about how William had died. He was also sad because his rendezvous with Adrienne was likely to be their last. He expected that they would lose touch, as had happened with so many of his favourite students over the years. A flurry of emails for the first year or two, requests for a reference, or a Christmas message, and then nothing.

Only ten minutes late, Adrienne burst into the café looking stylish and alive. She wore tight jeans and a grey denim jacket. She strode to the bar and gave Nick a big hug as he rose to greet her. He could smell the perfume on her neck and feel her body pressing against his. She sat on the barstool and removed her earphones. 'Peter Sutcliffe,' she smiled sheepishly. 'He's just been arrested. Before my time.' *Is that a dig at my age?*

Nick complimented her on her thesis, said he had read only parts of it, but that it looked good, and that progress reports from Darren Tobias had been encouraging. She admitted she was hoping for a Distinction but now that her life was moving on she said the grade was not such a big deal.

'Moving on?' Nick asked.

'Yes, I fly back to Korea on the eleventh of July. To Busan. Close to my Mum. I'm going to start up a business. A Korean-language true crime podcast series, concentrating initially on the best-known American serial murderers and a few famous Korean killings. There's a huge market for murderers in Korea.'

Nick joined her in her laughter. She said it would be a low-key podcast, Adrienne co-hosting with a former pop singer who had been a schoolmate. 'It will be chatty, and breezy, with lots of gore and sex. It's bound to be a runaway success.'

'I have no doubt it will be.' His smile faded. 'I'll miss you, Adrienne.'

She looked surprised. 'I bet you say that to all your sexy female students.' She regarded him with open, innocent eyes.

Nick looked at Adrienne. *Where did a comment like that come from? Was she flirting? Or luring him into an admission of sorts?* 'Absolutely not.' He resisted the temptation to ask her why she thought he found her sexy, and he didn't want to raise the matter of the harassment complaint, however obliquely.

'Besides,' said Adrienne, 'you've made no effort – zippo – to contact me for the last few months, so I hardly think you'll miss me. I'm sure you just forgot about me.'

Where was this attitude, this superiority, coming from? 'Hang about, Adrienne. You were the one who told me not to contact you. And I respected that. I didn't want you to think that I was harassing you for a second time.'

'You gave up so easily.' Adrienne smiled her sweetest smile. 'I like hanging out with you. Despite everything.'

'It's nice of you to tell me that now. Anyhow, despite everything, yes I will miss you, you know.'

She smiled, seeming pleased at his words.

Nick felt more comfortable reverting to their previous conversation. 'I saw the reference to my grandfather in your thesis. I'm afraid I couldn't find any reference to the Tamuang book or McDougall online, but you obviously know more.'

Adrienne's face fell, and her eyes moistened. 'Yes, I found the diary on the COFEPOW website. The reason we didn't find it by searching before is that Harrieson was spelt without the 'E'. Search engines are very literal. It's definitely William, though. The diary has never been transcribed into proper print, and it was hard to read. I took copies of the relevant pages and typed them myself. I have a copy for you in my bag. But I'm not sure I should give it to you. It's horrible. Horrible.'

Adrienne was beginning to cry. Nick wanted to wipe the tears away with his fingers, but he kept his hand on the table.

'Please let me see it,' he said gently.

She pulled a few pages from her bag. 'Tell you what. You read this now, and I'll go for a walk outside for ten minutes to pull myself together. Then we can talk about it, okay?'

There were three pages. At the top was written 'Extract from diary of Colonel Ian McDougall contained in the Tamuang Diaries.' Underneath was the date: 2 October 1943.

Readers of this diary – if there ever will be any – will know that I have recorded many dark days since I was captured in February last year. But today is the darkest of those days. May it be remembered eternally as a day of infamy, a day when the evil of man assaulted the very essence of humanity.

Today's entry involves the deaths of two fine Englishmen, Sgt Desmond Kember and Lt. William Harrison.

During an unexpected inspection of the sleeping quarters before dawn yesterday morning, Kember and Harrison were caught by the guards in possession of radio equipment. The equipment was in Kember's hut and by his bed. Harrison had been visiting from another hut.

The two men were dragged out into the quad part of the camp. They were interrogated noisily by Beaverface and the Rat. Neither man would reveal whose radio it was, and amid much shouting and kicking they were put in the bamboo cage by the latrines and left there until this morning. It seemed they received no food or water despite the extreme heat. This morning Beaverface hauled both men back into the quad when the rest of us were paraded for tenko. They could hardly walk, so weak were they. After ten minutes of abuse and interrogation, Kember confessed that it was his radio. Beaverface then gave a hefty piece of wood, like a cricket bat and with a handle, to Harrison and told him to kill Kember by clubbing him. We all protested loudly, and Colonel Dunlop as ranking officer said that he would complain to the commandant. Beaverface let him visit the commandant.

Meanwhile, Harrison refused to beat Kember with the club. Beaverface shouted at him, but he would not do it. Beaverface got more enraged, apoplectic even. In his awful English he told Harrison that he (Harrison) would die if he did not obey. Still Harrison refused.

Beaverface then made Harrison and Kember lie on the ground. He took out a parang and started hacking at Kember's neck. We watched horrified and shouted our protests as blood spurted from Kember's neck. After four mercifully quick hacks, Kember's head rolled loose. The men and I looked on in horror.

Colonel Dunlop returned, shocked at what he saw. He said that the Japanese would not intervene. May the Lord always curse the Japanese for their cowardice. Beaverface ordered O'Brien and Wilkinson to take Kember's body to bury it in the cemetery by the banana trees.

Beaverface then ordered Harrison to strip naked. He dropped his G-string and stood there without embarrassment. Beaverface then handed Wilkinson a tin bucket and told him to take it to the latrines and fill it with shit. He did that and returned. The bastard Beaverface then told him to pour it over Harrison. Again we all protested, but to no avail. Wilkinson refused, so the Rat grabbed the pail and tipped it all over poor Harrison. We urged him to be strong, as he stood there naked and humiliated.

Beaverface then left and returned two minutes later with a stone weighing about seven or eight pounds. Harrison was ordered to hold *it above his head. This he did, despite his desperately weak condition.*

The men were then sent off to work on the Railway three miles away. I stayed behind on account of my broken arm and watched Harrison from the shade of my hut. After quarter of an hour or so he dropped the stone. Beaverface swore at him and beat him several times on his back and head with his rifle stock. Harrison picked up the stone again. He struggled to raise it above his head.

After a few minutes, under the beating sun, he dropped the stone again. Poor Harrison stood, barely, with his shoulders stooped and his head down. It was pitiful to watch. I could see him bracing for the beating that was to come. Beaverface barked at him like a rabid dog and struck Harrison on the back with his rifle. The wretched man slumped forward on to the ground and Beaverface kicked him hard in his solar plexus. He then bashed Harrison on the back of his head with the butt of his rifle. Harrison grunted, like a docile puppy, and lay still. For two minutes he lay there in the beating sun, not moving. I broke ranks and approached Harrison to check his pulse. He had none. I looked at Beaverface and the other Korean guards with a scorn and a hatred I had previously never felt. I had to be restrained from attacking them.

Harrison's body was picked up by two of the Korean guards and taken away, to be buried by our men when they return from their work on the railway bridge.

I am sickened, beyond despair, and I grieve for two fine men of courage and decency who died for their country.

Nick folded the pages. He was rigid with shock and horror. *Poor, poor Grandpa. What an awful end to such a good and worthwhile life.* He lamented the loss of a young man in his prime, with a loyal wife and two young children. Thank God that Grandma Cecilia, his father and Mary never knew how William had died. They would have struggled to cope. He could not pass on to Mary what he now knew.

Adrienne returned to the café and sat down. He had ordered

her another glass of her favourite Provençal rosé, and she sipped from it as she looked at him closely. She saw his red eyes and his serious, hangdog face.

'Oh, Nick. I'm so sorry. I apologise for all Koreans, for my great-grandfather. I've wondered every day for almost three months whether he was Beaverface, or the Rat.'

Nick took her hand. 'Please don't think like that. It's not your fault. You're not responsible, in any way, for what Koreans did seventy-five years ago. And it's impossible to think that your relative was one of those guards. The odds of that are astronomically high.' Nick knew now why she had withdrawn the harassment complaint. 'People did terrible things in the war. War does that to people. It wasn't just the Japanese and the Germans and some Koreans. It was the Russians as well. The British and Americans committed atrocities too. Yes, there are hundreds of accounts detailing the brutality of the Korean guards on the Railway, but there are as many which describe the savagery of the Japanese military and camp commandants towards the Koreans. They were more brutal towards their own subordinates than they were to the prisoners.'

'Yes,' nodded Adrienne. 'I know. It's hard to even think about it.'

'One thing you must be very clear about. You personally are entirely blameless. Certainly in my eyes you are.' He squeezed her fingers.

'Time for a change of subject,' she said, withdrawing her hand. 'Tell me about Hem. I'm sure you've learned lots since you started ignoring me.' She flashed a grin at him.

He laughed and told her what he now knew. He talked of the books he had read and the things he had learned. She interjected often, and with insight.

'Actually,' he said, 'despite everything, I rather like Hem. He was his own man and didn't take crap from anyone. He did things his own way. And yes, there were casualties along the way, particularly his wives, and many of his friends, but who are we to criticise? And for what it's worth I still think Hem was a pig of a man, a buffoon and a sexist.'

They both smiled.

'What's more, I'm going to visit Pamplona in July for the *fiesta*. Bull-running and all that. I'm hoping I might be able to dig up something about William's visit in 1925.'

Adrienne perked up. 'Tell me the dates.'

After he told her she said, 'Wow. Can I come too?' Her eyes were bright, almost pleading.

He replied without thinking, 'Why not.' *How had the conversation taken such a turn?*

'Are you sure? It's a bit sudden, I know. Why don't you think it over for a while?'

'No, it's okay. No need to think about it. You will be very welcome.'

Adrienne's face darkened. 'But I can't. I'm broke. I maxed out my credit card to buy my ticket home to Korea. I'll be able to pay you back in a year or so when I get a decent job.'

Nick was smiling. 'No, I'd never ask that of you. You don't have to pay me back. You'll be on a working holiday, as my research assistant. We'll be on a mission. I'm happy to pay your air tickets. They won't be much, even at this late stage. EasyJet and BA fly to Bilbao. I've booked a large Airbnb in San Sebastian so—'

'Wowie! I've always wanted to go to San Sebastian. The pintxos, the Michelin-star restaurants, the beaches. How exciting.'

'It sure is. I've never been there either. The hostel in Burguete was very cheap, so that won't be a problem. I'm afraid the cost of hotels in Pamplona is extortionate at that time of year. The prices are ramped up seven-fold, I read somewhere. My room cost over four hundred quid a night, and I booked three months ago.' He let his words hang in the air. He didn't fancy paying upwards of £2000 for Adrienne's accommodation in Pamplona.

'Don't worry, I'm a big girl. I can share your room. But no funny business.' She smiled at him. *Such an earnest, innocent smile.*

'Don't you worry. Scout's honour.'

'Well, that's settled then. How exciting. All that wonderful food in San Sebastian, and what a thrill to be retracing Hem's footsteps. I can promise you I'm a good travelling companion.'

'By the most amazing coincidence, I have a spare ticket to the main Pamplona events.'

'See! Obviously you were subconsciously wanting me to go to Spain with you.'

'I don't think so.' Nick smiled at her. 'I was planning on inviting my sister. So you've saved me having to share a bedroom with her for the first time in about forty years.'

'Will you allow me to be in charge of activities in San Sebastian?' Adrienne was buzzing with excitement. 'I can dig up bars, restaurants, museums, all that. I'll leave Burguete and Pamplona to you.'

Nick had to admit that this turn of events was as welcome as it was unexpected. He looked forward to getting to know more about Adrienne. He knew nothing about her love life, little about her family and friends. How different her upbringing must have been from his. They had a few subjects in common (the law, London King's, Hemingway and the Burma Railway) but how would they get on in close proximity for a whole week?

That evening Nick rang Jo to tell her about what he had learned about their grandfather's demise. She listened in silence as Nick read the diary entry to her.

When he had finished she said, 'How awful. How simply awful. I weep for poor Grandpa, even after all the years. God, how war makes people act so cruelly.'

They went on to chat about other things, and Nick mentioned

that he would be heading off to Spain on holiday for a week or so early in July, to see if he could find anything about the Hemingway connection. He didn't mention that Adrienne would be travelling with him.

He decided that night that he would give up alcohol and take up a gym membership in the hope that he might be able to lose a few pounds before they travelled to Spain. Nick wasn't exactly fat, but his middle-age spread could not be denied. He also knew he was being silly. This wasn't going to be a romantic holiday. No, this was like travelling with a work colleague. Nevertheless, he didn't want Adrienne to be repelled by his paunch.

A few days before they were due to fly to Spain, Nick stood naked in front of the mirror in his bedroom. He looked himself up and down. He flexed his arms and was pleased to note that there was definitely more muscle in his biceps. He pinched the roll of fat around his midriff; that too was looking better. Overall he didn't think he looked too bad, at least for his age.

He looked down at his pubic hair. It was thick and straggly, black with a few unwelcome grey hairs poking through the unruly growth. He shuddered as he recalled a conversation at Friday night drinks in the common room the week before. Nick had been chatting away with the Dean. One of the younger women lecturers was talking loudly to Sharon from the Records section, both lamenting the absence of attractive men and the quality of men they interacted with online. Sharon, it seemed, had an active sex life. A fifty-ish blonde divorcee, she was fit and attractive, although a loose cannon once she had a couple of drinks. She said that she had a Brazilian, and all her boyfriends preferred it that way. All the other women in the conversation agreed that grooming was important. Then Sharon added the *pièce de résistance*: 'In fact, I don't think I'd date a guy if he didn't shave himself down there. Perhaps not completely bald, but whatever remains would have to be trimmed and shaped. And don't get me started on men with hairy backs.'

Nick whispered to Peter Hargreaves, 'I'll buy razors for us all on Monday.'

Nick looked again at himself in the mirror. He swivelled his hips and looked at his back. He was dismayed to see thickets of black hair all over the top half of his back. For a moment he considered making an urgent appointment at a beauty parlour to get an all-over wax, but that would be too embarrassing. Instead, he reached for his nail scissors and started chopping out the grey hairs and making the unruly ruly.

Later, in the shower, he applied his razor to his nether regions, removing what he thought of as the stragglers and tried to put shape and form into what remained. He cursed at the nicks and cuts he left behind. He then turned his attention to his back. All he could do there was stretch his hand over the opposite shoulder and let the razor remove whatever hairs it found in its way. He could feel himself straining muscles in his side as he stretched. He gave up in disgust after a few minutes.

It was a sunny day, so he decided to walk down to Oxford Street to buy clothes for his holiday. He took advice from a Jamaican thirty-something shop assistant in TopMan. He bought two pairs of shorts, some lime-green swimming trunks, a pair of light-blue chinos ('Dapper, man, dapper,' said the man with dreadlocks), a white-and-yellow T-shirt, and a light jacket. Even if he didn't feel the part he would at least look it.

16

They almost missed their flight from Gatwick. They had agreed to meet at Victoria Station at 11 a.m., which would give them almost two hours for an unrushed check-in and boarding process. Nick was on time as usual.

Adrienne was fifty minutes late, unapologetically so. Too many phone calls to make and she had to repack her bag twice. Nick hid his annoyance.

The flight was crowded, and the service on British Airways was perfunctory. Still, Nick and Adrienne were in the best of spirits as they set off on their adventure. Nick enjoyed the rubbing of shoulders and arms with Adrienne and the easy leaning into each other's space. She scrolled through the restaurant and bar listings, taking a careful note on her phone of recommended places to eat and to drink coffee. Nick read the section on San Sebastian in his *Rough Guide to Spain*. They had little trouble getting the bus from Bilbao airport to San Sebastian.

A young man met them on the street outside the Airbnb apartment in the Gros part of San Sebastian, less than two hundred yards from Zurriola Beach on the east side of the city. Adrienne was delighted with the location. It was an upmarket area, full of well-regarded restaurants serving Basque cuisine, and only fifteen minutes' walk from the old town.

The apartment was on the first floor, and spacious. There

was a huge balcony, populated with pot plants which Adrienne promised to water every day. There was one bedroom, with a king-size bed, and a sofa bed in the lounge. The young man showed them how the wi-fi worked, explained the lighting system, and wished them a pleasant three-day stay.

'You have the bedroom, Adrienne. I'll be very happy with the sofa bed.'

'Definitely not. You've paid for it, you deserve it. If you knew what couches and floors I've slept on over the years, you'd realise that this sofa bed is luxury for me.'

He insisted that she have the bedroom, and she relented after a few protests. 'Let's unpack, freshen up and go out and explore and eat some good food,' she said.

The weather was overcast and cold, with a brisk wind driving the rollers on Zurriola Beach onto the sand. They were glad of their jackets and headed into the old town. Adrienne had a better sense of direction than Nick, so he was happy to be led by her. Gros could easily have been mistaken for Milan or Geneva, with its neat boutiques, glossy travel agencies and technology shops. But once they were over the bridge they could see why San Sebastian was so loved by travellers. They marvelled at the tiny narrow streets, the quaint churches with gargoyles and saints' heads, the huge and stylish municipal buildings, the busy cafés with rows of pintxos and tapas on the counters, and the happy tourists and locals eating away. The easy charm of the old town enveloped them, and Nick knew that this was going to be a holiday to remember. Whatever they discovered or didn't discover about Hemingway and William, and however the relationship with Adrienne developed, a good time awaited them.

Adrienne let out a squeal when she recognised one of the restaurant bars that had been recommended, and she pulled Nick's arm as she walked under the canopy. She inspected the trays of pintxos: sardines, octopus, olives, chorizos, mushrooms, and roasted peppers. She was in foodie heaven.

They had a noisy dinner. Adrienne ordered for them both. They agreed there was a little too much bread in the local cuisine, but everything was fresh. Adrienne ordered a bottle of Txakoli, the mildly fizzy dry white wine produced locally. They had little trouble finishing the bottle.

On the walk home through the old town Nick felt sufficiently confident to put his arm around Adrienne's shoulder. She moved it off her. 'I'm not into PDAs, I'm afraid.'

Nick fell silent as they reached their apartment. Inside, she removed her shoes and left them at the door. 'It's bad luck to wear shoes in the home,' she said. Over the next few days he would learn a few more Korean customs: placing shoes on the bed or other furniture was not allowed and filling the kettle up to full was almost a mortal sin.

Adrienne went into the bedroom and came out ten minutes later in long white pyjamas then shuffled across the floor to the bathroom. When she emerged a few minutes later her phone rang. 'What a surprise, that's my mother,' she said as she threw an apologetic look at Nick.

For the next hour he listened to Adrienne shouting and crying and laughing and hissing as she and her mother conversed in Korean. By this time Nick was in his sofa bed, checking out TripAdvisor for things to do tomorrow.

Nick woke early and went for a walk through the deserted streets near the apartment. He loved travel, and particularly places he had never been to before. Nothing pleased him more than going for an early-morning walk along streets and through markets and parks for the first time. He found a patisserie and returned to the apartment with croissants and almond pastries.

There was no sign of Adrienne, so he went to her bedroom door and turned the handle. The door was locked from the inside. He knocked and said breakfast would be ready in a few minutes.

They had breakfast on the patio. Adrienne was able to work the coffee machine, the pastries were warm and fresh, and the morning sun warmed them up.

'It sounded like you had a pretty difficult call with your mother last night,' Nick ventured.

'Nothing unusual. She likes staying in touch.'

'But it sounded like there was a lot of anger. Does she try to boss you around?'

'Sure she does, but that's just her way of showing love. When I woke this morning I found seven voice messages from her on my phone. From last night alone. But don't worry. That's normal. Okay, I have mother issues, but who doesn't? All Korean girls have mother issues.' She said it as though that was the end of that particular conversation.

Their day as tourists started on the beach. They changed into their swimming costumes in the apartment and then ambled past the cafés and surf shops to Zurriola Beach. Even at 10.30 a.m. there were hundreds absorbing the sun's rays, and toddlers splashed in the shallows. A dozen surfers practised their craft at the western end of the beach.

Adrienne wore a pretty white bikini. Nick stood there self-consciously in his new swimming trunks.

'Very smart and cool,' said Adrienne in a half-mocking tone. 'I'm glad I brought my sunglasses.'

He tried to laugh, which wasn't easy, as he made a point of holding his stomach in whenever Adrienne was looking at him.

'Please take a photo of me standing in the water as I look out to the bay. To make my girlfriends jealous when they head out for a Nando's.'

She waded out through the cold water up to her knees. She stopped, and Nick took several shots of her looking away into the distance, the sun sparkling on the water. Again he appreciated Adrienne's beautiful neck. She looked so elegant and – he grasped for the right word – sophisticated with her hair up.

After changing, they returned to the old town, walking leisurely among the tourists and browsing the shops. Adrienne took particular delight in the bright green and red colours of the fruit and vegetables in the market by the big church.

Conversation came easily to them over a lunch of pintxos and beer in another of Adrienne's chosen cafés. Any doubts he had harboured about their compatibility had vanished. She asked many questions about his marriage and his girlfriends, and to his surprise he told her many stories about his romantic life. She always asked for more, and they both laughed when the recollections were, as was often the case, ones where Nick had made a fool of himself or had been rejected. He felt alive in telling her these stories, flattered by her curiosity. People who talked about themselves without showing interest in others or allowing them to contribute were bores in Nick's eyes.

'You've obviously been a Casanova over the years,' she said over a squid pintxos. 'I've counted fifteen different women, and it's only lunchtime on our first day.'

Nick laughed. 'Don't be silly. This is over a thirty-year period, and in half the cases the relationship never got going, or I made an ass of myself.'

He was aware that he and Adrienne attracted a steady stream of glances from passers-by and fellow diners. He soon came to realise that they were picking up on the incongruity of them being together. She, looking twenty-five, and being Asian and modern and altogether different, and he, looking fifty or more, balding and greying and looking like an English tourist.

He asked Adrienne what she thought people were thinking of them. 'Yes, I've been wondering about that too. Perhaps you're an international arms dealer and I'm your assistant and interpreter. Or you're a rich oil-baron sugar daddy and I'm a high-class escort from Tokyo or Seoul.' He laughed. 'Or how about you're a famous English law professor and I'm your fiancée? Perhaps we're having our honeymoon before the wedding.'

'You've got it. From now on I'll call you my fiancée.' And so he did. Twice on their trip he mortified her by referring to her as his fiancée when he ordered drinks or food in restaurants, each time getting a reaction (one quizzical, one smiling) from the waiter.

That afternoon they walked the mile-long Concha Beach and back again. Nick reminded Adrienne that Jake had swum from this beach near the end of *The Sun Also Rises*. He thought their shared connections with Hemingway were like bricks in the wall of their friendship. Each shared experience or reminiscence added to the whole.

They returned to the apartment in the late afternoon for a nap, tired but enchanted by San Sebastian. Adrienne said she had to post a few photos of her pintxos on her Korean food blog. She said that her loyal subscribers were always interested when she posted dishes of other cuisines. Nick caught up on the news, especially on the football world cup underway in Russia and Ukraine.

That evening Adrienne insisted they dress up for dinner. She had booked a nearby restaurant, renowned for its local delicacies. She wore a simple summer dress, pale yellow and sleeveless, and grey and yellow sandals with cork heels an inch high. Her shining hair tumbled over her shoulders. She looked a million dollars, and Nick wished that she really was his fiancée. He was glad to have refreshed his own wardrobe. He felt youthful and smart in his new linen jacket.

They sipped a mojito before dinner in a neighbouring bar and watched the sun set and all the families standing in groups chatting to each other. Adrienne insisted on ordering for them both at the restaurant: Jamón Ibérico, pork pābé and chanterelle mushrooms for Nick; raw tuna and a pesto-covered burrata for Adrienne, and a tomato salad with five different kinds of tomatoes to share. All were duly photographed by Adrienne for her blog. The food was washed down with a bottle of local garnacha red wine.

Adrienne sparkled that evening. It was as though there was an electric light in her. She emanated a radiance that everyone in the restaurant seemed to notice. The Argentine waiter was especially attentive.

It was Adrienne's turn to dominate the conversation. After a few gentle questions from Nick, she spoke about her own love life. Yes, there had been quite a few boyfriends over the years. There had been one keen young man in her final year of high school, a few desultory ones at Bristol University ('they were all so immature, and anyway I was concentrating on my studies'), and a few hook-ups on her travels. She talked of one lover, an American she met while travelling in Japan. They had lived together for several months in various places. 'He wanted to marry me, but I didn't love him enough. Plus, I didn't want to give up my freedom and my independence. My mother was so upset that I was not married by the time I reached thirty. Such dramas, I can tell you. The phone calls. She said I brought shame on the family. Perhaps it's no surprise that I live so far away.' She stopped, looking sad.

'But it's not as though my mom is alone in thinking that my being unmarried is so humiliating. Most Koreans, at least those over about forty, look at single people as losers, or objects of pity. Having said that, there's a new movement of sorts in Korea these days, of unmarried people in their thirties and forties mainly, who are proudly single. They even have a word for it. *Honjok.*'

'Koreans do seem to have a word for everything, don't they? And have you embraced the *honjok* lifestyle?'

'Shit no. I want to get married. And have kids too.' Adrienne laughed and took another drink of her wine.

'What about dating life in London?' Nick asked. 'There are a lot of eligible men around.'

'Hardly. They're either gay or married as everyone says, or they're football-obsessed, beer-drinking yobbos. My girlfriends and I all agree on that. It's very hard to find a half-decent man these days. We've all tried Tinder several times, and while you do meet the occasional good guy there it never ends up with a lasting relationship. That's how it is these days.' She looked at Nick. 'You're different. You're intelligent, and smart, and successful. You're funny, at least when you're not harassing me at law faculty functions.'

Nick laughed. It seemed such a long time ago now.

'And you're a pretty snappy dresser these days. It's just a shame that you're—' She stopped, and despite his protestations she wouldn't finish the sentence.

Too old? Too fat and ugly? Too old-fashioned and set in my ways? Perhaps all of those things.

On their short walk back to the apartment Adrienne skipped and swayed a bit, light-headed from the wine and, Nick liked to think, intoxicated by the romance and charm of this lovely Spanish city. She didn't object when he put his arm through hers.

In the apartment Nick made a pot of herbal tea ('Don't fill the kettle up too full this time.' Adrienne said) while she found a football game to watch on TV. They watched it for five minutes. It seemed such a tame end to an enthralling evening. Nick leaned over and took her right foot in his hands. 'Will you let me give you the famous Nick Harrieson foot massage?'

She looked a bit dubious, but then smiled. 'You mean the one that makes women swoon with pleasure and delight?'

'Yep, that's the one.'

'Okay then, show me, Mr Professor. I'll get some cream.'

She returned with some moisturiser, and Nick began the massage as she intermittently switched her attention between the football and Nick. He didn't kid himself that he was a skilled masseur, but he figured most people couldn't tell the difference between a good and a bad massage. He pushed his thumbs deep into the arch of Adrienne's foot, rubbed and pinched her Achilles tendon, pulled and beat at her toes, and gently rotated her ankle. He played with each of her dainty toes.

Adrienne smiled. 'You're good at that. Who would have thought it? *Le vieux Crosseur est un bon masseur.*' She laughed at her own joke and stood up. 'I must go to bed now. I need to Skype my mother and post a review of dinner on my blog. Good night and thank you.'

Nick felt disappointed. 'Well, if you're nice to me tomorrow I'll give you my even more famous back massage.'

He could see doubt on her smiling face. 'We'll see.'

Adrienne and Nick stood on Monte Urgull, surveying the old town and Concha Beach. The sky was a deep blue, and cloudless, but a chill wind blew through the trees, making them glad they wore shirts and sleeves. They were standing on the ramparts of the old La Mota Castle, parts of which dated back to the twelfth century.

They had climbed up the hill to reach the castle after an hour on the beach after their breakfast. It had been a strenuous hike, all the more satisfying because of that. They snapped photos of each other with the beach in the background. Hemingway had without doubt made this climb a dozen times or more, and the thought pleased Nick intensely.

At the bottom of the hill they found a large pop-up exhibition devoted to Picasso's *Guernica*. They hoped that the original painting itself might be on tour in San Sebastian, but there were only a number of copies. There were videos and descriptions of the painting on tour in the US in the late 1940s and early 1950s, and they were thrilled to see a number of familiar names among dozens of Americans listed as having donated money to allow *Guernica* to be shown to American audiences: Mrs Louis D

Brandeis, Mr Malcolm Cowley, Mr Theodore Dreiser, Dr Albert Einstein, Miss Lillian Hellman, Mr Ernest Hemingway. Ernest seemed to be following them around.

That evening they dined in a seafood restaurant that one of Adrienne's friends had recommended. Again, they talked and talked on all kinds of subjects: the burgeoning MeToo movement; gossip about some of the lecturers in the London King's law faculty; Kathy ('she used to be such a bully, but not so much in recent weeks' said Adrienne, and she seemed shocked when Nick mentioned that 'a long time ago' he and Kathy had had 'a bit of a thing, very low-key'); her thesis (yes, she said she was satisfied with the Merit grade that Darren Tobias had given it); her early life in Busan and the different life she would be returning to there.

Later, and without hesitation, she accepted his offer of a back massage when they returned from dinner. He suggested she change into shorts and a bikini top while he got a towel. She lay down on her front on the sofa bed, wearing the briefest of denim shorts and a white bikini top and put her hands under her chin. Nick slapped on some moisturiser and set to work. He started on her neck and shoulders and squeezed her between his thumbs and forefingers. Occasionally she would tense up, but then say 'That's so good.' Her bikini strap was in the way, so he unclasped it. She didn't stop him. By now he was kneeling astride her, and he gave her long strokes from her lower back to her shoulders. She grunted with the pressure, apparently appreciatively.

He started rubbing her calves and behind her knees, with strong firm strokes. Her body seemed to move on the bedsprings. He massaged her thighs from side to side, and her body rolled with his efforts.

'That's so nice, Nick. You're good at this,' she murmured.

After a while he returned to her neck and shoulders, and then finished. His arms were getting tired.

She sat up, covering her breasts while she refastened her bra. 'That was lovely, thank you. I was so relaxed I almost fell asleep.'

Nick smiled. 'Yes, I think we're both tired. San Sebastian has been such a fun place to come to, and you're the best companion.'

She looked at him, her eyes twinkling. 'You can be quite good yourself at times.' She scuffled off to the bedroom and shut the door. He could hear her lock it.

17

'It's a small town but we won't be able to miss it.' Nick was proven right as soon as they drove into Auritz-Burguete. Near the end of the town, on the left and up the narrow road, and slightly at an angle to the road, was the Hostel Burguete. As they knew from reading *Everyone Behaves Badly,* Hemingway used to stay there for several days before descending into Pamplona for the San Fermin *fiesta.* Presumably William had stayed at the hostel too, at the same time as Hemingway, if *The Sun Also Rises* could be relied on.

The hostel was a three-storey building, painted white and, like every residence in the town, with a steep roof so that the winter snow would not settle. Adrienne said how cute it was as they parked their rental car. The town itself was a well-manicured alpine village with a Hansel and Gretel gingerbread feel. It was the beginning of July, hay was being cut and baled in the fields and the roses in the gardens were blooming. Every minute or two some *peregriños* on the Camino de Santiago would stride past the hostel on their way down from the foothills of the Pyrenees to Pamplona.

They walked through the hostel door and into a dark and narrow reception area. A severe-looking woman came to attend to them. After exchanging *holas* it quickly became apparent that neither she nor anyone else at the hostel spoke English or even French (and France was only ten miles away). They were shown up to their room on the first floor, the heavily stained floorboards creaking with every step.

Their room had two queen-size beds. Nick had warned Adrienne that they would be sharing a room, and she had not expressed horror or anything else at the prospect. The room was spare, dark and dully furnished. The wi-fi was poor, the ensuite reminded Nick of his boarding school days, and the light bulbs were so weak that reading was difficult.

He suggested they explore the town before going a mile or two up the road to Roncevaux for lunch. The hot sun weighed on them as they walked down the main road of Burguete. There were only a few shops and cafés: the buildings were mainly residences, sited so close to the road that in places it narrowed to one lane. The town was slow and tranquil. It reminded Nick of a Swiss village in summer.

Back in Burguete, after a quick *bocadillo* at the only restaurant in Roncevaux, they decided to see if they could find the walking track that Jake and his friends had taken in *Sun* when they set off on their fishing expedition. Nick and Adrienne walked about half a mile back up the road to Roncevaux. Then, following Hem's description, they turned right through some trees and searched for a stream to cross and a field to traverse into the forest. They found neither the path nor the stream, and a taut barbed-wire fence prevented access to the yellow field of hay stubble.

Undeterred, they decided to explore the area by car and find the Irati River so beloved by Hemingway for its fighting trout featured in *Sun*. They headed east from below Burguete, through hay fields and forests and river valleys, taking in the peaceful beauty of the foothills of the Navarran Pyrenees. They found several streams and wondered if William might have fished them. Adrienne asked Nick to stop the car a few times so she could photograph a hayfield, or some horses, or a particularly handsome inn whose balconies were bedecked by rows and rows of vibrant pink and white peonies and begonias. 'For my Instagram page,' she explained.

They found the Irati River at a little village called Aribe. The river was at most twenty yards wide, and rarely more than a foot or two deep. The water was clear and bracken-coloured.

By late afternoon they had returned to the hostel for a rest before dinner. Nick read and Adrienne posted photos on her Instagram as they reclined on their respective beds. They decided to eat in the hostel's restaurant, for the history and the atmosphere.

The hostel was deserted, so they were uninterrupted as they explored it before dinner. Downstairs were two lounges and a dining room, full of dark furniture, old paintings and faded black-and-white photographs. Glass cabinets were everywhere, containing silver salvers, jugs and teapots. Large copper bowls sat on stools in the corner of one sitting room, not far from a piano that looked as if it had been there for decades. Nick wondered if it was the same piano that they had played in *The Sun Also Rises*. In one cabinet he was pleased to see two goblets that looked identical to the one on his sister's mantelpiece in London. There were no inscriptions on them. There were a few paintings and photos of Hem, but none from the 1920s. Time had stood still in the hostel. It was like a mausoleum to a simpler, cruder past.

The only other diner in the restaurant, and Nick suspected the only other overnight guest in the hostel, was an elderly German. They invited him to join them. It turned out that Hans always stopped there on his way to Pamplona to the *fiesta*. This would be his thirtieth visit for San Fermin, he said. Apparently there were hundreds, if not thousands, of Europeans and Americans who came to Pamplona every year in July. 'The bull-running is just a small part of it,' he said. 'It is the crowds, the old friends, the beer, the joy of Spain.'

They went up to their room early. It had been a low-key day, and the intimacy and warm embrace of San Sebastian hadn't continued into Burguete. Nick knew that Adrienne would not want another massage, or any other physical contact. They caught up on their emails and Facebook pages in silence, and then Adrienne's mother rang.

'God, I wish she'd leave me alone sometimes,' she said as she moved to answer. She chatted away in Korean, often raising her left arm in apparent anger and frustration. Frequently she would give Nick a wide-eyed look that indicated that her mother was mad.

After ten minutes, and frustrated that their TV was not showing the England v Colombia football match being played that night in Moscow, Nick decided to go for a walk to see what Burguete looked like at 10 p.m. He discovered it was deserted and cold. He saw neither people nor cars moving while he was out, and definitely no bar with a TV showing the football.

By the time he returned Adrienne had changed into her pyjamas. 'We had a good chat. Mum's in great heart,' she said with a straight face.

Nick changed into his pyjamas in the bathroom and after a few minutes he turned the light out.

18

They got lost on several occasions as they drove into Pamplona, which was bigger than they had expected. Adrienne had looked the city up on Wikipedia and informed Nick that it had almost 200,000 residents. Certain streets near the city centre had been closed off in preparation for the *feria*. Eventually they found the railway station to drop off the rental car and taxied to the Hotel Tres Reyes. It was reasonably plush, and its location a hundred yards outside the walls of the old city meant that it was close to all the festivities, but not too close. Their room was not ready, so they headed off into the city for a quick exploration. The old city was already full of pedestrians, many in the traditional San Fermin garb of white trousers and white shirt or tunic, with a red sash around the waist. The streets were narrow, cobbled in places, and vehicles had largely been excluded. There were many shops and stalls selling souvenirs, beer and *bocadillos*. Nick could feel a sense of mounting excitement.

They walked through the Calle Mercaderes, flanked on two sides by townhouses and apartment buildings five or six storeys high. Nick pointed out the balconies where they would stand to watch the next day's opening *chupinazo* ceremony and the bull-running the following morning. They walked up a small, shaded street into the light and colour of the Plaza del Castillo. This vast square was the heart of the city. They marvelled at its size, each side over a hundred yards long, and its big rotunda in the middle, and at the grassy knolls for people to sit on. It was surrounded by cafés, restaurants and hotels. The main cafés had outside seating for dozens of tables, some under temporary canopies.

It didn't take them long to spot the Café Iruña, famous for its Hemingway connections. Before taking a table under the canopy protecting the customers from being fried in the midday sun they explored inside and found the life-size bronze statue of the great man standing at the bar. Adrienne insisted that Nick take several photos of her draped over Hem's shoulders.

Nick was happy to oblige. She looked excited and joyful, with her hair flowing over her bare shoulders and her sunglasses riding high on her head.

Later, as they ate bread with olives and *jamon* washed down with beer and Rioja, Adrienne touched his arm. 'Thanks so much for bringing me here. It's going to be a very special few days.'

'My own thoughts exactly, *mi cara señorita*.'

Adrienne beamed. 'I love being called a senorita.'

They didn't say much, and Nick didn't feel that he should push the conversation. They were content to watch Pamplona ready itself for its famous *fiesta*. Workmen were still erecting tents, and hawkers were selling hats and sunglasses and bottles of water. American tourists, mainly men in their twenties and thirties, talked loudly of their plans for the bull-running. Women in summer dresses and wide-beamed hats promenaded in the sunshine.

They walked slowly back to the hotel, noting the beautiful monolith of the church of San Lorenzo only a hundred yards from their hotel. They were pleased with their room, which had a queen-sized bed. 'I'll have the left hand side,' Adrienne said. 'I prefer that side when I'm sharing a bed.' Nick shrugged, amused that she was still willing to share a bed with him, and said that would be fine.

They were glad to be out of the thirty-degree heat. After showering and unpacking they lay on the bed, Nick rereading portions of *The Sun Also Rises* and Adrienne making further inroads into one of her true crime podcasts while at the same time reading extracts from biographies of Hemingway and Hadley.

'I'm on to John Wayne Gacy now,' she said. 'Talk about a sick pervert.'

She had a talent for multi-tasking, able to listen intently to a podcast while scrolling through her Instagram feed or reading a book and painting her fingernails. Perhaps it was a generational thing.

Adrienne, seemingly able to elicit from her phone everything a visitor wanted to know, advised that the only two or three highly rated restaurants in Pamplona were fully booked for the festival, so they agreed that they would just try their luck that night and throughout their stay.

They headed to the Plaza del Castillo, like thousands of other tourists. They walked past groups of excited drinkers on the streets outside cafés, dressed in white and red and drinking lager. Many were boisterous and noisy, but unthreateningly so.

The plaza was teeming with revellers, and Nick could almost inhale their excitement. Most of the cafés were packed, and the waiting staff everywhere were rushing from table to table. First they found a clothes shop selling San Fermin clothing. An attractive and persuasive Spanish girl with little English kitted them out, Nick in long white trousers and a white polo shirt with a blue Pamplona crest on the breast pocket, and a bright-red sash and a neck cravat, each also with a San Fermin crest. Adrienne chose the same but opted for a white T-shirt instead of the polo. She also bought a white mini skirt that descended no more than a few inches below her crotch. Nick enthused when she modelled it for him in the shop. The shop assistant seemed transfixed by this apparition of foreign elegance. '*Qué mujer hermosa eres. Qué hermosa mujer.'*

They managed to seat themselves at a table at the Café Iruña. Nick ordered for them: *'Una cerveza y un agua mineral con gas, por favor.'* The waiter smiled, despite or even because of Nick's English accent.

Their drinks arrived as the sun was leaving the plaza. Nick raised his beer in a toast: 'Here's to you, my fiancée. Thank you for agreeing to accompany me in search of Hem.'

She accepted the toast: 'And here's to you, my oil billionaire sugar daddy. And thank you for paying for everything. I could never afford to come here out of my own money, or lack thereof. I do intend to pay you back. One day.'

Nick shrugged. 'Don't you worry. I learned a good lesson when I was a struggling student and people would pay for my beers or lunch. It's a noble and worthy thing for those that have the income to pay for those that don't. So please don't mention it again.' He paused, and surveyed the hordes in the plaza. 'It's funny what brings us here, to this place at this time. One of my pet theories is based on the sheer randomness of every minute of life. If you hadn't wanted me to supervise your thesis, for example, or even if you hadn't signed up for the Law of War optional class, then we wouldn't be here together.'

'More importantly, if you hadn't been accused of sexually harassing me, you wouldn't have been in the British Library that day, and we wouldn't have become research buddies. And neither you nor I would be here.'

'But it goes back even further than that. My own history, my backstory as you might call it, is very conventional. Born in England to middle-class parents, sent to a minor public boarding school, Cambridge, a law job in the City, and a lecturer for twenty years or so. So boring and linear. And yet you were born thousands of miles away in Busan, so far from Europe.' Nick remembered the terrible thought that a Korean guard had killed his grandfather. 'I've been thinking about your great-grandfather on the Railway. How difficult a time it would have been for him, as well as for the prisoners.'

'Yes, I've thought about him every day for months now. I think it's best that I don't know how he died, or where, or from what cause. It's just a dark episode. I included a chapter in my thesis on the treatment of the Korean guards by the Japanese. They were truly horrific times.' Adrienne paused. After a second, she brightened. 'But the whole process, the research by you as well by me, has been beneficial. I learned enough about my great-grandfather to satisfy my curiosity, and I got to study an interesting period of history. I got a good enough grade for the thesis, and you ended up finding out the truth about your Grandpa. An awful truth, but a noble one. You've got closure.'

'You're right. You might say we both found what we were looking for. I hadn't thought of it like that before. But yes, the Koreans in Thailand were victims too, I wholeheartedly accept. And there's certainly no animosity from me about how William died.' He squeezed her hand.

Adrienne seemed lost in thought for a few seconds. 'I was just speculating, wondering if you hadn't harassed me' – Nick smiled at her choice of word – 'whether you would have given me a Distinction for my thesis, instead of Tobias's rather stingy high Merit. What do you reckon?'

Nick toyed with his beer glass. He looked her in the eye. 'Without doubt I would have. It's a work of outstanding scholarship and research.' She laughed. After a moment he went back to what they had been discussing before. 'What was it like coming to England as a child? Was it easy to fit in?'

Adrienne took a sip of her water as Nick ordered another beer for himself. 'No, it was very difficult. I was fifteen then, not an easy age to move to a different country. I had to leave behind all my school friends in Busan, I knew only a little English, and many people in London were cold and unwelcoming. My mother spoke no English, and even now hardly speaks any. For our first six months in London she used to cry every night and used to have terrible rows with my father for bringing the family to England. I went straight into a local high school, speaking only a limited amount of schoolgirl English. My brother and I were given extra language tuition privately, which my mother refused to participate in. I can't tell you how hard it is to write an essay in a language which you have no proficiency in and where you can't understand the topic.'

Nick was enjoying seeing a new, passionate Adrienne. She had finished her water and said she would now like a glass of Rioja. 'I was one of only two Asian girls in my year group, out of about two hundred. Real Asians, I mean. There were twenty or so Indians and Pakistanis, but they were as English as the others. I was treated as a bit of a freak, a silent and uncomplaining outsider, who was good at music and spoke broken English with a funny accent. But I hung in there. My English got a bit better, and I managed to get a few A Levels in my second year. The Korean school education system was more rigorous and advanced than the English one, and I was able to use my maths and sciences background to good effect.'

'I had no idea. I can see it must have been hard on you and your family. So how was Bristol?'

'I liked it. The vibe was more welcoming, and I had a bit more confidence than at high school. I made a few Asian friends, girls from China, Singapore, and Malaysia. We all got on well, and we flatted together over the years. One of the guys we knew used to call us the Lucy Liu's. We all liked that.' She smiled. 'But it's not easy being Asian in Britain. We don't feel fully accepted. We look different and we sound different. Our differences put English people off. We're often pigeonholed, unnecessarily. I'm often referred to as the Korean girl, or the Asian woman.'

She took a good mouthful of Rioja. 'Tell me, Nick. You're a sociable man. Well known and well liked. How many Asian or African or black American friends have you got? I mean, decent friends. Not just fellow lecturers who you chat to for a few minutes.'

Nick thought hard for a few seconds. 'Well, I do know many non-English people. And yes, I regard them as friends. Granted, not close friends. And I had an Indian girlfriend for about six months when I came down from Cambridge to London. Rita. She was quite a character.'

'And was Rita as black as the ace of spades and came from Tamil Nadhu in the south? Or was she a light-skinned maharani from the Punjab or Kashmir?'

Nick would have applauded Adrienne's language had he not felt so defensive. 'Actually,' he admitted, 'Rita was fair-skinned, as light as me, and she was born in England.' Adrienne said nothing. 'From Chigwell, in Essex.' He laughed.

'And why am I here, Nick? Am I a China doll on your arm so that matadors and American tourists can congratulate you on your pulling power? Is it that you want to have sex with an Asian babe, just out of curiosity? Have you got yellow fever?' It was an expression he hadn't heard before.

'Not at all. You're here as my partner in crime, you could say, and my research assistant. We're here to find out about my grandfather and a great American writer. And I enjoy your company. Very much. You're different from my other friends. That's only partly due to your, ah, ethnicity, and your relative youth. I appreciate your worldview, if you like, your take on things. And you're a great conversationalist.'

Adrienne was laughing now. Her eyes were shining. 'So you *don't* want to have sex with me? You seemed to enjoy massaging my body the other night.'

Nick looked into her beautiful brown eyes. He wished he'd had more than two beers. 'True, I did enjoy that. But I didn't want to take advantage of you. You were in a vulnerable position, and you were virtually asleep. But yes, I don't believe I would say no. You're beautiful, and funny too. But I didn't come to Spain to have sex with you. You're a delightful travelling companion, and I'll have a splendid time in Spain, whatever happens or doesn't happen between us.'

Adrienne leaned forward and put her hand on his arm. 'Don't worry, *mon vieux*. I was pulling your leg. You promised me at the beginning that there would be no funny business, and I know you're a man of your word.'

'I most definitely am. I must say though, you're very hard to read. I never know where I stand.'

She stood up, with a triumphant look. 'Ha! That's how it always is.' She looked at her watch. 'It's almost ten and we haven't eaten. Let's wander around the old town a bit more, and we can grab something to eat on the street.'

They found a quiet café and ordered a *bocadillo* and a Rioja each. Nick talked of Hemingway, and how he'd had a fad for almost a year about Hem in his last year at school. He told her of the novels and short stories he had read, and the biography of Hemingway, and how the biography had led him into an appreciation of the life and works of F Scott Fitzgerald and other American writers.

'Have you never read any of Hem's short stories?' he asked.

Adrienne shook her head.

'Some of them are of the highest quality. The early ones are mainly based on young men in the forests and lakes of America near the Canadian border, so perhaps they won't be your cup of tea. There's one story I vividly remember, in part because it's so short, only a few pages long, but mainly because it was so shocking in its subject matter. It caused a minor furore at the time. I won't tell you the story. You should read it yourself. It's called 'Up in Michigan'.'

Adrienne picked up her phone. 'Here it is,' she announced after less than a minute. 'I've found a PDF of it. It's only four pages. Will you read it to me later?' Nick couldn't refuse.

They walked back to the hotel arm-in-arm, as the chill of

the night descended. The bar on the mezzanine floor hotel was jumping, with maybe thirty revellers getting in the mood before the opening of the *fiesta* the next day. A group of elderly men, all dressed in white and presumably long-time aficionados of San Fermin, were singing Spanish dirges to the accompaniment of a small guitar.

They were both in high spirits as they prepared for bed. Nick had a shower and changed into his T-shirt and boxer shorts in the bathroom. Adrienne walked around the room in her bra and underwear, with no appearance of modesty or shyness. Nick made a point of not staring when she might be looking, all the time wondering whether she was flirting with him or was just unabashed and confident, or even both. She sat down on a stool in front of the mirror and started applying face cream. 'Read, *señor*.'

Nick began to read 'Up in Michigan' from her phone as he leaned against the headboard. After a few paragraphs he stopped to ask if she was liking it. 'Oh yes. You have a great reading voice, so posh-sounding, and I like Hem's short sentences. Pray continue, *señor*.'

When he was about halfway through the story Adrienne jumped onto her side of the bed. She was now in her pyjamas. She lay back on the pillows and closed her eyes as she listened.

The story came to its dreadful end. The man was having sex with a lonely virgin on a jetty by a Michigan lake at night, and he fell asleep on top of her:

She was cold and miserable and everything felt gone.

'Hem was a misogynist even in his early twenties,' Nick said when he had finished the story.

Adrienne laughed and said, 'How awful. I wouldn't say he's a misogynist. I think he's portrayed it pretty well from the woman's perspective.'

They turned the lights out. Adrienne rolled on to her right side, facing away from him, and seemed to fall asleep straight away. Nick edged towards her and reached out an arm. He was disappointed that she had wrapped herself tightly in a sheet and there was no possibility that his hands might find their way on to her arms. Undeterred he moved beside her and spooned her. She seemed neither to encourage nor discourage that and ignored Nick stroking her hair. She was asleep. Nick rolled back to his side of the bed and closed his eyes.

He awoke early, at about six, as the morning light pierced the gap in the curtains. As he returned from his morning pee he could see her sleeping face in the gloom. *So serene.*

He got back into bed quietly and rolled over towards Adrienne. Her arms had come free from the cocoon of the sheet, and the sheet itself was a little loose. He began caressing her left arm, gently, and stroked her hair and her cheek. She remained asleep, or at least pretended to be so. Nick couldn't tell. After a few minutes he moved back to his own side of the bed and promptly fell asleep.

19

They laughed as they donned their San Fermin costumes for the first time. Nick felt a bit silly as he tied the red sash around his waist. Adrienne reassured him that he looked fine. Her long trousers and polo shirt fitted her figure perfectly, and he knew (and knew that she knew) that she would turn a few heads on the Pamplona streets.

Nick started to tie up the bright-red cravat around his neck. 'You can't do that yet,' said Adrienne. 'Not until the rocket is fired at midday. The *fiesta* officially starts when a rocket is fired at noon from the Town Hall. At that precise time everyone on the streets and in the plazas will go batshit bonkers and wave their cravats in the air. Only then are we allowed to tie our cravats around our necks.' She looked pleased with her knowledge.

They walked quickly to reach their destination by 10.30 a.m. Already the streets were filling up with happy *fiesta*-goers in their white-and-red garb. The plaza in front of the Town Hall was packed, and Nick and Adrienne had to push themselves patiently through the horde. At the appointed time they presented themselves at the foot of the apartment building in Calle Mercaderes, roughly half-way between the Town Hall and the Plaza del Castillo. A wholesome-looking American family was also there. The couple explained that this had been a bucket-list adventure for them ever since they studied *The Sun*

Also Rises at high school. They too had paid to share the balcony with Adrienne and Nick, and possibly a few others.

Their host Carol greeted them and led them up three dark flights of stairs into an old and smallish apartment. There were four people there already. One introduced himself as Carol's son and offered them a glass of sparkling wine as they came into the lounge. Carol was in her sixties, Nick guessed, with a baseball cap covering her short hair. She was no more than five foot tall, and her white trousers and shirt looked as though they had survived a number of *fiestas*.

'This will be our twenty-sixth San Fermin,' she said with obvious pride. She explained that she and her husband, both from Florida, had travelled here as young backpackers and fallen in love with the *fiesta* and the city. Even though they now lived in Hong Kong they owned two apartments in Calle Mercaderes – she pointed out one across the street, and said to Adrienne, 'That's where you'll be for the running of the bulls tomorrow morning' – and contracted the use of a few other apartments in the street during each year's *fiesta*. They ran a thriving business of renting out balcony spaces for the *chupinazo* and the bull-running, and also procured tickets to the bullfight for tourists at steep prices.

Nick and Adrienne found a spot on the balcony, soaking up the hot sun. Even with an hour to go the streets and small plaza below them were packed full of revellers standing shoulder to shoulder. Some held up banners and flags and were singing; many wore bright-red hats. A good number were drinking sangria out of plastic cups. Each building on both sides of Calle Mercaderes had several balconies, with each floor of most apartment buildings occupied.

They heard a loud boom to the right. *El chupinazo* had been fired, and the crowd cheered and roared. Red cravats were waved and hats were thrown in the air; gallons of sangria were tossed skyward, no one seemingly caring where the liquid landed. Nick and Adrienne tied their cravats around each other's necks. The occupants of balconies opposite them emptied jugs of water on the teaming mass of bodies below. Nick was apprehensive, comparing it to what would happen if you did that at a football stadium in England. But here the revellers queued up on the street, looked up and encouraged the people on the balconies to drench them.

Carol brought them a large jug. 'Here, go fill this up in the kitchen. And then let it all hang out.' Adrienne giggled as she poured water on the Spaniards below. A group of young men with sangria-sodden pink shirts spied her and pointed at her. '*Por favor, nuestra bella dama,*' they cried out. '*Mas agua, por favor.*' Adrienne delighted in pouring jugsful of water onto their heads. The young men moved on a minute or two later, making way for a slow-moving marching band in traditional green and black clothing.

Afterwards Nick and Adrienne inched their way through the crowds to the Plaza del Castillo, the *fiesta*'s epicentre, which in the 1920s had been known as the Plaza del Constitution. The thousands there were a picture postcard of white and red. The hot sun was beating down, well over thirty degrees now, and all shady spots and café tables under canopies were taken. Nick absorbed in wonder the vitality and exuberance of traditional Spain. Here there were no sullen teenagers or angry skinheads. Here young people were happy to dress in traditional clothes and be part of family groups.

Eventually they found a table, or at least half of one, at Bar Txoko. 'Another of Don Ernesto's haunts,' said Nick. 'Or so it is thought.' They sat next to four young Americans, college boys, fresh-faced and exuberant. The service was so slow that Nick went into the bar to order their drinks and a lunch snack.

When he returned a few minutes later Adrienne was engaged in animated discussion with the Americans. 'Oh, Nick, I've been entertained by these fine young American men. They're staying in our hotel and they hope to see us at some stage in the hotel bar. They say it's very lively every night during the festival.'

Nick had a grudging admiration for the Americans' easy manner. He was quite sure they had said that they wanted to see Adrienne, not both of them, in the hotel bar. They were from Cornell University, recent graduates about to take up jobs in New York, Boston and San Francisco in banks and management consultancies. This was their last fling as student friends. Last year it had been hiking in Yellowstone. All had read Hemingway at school or college, and all were planning on running with the bulls on three or four occasions. The first one was tomorrow morning.

'Isn't it dangerous?' Adrienne said. 'Don't people get trampled and gored, even killed?'

The Americans laughed. 'That's why we do it,' said one as he raised his glass of beer and drained it. 'No, you have to have shitty luck to be hurt. Four thousand people run with the bulls every morning. The chances of injury are tiny. Besides, we've hired a local to give us some tips on where to start the run from and how to avoid the dangerous areas.'

'Four thousand?' said Nick. 'I had no idea. The streets don't look big enough to take that many runners.'

The heat of the afternoon was becoming oppressive and they made their way through the throng back to the hotel. Nick said, 'I'm keen to watch Brazil play Belgium on TV tonight at a bar somewhere. Think you can handle that?'

'I'd be happy to. I love watching fit young men running around with a football.'

In their room Adrienne put on her earphones. 'Still on John Wayne Gacy,' she smiled. 'What a disgusting creep!' Nick checked out the *Guardian* and *Times* websites then fell asleep.

Nick suggested they do a pub-crawl that evening. It took them almost an hour to walk the six hundred yards to the Plaza del Castillo. Thousands packed the streets, drinking beer and sangria. The shirts and tops of many of them were pink from the day's festivities. Many had bright-red sunburnt faces and necks. Adrienne wore her white mini skirt. Nick had whistled his appreciation as she emerged from their bathroom, asking him how she looked.

'Fantastic,' he said. 'Stunning. You look like a million pesetas. A billion, in fact.'

Many of the bars had TV screens and it seemed that a good proportion of the *fiesta*-goers were keen to keep at least one eye on the football. Nick and Adrienne, who said she loved football but couldn't name a single player in either team, had made a pact that they would have no more than one drink in each bar. They worked their way outwards from the Plaza del Castillo – beers and sangria, gin y tonica for Adrienne and Rioja for Nick, and then mojitos in a bar that claimed Don Ernesto as a patron in the 1950s. They chatted with fellow British tourists, and even warmed to a group of Australian lads – 'Been drinking for thirty hours straight, mate. Love fucking Pamplona.'

They didn't have a late night, as they had an early-morning start to look forward to. They sauntered back through the night chill. Adrienne looped her arm around Nick's elbow, and occasionally nuzzled her cheek against his shoulder. They resisted an invitation to join a conga line of drunken Dutchmen in a hotel bar. They climbed the stairs to the lift lobby, past the packed bar on the mezzanine floor where guests were relaxing after the gruelling first day of the *fiesta* and were in their room by eleven. They were tired and happy.

Nick positioned himself in the middle of the bed, waiting for Adrienne to finish in the bathroom. He watched her as she walked around to her side of the bed. She was wearing a long black T-shirt, and he could see the bottom of her knickers. 'Why don't you take your top off?' he said gently. She looked at him, and smiled, and did as he suggested. She turned off the light and jumped in beside him as he took off his own T-shirt.

He enveloped her in his arms, feeling her breasts squashing up against his chest, and they kissed passionately, feverishly. Her lips were soft and her skin smooth. Nick was overcome with both desire and wonder.

He caressed her breasts and ran his hand down her belly. He felt her warm softness through her cotton underwear, and soon his fingers were inside her. She gave a small gasp, encouraging him, and his fingers delighted in her sticky wetness. Her aroma aroused him and he urgently found her mouth again with his. They were both breathing heavily. She moved her hand down inside Nick's boxers and circled his erect penis.

'Do you have any condoms?' she whispered. He shook his head, mentally kicking himself for his poor planning. It hadn't occurred to him that he might need any. 'We'll buy some tomorrow. No sex without protection, I'm sorry. Mind you, you may have to be quick as my period is due.'

They kissed and caressed more, and Adrienne lay back as Nick moved his mouth down her body, over her lovely flat belly to her waxy smooth mound. He thought he was in heaven. Adrienne responded as if she was too.

20

By 6.30 a.m. they were at their appointed place in Calle Mercaderes, waiting for Carol who would take them to their balcony. It was the first bullrun of the *fiesta*. Already large parts of the central city were off limits as the hundreds of police and other servicemen corralled the runners into various parts of the course. Tourists and spectators were kept well back.

When they reached their first-floor balcony, Carol explained how the bull-running operated. There would be six bulls, which would run from one side of the old town, uphill through Calle Mercaderes, and then around Dead Man's Corner, a ninety-degree turn to the right, down the cobbles of Calle Estafeta and then onwards into the bullring.

'The run lasts only about two and a half minutes,' said Carol. 'The bulls will be led through the streets by teaser steers. The teasers are tame and won't charge at the runners. The runners position themselves at various stages around the course. Only a few ever run the whole length. Many will start down there' – she pointed down to the street – 'or even further along around the corner.' Everyone was aware of the danger at Dead Man's Corner, where the bulls and runners converged and where it was easy to slip. In the lounge of their apartment the TV was showing live coverage of the morning's run.

At eight exactly there was the boom of a rocket being fired, and the run started. The hundreds of runners standing in front of their balcony became more alert and anxious, jogging on the spot. Nick could hear the rising crescendo of the cheering spectators, and then the bulls came into view thirty yards to their left. The runners took off. Five seconds later the bulls had turned Dead Man's Corner and were off to the bullring. No one had been trampled or eviscerated.

Carol could sense their disappointment. 'Most days there are no serious injuries. Every *fiesta* about twenty people end up in hospital with gore wounds or if they're trampled, and occasionally someone is killed. Anyway, let's head off to the *encierro* in ten minutes. That'll be a blast.'

They hurried on the cobbles with their tickets in their pockets and entered the bullring. Carol led them upstairs into the crowded seating. They sat two rows back from the arena. The scene was a glorious panorama of colour under the blue morning sky. The bullring was filled almost to its capacity of over nineteen thousand people. About half of them appeared to be teenage girls, in white shorts and T-shirts and bright-red sashes and cravats. Many were on their feet, in lines and groups, clapping and swaying to the loud music blaring throughout the arena.

In the arena were two hundred or so festival-goers and one steer. It was being taunted into charging at the revellers and occasionally would knock one over, to the delight of the crowd. These were not the half-ton bulls with sharpened horns that had run through the Pamplona streets half an hour before – those bulls would be slaughtered in the bullring that night. The steers were half the weight, with sawn-down horns covered in cloth padding.

Nick and Adrienne were caught up in the fun. This was the nearest thing that tourists could do to participating in a bullfight. Nick felt liberated at the giddiness of the occasion, the uniquely Spanish combination of colour, music, tradition and dance, with the unspoken subtext of danger and cruelty to animals. As each steer was tormented into near-exhaustion it was replaced by a fitter one.

Adrienne had spotted her American friends in the arena competing with each other to draw the steer's attention. Then one of them, Carl, a tall, laid-back preppie from Connecticut, spotted Adrienne and ran over to them. 'Come join us. It's such a blast.' Nick was doubtful, but Adrienne jumped to her feet and after a quick leap over the barrier, which wasn't permitted, Nick noted, Carl pulled her by the hand into the centre of the arena. The other Americans greeted her with backslaps and high-fives, and they set off to attract the steer's attention.

For ten or so minutes Adrienne chased the steers, occasionally being charged, to the delight of her new friends and others in the crowd who appeared to relish the bravery and energy of this elegant woman from a foreign world. Then she bade farewell to Carl and his friends with hugs and more high-fives and walked back to Nick. He jumped the perimeter fence to join her on the sand. Her eyes were shining with excitement, drops of perspiration on her forehead. 'Oh, Nick, that was such fun. God, I love Spain. I'm having the best holiday *ever*! Thank you so much.' She gave him the biggest of hugs and pressed herself into his chest.

In search of breakfast they walked hand in hand into the centre of Pamplona along the Ruta Hemingway Ibilbidea, the Hemingway Trail. They stopped for some *churros* and coffee at a busy little bar-café. A sign on the wall said that the café was on the same site as the former Casa Marceliano, where the sign said Hemingway loved the *ajoarriero*, a local cod dish.

Adrienne wolfed down her breakfast. *What an extraordinary woman*, Nick thought. *Always surprising me.* He wanted to reach over and run his hands through her hair, to caress her arms and her cheeks.

She smiled, her mouth full. He figured she knew what he was

thinking. She leaned forward and put a hand on his. 'Hold on a minute. I have to go to the loo.' Adrienne looked meaningfully at him. She picked up her handbag and walked to the back of the café.

'We have two main tasks for today,' he said when she returned. 'One, we're going to the offices of the *Diario de Navarra*, the local newspaper, to see if they have stories on Hem's 1925 visit or a photograph collection from then that might include some of William. Hopefully they'll have some English-speaking staff who will be able to help us out.' It was a long shot, but the paper had been in existence for over a hundred years. 'And second, we should try the police station, just on the off-chance that there might be a police report of a fight involving Hemingway and William during the 1925 *fiesta*.' This was even less likely to bear fruit.

Perspiring as they walked in the hot sun, they went straight to the offices of the *Diario*, with its navy-blue façade and its name in gold letters above the door. Inside it looked more like a travel agency. There were some desks at the back, with only one man there. He gabbled away on the phone for the ten minutes Nick and Adrienne waited to speak to him. They left the shop, none the wiser.

Later Adrienne used her online search skills to ascertain whether the *Diario* had an online database of photographs or old newspapers. She drew a blank. She couldn't ascertain whether the *Diario* published photographs in its 1925 editions.

The visit to the police station was even less productive. There were dozens of tourists in the queue, with the usual concerns of lost or stolen property. A few were being processed for disorder and drunkenness offences. There were two officers on duty, humourlessly processing the jetsam of the previous night's revelries, and only one appeared to speak English. It became apparent that any request for access to historical records, if they existed, would likely not be understood, and even if they could get their request across to the police, Nick sensed it would be met with disbelief and hilarity. He decided not to pursue it.

On their way back into the Old Quarter they looked for the six jewellers or antique shops that their online searches told them were situated in central Pamplona. Nick was hoping to find a goblet that matched the one on Jo's mantelpiece back home. Here too he was to be disappointed. Every one of the shops was closed for the *fiesta*. Nick thought that to be a typically Continental response to the hundreds of thousands of tourists who descended on Pamplona in July. In England the shops would be open, working long hours, making as much money as they could.

As they ascended one of the side-streets off the Plaza del Castillo they saw a placard advertising an exhibition of photographs of the *fiesta* during the 1920s and 1930s. They ventured into the building, a poorly-lit edifice in a state of decay, and found themselves going from room to room looking at a number of easels. Each was adorned by a series of black-and-white photos, assembled in chronological order. The pictures were of bulls in the arena and being run through the streets, and of the local citizenry milling around. Many were of the crowds in the main plaza and in front of the Town Hall.

Nick was studying the photos from the mid-1920s. There were a number of Hemingway, even though then he had not been famous, standing with Hadley or with local matadors or *ferministas*. The well-known 1925 and 1926 pictures of the Hemingways and their friends at the Café Iruña were there, and not far from them was another, similar, photo. It showed five men and a woman sitting at a table, maybe in a café. Nick immediately recognised Hemingway in the middle, with his strong jaw and bushy moustache.

And there too was William, two away from Hemingway on his right, a handsome and bemused looking figure with his gaze fixed on the camera. Adrienne recognised William a half-second after Nick, and she let out a stifled '*ssi-bal*', which Nick interpreted as Korean for 'fuck'. She clutched Nick's arm. 'Nick, we've found him. At last. The camera never lies. No one can doubt us now.'

The caption under the photo was in Spanish, accompanied by an English translation. It said that the photo was of the great American novelist Ernest Hemingway, taken in an unidentified café or restaurant during the *fiesta* of 1925. The caption said that the identity of the others in the picture was unknown. The photographer was also unknown. Nick looked at the fine print below the caption. The photo was reproduced by courtesy of the keepers of the Hemingway Collection of the John F Kennedy Library in Boston. On the back of the photo, Nick read, was the word *tarjeta*.

Nick looked at the picture again. There were similarities between the photo and the famous one on the cover of *Everyone Behaves Badly*. Hemingway was the centrepiece of the photo, and a white space behind his head gave him a somewhat saintly aura. William aside, Nick did not recognise the other men. The one at the back looked a bit like Pat Guthrie, Duff Twysden's lover in 1925. The woman on the right was wearing an apron, perhaps she was a waitress, or the café owner, invited into the picture because she knew the photographer or Hemingway.

'Well, Nick, we've got proof now that the two men knew each other and were here in 1925. It has to follow that everything else we know, which isn't much more than that they had a fight, must be true too. We've hit the jackpot. I'm so happy for you.' Adrienne's face lit up. She then took out her phone, and after tapping a few keys she announced that *tarjeta* translated into English as 'card'.

'Like a postcard, that seems to be its most common usage, but it's also used for credit card. Heaven knows whether that's of significance.' They took photos of the *tarjeta* picture on their phones.

Nick and Adrienne agreed as they left the exhibition that they deserved a beer, and walked up to the Plaza del Castillo. The plaza was packed, and the bars and cafés were mostly full. As they strolled around the plaza they spotted their elderly German friend Hans, their dining companion in Burguete. He had said he and his friends always congregated in the Bar Windsor, beside the glamorous Hotel La Perla. Hans beckoned them to join him.

Hans was sitting with four other older men, three Spaniards and an Englishman. 'Each year,' he explained, 'we meet in this bar every day during the *fiesta*. San Fermin would not be the same without my friends and this bar.'

The men were entranced by Adrienne, and offered her drinks and compliments, in Spanish and broken English, in equal measure. The Englishman, in his early sixties Nick guessed, eyed up Nick and Adrienne. 'Tell me, Nick, and I hope you don't mind me asking, but do tell me how you met.'

Nick was aware that Adrienne was listening in on the conversation. 'It's a long story, but we met in London about eighteen months ago.'

'I see. But you're so much older than your friend, and you, ah, look so different. It just seems unusual to see you together. Especially at San Fermin.'

Nick's dislike for the man was increasing by the second. He was about to rebuke him for his racist innuendo when Adrienne put her hand on Nick's thigh, smiled sweetly at the Englishman, and said, 'Don't tell everyone, but Nick and I are getting married next week. We're having a pre-wedding honeymoon, if you must know. You know the saying, "Try before you buy"? We're having the most amazing time together.'

The man blinked and concentrated on his drink. Nick looked at Adrienne with a new regard.

He reached for his phone and located the *tarjeta* photo and showed it to Hans and his friends. 'Do any of you recognise this? That's Hemingway, as you can see, and the picture was taken somewhere in Pamplona in 1925. Not sure where. I'm keen to know who all his friends are. One of them is my grandfather, who we believe met Hemingway and his friends here in 1925.'

Hans translated for his friends. They pointed to Hem but shook their heads at the other people in the photograph. 'Silvio thinks the location is the Café Iruña, but he can't be sure,' Hans said.

'The original photo had the Spanish word *tarjeta* on the back,' Nick said. 'Does that mean anything to your friends?'

Hans translated, but the Spaniards shrugged and shook their heads. One said a few words to Hans and laughed. Hans told Nick, 'My friend here has no idea why that word is on the back of the photo. Perhaps it was just a postcard. But he did say that he met Hemingway once, in 1959, when he had been called in as a teenager to serve customers at the Iruña.'

After a *bocadillo* washed down with prosecco Nick and Adrienne took their leave and walked through the bright sunshine and oppressive heat back to their hotel. A nap was called for after the day's early start – it seemed like yesterday that they had been on the balcony watching the bulls run by.

Nick marvelled how natural his relationship with Adrienne now was. She offered her hand to him when they were walking together, and they frequently touched each other in the casual, intimate ways that couples did.

They showered when they got to their room, Adrienne first, and when Nick came out of the bathroom after his she was fast asleep. Within minutes he was too.

They dined that night in the Plaza de Castillo, the hub of all the action. Adrienne finished her meal and took hold of her wine glass. 'Sad to say, but we've reached a dead end about Hem and your Grandpa. Finding the *tarjeta* photo's been a great step forward, but it doesn't actually give us any answers. Unless you can find old Beryl and William's memoir of his Pamplona visit, it'll have to remain a mystery.'

Nick looked up from reviewing the menu to see what desserts were on offer. 'Afraid so. If the information is in Pamplona, we're not going to find it.'

'Have you googled Beryl?' Adrienne asked.

He shook his head. 'There doesn't seem much point. It's just another woman's name, and I can't imagine it'll help if we dig up the names of two thousand Beryls.'

'Well, you never know.' She took her phone from her purse. Half a minute later: 'Listen, there's a mineral called beryl. I didn't know that, though I do recall beryllium in the periodic table from my schooldays. There's a porcelain-making company called Beryl Woods. And, yes, heaps of women called Beryl.'

Nick frowned. 'It hadn't occurred to me that Beryl may not be a woman.'

'Hey, there's quite a bit on a woman called Beryl Markham, who appears to have been in East Africa in the 1920s. Wasn't your grandfather there then?'

Nick was now on alert. 'I know her name. She was a leading figure in the Happy Valley set in Kenya. An aviator too. Have you ever read *White Mischief* or seen the movie?' Adrienne shook her head. 'That may be a connection worth following up. When did she die?'

Adrienne scrolled through her phone again. '1986, it says. Aged eighty-four. Born 1902.'

'A pity,' said Nick. 'William described her as 'old Beryl' in 1941. Beryl Markham would have been thirty-nine then, and I can't imagine that a gentleman like him would have referred to her as *old* Beryl. She would've only been two or three years younger than him.' He smiled. 'It's rather a nice thought, isn't it? Here's my Grandpa, whose story is completely unknown decades after his death, we know he interacted with Hemingway, and now there's a possibility that he may have known people like Karen Blixen and others in Kenya in the 1920s – not to mention being a prisoner in Changi and a forced worker on the Death Railway. Quite a memorable life, you might say.'

'Well, 'memorable' doesn't seem to be the best word to describe it. But I get your drift.'

A mariachi band paraded slowly past. They wore shiny lime-green jackets with tight black trousers, on the side of which were about twenty horizontal rows of three white braided buttons. A few women holding castanets wore flowing green dresses, with white frills at the edges. All the men wore huge white sombreros.

'I'm loving Pamplona in every way I couldn't have imagined,' said Adrienne through the din, beaming. 'I must say I had doubts about whether you and I would be compatible. But not anymore. You're quite good company for an old fella, knowledgeable and kind without being up yourself or pushy or patronising.'

Nick wanted to lean over and kiss her.

'What's more, I'm very happy to be your sugar baby fiancée.'

'I see you more as my escort.'

'I'll be happy with that too. And how do you feel about last night? Back in the hotel room?'

'I must say that I wasn't expecting that to happen. Definitely. We've been getting to know each other the last few days, and so it seemed natural to me. It was a lovely night, and you were sexy and loving, and I felt honoured by your ... attention.' He felt gauche and inarticulate. 'I hope you aren't regretting it?'

'Ha, it was a surprise to me. No, no regrets. I'm cool, though. It was fun. But it won't happen again.'

Nick's heart missed a beat. She'd been willing a day ago. He wanted to ask her why, but she stood up, walked over to his side of the table and gave him a big kiss on his forehead. 'Come on, big boy. Let's not linger. Let's go home. I need to call my mother tonight.'

They picked their way through the Plaza. The moon shone on the hundreds of pink-shirted revellers, standing in groups, still enjoying the night. Many carried their own huge plastic container of sangria. There was rubbish all over the plaza, bottles and plastic glasses strewn everywhere, but by the next morning it would all have been removed, the plazas and streets hosed down.

Adrienne darted into the hotel bar to see if their American friends were there. As it turned out they weren't among the forty or fifty *fiesta*-goers having a drink before heading back to their rooms.

While Nick had a shower and brushed his teeth he could hear Adrienne on the phone to her mother. Again her voice varied from laughter to lecturing to exclamations of disbelief, annoyance and anger. He wondered whether this performance, this exhibition, was actually the real Adrienne with her barriers down. He contrasted it with the demeanour she presented to him – calm, rational, competent, affectionate (at least recently).

Nick went back into the room. Adrienne, in her night T-shirt and underwear, took his place in the bathroom, the phone pressed to her ear. She gave him a look as they passed, indicating that her mother was being pig-headed and stupid. For the next half hour he couldn't avoid listening to the haranguing and protests from Adrienne in the bathroom.

When she finished Nick was barely awake. 'Sorry about that,' said Adrienne. 'Mom had a busy day yesterday. She's all good, though. She's looking forward to seeing me in three days when she meets me at the airport.'

'I'm sure she is. Tell me, have you told her that you are here with me?'

'Yes. I tell her everything. That's what mothers are for.' Adrienne got into the bed on her side and turned off the lights.

'Really? Isn't she concerned about your welfare?'

'God yes. She pokes her nose into every aspect of my life. She wants me to give her a grandson. Not a granddaughter, just a boy. She is a surprisingly liberal and modern woman, my mother. And she got angry when I told her that my period had come. That means no pregnancy this month. Plus, she always gives me a hard time about when I'm going to get married. She quizzed me all about you, to see if you were suitable. I told her everything about you, and that satisfied her.'

'What do you mean, 'satisfied her'? Do you mean that I'm suitable marriage material?' Nick knew immediately that it was a breach of the barrister's maxim that you should never ask a question in cross-examination that you don't know the answer to.

'*Au contraire, mon vieux*, or should I now say *mi viejo*? I told her that there wasn't a dog's-show of a possibility that you would be suitable for my dainty hand in marriage. Good night, Nick.'

He smiled. He knew that she would be smiling too.

21

Nick woke early and a little sad, knowing that this would be their last full day in Spain together. Still, on a personal level at least, their trip had been far more successful than he could have hoped. It had been a risk encouraging Adrienne to join him, but she had blossomed before his eyes into a woman of depth and substance.

He snuggled up beside her. Her body was warm, her breathing regular. He could feel himself getting aroused. He caressed her thighs and her arms and nuzzled little kisses on her neck and hair. If she was aware of his attentions she showed no sign. Her breathing was constant.

Nick was full of tenderness and attention for Adrienne now. He'd already decided that her comment the night before that things wouldn't happen again was just a gameplay. He wanted to hold her, and protect her, and to possess her and make her happy, and he didn't want to let her go. He didn't want their holiday together to end. He knew he was being sentimental and silly.

Adrienne continued to sleep, her soft and regular breathing a counterpoint to Nick's increased pulse. After a few minutes he rolled back to his side of the bed and promptly fell asleep again.

When he woke Adrienne was adding polish to her fingernails and listening intently on her earphones. She smiled at him, like a mother to her naughty son. 'Time to get up. You've had such a long sleep.' She pointed to her ears. 'I'm on to JonBenét Ramsey now. Some loser has just confessed, but I think he's lying.'

They had a lazy morning, breakfasting at a nearby café and otherwise staying in the room staring at their phones. Nick uploaded a few photos of Pamplona and the bulls to his Facebook page. He was only an occasional poster, but using it meant he could get information of his whereabouts and activities to his children and others without much effort.

Adrienne was disdainful of Facebook. 'No one uses Facebook anymore. It's so five years ago.'

Nick smiled. She was now an Instagram aficionado. She often posted three or four times a day, mainly pastiches of the dishes and drinks she consumed in a variety of cities and top restaurants, often teaser items to encourage people to check out her foodie blog.

Many times she had handed him her phone and asked him to take a photo of her in front of monuments, churches, bullrings, and so on. She would insist on about ten different snaps of each pose, with only one meeting the required standard for posting online.

Later they went to San Lorenzo's church next door to their hotel. On the balcony at the bull-running the day before, Carol had suggested that they would like the midday mass there. 'We'll get a good insight into traditional Spanish life,' Adrienne said, 'and it'll be cool for us to go there together knowing that Jake and Brett went there in the book.'

They walked the short distance in their white trousers and shirts, and red sashes and cravats, and joined about two hundred other churchgoers, most of them dressed in the same garb. There were very few obvious tourists.

The church was huge and ornate, with a central hexagonal tower adorned by a gazebo-style rotunda on top that dominated the skyline, five or six storeys high. Nick and Adrienne sat themselves on a pew in the main chamber. The walls were covered with gaily-coloured statues and paintings of the saints and apostles. The woodwork was dark, the prevailing impression being one of solemnity. To their right was another chapel, seemingly as big as the main chamber. There was a huge gold and silver effigy of San Fermin himself at the far end. That chapel was packed too. By noon there were thirty or forty people standing at the back.

A choir shuffled into the church, preceded by a few clerics. The choir was singing a chant in Latin. The troop moved into the San Fermin chapel and the service was conducted from there.

The congregation was called to pray. Nick bowed his head, as he always did when in church, which was mainly at funerals these days, not wanting to appear insensitive. Adrienne clasped her hands to her chest, her fingers interlocking, and bowed her head so that her chin rested on her knuckles. Her eyes were tightly closed. She looked deep in contemplation.

Afterwards, as they made their way out of the church into the bright sunshine, Nick mentioned that he didn't know Adrienne was religious.

'There are millions of things you don't know about me. Yes, I am religious, I s'pose. I prefer the word "spiritual". I hardly ever go to church, but I believe in God and the power of prayer. My mother is a Catholic, and I went to Catholic schools in Korea.'

He hadn't expected to hear that. They inched their way through the crowded streets in the old town. He knew that Christian missionaries had travelled far into Asia, but it still was a surprise to think that Adrienne had had a Catholic upbringing.

'Who did you pray for?' he asked as they sat down in a café in the Plaza del Castillo.

'None of your business, old man.' They both smiled. 'Well, if you want to know, I prayed for my mother, that she's healthy and that she'll live to be a hundred. And for my brother, that he'll pass his exams and find his way in life.'

'Your brother? You don't mention him much. Are you close to him? What does he do?'

'He lives in Hong Kong, working for a subsidiary of Hyundai. He's in marketing. He's fine, but he lacks drive and spends too much time on X-box. I text him every day. Yes, we're pretty close.'

'I learn more about you every day, Adrienne, and I've been wondering who you've been exchanging all those texts with over the last few days.'

'You'd be surprised to know who my texting friends are.' She smiled, her expression twinkling in the sun.

'And who else did you pray for?'

'I prayed for my flatmates in London, that they might find decent husbands and get better jobs. And I prayed for you, too.' Nick waited for her to continue. 'I prayed that you find what you're looking for. Not just information about your grandfather and Hemingway, but that you find some purpose, or calling, or partner, that will bring you a fulfilling future.' She looked down, apparently studying the menu.

Not for the first time, he realised she had an emotional intelligence far superior to his own. 'You are perceptive. The truth is, I've been a bit directionless and bored in the last few years. Divorced. I see my kids only every two or three weeks, and they show little inclination to want to see me unless they're short of money. My job is essentially the same as it was twenty years ago. Some lectures I could give in my sleep. I haven't found the right woman, and I fear that I'm getting so set in my daily routines that there wouldn't be room for her in my life. And I'll be fifty soon. I'm not looking forward to that.'

Adrienne was grinning at him when he looked up. 'Cheer up. You're on holiday with your high-achieving and beautiful fiancée. You're in a fabulous country, in a city and at a time unlike anywhere else in the world. The sun is shining. You've got money in your pocket. You're about to have some regional Basque food for lunch, washed down with a bottle of the local *crianza*, and tonight you're going to a bullfight. What more could you want?'

There *was* one thing more that he wanted, that he now wanted more than anything else. He reached out and touched her arm. 'Thank you, Adrienne, I feel better already. You've summed me up pretty accurately, funnily enough.'

'You're like many men. Outwardly strong and confident, and even assured, but inside a mess of insecurities.' She looked at him with humour and warmth. 'But overall the package is pretty good. It's just a drag you snore so much and hog the middle of the bed.' They both laughed. 'And by the way, my period should have finished by tonight. I usually have very light periods, you see.' She paused for a second. 'I could see what you were thinking a minute ago. You don't realise it but you give away a lot by trying hard to give away nothing.' She looked triumphant.

They each ordered a salad as a starter, and for the *segundo* course he ordered the *lomo de bacalao* and she the *merluza*, or salmon. The waiter poured them each a glass of sparkling water and one from their Rioja bottle.

'Are you sure you won't join me at the bullfight? It's not too late to change your mind.'

'Thanks, but no thanks.' Adrienne had said all along she would never attend a bullfight. 'It's the slaughter of innocent animals. They stand no chance, they're tortured and taunted and die a slow and painful and thoroughly undignified death. Spaniards should be ashamed that in the twenty-first century bullfights are still allowed.'

Nick wasn't unsympathetic to her position. He wasn't looking forward to the bulls being tormented and killed, but he wanted to see for himself what it was that had so entranced Hemingway. The pull of the corrida had transformed Hem's life. What would he have done with his life and his writing if he hadn't visited Pamplona in the 1920s?

Again Nick could sense that Adrienne knew what he was thinking. 'It's funny,' she said, waving her arm at the crowds in the cafés and the plaza, 'but I feel that you and I are in a special position. We have this unique connection to Hemingway, to the history of Pamplona, to this café even, because of your grandfather. I feel privileged, and alive. Thank you for bringing me here.'

'More to the point,' Nick said, 'thank *you* for coming. It's just such a pity we have to go home tomorrow. And it's an early start too.'

'We have the rest of the day to look forward to.' Adrienne raised her glass. 'To Hem. To William. To you. To us.' Their glasses clinked.

'We're lucky to have this shared connection, and purpose.' Nick smiled. He spread his arms at the crowds. 'All those people in the Plaza today, they're all here because of the great Ernesto. If he hadn't written *The Sun Also Rises*, Pamplona may never have been discovered by the rest of the world, or at least to the level of interest today. San Fermin would be just another Spanish festival, like throwing live goats from church towers or having a tomato-fight in the streets.'

'But tell me, Nick, what's so special about *The Sun Also Rises*? Nothing really happens in it, and most of the characters are people you want to avoid.' Adrienne gave Nick a cheeful smile.

Nick felt a need to impart his knowledge to Adrienne. 'I'm so glad you asked me that. *Sun* had a tremendous impact when it was published. For two reasons, really. One, the subject matter was this group of decadent, disillusioned young people still processing the Great War. People who had sex with each other, who hit the booze, got into drunken brawls. That was quite shocking in 1926.

'More than that, though, the second reason, was Hemingway's

writing style: lean, spare, economical with words. His iceberg theory of writing. Less is more. Hardly any adjectives or adverbs. Short sentences. Sentences beginning with 'and' or 'but'. You know the classic style: Jake looked at Brett and at his glass and drank deep, and the sun shone on the balcony and it was good.'

They both laughed.

'But because of all that, it was a literary sensation when it was published. One of the first 'modernist' novels. Instantly he became one of the leading novelists of the times. And, remarkably, he was only twenty-six. There are many things to admire about our friend Hem. Our mutual friend.' Nick leaned back and sipped his wine.

'And the Rioja was good and the sun beat down on the man and the woman in the plaza,' said Adrienne, and burst into loud giggles. Nick thought she had never looked more desirable. They were silent for half a minute.

Adrienne stared into the distance. It was as if she had withdrawn into herself. 'A penny for your thoughts,' Nick said. 'Or perhaps a peseta or euro.'

'I was thinking about what awaits me back in Korea. You realise that within forty-eight hours I'll be on a flight from Heathrow to Seoul? I've only packed half my belongings, and I've been thinking about other things in recent days and weeks.'

Nick waited for her to continue. 'I haven't lived in Korea since I was fifteen. Almost twenty years ago. I hardly know what I'm going back to. I've visited a few times over the years, but they were just visits. To see family, eat kimchi, and that was about all.'

'But you have your mother to go back to, and I know how close you are to her.' Nick resisted the temptation to say more about her mother.

'Yes, but she's so controlling. She'll want me to live with her, and she'll make life miserable for me.'

Nick smiled. He knew that he'd never understand Adrienne fully, and he knew too he would never get to the bottom of mother/daughter relationships. One of life's eternal mysteries. 'But at least you won't be on your own. You have your mum, your brother is only two or three hours away in Hong Kong, you have the project of setting up your true crime podcast, you have your Korean food blog, and all your friends on social media. And you'll even have me, halfway around the world, your oil-billionaire fiancé and Hem co-investigator.'

They both laughed. Nick wanted to reach out and hold her, to let her doubts escape while she was in his arms.

'And will you visit me, Nick? I hope you will. Perhaps you could do some lectures at one of the Korean law schools. In English, obviously.'

'It's a nice thought. We shall see. But you'll have forgotten me in a few weeks.'

She shook her head. 'No. I won't. I never forget good people.'

They sipped their drinks. An early afternoon torpor had fallen on the plaza. The bands had stopped playing. A few African immigrants peddled hats, scarves and handbags around the café tables.

Adrienne hadn't finished. 'I know Korea has come ahead in leaps and bounds in the last twenty or thirty years, and is famous for its cars and electronics, its K-Pop and Gangnam Style, and ultra-fast internet, but it's also a tough country. If you're born rich, or have become rich, life is great. But my friends all tell me about the inequality. We have this expression which translates into English as 'dirt spoon'. This is something you're born with, and it's only the tiny minority who are able to escape that. My family was neither rich nor poor. Middle class, I suppose. But, for the 'dirt spoon' people, there's no way out. Their young have a sense of hopelessness, of being crushed by the system. They know they'll never be able to afford a house, so all spare money is spent on living as best they can. They're all massively in debt. And I'm thirty-four, and broke. I have no savings, and hardly any possessions too. I have no husband to keep me, no kids to look forward to, no certainty of income, only a few old school friends from my upbringing in Busan.' Her brown eyes seemed to darken. Nick reached over and squeezed her hand.

He settled their bill, and they slowly walked back to their hotel through the narrow streets of the old town. Adrienne clung to Nick's arm as the sun shone brightly on them.

'Don't forget,' Nick said, 'I'll see you in the Bar La Mafia after the corrida.'

Adrienne looked up from her phone and said she'd be there. Hans had said that it was a long-standing tradition that the true aficionados of bullfighting, and a few matadors too, would meet for a couple of hours in the Bar La Mafia after every bullfight. He had promised that Nick and Adrienne would meet some interesting people there.

It was still thirty degrees or more outside as Nick hurried to the bullring. There were a few people near the entrance seeking to buy tickets, and he selected one woman, fortysomething and healthy-looking and obviously American, and gave her his spare ticket. 'Why, thank you, sir,' she said with the good manners that, in Nick's experience, most Americans had. 'Please let me pay you for it. How much do I owe you?'

'Oh no. It's free to a good home.'

The woman smiled. 'Thank you again then. My name's Karen.'

'And I'm Nick.'

She joined him as they clambered up the steps in the arena. Their seats were near the back of the upper of the two tiers, in the shaded *sombre* section. The arena was magnificent. The sell-out crowd was excitedly chattering, virtually all spectators in their uniforms of white with bright-red cravats and sashes. The sand in the arena was ringed by a hundred concentric circles left by the raking, giving it a manicured, stylish look.

Karen was from Wisconsin. She was in Pamplona for only

two days, enough to see the running of the bulls and a bullfight. 'I don't actually approve of the bullfight, as it's cruel and I'm sure it'll be upsetting, but I'm curious to see what all the fuss is about.'

'That summarises my own feelings on the subject. Where does your curiosity come from?'

'I studied Ernest Hemingway when I was at college,' she said. 'We devoted one whole semester to *The Sun Also Rises*. It opened my eyes to Europe and Spain and travelling. And the energy that Hemingway described in the bullring – I felt I had to experience it myself first-hand, and now I'm divorced and my son has left home I can make the trip.'

'I've come to Pamplona because of Hemingway, too,' said Nick. 'We owe him a lot.'

The corrida began with a parade around the ring by the main participants. They were led by the picadors on horseback, their horses blindfolded and covered in thick protective padding. The matadors followed them, waving to the cheering crowd. Loud band music filled the arena.

A few minutes after the matadors had left, the first bull ran onto the golden sand, greeted by cheers from the spectators. It looked lost and frightened. Periodically it chased at the men in shiny silvery suits who waved bright-pink capes to attract its attention. Each time the bull charged, the man with the cape would step out of sight behind a wooden barrier, and the frustrated animal would stop and paw the ground, and then set off to chase down one of the other men waving his cape from the other side of the arena.

The bull panted and snorted when it stopped to rest, and each of its charges was slower than the previous one. The picadors then entered the arena and encouraged the bull to attack their horses from side on. The bull seemed to need no invitation and lowered its horns in a sustained charge into the flank of one horse. The horse lurched to the side, unable to see, no doubt uncomprehending and, Nick hoped, not gored. The picador lanced the bull in its shoulder. Thick red blood seeped from the wound. Nick felt queasy as the bull stumbled. Twice more the picador lanced the bull's shoulder. The area below the bull's shoulder was now dark and shiny.

The matador replaced the picadors. He strutted out like a bantam, with his tight trousers and braided silver epaulettes, lapping up the cheers and the occasional *olé*. Responding to the matador's flamboyant gestures with his red cape, the bull charged, half-heartedly thought Nick, and the matador allowed the bull to pass him at a distance of less than a foot. This happened several times. After a few minutes, at the time of the next pass, he stabbed a knife-like instrument, adorned by bright red and yellow flags, into the bull's shoulder. More blood seeped out, and the bull staggered a bit more. The procedure was repeated two more times.

After a few minutes of what Nick thought was pointless and cruel posturing and increasingly less-threatening charges by the bull towards the cape, the matador took out his *estoca*, his sword with a foot-long blade. He hid this behind the cape. After some short charges from the bull at close quarters the matador thrust the sword down through the bull's shoulder blades into its heart. It staggered onto its front knees, and after a second or two keeled over.

The crowd roared its appreciation. Nick looked on appalled. Karen had covered her eyes for the last few minutes.

A cart pulled by three horses drove onto the area. A man tied the hind legs of the dead bull to the cart and dragged the carcass into the bowels of the arena building. The crowd clapped. Nick wondered how Hemingway could have been so captivated by this tawdry scene. Yes, there was the theatre and the tradition, and some artistry from the matador, but Nick couldn't take his mind off the brutality and the needless slaughter.

There were five more bulls chosen to have their final moment in the arena. Nick barely watched them, preferring to chat to Karen about unimportant things, and he was glad of her talkativeness. They both left early after the fourth bull had met its end and headed off in different directions.

Nick made his way to the Bar La Mafia, only two hundred yards from the bullring. Adrienne was not due there for half an hour or more. He found a space at the bar area at the front of the restaurant, downed a beer and waited.

He texted Adrienne: *Je suis en place.*

She replied straight away: *bon c u soon.*

He finished another Estrella as he waited, and still Adrienne didn't arrive. After half an hour he texted her again but received no answer. Had she been run over by a bus? He became irritated by her lateness and felt a bit silly drinking by himself as all the other diners made merry in their happy groups. He couldn't see Hans or any other old-timers he recognised. Nor could he see anybody who resembled a matador.

After an hour or more, and having consumed three beers and a small pizza, Nick left the bar and walked back to the hotel. He was disappointed, and a little angry, that his last night in Pamplona had taken such a poor turn.

As he walked into the hotel lobby he could hear music and singing from the bar on the mezzanine. Entering the bar he could see three middle-aged couples dancing, an old-fashioned waltz with elbows and hands held high and away from the body. Everyone in the bar was in their white-and-red *fiesta* uniform. To the right stood an elderly man with a black broad-rimmed hat, like a small sombrero, with red lace on the outer edge from which dangled little red balls. He was playing a piano accordion. He swayed with the rhythm, from side to side and backwards and forwards, a smile on his face.

To his right were half a dozen young men standing by a piano, some with cocktails in their hands. They were loud and excitable. Nick recognised them as the young Americans staying in the hotel. Adrienne and Carl were playing the piano in a duet.

On the piano lid in front of Adrienne were three tall-stemmed cocktail glasses, two empty and one full. They were playing 'Alone Again (Naturally)', with the Americans belting out the words tunelessly but with gusto. Adrienne's face was shining, at times serious as she concentrated on the piano-playing and then with a broad smile and blazing eyes as she played up to her admirers at the piano.

Nick walked over towards them. One of the Americans recognised him, and Nick heard him say, 'Hey your old man's arrived.'

She turned to him, and Nick thought he saw a flash of anxiety in her eyes. She stood up. She was wearing her white mini skirt. She hugged him and said, 'I'm having the best time with these American boys. They're such fun, and they know the same songs as me.'

He knew there was no point in asking her about their missed rendezvous. Adrienne was having a much better time with these young men than she would have had with him. 'Please carry on', he said, sounding more generous than he felt. 'Play some more toons,' he added with an exaggerated American accent.

Adrienne hooted and went back to her seat. She whispered to Carl as they sat shoulder to shoulder, and they started on 'What a Wonderful World'. Carl sat on the left and played the chords, and Adrienne played the melody on her left hand, occasionally augmented by her right hand. The Americans started singing the words to the song, pretending they were a barbershop quartet, swaying together and stretching out their hands for the rest of the chorus. A waiter put a beer in Nick's hand. He couldn't remember ordering it.

A group of Spanish men moved over to join them. They joined in the singing, but in Spanish. Nick felt himself getting carried away by the camaraderie and by the joy to be found in music and strangers. He too began to sing.

The song ended with a flourish from Adrienne, tinkling

furiously. Everyone clapped and cheered when she finished, and she stood and bowed. Nick had never seen her more alive than now. All the Americans, Carl in particular, were vying for her attention, drawn into her aura. Carl kept on putting his arm around her shoulder or trying to put his hand on hers. Adrienne didn't seem to be encouraging him.

Next on the repertoire was 'Yesterday'. The accordionist immediately joined in, and soon the whole bar was singing the familiar words. Again the chords were mainly provided by Carl, who kept on trying to maintain eye contact with Adrienne. There were now six couples slowly dancing on the floor of the bar.

Nick couldn't take his eyes off Adrienne. It was as if the spotlight was on her alone and everyone else in the bar was peripheral. She looked delighted to be the centre of attention.

They started playing 'New York, New York', but not before Adrienne had taken a slug of her cocktail and had patted her brow with a serviette. Her mini skirt was riding high on her thighs, the Americans admiring the view. They were belting out the words of the song, aided by a couple of young Spaniards in tight matador clothing. Nick remained detached, silent, transfixed.

The song finished, and Adrienne played on alone for a half minute, giving it a wholly original finale and a dramatic ending. The Americans cheered and hooted, and twenty or so of the others in the bar got to their feet and clapped. Adrienne stood to face the bar, her face flushed, looking a little embarrassed, and gave an extravagant bow. She walked up to Nick and whispered, 'Take me home now please. I want you to make love to me.'

He smiled his agreement.

Adrienne started saying her goodbyes to the Americans. They begged her to stay, putting their arms around her. One tried to dance with her, and whispered something in her ear. Adrienne shook her head and smiled. Others insisted on selfies.

Carl looked crestfallen and sullen, but she was firm and friendly and told him and his friends that she and Nick had an early start for the airport next morning. The Spaniards in the bar gave her kisses on both cheeks. It was as though she was now their adopted daughter, a gift of stardust from a far corner of the Earth.

Eventually, hand in hand they made their way out of the bar and up the stairs to the lift. Nick felt pride in Adrienne, mixed with affection and desire.

As they stood waiting for the lift, their fingers entwined, Carl stumbled up the stairs and into their space. He tottered and weaved. 'Hey, China doll, don't go with that old asshole. Come with me.' He grabbed Adrienne's free arm and pulled her towards him.

Adrienne said, 'No. Please leave me alone,' and tried to remove his hand, but without success. By now she had been pulled a yard or two towards the staircase.

'How dare you, you little prick,' said Nick, now trying to prise Carl's hand from hers. 'Take your fucking hand off my fucking fiancée.'

Carl snorted. 'Fiancée? You're kidding me. You're old enough to be her father. She doesn't want you, old man.' He addressed Adrienne directly. 'Babe, we had a thing there, at the piano. You and me, I know you felt it too, giving me all those come-ons.'

'No, I didn't. You're dreaming. It was just harmless music-making. Nothing more than that.'

Nick shoved Carl away. 'Now leave us alone. We're tired. And you're drunk.'

Carl stumbled, and then launched a swinging left hook. Nick swayed back out of harm's way, and as Carl's fist swung into the empty air he lost his balance. Nick took advantage and punched him on his left temple. It was not a particularly forceful blow, but enough to topple him over, and he fell to the carpet as if he had been shot in the heart.

Just then two of the Americans joined them. One knelt to restrain Carl, and the other, a fresh-faced blond boy, tried to placate Adrienne and Nick. 'I'm sorry about Carl. He's like this most nights. He's a fucking embarrassment at times. We'll look after him.'

Fortunately the door to the lift opened, and a shaken Adrienne and a still angry Nick stepped in. As the door closed they could see Carl scowling at them, nursing what Nick hoped would be a big and painful bruise.

Adrienne looked up and smiled at him with a look that Nick, still breathing hard and his heart beating on overdrive, interpreted as one of love. 'Thank you, *mon vieux*. My hero.' She squeezed his hand. 'I love it when you call me your fiancée. Especially—' Adrienne's left hand was now gently caressing his crotch—'when you call me your *fucking* fiancée. What girl could possibly resist that?'

As soon as they were in their room they were kissing frantically, passionately. Nick could feel the heat in her body and tasted the perspiration on her brow and her neck. He removed her cravat and sash and pulled her T-shirt over her head. He found the zipper on her skirt and it fell to her ankles, revealing a tiny red thong. She looked beautiful and ripe. The fuzziness from all the beer and the late hour had left him, as had his anger at Carl, replaced by a lust and a love – yes, it was love, he knew – for this remarkable woman.

She broke away to go to the bathroom. He undressed and got into bed, turning down the lighting so that there was only a light in the entranceway of their room. After two minutes she came out of the bathroom, and Nick said he too had to have a pee and clean his teeth.

When he returned Adrienne was sitting on her side, still wearing her bra, talking agitatedly on the phone in Korean. She covered the mouthpiece and said, 'My mother. She's got a crisis. I'm trying to deal with it.'

Nick said 'Okay,' but he could feel the moment slipping away. He got into bed naked and sidled up to her. He caressed her thighs and her belly and tried to ignore the loud and incomprehensible arguments she was having with her mother. He could hear the mother crying and shouting. Occasionally Adrienne would hold the earpiece a foot away from her ear and make an exasperated face at Nick.

He slipped his fingers inside her thong and briefly felt her smoothness, but she pulled his hand away with an annoyed look.

Still the conversation raged, and after a while Adrienne left the bed and continued the call in the bathroom. At one stage he could hear her sobbing. It was undoubtedly a crisis of epic proportions. How awful having such a difficult mother. He could feel his ardour subsiding as she returned to the bed, still on the phone.

Nick slumped into the pillow. He moved back to his side and checked the alarm on his phone. It was set for six, in time to get the bus to Bilbao for their easyJet flight. Adrienne put her hand on his shoulder, as if to say, 'Don't fall asleep.' But he couldn't keep his eyes open. His last memory of the night was of Adrienne shouting at her mother.

They were both tired and irritable in the morning as they showered and packed. They had had only a few hours' sleep, and Nick had trouble waking Adrienne up.

As he packed his case he said, 'Your mother sounded in real distress. I hope she's okay.'

'Don't worry. She's fine. It was nothing. I think she just wanted a chat.'

Nick looked at Adrienne, uncomprehending.

On the bus Adrienne took his hand and said that she had had an amazing trip. 'I'll never forget it, and nor will I forget you. You've been the best travel buddy, relaxed and funny, and you've put up with me and all my foibles. I'll miss you.'

Nick was at a loss for what to say. Adrienne looked anxious and tired. 'I've had the best time too. Getting to know you, learning more about you every day, has been a pleasure. And exciting too. It's just a pity that last night—'

'Don't say it, Nick. Probably it was for the best. I might have fallen in love with you, and we won't see each other again after today. I would've been unhappy for a long time. At least now we're good friends, and we will *always* be good friends. We can still message on WhatsApp.'

Nick felt wrung out, as though he had been promised a drink of the finest champagne and the glass had been knocked from his lips as he was ready to drink deep. 'We'll always be friends. I'm your number one admirer, Adrienne,' he said, cursing himself for not saying what he wanted to say. 'I always will be, and I'll follow the rest of your life with interest and, ah, concern. It is, after all, a wonderful world.' She looked at him with what he took to be gratitude, and possibly more than that, in her eyes. 'And perhaps one day, twenty-five years from now, we might meet in New York, New York and all our troubles will be far away.'

Adrienne gripped his hand and put her other hand over his. 'Thank you for being so understanding.' She gave him a little kiss on the cheek.

At Stansted Airport they parted to take separate transport into London. 'I hope you have a safe flight tomorrow,' Nick said. He had never been good at goodbyes.

As they hugged for the last time, Adrienne said, 'Make sure you let me know if you get any more info about old Beryl.'

22

Nick struggled to adjust back to a London routine. He frequently relived his time in Spain with Adrienne, over and over recalling and examining little incidents and conversations and impressions. He decided that she had been right when, as their plane levelled out from its climb from Bilbao, she described their week together as a bubble. She had said that when he took her hand and said that he would miss her terribly.

'No you won't, silly. Sure, we had a lovely time. The best. And you're a great guy and everything, but I'm not sure it was all that real. Yes, it was intense at times, and we had some, ah, intimate moments, but I'm sure that in a week or two we'll realise that we were in our own little bubble, like having a holiday romance, and all holidays come to their natural end.'

'I'm not so sure about that. I'll definitely miss you heaps.'

She looked him in the eyes and held his gaze. 'In a few days you'll have moved on. And when classes start in September I'm sure you'll find another research assistant, perhaps a ravishing young beauty from China or India.'

'I don't think so. Besides, as you know, academics aren't allowed to have relationships with their students.'

How he remembered her kisses and her smooth skin, her giggles and her directness, her idiosyncratic take on things, her unpredictability and warmth, her jet-black hair that cascaded down over her shoulders to her breasts. How she held his hand as they walked, at times a vulnerable young ingénue and at others fifty times wiser than him.

Nick reflected on how close they had come to consummating their relationship on their last night in Pamplona. At nights and in the Tube, and while writing, he would pause to contemplate what making love to Adrienne would have been like. He knew it would have been tender and loving (at least on his part), and he knew too that for the rest of his days he would regret not having made love to this woman who had so entranced him.

And all because of her mother. Her fucking, intrusive mother. Parents always screw up their children, but poor Adrienne, in her mid-thirties, for God's sake, suffered badly from it.

For weeks Nick and Adrienne would send WhatsApp messages to each other for an hour or more a day. They were affectionate and intimate, and funny too, a mangle of English, French and Spanish. The messages gradually became less intimate, dwelt less on Spain and more on their daily lives, and Nick realised, with sadness mixed with relief, that they were 'moving on'. Adrienne seemed to be moving on with more speed than he could muster. She told him about how she would record her first three podcasts soon, as she was spending twelve hours a day researching some particularly gruesome murders from her hometown in Busan.

Nick had a few weeks to kill before he needed to start preparing for lectures for the opening semester of the 2018/2019 academic year. Lecturers were always encouraged to do some legal writing, to get an article published in a law journal, but instead Nick decided to write a brief memoir of what he knew about his grandfather's experiences in South-East Asia in World War Two. It was a grim story, but not without interest. It took him only two weeks of research and writing and ended up being just over forty typed pages. He was pleased with his effort. He printed copies for Jo and his children, and posted it on the

COFEPOW website, but he couldn't bring himself to send a copy to Aunt Mary in New Zealand. She didn't need to know the details of her father's terrible fate.

About a week after his return from Spain, Nick rang Suzanne, his occasional lover from Durham University. He invited her to stay that coming weekend. They spent most of it in bed. A number of times she remarked on his ardour and energy, and on her subsequent visits she suggested that perhaps they could 'up the stakes' of their relationship by spending most weekends together. Nick gently let her know that he would prefer that things stayed as they were, that they had a beautiful friendship, which they might lose if they were to escalate things. He knew he was being selfish, but despite her goodness, intelligence, sincerity and loving nature he wasn't willing to give more to the relationship.

He felt bad about himself, questioning his values and his settings. He wondered if he was just another selfish shit, taking advantage of the vulnerability of others, someone too emotionally stilted and old-fashioned to commit, to open himself up. Yes, he decided, there was something in all of that. He had always envied the passionate and emotional Italians and Spaniards, with their dramas and shouting and laughing and crying and arguing, but always tactile and loving. The contrast with the reserved English, and especially with him, was one he was always conscious of. He decided that, for Suzanne's sake, he wouldn't encourage more of their weekends together. She had come to her own decision: she never contacted him again. Nick didn't blame her.

The new academic year was looming, and Nick directed his efforts to preparing for the first semester's lectures. There were recent judgments and articles to read, and he liked to have each lecture planned out in a series of headings and bullet points long before the start of term. Plus, and this was an important thing for his vanity and reputation, he needed to prepare a crossword for the first lecture.

His messaging with Adrienne dwindled to one or two a week, and now she would often take two or three days to respond. She continued to be affectionate towards him ('miss u xxx') but she gave the impression of being busy with other things. That was to be expected, and he had now come to terms with the fact that his interlude with Adrienne had indeed been a bubble, albeit a glorious one, incongruous and opportunistic, and it had burst. As the autumn advanced and the days grew shorter, his mind wandered away from Adrienne, and from his grandfather too, and he poured his energies into his job.

His gloom and introspection lifted when, in late October, he received a call from Sadie. They hadn't spoken since June, and he was delighted to hear her crisp, deep tones on his phone. She had sent him an invoice for £8000 for her work for him, which Nick had thought to be swingeingly high, but he paid it without complaint within two days.

Sadie was calling to suggest dinner. 'My shout,' she said. 'There's a new French restaurant not far from my flat. They do an amazing lamb rack.'

A few days later they had dinner. The restaurant was packed, noisy, a little dark, with excited chatter. Conversation flowed easily. Sadie told Nick about some of the cases she was working on and how busy she was. She never betrayed client confidentiality, but she often dropped a clue or two which fed Nick's imagination. 'The real killer, in a time sense, is time spent away from the office. If you're not there to deal with them, the emails and the telephone calls just pile up, and often it takes half the night to get through them. Waiting around in court is the biggest time-waster. But it's also the travelling time, in taxis, and waiting for them too. Take yesterday. I had to get an affidavit sworn at Kensington Palace.' Nick's interest was piqued. 'The actual taking of the affidavit lasted no more than fifteen minutes but I was away from the office for about two hours for a journey of little more than a mile. Waiting for the taxi at both ends, traffic congestion, going through security, waiting to be seen. All very frustrating.'

'Kensington Palace, eh? You *are* moving in top circles. I take it your client remains at the Palace?'

'I shouldn't have said that. Please forget I mentioned it.'

'And will I read about it in the papers at some stage?'

'Not if I do my job well.' She gave a steely smile, making it clear that was the end of that particular line of conversation.

Nick told her about William and Hemingway and his visit to Pamplona. He mentioned that Adrienne had accompanied him, but he allowed Sadie to think that they had separate rooms and their friendship was based on their shared research into the Burma Railway and Hemingway. He also told her about Suzanne. She listened with apparent interest and sympathy, often with a humorous interjection. She smiled as he talked about the pleasant weekends with Suzanne and how he had not been able to offer her what she wanted.

They drank their way through a bottle of Châteauneuf-du-Pape, and Sadie suggested they finish off with a coffee and a cognac at her place, only two hundred yards away. They idled back through the quiet Pimlico streets, gossiping away about legal figures they both knew. Sadie's apartment was small and dark, with framed paintings and drawings covering nearly all the walls of the hallway and the sitting room. Ornate Victorian and Edwardian glassware and porcelain covered many of the side-tables and mantlepieces. It was not a room that children had frequented over the years. Nick complimented her on her collection.

'You're too kind. It's more like an antique-shop jumble sale. I have trouble decluttering.' They sat down with their cognacs, an enticing brown swirl in the bottom of enormous bulbous glasses. Nick raised his glass and looked affectionately at his old friend, 'Here's to thirty years of knowing each other.' Their glasses clinked.

'You were such a gawky, gangly lad back then. All height and no flesh or muscle. You were shy and awkward, but we could all see that you were clever and witty. And those curls of yours were adorable.' Nick smiled. It had been a long time since he'd had curls, and over ten years since he'd had any hair to be proud of.

'But you know the funny thing? We all quite fancied you.'

'You're joking.'

'Yes, we had the noisy, rich, good-looking boyfriends, with their public-school accents, their MGs, their rugger and their matey-ness. I'm not knocking them. It was good fun, and it was fun waking up on a Sunday morning with a Toby or Henry in your bed. But we could never figure out why you made no effort to ask me or Fiona or Katy out.'

Nick cleared his throat. 'I *wanted* to. But I was terrified of you all. You were all so pretty, outgoing and ...' He searched for the right word. 'So *popular*. The guys were all over you. I didn't think I stood a chance. I just had no confidence with girls. And no experience, either. It didn't occur to me that any of you might be interested.'

Sadie's face was shining now. 'You must remember that ball at Christ's, towards the end of our first year? Your date was Katy. I had bullied her into asking you to accompany her. She fancied you. She said she admired your kind face and that you read books. And she was desperate to lose her virginity. She hoped it was going to be with you, after the ball. But sadly it didn't happen. She never explained why, but she was determined all right.' Sadie laughed. 'She lost her cherry a few days later to her French Lit tutor.'

Nick felt a little embarrassed at these stories from the past. 'I remember that night. Katy looked so stylish and upmarket, and sexy too, with the big cleavage and the red lipstick. But I'm afraid she got drunk and came on to me too aggressively, and she was beginning to make an ass of herself on the dance floor. She spilt red wine all over her white dress, so I took her back to her college early. I had no idea that she was still a virgin. Hell, she could've had *my* virginity that night. One that got away, you might say.'

Sadie took a sip of her drink. 'You know what, Nick? Hey, come sit next to me.' He moved beside her on the couch, their knees touching. 'It's not too late. I think we'll find the wait's been worthwhile.'

Nick turned to her, took her hand and stood up, all the time meeting her eyes. They walked slowly and in silence to her bedroom door.

And so began the next chapter of their friendship. He delighted in Sadie's luxurious body, curvy and generous in every way, and was surprised by their mutual passion. He felt like they were naturals, meant to be lovers. Intimacy came effortlessly, and soon they were spending two or three nights together a week, usually preceded by dinner or a movie or concert. Nick could not believe his luck. She was a stimulating companion, full of wisdom, and warmth, with a dry wit and a keen sense of gossip, and she seemed to love the physical intimacy they offered each other.

Nick had now moved on from thinking about Adrienne and, without mentioning it, he gave all the credit for that to Sadie. He had smiled when Sadie had whispered in his ear, when he woke that first morning with her, that the Law Society would strike her off if she continued to act for him. He said that he wasn't planning on needing a lawyer for a long time.

The winter came, with its bleak and brutal regularity, and then had come and gone. Jo invited Nick and Sadie around for dinner at her house after they had been seeing each other for three months. Jo regaled Sadie with a series of stories from childhood and adolescent days that portrayed Nick as dim-witted and accident-prone, and Sadie laughed with delight. By the end of the evening the women were like sisters who hadn't seen each other for years, planning a lunch together the following week.

Nick was anxious that Jo and Sadie might spend the whole of their lunch talking about him. 'Not at all,' Jo said when he rang her afterwards. 'Your name hardly came up.'

'I'm so glad that you like Sadie, Jo. It means a lot to me.'

'I most certainly do like her. She's wonderful. Witty and empathetic and so successful in every respect. If you weren't my brother I'd be thinking she was too good for you. She's a keeper, Nick. Make sure you don't stuff it up or you'll have me to answer to.'

Nick's lectures went well, too. The University had recently introduced a Student Feedback programme, where students were encouraged to rate their lecturers. The ivory tower wobbled at the prospect, but there was no resisting it. *In the competitive world of Britain's tertiary education institutions,* the Vice-Chancellor emailed the teaching staff, *there can be no lowering of standards. There will be casualties. We cannot risk losing students, or our rankings in the league tables, because we are carrying or indulging poor performers.* The email was met with howls of outrage, particularly from those in their sixties or seventies. Academia is not a beauty pageant, or a competition, they said. What about publications, experience, leadership, and contributions to legal scholarship? These were surely more important? Yes, they were valued, replied the V-C, but the students (or 'entitled little shits' as some of the older lecturers called them) knew best.

Nick had no fear about the new regime. He could see the laughter and the smiles in his students, and he never had trouble filling up his lecture theatres. He was not surprised at all that he was by a few percentage points the most highly rated lecturer in the law faculty at London King's. He was assured that at the next round of salary reviews his pay was likely to move to the top of his band.

He gave little thought to his grandfather now and to his interactions with Hemingway. Things had come to a dead end.

He had talked things over extensively with Jo, and she was bereft of ideas about how he could find out more information.

That all changed when a postcard came from New Zealand. On its cover was a photo of the Sky Tower, dominating the Auckland skyline, with the blue Waitematā Harbour in the background.

23

Kia ora, Nick

It's probably not relevant anymore, but I've remembered who old Beryl was. Beryl's a man, not a woman. It came to me in the shower yesterday, of all places. He was Dad's solicitor. In Aylesbury, I believe. He'll be long dead, but you never know. Anyhow, I hope all is well. You are always welcome to visit again.
Love, your Aunt Mary xox

Nick's heart beat with excitement. How blinkered of him not to have realised that Beryl could have been male. He went straight to the website of the Law Society, to its 'Find a Solicitor' page. No law firm had Beryl in its name. There were eight people called Beryl practising law in England and Wales, but none had it as the surname.

Nick considered his next step. He knew his limitations on searching online, and so adopted his usual default solution: get someone else to do it for him. He dialled the Law Society's Support Centre and was put through to a woman called Priti. He introduced himself and explained that he was doing some historical research and was trying to find out more about a solicitor whose surname was Beryl who had practised in Aylesbury or possibly elsewhere in Buckinghamshire in the 1920s and 1930s.

'Well, that shouldn't be too hard,' said Priti with a Liverpudlian lilt.

Nick explained that he was trying to track down a document that Beryl may have had in safekeeping, so he was keen to know if Beryl's practice had been sold to another firm when Beryl retired or died. Priti took Nick's email address and said she would get on to it 'prontissimo'.

Within two hours she had emailed him with everything he needed to know. Albert Edward Beryl, OBE, had practised in Aylesbury from 1909 to 1949, with a break for military service in World War One. At the time of his retirement his firm was taken over by another, and that firm morphed in due course twice more. It was now known as Sweeting and Holt LLP. Priti supplied a phone number too. Nick made a mental note to send an email of commendation for the wondrous Priti to the chief executive of the Law Society.

He rang the number in Aylesbury, introduced himself, and asked to speak to the oldest lawyer in the firm. He gauged that the old-timers would know more about the firm's constituent parts in earlier days. The telephonist giggled. 'A lot of them are quite old, sir, but I'll put you through to Mr Sweeting.'

Mr Sweeting sounded old, unfailingly polite but a bit absent-minded. Nick explained it was a long shot, but he wondered if someone could search the firm's files or deeds records to see if they had anything belonging to or relating to one of Albert Beryl's clients called William Forbes Harrieson. 'Yes, with an E.' Sweeting said he would look into it. He said it was doubtful there would be anything there, what with records being moved during World War Two and boxes of documents going AWOL during all the mergers of the law firms. 'Give me a few days,' he said.

As good as his word, Sweeting rang four days later. 'To my great surprise, I think I may have something for you.' Nick held his breath. 'I was able to find the packets. There was nothing in the firm's deeds safe at our office premises. No surprises there, as anything over thirty years old is stored off-site, as my younger colleagues say. But the firm rents a secure storage facility on the outskirts of Aylesbury, where we store all our bulky files in boxes until we're allowed to destroy them. Leanne, my secretary, was able to find a trove of documents and files that belonged to our predecessor firms. Some went back even to the early 1900s.'

Sweeting paused, it seemed for dramatic effect.

'To cut a long story short, Leanne found a few boxes of documents that had come from Albert Beryl's practice and, bless, there were two documents held in the name of William James Forbes Harrieson. With an E. I have them on my desk as we speak.' Nick's pulse had steadily increased. 'One is a grant of probate for the administration of Harrieson's estate, dated May 1946. Attached is your grandfather's will, itself dated in 1932. Apart from a few minor bequests of personal items to his children, everything went to his wife Cecilia. Nothing unusual there.'

'And the other document?' Nick asked.

'I'm not sure what it is. It is a large envelope, sealed with red wax on the back. On the front it has your grandfather's name and the writing on the front, apparently signed by Mr Beryl himself, says the following: *'Private and Confidential. This envelope is to be kept with the will of the above-named and is not to be opened during his lifetime. It is to be given to his widow Cecilia Mary Harrieson or if she shall predecease him or not survive for more than thirty days after his death it is to be bequeathed as set out in the will.'* It's dated 16 June 1932.'

'I'm so excited to hear that, Mr Sweeting. That envelope may contain exactly what I've been hoping to find. Can I come and collect it from you?'

'You certainly may. Bring your passport and evidence that you're a direct descendant. I can't imagine that any of his children are still alive, so there's no reason not to give it to you.'

'Yes, my father died in 2007. I can bring you his death certificate.' Nick didn't feel it necessary to mention that Mary was still alive in New Zealand.

'Good, that will be sufficient. I'm afraid I have no explanation why we still hold the document. It should have been given to your grandmother when he died. But evidently it wasn't.' They agreed that Nick would visit in the next day or two to collect the documents.

Nick sat in a quiet, well-lit corner of the King's Head, two hundred yards from the offices of Sweeting and Holt LLP. He had the documents in his briefcase and sat down to lunch on his fish and chips and savour a pint of IPA.

He looked first at the will attached to the Court order granting probate of his grandfather's estate. The will had been typed on a thick parchment paper, now yellowed and stained. It was a fairly routine will, Nick thought, what one would expect. The only item of note was a personal bequest of a 'brief memoir, made by me in 1927, which is in a sealed envelope held with this will. It is to be bequeathed to my wife Cecilia, but if she shall die before me or not survive me for more than 30 days, to the child of mine who, having reached the age of 21, shall display the most literary curiosity.'

Nick smiled. Good old William. Trust him to make life difficult for his executors. Nick looked at the second envelope, still sealed on the back. Why hadn't it been given to Cecilia?

She must have declined to take it, because the seal was unbroken. If so, why? The executors, Cecilia and old Beryl himself, would obviously have been aware of the envelope's existence. Perhaps Cecilia said she would take possession of it at a later time, or suggested to Beryl that he kept it and give it to Nick's father or Mary when they turned twenty-one? If that was the reason, people must have forgotten about it. Nick surmised that Grandma Cecilia knew the contents of the envelope, as curiosity about it would have got the better of her if she hadn't.

Another thought came to him. Perhaps Grandma didn't want the contents of the envelope to see the light of day? Was there something in there which was hurtful, or scandalous? It was all a mystery, but shortly he would have a better idea of what the reality was.

Sweeting had insisted on meeting Nick when he called at the law firm's offices shortly before lunch. He was tall, probably about seventy, with a fine head of white hair brushed back from the front. Nick thought of Michael Heseltine. He had an angular face, with red blotchy cheeks and white sideburns. He was the model of a trusted old solicitor, the keeper of family secrets over generations.

'It's a pleasure to meet you, Mr Harrieson,' Sweeting said as they sat down in a large boardroom. He had the two document packets under his arm. 'Your reputation precedes you. My grandson started his law studies at London King's in September. He turned down a place at Oxford because of you. Old Crosser, eh?' Sweeting was chuckling as he looked keenly at Nick, as if trying to see what all the fuss was about.

'Truth be told we're very glad to hand these documents to you. Law firms are full of old records, in a few cases dating back as much as two hundred years. It's impossible to trace descendants and the documents can't have any legal relevance today. Yet we dare not destroy them, as they might have some historical significance. So they just gather dust in old storage spaces.' Sweeting looked at the sealed envelope. 'That one looks more interesting than most. Any idea what it contains?'

'As a matter of fact, I have. I'm hoping it contains my grand-father's account of a trip he made to Spain in the mid-1920s. I think he had a few adventures there and met one or two inter-esting people. Enough to warrant recording it all for posterity.'

'I hope you're right. It would be a terrible pity if it was just a shopping list or press cuttings of the 1930 First Division football season.' They both laughed.

Nick finished his lunch. He ordered another pint and wiped the white flecks of fish off the knife on his plate. Gently he inserted the knife into the flap of the envelope and cut open the short side, careful not to break the seal. Slowly he pulled out the handwritten document, dozens of pages held together by a single staple and a small corner of another envelope in the top left corner. The manuscript was in prime condition, and had survived the years untouched by bombs, law-firm mergers, floods, mould, fires, dust and neglect.

At the top of the front page, in capitals and underlined, it said simply 'A PERSONAL MEMOIR'. Directly underneath were additional words, which appeared to have been written using a different pen: '(or setting the record straight)'.

Nick was intrigued. He had found his Holy Grail. He cursed himself for his nervousness. He took a long slug of his beer and slowly began to read.

When he had finished, he looked unseeingly around the by now busy pub. He struggled to collect his thoughts. He ordered another beer. He sat there, content in his own world, his thoughts zooming in competing directions. He thought of Jo, and Adrienne, and dear Aunt Mary, and he thought of Grandpa. Poor William, who came to such a ghastly end but who had produced this masterpiece. Yes, masterpiece. Nick knew he had stumbled on the right word. William's goodness and optimism and intelligence, naïveté also, permeated the memoir. How cruel it was that his life had been cut short in the war. His death was a loss to his family, but Nick now knew that the world had also lost a fine citizen whose contribution was about to be recognised for the first time. He slowly slid the memoir back into the envelope, holding it as carefully as he would a stick of dynamite. And it was dynamite. He looked at his watch. He had to hurry to get the train back to London.

He went straight to his office at the law faculty. He photocopied the manuscript, page by page, and then scanned and emailed the copies to himself. Later, when he got back to his cold flat in Kensington Park Road, he forwarded the manuscript to Jo and Adrienne. He sent the same accompanying message to each:

Hiya. Guess what? I've found Grandpa's manuscript. I'll tell you how I got it later. Here it is. It has more information in it than we could have hoped. Now I have to figure out what to do with it.

He couldn't be bothered cooking that evening, so walked to a nearby takeaway place. By the time he had finished the doner kebab, halfway through his second reading of the manuscript, Jo rang.

'Un-fucking-believable,' she said. 'What an amazing story. Tell me how you got hold of it.' He told her about Mary's postcard, Priti at the Law Society, old Beryl's firm, and Mr Sweeting. Jo said she was impressed by his detective skills. They talked for half an hour about the stories and the people in the manuscript.

Jo put her finger on the crux of it early on. 'You realise this is a memoir of international significance? It casts a hugely different light on the most famous novelist of the twentieth century, and now we have to re-examine the origins of one of the seminal works of fiction of the last hundred years. Global interest will be massive. You'll be famous, Nick.' She checked herself. 'Even more famous, I meant to say.' They both laughed. 'What's more, it could be worth millions.'

'Really? You think so?'

'God, yes. The world is full of Hemingway scholars and students, and he's still a figure of major interest. One of the big American universities would pay a humongous sum for it. *TIME* magazine, the *Daily Mail*, Netflix or Amazon would jump at the chance to have exclusive publication rights.'

Nick was struggling to absorb this. He liked the idea of the millions, but not the publicity. 'The memoir is yours as much as it is mine. Any money will be split fifty-fifty.'

'I was hoping you'd say that.' She laughed. 'Why don't you send it to your old mate Andrew McGregor? As one of the leading lights in the UK on Hemingway he'll be able to give you a more informed view of the memoir's literary and historical value. But swear him to secrecy first. You can't allow a copy to get out in the public domain. Ask Sadie to draw up a confidentiality agreement.'

Jo had always been the more sensible of them both. She always used to say and do the right things while he blundered about in his gauche, childlike way.

He looked up Andrew's phone number in his little green address book. He hadn't talked to Andrew for seven or eight years, but they knew each other too well for that to be a problem. They had met in their first year at Cambridge. Andrew was tall and good-looking, the son of a Foreign Office bigwig. He had spent the summer holidays of his school years in European capitals and as a result was near-fluent in French, Italian and Spanish. He seemed experienced for his years and allowed Nick and his other friends to assume – probably correctly – that for years he had been having sex with girls with names like Simone, Francesca and Caterina.

In his university years he wore the tightest of jeans, with a blue denim jacket and ankle boots that gave everyone the impression that Keith Richards' son was now studying at Cambridge. Girls fluttered around him, drawn by Andrew's worldliness and sophistication, but he kept them all at arm's length. He studied languages and history to begin with, but once Nick introduced him to the novels of Fitzgerald and Hemingway there was no turning back on his interest in American fiction. He had been an academic now for over twenty-five years and was professor of twentieth-century literature at Oxford.

Over the years he had become more and more eccentric. He

would wear yellow shirts and socks, yellow berets and cravats too. Andrew's wife Jane answered the phone when Nick rang, and they chatted for a few minutes as they caught up on each other's family news.

''Allo, my learned friend,' cooed Andrew as Jane handed the phone to him. He had greeted Nick like this for years.

Nick explained what the manuscript was, that he wanted to send it to Andrew for his assessment and reaction, along with William's 1941 letter and monograph, as they involved the great man too.

Nick was embarrassed to raise the confidentiality agreement with Andrew, who bristled a bit but his interest was hooked by now.

The next day Sadie prepared a non-disclosure agreement for him and Andrew to sign. Nick emailed it to his friend. It came back within ten minutes, unsigned, but with the simple email message: 'I agree'. Nick emailed the documents to Andrew. He knew it would be only a matter of hours before Andrew called him back.

Nick sat down again, now at his desk, and reread the memoir again. This time he kept notes with a view to identifying those portions which were previously unknown or scandalous, or which changed the known factual narrative. After a while he stopped. There were just too many things to record.

24

A PERSONAL MEMOIR
(or setting the record straight)
by
William James Forbes Harrieson
Assistant District Officer
Colonial Office
Nanyuki District
Protectorate of Kenya
February 1927

I feel compelled to record my involvement with Ernest Hemingway, the American writer, and the events and people described in his recently published novel 'The Sun Also Rises' (which I shall call TSAR). The character Harris is undoubtedly based on me. I am surprised and even shocked at some of the portrayals in the book, and I want to put the record straight, or at least to set out my recollection of events.

Below I will refer to actual conversations. These are recreations of the sense of what was said, but I believe they are accurate and do not distort anything that was said or unfairly malign any individual. In my defence I point out that I maintained a detailed journal throughout my fishing trip to Spain last year, which was towards the beginning of my home leave from Kenya. I recorded in my journal, usually on the same day, the vast majority of the recollections below.

Part I—Burguete–Auritz. 29 June–2 July 1925

I travelled south from Paris, armed with my new Hardy's rod and reel that I had bought in London. After spending a night in Saint-Jean-Pied-de-Port, along with groups of pilgrims on the famous St James' Way, I joined a few pilgrims and walked over the mountains to Burguete–Auritz across the border in Spain. Burguete is a delightful little town. It consists of only a few hundred residents, all seemingly living in stone houses with steep roofs and which border the road downhill from the nearby Pyrenean foothills. The town is well placed as a base for fishing the local trout streams.

I was booked into the Hotel Burguete, a little inn at the northern entrance to the town. As I walked into the hotel to book in, late in the afternoon, I could see that there were four other people (three men and a woman) ahead of me in the small lobby. They were obviously Americans and seemed to be remonstrating with the woman receptionist. They were speaking in a curious mix of French, Spanish and English, and it appeared that they were talking mainly about the local fishing conditions, which I was learning were poor because of pollution brought on by a forestry company which had destroyed the best fishing areas in recent months.

The most vocal of the group was a man about my age, a striking and handsome fellow with a strong jaw and broad shoulders. I would learn shortly that he was Ernest Hemingway, whose name I was vaguely aware of from various reviews and articles about the Paris literary milieu. He introduced himself, as Americans do, and then introduced me to his wife Hadley and to their friends Bill Smith and Donald Ogden Stewart. Stewart was even better known than EH. They kindly invited me to dine with them and to have a drink before dinner. I was grateful for the company. It soon transpired that Smith and Stewart had travelled separately from the Hemingways and had checked into the hotel some time before.

When I told them my name was William, Donald was quick to note that there were now two Williams in the group and that we now had a Double Bill.

When I went downstairs at about 7 p.m. to join my new friends in the hotel's lounge I could see that the party was well on its way. The lounge was dimly lit, with a piano against one wall and cabinets holding glass and silverware along two sides. In the centre was a smallish coffee table, around which were placed armchairs and a sofa. As I walked in Ernest beckoned me over, finding a chair for me and drawing me into their midst. Bill Smith put a glass of wine in my hand.

'Welcome, our new friend,' said Donald, declaiming as if he was on the stage. 'Should we call you William, Willie, Billy or Wilhelm?' I replied that any of them would do, but William was what my parents, tailor and bank manager called me. That broke the ice nicely, and I could feel their goodwill already.

'What brings an Englishman to Burguete?' asked Bill. 'The moustachioed señoritas? The bulls of Pamplona? Or the fat trout of the Irati River? I saw that you had a rod carrier bag with you—unless you keep a horsewhip in there to beat off all those inquisitive Americans you run into in strange out of the way villages in Europe.' It was not just Donald who liked the sound of his own voice.

I told them why I was there, and when I mentioned Kenya I could sense Ernest's interest in me increasing. He said he knew little about Africa – Donald interjected, 'Hemingstein knows everything about everything else, though,' to much amusement – and asked me about the trout fishing there. I said that even though Kenya was on the Equator there were many mountains and highlands and the fishing was good. Whenever I mentioned something he always had a question or two more and was noticeably serious in seeking to elicit information.

I told him about the little streams in the Aberdares and in the foothills of Mount Kenya (I described them as the green hills of Africa), and how you could often look across the rivers and into the trees and see a group of chimpanzees playing or giraffes walking past. He seemed fascinated, as though he was committing what I said to memory. He even took notes of a few expressions and phrases that I used, which I found both flattering and disconcerting.

The gaiety and the wine flowed hand in hand. I couldn't believe how much they all drank. Whenever my glass was down to half-full one of them would fill it up. I reckon that that night, including drinks before dinner, we must have consumed about a dozen bottles of wine among us, plus a few whiskies and absinthe. Hadley matched the men drink for drink too. Drinking on this scale was new to me (it was like this every day and night), and when I left Spain I abstained for a few weeks away from liquor to let my body refresh itself.

Dinner was a loud and raucous affair. The only other diners in the dining room were a few pious peregriños who kept to themselves. We were served by a pleasant waitress whose name sounded like Sandra – she was tall, with yellowy blonde curly hair and the sweetest of smiles in her pretty face. Ernest and Donald took a particular interest in her, and I could sense that Hadley was not altogether pleased to see her husband fawn over the pretty girl so openly. Poor Sandra, embarrassed by the attention, told us under interrogation from Ernest that she was from Latvia and that she was planning on becoming a nun. That revelation caused much amusement at our table. It transpired that after spending a few years in a seminary of sorts in Latvia she had become a novitiate and was spending a year or two to consolidate her vocation before taking the vows to be a nun. As part of that she had walked hundreds of miles with a fellow novitiate along the St. James' Way and had liked Burguete so much that she stayed to help out in the hotel for two months. All this we learned in a combination of French and English.

The poor girl was run off her feet fetching more wine or bread and taking everybody's order. She put up with it with the good grace and patience that one would expect of one with her calling and did not appear to be offended by some coarse language from my new American friends.

Ernest continued to appear to be taken by the charms of the young woman, frequently calling out to her for more provisions for the table.

Hadley was seated on my left, and I could see her shooting disapproving glances at her husband. Ernest simply ignored her, which struck me as unkind.

While the men reminisced about the successful fishing they had had exactly a year earlier on the Irati River and nearby streams, Hadley and I had a one-on-one conversation. She had the attractive trait of fixing her gaze on the person she was talking to. In a funny way I felt blessed by her attention. She had a warm smile, accentuated by her cheekbones. We talked of the food in Spain, and in the Basque country in particular ('too oily and gritty' and 'you need an axe to break the bread'), and of their son Jack whom she called Bumby and who was being looked after by a nanny somewhere near Paris. She was several years older than Ernest. 'I don't think I'll join you all for the fishing tomorrow,' she said. 'I love the fishing here, and believe it or not I caught six fat trout on our visit to Burguete last year, but I think a quiet day on my own will be good for me.'

She then began to speak about Ernest's talent as a writer. She described him as a genius, an original thinker, and said that her role in life was to make sure he succeeded in becoming a first-rank writer. This struck me as a selfless and un-American attitude, as everyone will tell you that post-war American girls are very independent and not as docile as English girls. She went on to say that EH was undoubtedly going to be one of the most well-regarded and successful writers in the United States. Her eyes lit up, emphasising the certainty of her convictions.

I said I regretted that, while I had heard of Ernest's growing reputation, I had not read anything of his yet. She patted me on the wrist, as if to say that that was not a problem. She then said there had been a 'terrible tragedy' two or three years ago when, at a Paris railway station, she lost a suitcase full of Ernest's unpublished writings, including an unfinished novel. This had caused her 'untold grief and anxiety', but Ernest had been an 'angel' about it. I sensed that one would not wish to cross Ernest.

Still the wine flowed. Table conversation moved from tales of last year's fishing, when Ernest and Donald caught many 'big fat bastards', to this week's. They kindly invited me to join them on the morrow for a day's hike to see if the Irati was in fact unfishable, and there was talk of a second expedition to different rivers to see if some good fishing could be had.

As the cheese plates were taken away Ernest proclaimed that a round of what he called 'the green fairy' was needed. Hadley explained that he was referring to absinthe. I had heard terrible things about its occasionally poisonous and addictive qualities and was quick to say I did not want any. The others, however, thought it was a capital idea and the hardworking Sandra was despatched to find a bottle. I made my farewells to the increasingly boisterous Americans, who entreated me to stay, but I told them that I'd drunk more in one evening than I had all year and I needed a good night's sleep. Sandra smiled at me as I passed her at the foot of the stairs.

In my room, as I wrote up the day's events in my journal, I could hear the piano downstairs – Hadley was the pianist among the four of them – and some loud voices singing 'For Me and My Gal'. I had to take my hat off to them for their stamina.

Everyone was subdued over breakfast. Donald and Bill claimed they had sore heads. Hadley said she hadn't slept well and so was glad that she wouldn't be joining us on our fishing trip. Ernest alone looked lively and spoke animatedly about the big fish he was hoping to catch that week. Breakfast was as basic as one would expect in a small Basque hotel: bread and cheese and some knotty local sausage, helped down by scalding tea.

The hotel had packed us some lunch and wine to take on our expedition. Ernest pretended shock and dismay when the hotel supplied only three bottles of wine. He insisted on three more! We set off shortly in the crisp sunshine, joining a few pilgrims as they walked downhill through the village, and after a few hundred yards we turned left and walked through some hayfields towards some forested hills in the distance.

Ernest and Bill kept up a ferocious pace, up and down dales and through wooded areas that seemed to have no discernible path. Ernest kept assuring us that he knew where we were going. This was the third year in a row he had been fishing in Burguete before heading to the San Fermín festival in Pamplona.

There was little time for conversation as we huffed and puffed our way to the Irati River. When we arrived, at around noon, I was dismayed at what we saw. Logs and branches and other pieces of tree flotsam made fishing impossible, as we had been led to expect. None of my companions was particularly disappointed by this apparent setback. When we had located a grass lunch spot Donald took the wine bottles from our rucksacks and placed them in the cold shallows so they would be nicely chilled when it came time to have lunch. Ernest was keen to hike off to a tributary of the Irati to see if that might hold a few catchable trout, but Donald and Bill said no, they were tired and hungry, and wanted to stay put. And so we had a most pleasant lunch for two hours or so, mainly sausage and tomato bocadillos made by the hotel, washed down with many cups of wine. We all took our shirts off as we took advantage of the hot sun.

I asked Ernest about his fishing experiences in America. He and Bill were only too keen to reminisce about their days at high school and after in the northern regions of Michigan, when they would head up to the lakes for camping and fishing trips. They had all sorts of hair-raising adventures, involving bears and eagles and floods and injuries, and monster trout (for reasons unknown to me, Bill and Ernest called trout 'lainsteins') and carp that were caught and others that got away. I suspect that half of the stories were exaggerated, but that is the habit and the privilege of the fisherman, and no one objected.

Donald often interjected with witty jibes, trying to get the conversation onto art or politics, but Ernest and Bill were not to be swayed. As the final bottle was emptied, Donald reminded me that all of the fishing stories had been embellished and recorded as fiction in a number of Ernest's short stories that had been published already. I said that I was aware of that, but I had not read any of them. 'Well, make sure you do buy them, William. You don't have to read them, and anyway one or two of them are scandalous. But poor Ernest needs the money. It's not easy being a struggling writer and reporter in Paris, with a young family and a wife who has a trust fund and spending several months a year on vacation in Italy, Spain and Switzerland.'

Ernest led the laughter, and I promised that I would seek out his collections when I returned to London.

The walk back to Burguete seemed to take longer, despite the leavening good spirits of my companions, but the hot sun and the effects of the wine combined to make it an arduous and tiring afternoon. How I rued not following my father's wise advice never to let alcohol pass my lips before 5 p.m.

The evening began much as the previous one. We met again in the lounge of the hotel for some drinks before dinner, again served by the demure Sandra. A few of us had had a lie-down, but it seemed Ernest had not, as Hadley told us that they had had a pleasant walk through the village after we returned from our outing.

I was astonished at my new friends' capacity for whisky and wine. Ernest ordered wine two bottles at a time, and five whiskies for us all without enquiring if we wanted one. All this on top of 1½ bottles of wine each for lunch. I wondered to myself whether this was a habit of American youth, or even of competitive literary types, or perhaps a reaction to Prohibition. I think it is probably a combination of the three.

Ernest regaled me about the history and charms of the village and the local area. He talked knowledgeably about the local economy and surprised me with tales of witchcraft and sorcery for which Burguete (and the whole of the Navarra region) had been known for hundreds of years. He also knew about the village of Roncesvalles, just two miles up the road and through which I had passed the day before, and the legend of Roland at the pass. Ernest was impressing me as a man who had a great thirst for knowledge.

Over dinner Hadley whispered to me that I shouldn't be too impressed by what Ernest had recounted before dinner. She had obviously had one ear listening to our conversation. 'All that talk about witchcraft, and

Roland? The only reason Ernie knows about it is that on our walk through the village before dinner today we ran into the local priest, who spoke good English and was keen to tell us all about the local area. He'll probably have forgotten all about it by tomorrow.' She smiled affectionately at her husband. In his defence I should note that TSAR contains a few references to Roland and Roncesvalles.

The dining room was almost full of pilgrims, stopping off on their way to Pamplona and, in time, to Santiago di Compostella. They were young and old. The men all had beards, evidencing days and probably weeks on the Camino, and the few women had long hair. All had a disciplined and modest demeanour. The contrast with our own merry band could not have been starker.

The three men dominated conversation. It came down to a contest about which of them could be the funniest. Ernest was more bombastic than witty or humorous – he got his laughs by force of willpower, fixing us with his piercing gaze when he finished a story, not releasing it until we laughed with him. Bill did not say much, being more reserved and cautious than the others despite his rapid drinking. His interjections were often hilarious. Donald introduced me to a new Americanism by describing Bill as a 'wisecracker' extraordinaire. Donald himself was a comedian through and through. He had wonderful comic timing, augmented by a theatrical manner and a fine memory for names and places.

Over dinner Hadley remarked that I used lots of proverbs and quotations in my conversation. She was not the first, and certainly will not be the last, to make that observation. I explained that my dear father was a traditional educationalist and teacher and insisted that at every dinner his children had to recite a proverb or quotation from a poem or the Bible. 'Once learned, never forgotten,' I said, and Hadley smiled.

She then seized on the idea that we should have a competition of sorts – going around the table, clockwise and rapidly, each of us had to recite a phrase or expression which was generally well-known until one of us could not remember any more, or could not remember one correctly, at which stage that person would cease to participate.

All of us liked words, so we were in our element. Donald's quotations were always funny. He quoted often from his friends Dorothy Parker and Robert Benchley. Bill obviously had spent long days at Sunday school, as he appeared to know much of the Bible by heart. Ernest mainly quoted from Shakespeare, which was not difficult, but also from Dickens and, to the great mirth of the others, from his Paris friends and acquaintances – James Joyce, Ford Madox Ford and even Gertrude Stein ('Rose is a rose is a rose is a rose'). Hadley stuck to commonplace proverbs, mainly from the Bible, and a pair of quotes from Ernest's short stories which Bill and Donald protested were not well known enough.

I decided to show off my love of English poetry, working back from the war poets to Oscar Wilde (a feast of memorable lines there) and further back to Donne and Milton. My new friends were impressed by my ability to quote, exactly, the immortal lines: 'If a clod be washed away by the sea / Europe is the less ... And therefore never send to know for whom the bell tolls; / it tolls for thee.' Ernest seemed struck by those words (he said he was vaguely familiar with them, as Gertrude Stein had insisted he read John Donne's poems) and made a little note on the pad which he kept in his coat pocket. Another quote of mine, this time from Ecclesiastes, ending in 'the sun also ariseth, and the sun goeth down, and hasteth to his place where he arose' was also well received. Ernest made another note in this book.

Round and round the table the game went. Fifteen, twenty and then thirty times. Donald was keen to claim that Ernest misquoted frequently, but no one could fairly accuse me of that. My father had done his job well. Bill was the first to fall, saying he was a bit 'tight' from the evening's wine. Then Hadley, who I think felt the game was getting tedious, decided she had no more quotations to offer. Then Ernest started a lengthy quote from Macbeth, but completely lost the sense of it and ended up in Hamlet! That left me and Donald – each of us could sense a long night of jousting ahead, so we quickly shook hands on a memorable draw. Ours was the last table to leave the dining room, and I suspect the peregriños thought the Americans were loud and brash drunkards!

We retired to our respective rooms, and I recorded the day's events in my journal.

At breakfast the next morning Hadley made a point of sitting next to me. The whole group seemed in good humours, not too tired from the previous night's drinking, and talk turned to the day ahead. Another day's fishing was planned, this time seeking out different rivers. Again Hadley said she wouldn't join us, saying she had some letters to catch up on.

While everyone else chatted away, Hadley leaned in to me and said in a quiet voice, 'I'm not sure Ernie should really be doing a long walk today. He didn't have a great sleep last night.'

'Well, that's hardly surprising. I suspect none of us did.'

She smiled at me. 'Yes, I know. But poor Ernest has had a flare-up of his old bête noire.' She looked down, and I wasn't sure what she was referring to. 'What I think you English call piles.'

I gave her a sympathetic look. She went on: 'All that walking yesterday wasn't very wise, and he was in real pain when he got back. Not that he showed it to you and the others. He'd be much better off staying in today and resting, but you can't keep him away from a day's fishing.'

I said I'd try to make sure we didn't do too much walking today. 'Thank you, William. But please don't mention I've told you about his ... his condition. He wouldn't be pleased with me.'

I assured her of my discretion, and we rejoined the general conversation.

After our teas and coffees, Sandra brought us our lunch all packed neatly in two canvas bags, and six bottles of wine. Bill joked that there would be only enough wine for him and one other.

Soon we were on our way, this time heading north for half a mile or so, towards Roncesvalles, before turning east and walking through yellow hayfields towards the wooded hills. Ernest led the way, and at a smart pace. He was in ebullient spirits and did not appear to be suffering any discomfort.

After an hour or so Ernest found a little river, no more than five or six yards across at its widest, beside which was a deserted brick factory building. We put down our packs and soon assembled our rods and reels and tied flies to the leaders at the end of our lines. We set off to different spots on the river, and so began a few agreeable hours of fishing. The sun shone intermittently, there was a gentle breeze, and the brook gently rippled by over stones large and small. It reminded me of the little streams in the foothills of Mt Kenya.

Bill and Donald maintained a constant banter, mocking each other's casting abilities and lack of success. Eventually Bill caught a trout, and then Ernest caught one, about 12 inches long. He was delighted with it and was particularly pleased that his catch was a larger specimen than Bill's. We then set about our lunch preparations. I gutted the fish by the riverbank, and Bill and Ernest used their skills, no doubt practised over many years during camping trips in Michigan, to get a fire going and grill the trout. Donald unpacked the rest of our lunch and poured wine into our cups. Trout had never tasted so good. Again I marvelled at the thirst and energy of my new friends (perhaps something to do with growing up in the New World?), exemplified by an uninterrupted barrage of repartee and jibes. The others were calling me Guillermo, which Ernest said was the name of one of his matador friends.

Eventually we drifted off to sleep. Six bottles among four people on a summer's day has that effect. I woke up after about an hour, and since the sun was still high in the sky I decided to continue fishing. I let the others sleep. Within a few minutes a trout snatched at my fly and after a vigorous contest I managed to land it on the bank. It was a fine fish too – rich, red rainbow colours, and 14 inches long, weighing about a pound and a half. I was delighted with it and was even more pleased with myself when I caught another one of the same size and quality a mere 15 minutes later.

I shouted out to the others to watch me playing the fish, and they emerged into the sunlight rubbing their eyes as I pulled it into the shallows and netted it. Donald and Bill were delighted for me.

Ernest also congratulated me but without enthusiasm. Later, as we trudged back towards Burguete, Donald whispered to me that Ernest hated being bettered at anything, and that he was 'the most competitive son of a b—ch' he had ever met. 'But don't worry, Billyboy, his sulking will wear off after an hour or two, and he'll be right as rain, as you English say, by this evening.' And so it proved.

That night was my last night in Burguete, as I was to set off to Madrid on the morrow. The others had two more days there, before heading to Pamplona a mere 20 or 30 miles away. Our whole group was in good form, and Donald made a point of telling Hadley that I had caught two monster trout and Ernest had sulked about that. Hadley looked concerned, and I felt embarrassed, but Ernie took it in good stead and pointed out that Donald had not caught anything.

Donald was not to be outdone. 'But I fish for the companionship, for the peacefulness and the tranquillity, and not for the pleasure of the kill.' Later Ernest graciously toasted my success after eating a mouthful of my trout, poached skilfully by the hotel's chef.

Over dinner they all talked about their friends and acquaintances in Paris and in America. I was amazed at how many leading writers they all knew. Ernest talked about many well-known names, like Ezra Pound, Gertrude Stein, Sherwood Anderson and F. Scott Fitzgerald. Donald too had his own famous friends, like Dorothy Parker and George S. Kaufman. It was a genuine thrill for me to hear them gossiping (Ernest called it 'giving the dirt') on these eminent writers. Mind you, he was hardly complimentary about many of them, and he was apt to describe various of them as whoremongers, adulterers, drunkards, liars, thieves and sons-of-b—ches. I was glad that the saintly Sandra did not know much English, as she would have heard words that night she had never heard before.

Ernest again appeared to be showing off to Sandra, loudly demanding a further bottle or two of wine. At the same time he grinned at her like a madman. I thought it was poor behaviour, especially in front of Hadley, who pretended not to notice. I could tell she was accustomed to Ernest behaving like that.

Conversation turned again to the behaviour of their friends in

Paris. Ernest said that Ford Madox Ford and Gertrude Stein behaved particularly badly. I protested about Ford, saying you could forgive a man who had written some of the best and smoothest prose written in the English language. Donald agreed with me, but Ernest snorted. 'Not anymore, he doesn't.' We all laughed.

I said: 'Yes, people do behave badly on occasion. I do too. But that doesn't make me, or Ford for that matter, a bad person. The simple fact is that everyone behaves badly. It's just a question of degree, and frequency too.' Ernest looked at me as if I had said something profound or insightful.

'Guillermo, you've hit the ball out of the park with that observation. I must remember that expression.' He looked in vain for the little notebook he carried around with him. Needless to say I smiled with pride when I saw that he used the 'everyone behaves badly' quote in TSAR.

Hadley left the table for a few minutes to go to the washroom, as she quaintly called it. I knew she didn't like Gertrude Stein; Hadley had called her a 'cow' earlier in the evening because she apparently used to ignore Hadley when she and Ernest would visit her and Alice B Toklas in their Paris abode. Hadley told me later that she regretted agreeing to Gertrude and Alice being Bumby's godparents.

While Hadley was out of the room there was unsavoury talk of Gertrude Stein's living arrangements and her undisguised sapphism. Ernest then proceeded to shock me – but not Donald and Bill, because they laughed – when he said that the 'ugly old b—ch' was constantly trying to 'f—k' him, but he said he didn't want to go near any of 'her bases'. I hope Ernest was joking, and that it was the wine talking, but I couldn't be sure.

When Hadley returned conversation moved to the main purpose of their trip to Spain, to attend the San Fermin festival in Pamplona which was due to start in a few days. All of my new friends spoke excitedly about previous fiestas in Pamplona, of the bulls running through the streets, and of the bullfights, of the general merriment of the locals and the all-round gaiety of the occasion.

Ernest turned to look at me. 'Guillermo, why don't you join us in Pamplona? You'll have a swell time.'

I was taken aback by the suggestion and said that I couldn't because I needed to be in Madrid to stay with my friend Robert Jordan at the Embassy.

Hadley put her hand on my forearm. 'We'd love to see you in Pamplona. Some of Ernie's ghastly other friends will be there too, and you'll be a calming and civilising influence. Please, William, for my sake.' She looked at me with those wide eyes. How could a man refuse?

'Well, I'll try,' I said. 'I may need to rearrange a few things, but hopefully I'll be able to join you for two days or so towards the end of the festival.' Hadley looked relieved, and the others cheered. Ernest ordered another bottle of wine, which arrived quickly. I noticed with some satisfaction that it was a bottle of Sauternes. Earlier that day, on our walk back from fishing, Bill had mentioned to me that Ernie was suffering from haemorrhoids. I didn't let on that I knew already. I did however recall to Bill that I had once seen a poster of traditional French wine remedies for afflictions, and that trois verres de Sauternes was recommended for les hémorroïdes. Bill must have passed this information on to Ernest.

'You have to realise that my apparent reluctance to join you is not just a question of convenience, or of my ingrained English reserve about new things and experiences. It's because I'm worried about my health, my safety.'

Hadley interjected. 'Don't be silly, William. It's not compulsory to run with the bulls. I certainly won't be doing that.'

'No, Hadley, it's not that actually.' I paused for effect. 'It's just that I'm not sure if my body will be able to tolerate another few days of so much drinking.' My new friends all roared with laughter.

The dinner continued its merry course, as the other diners slipped away and gradually our own group got smaller as one by one the others left to retire for the night. Soon it was just Ernest and me left. Ernest called Sandra over and ordered a bottle of Rioja as a nightcap. I acquiesced under protest, as Hadley's parting words to me were: 'Don't keep Wemedge up too late. He needs his beauty sleep.' They had the strangest names for each other.

By my rough calculations Ernest would have drunk about four bottles of wine already that day, as well as two glasses of absinthe at lunch. He was now in full flight, telling me all about the previous two trips to Pamplona and his friendships with the matadors and the owners of the hotels and cafés there. He talked about his friends who would join their group for the fiesta. One was called Duff Twysden, apparently a titled English woman (her name meant nothing to me), whom he described as full of 'sex-appeal' and great fun. Another was a man called Pat Guthrie, Duff's new lover, 'a drunken wastrel and a non-entity'. A third was Harold Loeb, an American from a wealthy Jewish family. Ernest unkindly called him a 'poor little jew-boy. He follows me round like a toy poodle.' Loeb had taken Duff away for a tryst near Biarritz only a few weeks ago, which Ernest said was a treacherous act, and he wished that Loeb would not join them in Spain. I must admit that I was rather looking forward to meeting these characters.

It was getting late, and the bottle was almost emptied. Ernest excused himself to go to the lavatory and lurched out of the dining room. I waited at the table. After a minute or two I heard a bit of a commotion in the hallway, and I could hear muffled voices. I was concerned enough to investigate, and I was shocked to see Ernest and Sandra in close contact. He had shoved her against the wall and was trying to kiss her. She had turned her face away from his, and held her hands up, trying in vain to push him away with her elbows. He was too big and strong. With his right hand he was trying to lift her skirts.

I was shocked and outraged and rushed to the poor girl's rescue. 'Stop! Stop!' I hissed as quietly as I could to avoid waking up all the guests. Ernest tried to push me away, but I would have none of it, and soon I prevailed. Sandra scurried away, shaken. Ernest looked at me drunkenly. His face was red, and his moustache seemed to rise and fall.

I sensed anger and aggression in him, but these quickly subsided. He then had the gall to smile at me. 'Just a bit of harmless fun. Prep for

Pamplona.' And with that he stumbled off up the stairs.

It took me a minute to compose myself, and I went into the kitchen to console Sandra and to apologise for Ernest's behaviour. She was sitting on a bench, quietly weeping, and apparently entreating God in Latvian to give her pity or forgiveness. In a mixture of poor French and extremely basic Spanish, I explained that Ernest was a great writer but was not the same when he drank too much. I said he was a good man, but difficult at times. I am not sure whether I made things any better, but at least she thanked me.

The next morning Ernest and Hadley did not come downstairs for breakfast. Sandra served us as if in a trance, but she did give me a pinched smile, which I took to be an acknowledgement of gratitude. My car to take me to Logroño arrived after breakfast, and I was unable to say farewell to the Hemingways.

As I settled my account at the hotel reception I handed the woman an envelope to be given to Ernest. I had put in it a few flies that I had tied in Kenya. I left a little note too, thanking him and Hadley for their companionship, and suggesting that East African trout had difficulty resisting these flies.

Nick stood up to pour himself another glass of wine. Rereading the memoir brought to light details and nuances he had failed to identify during his first two readings.

His phone bleeped. It was a text from Andrew:

Have read only the first 5 pages. You've found a goldmine. Will call later when finished.

Nick smiled. He texted back:

Good, it gets better. Talk soon.

25

Part II—Pamplona, 9 July–11 July 1925

I decided not to stay at La Quinta, the hotel where the Hemingways and their friends were staying. I thought, rightly, as it turned out, that a bit of distance would have its rewards, and I didn't want to be prevailed upon to join them for late-night drinking sessions in the hotel. I stayed instead at the Hotel Tres Reyes, a perfectly pleasant inn just outside the city wall. The manager assured me it was much quieter than the hotels like La Quinta in the Old Town.

By happy coincidence I had travelled from Madrid with my diplomat friend Robert Jordan. He was pleased to be able to leave Madrid a day or two earlier than planned to join his wife and baby at their summer holiday location in San Sebastian, about 50 miles away, and could take me to Pamplona.

Robert was a well-read man who had been fascinated to learn that I was now friends with the up-and-coming writer Ernest Hemingway and his more famous compatriot Donald Ogden Stewart. I offered to introduce them to him. An exchange of telegrams with Ernest quickly resulted in Robert and I meeting Ernest and Donald at mid-afternoon on the day we arrived, and Ernest led us to a café in the Plaza del Constitution. Already we were struck by the number of happy revellers and bands of musicians of all kinds. I could smell the liquor on my friends' breath and was surprised and relieved when they expressed a preference for coffee rather than wine.

They were both friendly to Robert and me. I was profoundly grateful that Ernest did not mention or allude to the last occasion I had seen him. In fact, he never mentioned it again for the rest of my visit. In recent weeks I have seriously wondered whether he had any recollection of the incident with Sandra. At one stage he warmly thanked me for the flies I had left for him at the Hotel Burguete and said he would love one day to prise some fish out of the African mountain streams.

Robert asked many questions about Ernest's short stories and was evidently familiar with them, which pleased Ernest immensely. He also quizzed Donald about the Algonquin Round Table, which Donald described as like a lion's den of competitiveness. After about half an hour Donald abruptly stood up, saying he had another appointment and bade farewell. Later Ernest casually mentioned that Donald had had an assignation with some ladies who worked in a local bordello – to this day I do not know if he was joking.

Robert was keen to get a photograph of him and Ernest together, so we hailed a local photographer walking past with a big camera. By this time our table had been joined by two other men whom Ernest knew from a previous fiesta, as well as by a garrulous waitress of a certain age who flirted with Ernest at every opportunity. The photo was taken. Robert, with his excellent Spanish, said that he wanted the photo for a postcard to send to his friends (he called it a 'tarjeta') and asked for ten copies to be mailed to him in Madrid. He tipped the photographer handsomely. I hope the photographs duly arrived and that the photographer did not simply pocket Robert's money!

Robert had to resume his journey, and Ernest entreated Robert to look him up on his next visit to Paris. He then said a curious thing: 'By the way, Robert, I like your name. Robert Jordan has what I would describe as distinction. Would you mind if I use the name in a story one day?' Robert was delighted at the prospect. No one of that name appears in TSAR, I note.

I had arranged to meet my friends before dinner at what appeared already to be the main meeting place in Pamplona – the Café Iruña, in the Plaza del Constitution.

It was in an old building three or four storeys high, with elegant facades on the outside and chandeliers and mirrors on the inside. Twenty or so tables were placed on the terrace outside, sheltered from the sun by umbrellas.

As I walked into the plaza I was struck by the vitality and energy of the local population. Hundreds were standing around, dressed in colourful national and regional costumes, many of them in bands and carrying musical instruments. Others were dancing gaily.

The group was now much bigger, and I could hear them before I could see them. Hadley gave me a big smile and waved me over, and soon she and Ernest were introducing me to the Hemingways' new friends – Duff Twysden, the English 'lady,' her companion Pat Guthrie, who smiled at me in a friendly manner but said little then or later, and Harold Loeb, who had a pleasant and intelligent face but seemed a bit withdrawn.

Soon the wine was flowing, and Ernest was in his element. He was the centre of attention and decision-making (despite being the youngest person in the group), which I suppose was not surprising as the group was made up of his friends. He introduced me as the best English trout fisherman currently in Spain, and we all laughed. He asked everyone to put their manuals (his strange word for hands) together to welcome me.

I explained that I would be in Pamplona for only two nights as I had to head back to London. Ernest immediately took charge and said that I had to run with the bulls the next morning and go to the bullfight that evening. I said, 'Why not?' There ensued a lot of talk about the bullfights and the bull-running. Hadley said, 'You're lucky, William. Ernest has never run with the bulls before, so you should be honoured that he'll run with you. His war wounds in his legs make running difficult. And you'll enjoy the encierro afterwards.'

Ernest explained that the encierro de plaza took place after every bull run. The runners and other festival-goers congregated in the bullring, and a number of young steers, with padded horns to make them less dangerous, were let into the ring amid general chaos and hilarity.

The trick was to touch the steer but not to be knocked over or trampled. Hadley said that Ernest and Harold Loeb had become famous locally a few days earlier at the encierro for their antics. Harold especially was now much fêted because he had managed to sit on the head of a steer and was tossed up in the air – the first foreigner ever to do that, said the locals, and a spectacular photo of it was printed in the New York Times. Loeb didn't strike me as the daring type. He looked scholarly and quiet and a little bemused by the attention, but I could see that he did have a celebrity of sorts as two Spaniards passing by pointed to him and said excitedly 'El jefe', which means 'the boss'.

Plainly Ernest didn't warm to the idea that his friend might be thought to be braver or more daring than him. Hadley seemed to see that too and quickly added that Ernest had distinguished himself at the same encierro by seizing a steer by the horns and wrestling it to the ground. Ernest looked pleased to have the balance righted. I said to the group, more formally than I intended: 'I am impressed by your bravery. Please don't have great expectations in the encierro for me, a mere callow Englishman. I think Ernest and Harold are more like Don Quixote and I am more like Sancho Panza.' They were all kind enough to laugh.

It was a curious group of people. Duff Twysden had a rather dangerous look to her, like a femme fatale from a Valentino film. I could see that Hadley and she were not close friends, as their conversations were short and no more than perfunctory. In fact Hadley seemed wary of Duff, who was ignoring Patrick Guthrie, Duff's lover, and Loeb (her former lover), and Ernest appeared to be trying to flirt with her. I could see Hadley was ill at ease in this company and displeased with her husband. Poor Loeb appeared to be withdrawn and sulking and was the butt of the occasional anti-Semitic barb from Ernest and Donald. I was alert enough to realise early on that there were tensions within the group and I would need to use all my diplomatic skills to ensure I did not unintentionally offend anyone or take sides. Donald and Bill appeared to be the most relaxed, jousting with each other goodnaturedly in search of the wittiest ripostes.

As the light faded the plaza filled up with even more revellers and musicians. Ernest lamented the fact that the annual San Fermin fiesta was losing its local character and was being corrupted by foreign tourists. He evidently saw himself as a local and seemed oblivious to the irony that his group of friends, including me, were all tourists too.

Ernest took control of the dinner arrangements as we moved inside the café to our table. He ordered for everyone and asked for no fewer than eight bottles of wine to be put on the table. I sat next to Hadley; on my left was Loeb. Duff sat opposite me, between Ernest and Patrick. Ernest was evidently trying to monopolise Duff's attention, to Patrick's and Hadley's chagrin, but I was glad to see she was not giving him much encouragement.

Hadley put her hand on my wrist and said in a low voice: 'I don't know what happened on your last night in Burguete, but thank you for looking after Ernest. He came up to our room and muttered again and again how you had saved him from embarrassing himself and how Bill had passed on some unspecified, wise advice you had offered. I'd rather not know any more than that. But he and I are both grateful to you. He's not the same man when he gets tight. The funny thing is he now seems to prefer Sauternes to his usual clarets and Riojas.'

I had to smile at that last comment. I was a bit surprised at the rest, but glad that she was not seeking information about what had happened. 'Don't worry,' I said. 'It was nothing. Friends help each other. But, yes, Ernest does seem to like his drink.'

We moved on to safer topics. Hadley talked of her son and their life in Paris, and how homesick she was for her family back in St. Louis. She said she would much rather raise Bumby in the U.S. than in Paris. I warmed to her as she told me many personal things – how strained her relationship with her mother had been, how her sister had died in a fire when Hadley was studying at Bryn Mawr, how miserable and lonely she had been at college, and how she had left Bryn Mawr and gone back home. She had been 'down and low' for a year or two, not always in good health, and meeting and courting Ernest had done wonders for her confidence and well-being. I could see she warmed to me (on reflection, probably because I was not like the others in the group). She was kind and maternal by nature.

I noticed that Loeb (who Ernest had called a 'moron' in an earlier conversation with me) had hardly joined in any conversation, so I began talking to him. Gradually he emerged from his cocoon. He explained that this was his first trip to Pamplona, and that his bravado at the encierro owed more to incompetence and luck than skill. He was a New Yorker, and I said that I had heard that he was part of the Guggenheim family. 'Yes, but not 'the' Guggenheims. My mother is from the lesser Guggenheims, the poor ones.' I could see he was jesting, as the life he described was not one which could be described as unprivileged. He had been at Princeton before the war, and had been married, had two children, been divorced in 1923, and had been owner of a bookstore and editor of a literary magazine in Paris and Berlin. He was also a boxer, wrestler, tennis player and writer. Harold was what the Italians call an uomo universale, a universal man.

Harold quietly explained that he felt he had a vocation to shine the light on the new crop of American writers who had burst onto the literary scene in the 1920s. 'Guess what, William? It may not seem that obvious now—' he looked at Ernest, who was swilling his wine and telling Duff an unlikely story about some ménage à trois in Paris—'but the prince of them all is our friend Hemingstein. He has a rare talent, you know. Raw, unformed, yes, but he is his own man, and one day soon he'll be known as one of the best. You heard it from me first.' He beamed at me through his round spectacles. In fact, he was the second to say it to me, after Hadley.

Loeb often glanced at Duff, who chatted away to Bill and Donald, seemingly unaware of his presence. I mentioned to him that I was aware he had had a fling with Duff a few weeks back. He appeared glad that I knew. 'Oh, does everyone know? Actually, it was more than a fling. We had what we Americans call a beautiful relationship.

But women are fickle, and she decided she didn't want to be with me anymore. So she took up with that dimwit over there instead.'

I was still weighing up my response to that when Duff's voice boomed across the table. 'Hey, I can see you're talking about me. At least I hope you are.' She led the laughter. 'Welcome to the group, William. It's so good to have another English person in the gang. So civilised. Not like all these Yankee upstarts from the colonies.' Ernest and Bill protested goodnaturedly. Duff had a presence about her. She wore a fedora, had a strong face, wore no rouge or lipstick, and had a direct way of looking at one that gave the immediate impression that she was interested, that there was no one else that mattered. I didn't return her gaze, as to do that would have been disloyal to Loeb, and to Hadley. Instead I tried to think of something witty to say, but I couldn't think of anything.

More bottles of wine were placed on the table – two Sauternes too – and Ernest made a point of filling everyone's glass. One of the wine bottles was champagne, which Duff had been drinking. When the waiter filled her glass, she raised it to the group, and in a loud and confident voice said: 'A toast, chaps. To royalty!' She laughed, as we all did, and we drank from our glasses. Brett makes the same toast in TSAR.

Occasionally locals would come to greet Ernest or Harold, and on one occasion Ernest absented himself for about twenty minutes to speak to a few matadors sitting quietly at another table. Everything about the café, and Pamplona, and the people around me, created a distinct sensation of our being in a special place at a unique time. The passage of time since has served only to reinforce that impression.

Hadley interrupted my reverie by whispering, 'Don't be drawn into her web, William. She'll eat you up and spit you out, just as she did with poor Harold and as she will do with Pat. Stupid old Ernest is infatuated with her. He meets her for drinks or dinner two or three times a week in Paris, which I hate. He swears he's not having an affair with her, and I believe him, thank God. I don't think I could survive that. I hate how he makes such a fool of himself and insults me by fawning over her. She's just a spoilt b—ch.' I had never heard Hadley use such sharp language before, and my heart melted.

It was my turn to pat her on the arm. 'Dinnae fear, bonnie lassie,' I said, adopting a Scottish accent. 'Saucy women dinnae interest me.' Hadley laughed, and I thought I could detect Ernest giving me a dark look.

After a decent interval, at about midnight, I made my excuses and headed back to my hotel. Many bars and restaurants were still packed with ferministas enjoying their night.

As arranged I met Ernest after 5.30 a.m. in the Calle Mercaderes. Even at that early hour there were hundreds of men milling around, including a number of policemen and medical people. Ernest was dressed, like me, in long white trousers, dark shirt and jacket, red cravat and a beret. Many others were similarly attired. Ernest explained that no one else from the group wanted to run with us.

He said that the knowledgeable joined the run about halfway through, where we were standing. 'At the end of the street it veers 90 degrees to the right. That's called Dead Man's Corner, so you have to be careful you're not trapped against the wall as the bulls go past. They say the trick is to stay out of harm's way by keeping your ass against the walls on the side of the street, and if you fall over cover your head and let yourself be kicked and trampled. And try to slap the bulls on the ass as they run past.' Ernest laughed, but I sensed that he was nervous, like me.

After a long wait we heard a gunshot in the distance, and the bulls were on their way. We positioned ourselves in a group of about twenty men, waiting for the bulls to arrive. The spectators on the balconies above us cheered and yelled as the bulls swept into our street. The bulls looked huge and menacing. My heart pumping at a terrific rate, I waited with Ernest and then sprinted with him when the bulls were about twenty yards away. Away we went, frantically looking over our shoulders every two seconds, as the bulls descended on us.

Just before Dead Man's Corner, Ernest lost his footing and fell heavily, and other runners tried in vain to get out of his way. His face indicated the pain he was experiencing, and I could see genuine fear in his eyes as a huge bull bore down on him with its razor-sharp horns lowered to gore him and toss his body in the air. Poor Ernest was immobilised with terror, but I managed somehow to manhandle him onto the side of the street by a railing as the bull rolled past, its right horn ripping into my trousers and making a small gash in my thigh. I noticed that only a minute later.

Ernest and I said nothing as the bulls and the other runners swept round the corner and down the street to the bullring. We were both badly shaken, but we managed to compose ourselves and walk slowly down the street to see the encierro de plaza. Neither of us had any wish to join the festivities in the middle of the ring and just sat and watched. I felt sorry for the steers as they futilely chased the men taunting them without often hitting one, all the time looking terrified and being goaded by dozens of men waving cravats and rags at them.

As we walked back to the town centre Ernest put his arm around my shoulder and said, 'Thank you, Guillermo. That's twice now you've saved me from a dicey situation. It was nearly three strikes and out for me there. I am very grateful. I don't think I'll be trying that again.'

'Think nothing of it, Ernie. You'd have done the same for me. It was just bad luck that you fell. And don't you worry, I don't plan on mentioning it to Hadley or your friends.' Ernest seemed relieved.

'One thing, Guillermo,' he said after we had walked in silence for a minute or two. 'I've been thinking about that quote of yours during that dumbass game we played after dinner in Burguete. The one about the sun setting and rising.'

'Yes, it's a wise saying. Whatever we do, life goes on. And we're only on earth once, and so if we don't seize the moment – carpe diem, my father used to say – then more's the pity. The sun will still set tonight and rise tomorrow morning, and each of us will be another day older.'

'Exactly, Guillermo. Every night we are one step closer to the grave and—'

'Especially if we drink so much wine and whisky.'

'True.' For a moment he was lost in thought. 'But when I think of *my life I see so many things I haven't yet experienced, places I haven't been to, like Africa, women I haven't f—ed, books and stories not yet written. I feel as though I'm stuck on second base. Luckily I'm still young, but I look at some of the people at dinner, they've got no drive, no cojones. Look at Loeb, he's just a bitter boy, gets his kicks from others. He's never got off his ass. Donald, his best games are way behind him, so he lives off the memories, like a punch-drunk retired boxer. Patrick? What a waste of a man, a nonentity. Boring and with nothing to say or do except get tight every day.'*

'Well, I can't comment on your friends, Ernest. I've only just met them.'

'Another day I can give you all the dope on Donald, Robert and Duff. And on Bill and Pat Guthrie. Too tired now.' It was a curious use of the word 'dope'.

Lunch, this time at the Hotel La Quinta, was more subdued than the night before, but everyone was in good spirits. The others were delighted that I had successfully run with the bulls, my small injury serving as proof that I was now one of them. Neither Ernest nor I mentioned his fall and his flirtation with serious injury.

I was keen to do some sightseeing, as this was my only full day, and when I said I wanted to see the church next to my hotel Hadley leaped at the opportunity to join me. She said it was her favourite church in Pamplona. Ernest said he wanted to do some work on a book he was planning.

Hadley and I walked slowly in the afternoon sun to the Iglesia de San Lorenzo. It was a beautiful church, with big trees on two sides, built in what I believe is called the Spanish baroque style. It had a large yellowish stone outside. We entered through the main door, into a room about 25 yards long, full of pews and with ornate Roman Catholic statutes and icons on all of the walls. At a right angle was an even larger area, which was the Chapel of San Fermin, the patron saint of the festival and of Pamplona. The church was completely empty of people, so we were able to explore it at will, and talk without fear of interrupting others.

After a few minutes Hadley sat on a pew near the front. When I joined her she said, 'Are you sure you can't stay a few extra days, William? You're such good company. You're friendly to me and everyone else, you don't criticise people, you're decent and you're funny too. I fear that things will descend into bitterness and tears when you're gone. And I think you're a good influence on Ernest.'

'Me? I'm not sure about that. Sometimes he gives me a look of disapproval, especially when he sees you and me chatting away. But no, I'm sorry, I have to leave tomorrow. I have people to see in London, interviews and other meetings, and then I have to get the boat to Mombasa.'

'That's a shame, but I understand. Ernest thinks the world of you. As we were walking to lunch today he said that twice now you've helped him out. He even said 'saved his bacon'. He wouldn't tell me how you might have done that.' She looked at me, perhaps hoping that I would spill the beans.

I said that Ernest was overstating things and was probably just referring to the companionship that I have offered since we first met 10 days before.

Hadley did not seem convinced. 'Anyway, he credits you with his new-found passion for Sauternes, so that is perhaps a lasting influence you have had on him.' She smiled. 'It's been good seeing you here, and in Burguete. You're so different from the others. They're so pompous, self-centred, and they all think they're so clever. I know they call themselves artists, but that's no excuse for a lack of basic human decency.'

I protested that individually people were fine, but in a group things did change a bit.

'They treat me as Ernest's appendage,' she said, 'almost as though I don't exist. It's humiliating when they ignore me during their conversations. And don't let me get started on that cow Duff.'

Hadley burst out laughing, as if surprised by her immoderate language. I took her hand. 'I won't.' She looked gratefully at me and made no effort to pull her hand back. We sat there in silence, holding

213

hands for about a minute. I realised how out of order it was for me to hold the hand of a married woman in such a manner, so I stood up and suggested we might leave.

'Don't leave, William. Not yet.' She looked seriously at me. 'It's just that Ernest has been so depressed and angry this year. He has what he calls his black-ass moods. Between you and me he may even need medical help. He says he hates all the phonies and bums in Paris, but he won't leave. His work isn't getting the recognition he feels he deserves. Other pals of his, like Scottie Fitzgerald, are leaving him behind in terms of critical reviews and book sales, or so he thinks. And he's always getting drunk and trying to have fights with his friends. He's not an easy man to live with.'

I felt a bit embarrassed, not being used to relative strangers telling me about the state of their marriages. All I could manage was, 'Genius is often unpredictable.'

She laughed. 'The trouble with Ernest is that he's so predictable. But the days in Burguete were great for him. The fishing wasn't great, but the fresh air and the hiking do wonders for his well-being. Spain has that effect on him. And meeting you, with your level-headedness and wisdom, well, he likes you. I do too.' She looked sad for a second, then hastily added, 'We all do.' We both laughed. It was only after she finished speaking that I realised she had taken my hand again.

We left the church and headed back towards the city wall, where we parted. She looked at me intently, almost as though embarrassed. 'Thank you for being so understanding. You are a fine, sensitive man. If only—' She didn't complete the sentence, and to this day I do not know what she intended to say. She must have thought the better of it, because she said she looked forward to seeing me at the bullfight and turned away into the city.

We all met up again at about 6.30 pm, outside the bullring. Ernest had our tickets, and his excitement was infectious. I had never been to a corrida before, and I was curious to experience it. Our seats were in the second row up from the arena, which Ernest said was a prime location to get the most out of the occasion. 'You can hear the bull breathing,

214

and the scrape of the dagger being taken out of its metal scabbard. You can almost hear the racing heartbeat of the matador.'

I took my seat between Ernest and Duff. She whispered how keen she was to get to know me better ('Ernie and Hadley say you're such a darling man,' she cooed) and said what a pity it was that I wasn't staying in Pamplona longer. She confided that she found the bullfighting dull and cruel, and that she attended just to humour Ernest.

I will not bore the reader with a description of the bullfight. I expect it was like any other, with the same result for the bulls. All I will say is that I was repelled by the violence and cruelty and by the absence of any sympathy for the unfortunate animals from anyone in the crowd. The poor bulls never stood a chance. They were teased and taunted to the point of exhaustion, and then lanced and stabbed to death. I decided there was no point in telling this to Ernest. He saw it as his mission to inform and educate me about the finer points – the history, the pageantry, and the subtlety and the finesse from the matadors, and the nobility of the ritual. Above all, he said, there was respect from the matador and the spectators for the bull and its fighting qualities. I saw little nobility or respect in watching men in tight-fitting costumes slaughter defenceless animals in front of a rabid crowd. Ernest hardly stopped talking throughout the corrida, oohing and aahing at every pass of the bull and shouting 'Olé!'. He seemed pleased when a horse was gored on its side during one fight, with some of its entrails hanging out. I was horrified, but Ernest acted as if it was all part of the fun.

There was a pause of a few minutes between the fights. 'What are you writing at the moment?' I asked.

'Not a helluva lot these days. Too much talking and carousing. But I'm here on a commission from a German publisher – did I tell you that Ernest von Hemingstein is big in Germany? – to do a book on bullfighting. Non-fiction. And all being well Picasso and Gris will provide some illustrations for it.'

'Those are impressive names to be associated with.' A thought suddenly came to me. 'Why don't you write a novel? You mentioned last week that you plan to write one one day. But look around you. A

215

novel set in this city, during the fiesta, and with characters based on your friends, I'd buy it. There's definitely enough scandal, humour, conversation, colour and intrigue among all your friends to fill up several books.'

Ernest looked pensive. I could see he was thinking hard. 'You know what, Limey, I think you just might have hit a homer there. Let me think about it.' The next bull sprinted out into the arena to the cheers of the crowd.

Fifteen minutes later, as the poor bull, having sucked its last noble breath as the brave matador plunged a dagger between its heaving shoulder blades, was towed off the arena by two horses, Ernest leaned over. 'You're a genius, Guillermo. I see it so clearly now. Duff the upper class c—k-tease, Loeb the sulking Jewish intellectual, Donald the witty and clever New Yorker, Pat Guthrie the drunken bore, you as the know-it-all good guy, and me as the hero, the good-looking American writer, veteran of the war and many battles since. Yes, and the beauty is no research will be necessary. I could start writing next week.'

For the next few hours, until his mood changed without warning (as I will relate), Ernest was like a man possessed of a rare exuberance and confidence. He exuded an aura of masculinity, as though the sun and the moon were focused on him, chosen by God. The combination of the passion of the bullfight and (I like to think) the idea of writing a novel seemed to have brought on this special state.

Duff noticed it too. After the next bull was despatched she leaned into me and whispered, 'What's up with Big Boy? Did you give him some opium or put some pepper in his absinthe?' I shrugged and pointed to the arena and the colourful spectacle we were witnessing.

'William, do sit next to me at dinner tonight. You're today's hero, with that wound you got this morning, and I'm dying to hear all about your bravery. And after dinner you can show me your injury, and I'll kiss it better.' I was quite shocked at how forward Duff was. I had not encountered women like her in my whole life. She then said, 'What a mistake I made bringing Patrick to Spain. He offers me nothing. He just drinks himself silly every day and says mean things to Harold.'

I found myself at a complete loss for words. 'Hadley's been stealing you all to herself,' she went on. 'It's not fair. And she wears such ghastly clothes. You can see she's bought nothing this year.'

I am clueless when it comes to assessing women's fashion, so I had no opinion on what Duff said about Hadley's clothes, except to note that it was needless and unkind. I was determined to give her no encouragement, and fortunately the next bull ran into the ring and conversation became too difficult. She squeezed my knee and turned to watch the bullfight.

When she joined our group that evening for dinner at the Café Iruna, she made a memorable entrance. She had a jersey draped over her shoulders, and her clothes fitted tightly to her womanly curves. Donald spoke for all of the men when he said as we all stood: 'My dear Lady Twysden, you are dressed to kill.' It was the reaction she was no doubt looking for. I thought I saw Hadley scowling out of the corner of my eye. Duff looked around to find a seat at the table, and I made sure that there would be no seat for her next to me.

We were all in high spirits that evening. Ernest was waxing on about the artistry of the matador in the last two fights, but none of the rest of us showed any appetite for that topic. Everyone knew it was my last night, and they were keen for me to tell them more about my life. I talked about boarding school in England, and fagging (which caused no end of mirth for Donald and Bill, prompting them into a hilarious routine on homosexuals in the Paris and New York literary worlds), and I talked of the beauty of Kenya and Tanganyika, of the wild animals and the beaches, but also of the poverty there and the challenges of the British in governing protectorates and colonies in Africa.

'The difficulty in Kenya,' I said, 'is that you have those who have a lot and those, the vast majority, who have nothing. It is a case of the haves and the have-nots. Much of the best land is owned by rich British and European settlers. They all have servants, paid a pittance but grateful for the work and the security. It's not a question of to have or have not. We all want everyone to have. But it'll take fifty or more years to bring the region into any level of prosperity. It's a gradual

217

process. *Every year progress is made – new roads, schools, railways. And like all gradual things all of a sudden it's done, and you realise that you've reached your goal, or at least as close as you'll ever get. That's the plan anyway.' Ernest was listening intently.*

'True, the poverty among the native population is a nightmare, but it's actually a wonderful nightmare, because it will all change for the better. The Kenyans have a drive to improve themselves. The future is bright for them, but it will take many years.' Ernest looked thoughtful.

Hadley asked me if the Kenyans were a happy lot, whether they felt oppressed by the colonial rule. 'On the contrary,' I said. 'I believe they're grateful for Britain's administration and protection. Roads, schools, courthouses, sewage. The country is vastly better off. The people of British East Africa are definitely on the pursuit to happiness.'

Ernest said he liked my choice of words and scribbled some things in his notebook. He said he was all fired up to visit Africa, to see it for himself, and talked about a trip Theodore Roosevelt had made to Kenya fifteen or so years ago. Ernest and Bill were the only ones in our group who thought hunting and killing wild animals was a good idea. Hadley said she was ashamed that Roosevelt and his son had shot over 500 animals on their safari.

'Don't be such pussycats, you miserable sons-of-b—ches.' Ernest definitely had his own way with words. 'Man against beast is an equal contest, native untamed cunning against a single bullet from a rifle held by a man who is in unknown territory. Hash, we must go to Africa as soon as we can afford it.' Hadley looked doubtful about this suggestion.

'I'd be happy to introduce you to some people in Kenya,' I said. 'I'm quite friendly with a hunter called Finch Hatton. He's a larger-than-life character, and you'd like him. Moreover, his lady friend's a writer who's beginning to make a name for herself. Karen Blixen, a Dane.'

'Makes it even better. We must stay in touch, William.' I agreed that we should. I have to say that I was most pleased to see that Ernest made a small reference to British East Africa in chapter 2 of TSAR. It had no relevance to the plot, but I like to think it was a nod of sorts from Ernest to me and my description of Africa.

Conversation flowed as easily as the wine. Loeb seemed a different man from last night, warm and witty. Donald was as droll as ever, and even Duff and Hadley were chatting away about the pros and cons of living in Paris.

The café was full of happy people, many of whom had been at the corrida. The waiters were run off their feet fetching more wine and whisky at Ernest's behest. I had more to drink than I would normally permit myself. It reminded me of some of my student dinners at Cambridge. By now Ernest was calling me Don Guillermo and insisted that everyone call him Don Ernesto. People were happy to oblige. Donald exhorted us to call him Don Donaldo Ogdeño Stéwarto too!

As our dinner plates were taken away Donald suggested we play a word game, to see who could use the same word the most times in the same sentence, preferably in a row. That made us all think furiously, which wasn't so easy bearing in mind that there were about 15 wine bottles on our table.

Donald started us off with something like 'Will, will will will Will's will,' which we all thought frightfully clever. Duff, surprisingly as she was well-read and had a fertile mind, and Pat declined to participate: 'Not my specialty, sorry,' she said. Hadley and Bill mentioned the well-known 'John, where James had had 'had' had had 'had had.' 'Had had' had been the preferred expression,' or something like that.

Loeb looked pensive, then offered something along the lines of 'in the accommodation sign outside my house should I put a hyphen between the Bed and And and And and Breakfast?' Hadley clapped, and even Duff seemed to be impressed. Ernest suggested, 'But Butt's butt butted butter to Butterworth,' which we all acknowledged was a decent attempt.

'All yours, Don Guillermo,' said Ernest and attention moved to me. I had desperately spent the last few minutes trying to come up with something original. The occasion and the wine combined to embolden me to say the following: 'When the doctor had finished his examination of a famous American writer's bottom at a reception at Windsor Castle he was asked by Queen Mary what he'd seen. He said, "Ahem,

Hem's hems, he-Majesty."' I had no idea that Ernest's piles were so well known, but my offering was greeted with howls of laughter and applause, especially from Duff, Donald and Bill. Hadley laughed too but a bit nervously.

Ernest was most definitely <u>not</u> laughing. He glared at me, contempt written all over his red face. 'Not f—ing funny.' He stood up, muttered something about finding decent company for a drink, and stormed out into the Plaza. I was distraught, but people were quick to comfort me. Donald told me not to worry: 'He's just a bit red between the cheeks. He'll get over it.' That eased the tension.

Hadley leaned across the table. 'Don't worry, William. He often gets on his high horse when he thinks people are laughing at him. He'll just go and get tight, even more tight I should say, and he'll be fine tomorrow.'

The rest of us stayed on talking and drinking wine for a little longer, but the fun had gone from the evening and it felt a bit strange. People peeled off one by one to retire for the night. Duff came up to me after she rose to leave, and said, 'Sorry we didn't talk much tonight. Look me up sometime in London, or wherever,' planted a kiss on my cheek, turned dramatically and pulled the hapless Pat out into the night. Donald and Bill left a few minutes later, Donald saying something about going to find some señoritas.

It was just Hadley and me left. The waiters were clearing our table. I suggested we finish up. I pointed out that Ernest might be waiting for her back at their hotel. 'Let him wait, then. Bad manners shouldn't be rewarded. Come on, William, it's your last night. Let's have a nightcap.'

I was a bit dubious, but it was not easy to say no to Hadley, and she led me to a little bar a street or two away down the hill. There were only a few locals in it. Hadley ordered a whisky, and I a coffee. I felt uncomfortable being alone with her, but she said, 'Serves him right. He gets so jumped up at times, so pompous and self-important. He makes a fool of himself, carrying on with other women right in front of me. I feel so humiliated.'

For the next hour she told me all about her marriage: about how Ernest had rescued her when they first met; how she hated Paris and all of Ernest's self-obsessed literary friends; how he drank too much (she smiled ruefully when she said this, as the waiter brought her another glass of whisky); how he became angry and violent towards others for no good reason yet could be as soft and adorable as a little boy. She talked of their financial struggles, and how lucky they were that she had a trust fund to support them.

Her eyes welled up on occasion, and I held her hand tenderly. My heart wept for her unhappiness, and I was not surprised to learn only recently that they separated a year after we had all been in Pamplona. But Hadley was fair and loyal too, as she spoke about Ernest's talent and his burning ambition to succeed.

Just then Ernest burst into the bar, with a loud shout and the look of a maniac in his eye. He was clearly intoxicated. I immediately withdrew my hand from Hadley's, but not before he saw it. We both stood up as he lurched towards us, fearful of what would happen next. He looked at me, and then at poor Hadley, and then raised his left arm and gave Hadley a hefty smack on her cheek with the back of his hand. She stumbled to the floor, now covered in sawdust. I remonstrated loudly, stood between the two of them and told him not to be a bl—dy fool.

Ernest would not be placated. His anger knew no bounds. His breath stank of wine and absinthe. He started pushing me on the chest with his open palms, muttering about fighting like a man and how dare I put my hands on his wife. I protested, struggling to keep my balance, and said I had no wish to fight, that I had no intentions whatsoever towards Hadley. He did not seem to be listening.

He put his fists up in front of his face, like a boxer, and started bouncing around on his toes and urging me to fight. Hadley, by now back on her feet, tried to intervene, and told Ernest to stop it, that I had been completely blameless. He would have none of it. He was much bigger and stronger than me, and I had no fighting experience. I am a pacifist by nature. While my hands were still largely down by my hips

221

I felt a big blow on my jaw from Ernest's right fist, and it stung badly. I shouted at him, begging him to stop. He wouldn't listen. A second swing at me missed narrowly, and I immediately punched him back, landing my fist on his chin. It felt like granite, and my knuckles ached.

Hadley then grabbed one of Ernest's arms, and the bartender tried to seize the other arm. Ernest shook them both off and swung another fist at me, hitting me on the side of the head. While he was getting his breath, I lunged at him and landed a very decent blow on his jaw. It struck home, and he staggered back. Straight away his aggression just evaporated. He looked at me, with a half-smile on his face, and stroked his jaw (which I hoped was sore and painful). 'Hah, the limey has cojones after all.'

He then nonchalantly walked across the bar to the door, pulling Hadley with him. I looked at her imploringly, fearing for her safety, but she motioned to me that it would be all right. Just before they left the bar I shouted to them something stupid. I have no idea what made me say it. I said something like, 'You know, it's not pretty to act like that.' Ernest stopped for a second and give me a strange, piercing look, then smiled and they were out the door. I waited a minute or two, tipped the barman handsomely, and set off to my hotel.

Straight away I started recording events in my journal, my hand still shaking. It was hard to believe that I had been in Pamplona only a day and a half. No one could ever say that being with the Hemingways was dull.

I was not due to leave Pamplona until noon, but I had no desire to see Ernest again so did not try to seek out my friends for breakfast or at their hotel. Shortly before I left I heard a footfall outside my room and saw an envelope had been pushed under my door. I opened the door, but whoever had delivered the envelope had vanished.

The envelope contained a letter from Hadley, and included the following:

Dearest William, I am so sorry about last night. The man can be a brute and an animal, and as you have seen he does not respond well to too much liquor. It is very un-American of him in that regard. What's more, his 'hems' have been playing up, and while that is no excuse I know that will provide a little consolation for you.

Do not worry about me. I can look after myself. I fear I will not have to worry about a recurrence of this kind of activity for too long into the future, as our marriage ties have sadly weakened over the last two weeks.

Please do your best to forgive Ernest. He is a little boy at heart, and often sees things that are simply not there. I know him well enough to know that he won't bear any grudge towards you. Already this morning he is remorseful, although he will not come to see you to apologise. And he has a red bruise on his jaw!

I have so much enjoyed meeting you and talking with you in the last few days. I do hope there will be other occasions in the future.

Yours,
Hadley

As I finished the letter I was overwhelmed with sadness for Hadley's plight. She was too good a woman for a man like Hemingway, with his rhinoceros-like qualities, his aggressiveness and instabilities. Never before had I seen a man hit a woman, let alone his wife.

I was a bit shaken for the next few days, but I soon rejoined my earlier life once I returned to London. I got the boat from Southampton to Mombasa, via the Cape, and in only a few weeks I had taken up my new position in Nanyuki. Gradually the events (and excitement) of my visit to Spain and my involvements with the Hemingways and their friends receded in my mind. Luckily I had kept a full journal and I made sure that all the main events and signal conversations were faithfully recorded.

But that is not the end of this little story, or the parts of it that I have chosen to record here. After a few months back in Kenya I received a package delivered through Colonial Office and diplomatic pouches from London. Inside it was another package, which had been addressed to me (described as 'Mr Wm Harrison'—no E) care of the 'Colonial Office in London (believed to be serving somewhere in Kenya)'. It had a Paris stamp. I opened the package, and in there was a silver-plated goblet, of the kind that I had seen in jewellery shop windows in Pamplona. On it was an engraved inscription: 'To Don G, you were damned right. Everyone does behave badly. Especially me. Don E.' The date July 1925 had been added. There was no accompanying letter or note.

The man does have some class after all, even if he hides it well. The goblet is on my mantelpiece here as I write. I am not sure how I will ever explain to anybody what the inscription means or what the background to it is.

I remember reading in the middle of last year that the 'up-and-coming American writer Ernest Hemingway, based in Paris' was shortly to publish his debut novel which was rumoured to be ground-breaking. I was on the lookout for it. Eventually in a copy of the New York Times I borrowed from my friend at the U.S. Consulate in Nairobi I saw a rapturously positive review of TSAR – I laughed long and hard when I saw the title – and promptly ordered a copy. It took about six weeks to arrive, and when it did I was impressed by how slim it was and also by its confident and spare tone. I read it in 24 hours over one weekend and was stunned by it.

In so many ways the book was simply a recording of the various interactions that I had observed in Burguete and Pamplona, although with a number of major differences which I have been pondering in the intervening weeks. It is not for me to write a review of the book, but I do note for the record a few major differences:

1. The most obvious one in the Burguete section of TSAR was that the fictional portrayal was one of an idyll – of sunshine, plentiful trout, good regional food and witty company. I assume the descriptions were based on his two previous visits to Burguete, which he often said had been great successes, when the weather and the fishing had been perfect. There was definitely witty company, though. Ernest was seeking to use his novelist's licence to create two markedly different worlds – one, in Burguete, the idyll of simpler times, of outdoor pursuits and decent

people; the other, in Paris and Pamplona, a corrupt and venal grouping of men and women of doubtful moral values.

2. He made a number of character changes. Donald and Bill were combined into Bill Gorton, a character not (in my unbiased opinion) as funny or as likeable as either of the originals; Hadley was ignored; I was changed into Harris, a dull but inoffensive Englishman, and I dare say I should be grateful for that; and Sandra, poor angelic Sandra, was transformed into a Spanish girl with no apparent significance or personality. I accept that all the changes – similarities too – entirely fit within the broad rights of the author to write his novels as he sees fit.

3. Even though the book is dedicated to Hadley (and their son Bumby), she does not feature in it. The narrator Jake is single. I have wondered whether that was at her request (that would not surprise me in the least) or if it was his decision. Perhaps he omitted Hadley as revenge for her being open and friendly towards me. I have read that since Hadley and Ernest separated he appears to have a new girlfriend, an American called Pauline. Against this background it does seem perverse that TSAR should be dedicated to Hadley.

4. My character Harris was in the Burguete segment but omitted from the Pamplona episodes. The character did not add much to the plot, except perhaps to act as a contrast to the other loud, petty, violent and morally loose characters. I interpret the inclusion of my character as an attempt by Ernest not to cause further misery for me and that he had been genuine when he apologised for his behaviour towards me. In case anyone reads this little self-indulgence, and doubts that Harris is based on me, I offer the following:

(a)   the similarity of the names, Harris and Harrieson.

(b)   the fact that Harris says in the book that his real surname is Wilson Harris (unhyphenated). I had told EH that my full surname is Forbes Harrieson, also unhyphenated.

(c)   Harris, like me, walked from Saint-Jean-Pied-de-Port to

225

Burguete, and he went fishing with Jake and his merry band to the Irati River. I fished there too with Ernest and <u>his</u> drinking companions.

(d) Harris, like me, tied his own trout flies, and presented some as gifts to Jake. I gave five or six flies to Ernest, too, but not as many as the dozen that Harris gave Jake.

(e) There is reference to Harris having been in the war, as I had served, if only briefly. Ernest's war service was even briefer.

Another difference is that Jake, the main character in TSAR who is obviously based on Ernest, is portrayed as a war hero (true, Ernest did have war wounds in his leg), a reliable man and a stable influence. Nowhere is there a suggestion that Jake is lecherous towards servant girls, a plagiarist (or at least someone who borrowed phrases and quotes off another person without attribution or apology – even the word 'pretty' makes a startling appearance at the end of TSAR), a drunkard, a coward, a man who hits his wife, a man prone to violence and a petulant child.

In saying all this I defer to the author's licence to portray himself and others as he sees fit. Ernest is without doubt an extraordinary talent, and I know enough about literature to know that this book is worthy of the sensation which it has created and of the laudatory reviews it has received. I know too that I have had a small part in its origins. His career is one which I and the rest of the world will follow with some interest in the years to come. Hopefully he will be able to avoid altercations with others in the future, although I doubt that very much.

I feel better for having written all of this down. I sense somehow that my observations of Ernest and his friends in Spain in 1925 will have some historical value. I will make sure that I send this little memoir to my solicitor in Aylesbury for safekeeping.

William Forbes Harrieson

26

It was almost 10 p.m. when Nick's phone rang. 'What took you so long?' he said.

Andrew launched forth. 'I can honestly say, old chap, that I haven't read anything more sensational since I re-read my student diaries ten years ago, as our old friend Oscar has Gwendolyn say. I hardly know where to start, but I'll give it a try. The first thing we have to nail down is the authenticity of these two documents. How sure can we be they're the real deal?'

'One hundred per cent real, no doubt at all. I have the originals, and I'm sure tests could be done if need be to prove they were written when they claimed to be. The 1927 memoir came from an unopened envelope which I found in a solicitors' office. It had been there since 1932, for God's sake. I still have the envelope.'

'Amazing,' said Andrew. 'That's good enough for me. Any publisher will still have to be convinced, though.'

'We can talk about publication another day. I have the original of the 1941 letter including the monograph appended to it, and also the envelope which they came in. I got them from my aunt in New Zealand, my grandfather's daughter. I'm sure we can get an affidavit from her that they've been in her continuous possession since the death of her mother, William's widow. And the handwriting is the same in both documents.'

'Yes, yes, that all helps. We'll need to get experts in to give their two pennies' worth. We'll need manuscript and handwriting tests done, and probably some kind of chain-of-title timeline so that we can eliminate the possibility that these are elaborate forgeries.'

'Hang on, Andrew. One step at a time. Publication hasn't crossed my mind yet. Let's park that possibility. Now, tell me what you thought of the contents?'

Nick heard Andrew breathe in. He could imagine him standing to attention. 'Where do I begin, my legal friend? The documents are chock-full of revelations of massive interest to Hemingway scholars, and to anyone who has read *The Sun Also Rises*. I've been so excited – almost orgasmically so, I must confess – by what you sent me, that I've made a few notes, and even put them into different headings.

'The first is the book itself. We now have an account from someone who, unwittingly, was a key figure in the origins of the novel. For example, your grandfather claims it was his idea, which Hemingway acted on, that Ernest write a novel rather than a non-fiction book. To date there have been conflicting stories and theories about whether Hemingway went to Spain in 1925 with the intent of writing a novel. We now have some strong, contemporary evidence to indicate that he didn't. We know that in April 1925, a little over two months before travelling to Spain, he wrote to his editor Maxwell Perkins that he had no intention of writing a novel, happy instead to keep writing longish short stories. So your grandfather's account may settle this particular debate.

'More importantly, we now know that Hemingway was fed a lot of phrases in his books, shamelessly taking ideas and quotes from your grandfather. Even the titles for *Sun* and a few other books. And all without attribution or acknowledgement. This will be a dent to his reputation as an original and creative writer and modernist. Mind you, writers get their ideas from a number of sources, so we shouldn't be too critical here.

'And regarding the title, it's been generally thought that it was inspired by a visit he made to Chartres Cathedral in August 1925. Now we know that's probably not the full story.'

Nick was struggling to absorb what his friend was telling him.

'We now have more colour, and nuance, about the inter-relationships within the merry band of travellers in Pamplona,' Andrew went on. 'Harold Loeb emerges with more credit and depth than Hemingway and many others gave him. And Hadley too; she emerges as warm, and long-suffering and a hugely sympathetic woman. Nothing particularly new there, but it's good to have it confirmed.

'And your grandfather's observations about Hemingway's cronies, Duff, Stewart, Guthrie etcetera, they all ring true. They add to the authenticity of the sensational revelations. And the most sensational of all, the most gobsmacking feature of the whole shebang' – Nick could imagine Andrew in a packed press conference or lecture hall – 'is the suggestion that Hadley and your grandfather may have had an affair. What a thought.'

'Yes,' said Nick. 'I thought you'd pick up on that. It's only hinted at, though. They obviously took to each other, but everything I know about my grandfather's character tells me that it's most unlikely that anything ever happened between them.'

'That may be true, but who are we to know for sure what happened? Those were heady, passionate days at the *fiesta* in 1925. That letter from Hadley to your grandfather was very, how can I put it, affectionate. The fact that Hemingway attacked him on account of Hadley. The odd, otherwise unexplained questions and comments about her when he visited Hemingway in Hong Kong in 1941. You would have to say Don Guillermo had a very soft spot for Señora la Doña Hemingway. And he would have us believe it was reciprocated. That all amounts to a credible narrative.'

'I suppose so,' said Nick. He was about to mention the curious detail that Aunt Mary's middle name was Hadley but decided not to. Andrew was excited enough as it was. Instead Nick said, 'Did you notice that the letter from Hadley at the end of the memoir appeared to be only an extract, so may not have been the full letter? William quoted various paragraphs which were "included" in the letter. And did you notice that line at the end where he talks about having recorded only those things he chose to record? He must have left bits out. I wonder what he decided he couldn't or shouldn't tell us.'

'God, you're right, I hadn't noticed that. It does add up to what you lawyers call a good circumstantial case. But whether or not the two of them did have a thing, we now have a very fact-based reason for Hemingway omitting Hadley completely from the novel. He was angry at her. This was his means of revenge, although admittedly the book was dedicated to Hadley, and as part of the divorce settlement he assigned her all the royalties from it. Perhaps your grandfather was right, that he subsequently had remorse about excluding her? Anyway, by the time of publication in late 1926 Hemingway had moved on with Pauline Pfeiffer and possibly he felt guilty. She'd returned to America by then.'

Another thought came to Nick. Hadn't Aunt Mary told him that her father was on a fishing trip for several weeks in the midwest of the U.S. around the time she was born? Surely William was not there to meet up with Hadley? He put the thought out of his mind.

Andrew continued. 'The slap that Hemingway gave Hadley in Pamplona will reverberate around the literary world when it sees the light of day. No one can forgive a man hitting his wife, and drunkenness is no excuse. Mind you, there is other evidence that Hemingway on at least one occasion did slap Mary, his fourth wife, so perhaps this particular revelation will not be quite so scandalous after all. It all goes to show how excess drinking can change a person's character.' Andrew paused, as though to get a second wind.

'It also explains why the character Harris didn't feature in the Pamplona section of the book. Harris is clearly based on your grandfather. He's portrayed as an unremarkable and decent man, and it sounds like it may have been a fair portrayal.' Andrew had a way of praising and damning someone in one sentence. 'If your grandfather had been such a central figure during the Pamplona visit, Hemingway must've had a good reason for excluding him from that section of the book. Continuing anger at his closeness with Hadley? Probably. Hemingway was famous for not letting go of grudges and slights. But then why include Harris at all in the book? The scholars will have a field day over this.

'Hemingway himself emerges from your grandfather's writings as even more grotesquely a caricature of the man the world knows. Boorish, aggressive, anti-Semitic, a drunkard, volatile, misogynistic, a sexual predator. The list could go on. It all rings true and only serves to underline the authenticity of the documents. Even the expressions used by Hemingway in your grandfather's accounts are consistent with all contemporary and historical biographies – references to boxing and baseball, for example, and the use of words like 'swell', 'dirt', 'dope', 'moron' and 'Limey'. Pure Hem.

'Your grandfather mentioned a number of phrases in his 1927 memoir, all of which found their way into Hemingway's novels and short stories later on. *The Green Hills of Africa, For Whom the Bell Tolls,* even *Across the River and into the Trees* and *To Have and Have Not.* Your antecedent gave those titles to the most famous novelist of the twentieth century, without even knowing it. Let's not forget that Hem used the name Robert Jordan as his protagonist in *For Whom the Bell Tolls.* And he wrote them all down on his notepad during conversations. The great man himself was perhaps not as original as many of us have thought.'

Nick remembered something else. 'And what about the three prostitutes in Hong Kong? The mention of Russian spies? I've read of the rumours about these things, but they've never been properly established, have they?'

'You're right. Just rumours. Hemingway himself used to tell the story of the prostitutes at the Peninsula, and even mentioned them in *Islands in the Stream*, and now we have corroboration. Mind you, Hemingway's story is that the three girls were in his room when he returned from some errand, as opposed to them visiting him when he was in the room. But that's a mere detail. He used to say that he just had a shower with the women and didn't have sex with them. Not that it matters, but the new account certainly validates the rumours. And one or two academics believe that the visit of the prostitutes to the Peninsula did in fact happen.

'And Russian spies? Well, that too is part of Hemingway legend. It's well known that he did various assignments for the CIA during World War Two, in China, and also in Cuba, and he often used to say that Russian agents were trying to get him to spy for the Soviet Union. Some writers believe Hemingway had agreed to help out the Russians. He probably never did, but we now have a bit of supporting evidence that they were at least interested in him.

'In addition, we have confirmation that Ernest's marriage to Martha was on the rocks even as it began – on their honeymoon, what's more. Again, that's not new to Hemingway scholars, but it does add a little bit of information to the mix. Plus, before I forget, William talks of Hemingway running with the bulls. The accepted wisdom is that he never did that, so there's something else to chew on there.'

It seemed to Nick that Andrew had been speaking non-stop for half an hour.

'Getting back to the question of the authenticity of your grandfather's writings. It would help if there was any other evidence that he knew Hemingway. Do you know of anything? Any other letters to friends or family referring to him? I don't recall there's anything in Hemingway's collected letters about your grandfather.'

'Well, now you mention it, there are some things. A fellow prisoner of war in Thailand mentioned William's story about the punch-up with Hemingway in Spain. And then there's the goblet.' Nick explained how the goblet referred to in the memoir was in Jo's possession.

Andrew squealed with excitement. 'Wonderful,' he said.

'But wait, there's more,' said Nick, and paused for a second. 'We have the photo of the two of them together in Pamplona, the one referred to in the manuscript. The *tarjeta* one. The original is with the JFK Library in Boston. I saw it when I visited Pamplona, at an exhibition. I'll send you a photo of it.'

'Holy fucking shit. You've got that? That'll seal it. What we have – what *you* have – will be the biggest literary sensation of the last thirty or forty years. It's as though Hemingway's lost manuscripts had been located in the lost property section at the Gare de Lyon. It's that big.'

'Calm down, Andrew. We need to think about things for a while, and not rush into any decisions. Let's sit on it for a week or so. And I need hardly remind you about the importance of confidentiality. No one else can know at the moment. We have to be sure about our next steps.'

'Okay, old chap. You have my word, as a scholar and gentleman.' Andrew sounded deflated. 'Let's talk again soon. It's getting late anyway. Good night.'

Nick sat back, stunned by everything Andrew had told him. He poured himself a glass of merlot and wondered what all this meant for him (and Jo too) for the future. Money? Media exposure? Being hounded by journalists? It was all too much to take in. He wanted to speak to Adrienne, who was now only occasionally in his daily thoughts. He planned to call her on

WhatsApp tomorrow.

Before he went to bed he heard a ping on his phone. It was an email from Andrew. It was headed, simply: 'Hem's hems'.

I forgot to mention it. The great man did have piles. He mentioned it in a letter written in 1927. It is in the third volume of his Collected Letters. I also understand there's a letter he wrote to AE Hotchner in 1949 which referred to him having terrible piles as a high school footballer. If he had piles in 1917 or 1918 and also in 1927 it stands to reason that he would have had them in 1925.

Cheers, Andrew

Nick knew he would sleep well.

When he woke there was another email from Andrew, sent just before 1 a.m. and headed 'Flashy?':

Your grandfather reminds me a bit of the much-missed Harry Flashman. You will remember we read a number of those books in our first year or two at Cambridge. Well, your grandfather seems to pop up knowing a lot of famous types, interacts with them at key times, and then sails off into the sunset, unscathed, to face a new adventure. Just like Flashman. I wonder who else he came into contact with.

27

'*Oh, c'est toi, mon vieux fiancé.* How are you, Nick?'

'I'm well, thank you. How lovely to hear your voice. It's been almost three months. How've you been? Korea's working out okay, I hope?'

'It certainly is. I'll tell you all shortly. But first we must discuss Don Ernesto and Don Guillermo. What an amazing story. I've read it three times and almost cried with happiness. And fancy 'old Beryl' being a man. No wonder we never knew where to look for the manuscript. And what a blast that you and I stayed in the same hotel in Pamplona as William.'

Nick told her about what Andrew had said, and they chatted about William's revelations. 'It's a real hoot that he was a bit of a ladies' man,' Adrienne offered. 'Just like his handsome and dashing grandson.'

Nick laughed. 'Hardly. You've seen the gauche incompetent at work. Anyway, enough of that. Tell me about your podcasts, and then your love life.'

Adrienne chuckled. 'The podcasts are going great. We've recorded twenty different half-hour podcasts, covering five or six well known Korean crimes, and already we have about ten thousand subscribers, each one paying about six US dollars for a year's subscription. I reckon we're on our way to riches and world-wide fame. My poor food blog is suffering neglect.'

Nick was delighted but wasn't in the least surprised. He had long realised that when Adrienne set herself a task she would do it with enthusiasm and success.

'And guess what, I've got myself a boyfriend. He's a top guy, funny and cute. Solvent too.' She laughed. 'I hope you're not jealous. Are you?'

'Gosh no. I'm thrilled for you. You deserve only the best. Tell me all about him. Age? Occupation? Nationality?'

'Well, he's thirty-five. A good age, you'll agree.' They both laughed at that. 'And he's Korean.' They laughed at that too. 'And you'll never guess what he does for a job.'

Nick was thinking K-Pop, a Hyundai manager, or perhaps a film producer.

'He's an international lawyer.' Adrienne shrieked with laughter.

'He sounds great. You obviously have a thing for lawyers. Do tell me that he loves you and that he's romantic.'

'He most definitely is. He treats me like a movie star. Gifts, unexpected texts, lots of TLC. I couldn't be happier.'

'And are … wedding bells in the air?' There was silence for a few seconds. 'I'm sworn to secrecy, but yes, he proposed last week. I'm so excited. I'm going to get married at last, and I'm going to have three children, and we're going to be a happy middle-class couple living in Korea. The wedding will be in November, and you'll be invited. You'll come, won't you? You're one of my closest friends.'

'I would love to, thank you. No promises, but I'll do my best to be there.' Nick knew that neither Adrienne nor he wanted him to attend the wedding. He would know no one there, and it was so far away. More importantly, he would feel jealous.

'I'm so glad, Nick. My mother's dying to meet you.' Nick wondered whether she was having him on. 'I've told her so much about you. Nothing about Hem, I promise. And guess what? Mum and I are coming to Europe in May for a bit of a pre-wedding shopping trip. Paris and Milan, mainly. I'd love to see you, but we're not planning on going to London. So how would you fancy a weekend with me in Spain somewhere? We have so much to talk about, especially about Don Ernesto and Don Guillermo. How does that sound?'

'I'd love to see you again. But won't your husband-to-be object? It's hardly proper for you to be holidaying with another man. Won't he be jealous, even angry?'

'Oh no, don't worry about that. I've told him lots about you, not everything, just that you're my wise mentor and my lecturer and a man of good manners. And there won't be any funny business anyway. I'm spoken for now.' She giggled down the phone.

'Are you sure? I'm not sure I would be so generous if I were in his shoes. But I do want to see you. Anywhere special in Spain? How about Barcelona, or Seville? Both great cities.'

'No, been there before. Somewhere new, please, and sunny. And not Benidorm.' Adrienne laughed at her own little joke.

'How about Alicante? I've heard it's a charming little place, and you can fly directly there from London and Paris, and I'm sure Milan too.'

They agreed to meet in May. Adrienne said she would email through her preferred dates, and Nick said he would book an Airbnb apartment for them.

Nick knew he should tell Sadie about his plan to see Adrienne in Alicante. He had told her that Adrienne had accompanied him to Spain the previous July but had given no indication that they had had an intense relationship. He had told her that they had had separate bedrooms – which was only half-untrue – and that while he found her company agreeable, they had little in common. Sadie had been bemused by the fact that Nick and Adrienne were friendly at all, just months after her allegation had nearly ruined his career.

The opportunity arose over dinner the following day.

'Alicante, eh? I've never been, but I've heard it's a pretty town. And are you going to invite me along? I'm keen to meet the chic young Adrienne. The three of us could eat paella and drink sangria in a pretty little café near the sea.'

Nick hesitated for a second. He had anticipated her question and couldn't think of a valid reason why she shouldn't join them. 'You'll be very welcome. I'm sure you'll like her. She's quite a character, and intelligent too. But I hope you won't give her a hard time about all that unpleasantness last year.'

'Me? Give the vixen a hard time about putting you through the wringer on the basis of a spurious claim?' Sadie laughed, and gently put her hand on his. 'Relax, Nick. Don't be alarmed. I won't spoil your party or your reminiscences. I have no wish to meet Adrienne. She's bound to be gushing about her husband-to-be and her wedding dress. I can do without all of that. No, you go alone. All I ask is that you don't return in love with her again. As you were last year.'

'Don't be silly. I was never in love with her. Sure, we got on well in Spain, and were able to put the harassment claim behind us, but no, definitely not in love.'

'You could've fooled me. When we had that first dinner, three months or so after your return you couldn't help yourself. You were waxing on about the bulls and the plazas and the throngs of party people, and every time you mentioned her I could see this love, desire too, in your eyes. Women see these things, Nick. We're not stupid.'

Nick had underestimated his admirable friend and lover, and not for the first time. He could see she wasn't jealous or hurt, just telling it as she saw it. 'I suppose I did take a shine to her. She was so completely different. But I certainly wasn't in love. Anyhow, she's engaged now, so you needn't be concerned.'

'And don't forget. You're not yet out of time for Adrienne to lay a complaint about the harassment, the incident. There's a month to go, so don't mess it up.'

'Thanks for the reminder. I doubt she even knows about it.'

That night, back at Sadie's flat, their lovemaking was more passionate than usual. Sadie took charge and showed an ardour that had been missing since their early trysts. Afterwards, she held him tightly.

The next two months passed in a whirl. The bitter winter cold departed, to be replaced by a grey and wet spring, and daily university life increased in intensity as the academic year sped to a close. There were lectures to prepare and deliver, theses to read and critique, tutorials to attend and planning sessions for the next academic year to endure.

During this time Nick received a number of emails and texts from Andrew McGregor, begging to receive the go-ahead to publish William's Hemingway materials. Nick would reply that he and Jo were still considering what should be done with them. This was a fib. Conversations with Jo on the subject were brief. She had no wish to be in the public gaze. She was content, she said, to leave the decision to publish or not up to him.

He was surprised at his own reluctance to avoid the publicity that would inevitably follow any public release of William's writings. Nick was a public figure anyway, at least in certain narrow circles. He had lectured thousands of students, tens of thousands even over the last twenty years. He had a minor national reputation, and his crossword gimmicks in lectures were, he knew, attention-seeking and brazen. Every two months or so he would pop up on radio or TV, commenting on a new court case or a proposed new law. He was comfortable with all of that, but a wider, international glare was one which didn't appeal.

He and Adrienne settled on the dates for their trip, Nick insisting on booking her flights from Paris to Alicante and back. He said it was his wedding present. After spending an hour on Airbnb's website he selected a two-bedroomed apartment just up the hill from the centre of the Old Town. He booked it for Friday and Saturday nights.

Unlike the year before he didn't feel he needed to spruce himself up before the trip. He had stopped his visits to the gym, which had been intermittent at best, and didn't bother to lose a bit of his belly or groom himself in any way. She would just have to take him as she found him.

28

Nick took a morning flight to Alicante, keen to settle into the apartment and have a quick look around the Old Town. He had read that Alicante boasted three hundred days of sunshine every year. The sun shone brightly through the clear-blue sky as the plane descended over the parched red hills and valleys. The aircraft was full of boisterous British holidaymakers.

TripAdvisor had recommended that visitors take the bus into town, as taxis were unlikely to get their passengers much closer to their Old Town accommodation because of the narrow streets, many of which were steep and interspersed with steps.

Nick knew immediately that Alicante was the right choice. It was small enough, with a population of just over 350,000, and its centre was small and quaint, overlooked by a grand-looking castle perched on a rocky hill. The centrepiece was a pedestrian promenade, almost a kilometre long, parallel to the main marina, and with majestic Phoenix palms on either side. The overall impression was of a city of elegance, refinement and history.

The apartment was a fraction tattier than it had appeared online. There was one big bedroom and one small one: Nick took the smaller one for himself. The kitchen was narrow, but the living room was comfortable and big enough. From its ornate window he looked out over sandstone houses, tabernas and churches.

By the time he boarded the airport bus to greet Adrienne, he had already explored the Old Town. Adrienne took over an hour to navigate Customs and baggage handling. Tourists emerged by the hundreds while Nick waited in the arrival hall. Most were British, but there were groups from all the other usual European countries. Many of the young men and women were noisy and apparently drunk already. It looked as though there were a few stag and hen parties starting that weekend.

Adrienne emerged at last. His heart leaped when he saw her dark hair and wide cheekbones, her sunglasses perched on the top of her head. She looked just as he remembered from the year before. She waved when she saw the bright-red straw hat he had bought in Pamplona and soon they were hugging each other as though she had just been liberated from prison. She felt warm and generous, and he enjoyed the faint aroma of the perfume that she had worn in Pamplona.

They chatted away from the moment they met until the moment he unlocked the door of their apartment. He asked about her shopping trip and her mother and her wedding plans, and she asked about the apartment and Alicante and the food and the castle. Adrienne, in charge of planning for the weekend, said she had booked good restaurants for their two nights and that in the morning they would take a ferry to the island of Tabarca for some swimming and a long lunch.

Adrienne gushed about the apartment. 'Oh Nick, it's so cute and adorable. I love the door and the window grills, and the colourful shutters and balcony flowers. It's just perfect for us.' For all her discernment and taste in so many other parts of her life, Adrienne was a sucker for all things European.

'And here's your bedroom,' he said as he lifted her carry-on bag onto the bed. 'It looks pretty comfy, and it's a bit bigger than mine.'

Adrienne looked doubtful and went in search of the other bedroom. She returned in seconds. 'You can't possibly sleep in that cubbyhole. You'll never get any rest there, all scrunched up in that tiny bed. Come. We can both sleep here. It's a queen size. Definitely room for two, and I know you won't try to take advantage of me. I'm already taken,' she laughed. *How often had she said that to him?*

She brushed aside his feeble protests. 'It's settled,' she said, raising her right hand.

Nick always felt his age when he was with Adrienne, and never more than now. She had the looks and energy of a twenty-year-old. She wore her moods and thoughts as easily as Nick hid his, and he loved her for them at the same time as he lamented his own emotional shortcomings.

Adrienne had booked them into a restaurant which had been recommended to her, and she was keen to see what all the fuss was about. She put her arm in his as they navigated the steps from their apartment, she in a white frock and a faded denim jacket, he in some beige chinos and a Hawaiian shirt.

Google maps took them straight to the Taberna del Gourmet. They entered the bustling restaurant, where the diners were obviously locals. They were shown upstairs to a table for two in an equally crowded room, and soon a waiter in his sixties or seventies came to explain the menu. His English wasn't much better than their Spanish, and he was plainly smitten by Adrienne, who smiled at him at every opportunity. Nick ordered a bottle of the local rosé; Adrienne ordered a seafood paella to share, preceded by *gambas* and some salted fish. The waiter whispered to Nick that his companion was *muy hermosa*.

Nick knew they had a thousand things to talk about and that they would get around to all of them over the weekend. She talked of her life in Busan and showed him photos of her fiancé. His English name was Bobby and he was now her *yubo*, or honey-bun. Bobby looked like a serious young man: he didn't smile in any of his photos. He too looked younger than his age and was smartly dressed. 'Every day he tells me he loves me and that he will love me forever. What girl could say no to that? You know what, though? I think I've hit upon the secret of the attraction men have for women. My mother put me on to it. She said that whatever I do with Bobby, don't let him have sex with me until I have a wedding ring on my finger. And it's as simple as that. We have lots of sexy times together, but we've never had proper sex.'

Nick's reactions were a mix of incredulity and surprise, combined with a new respect for her discipline. 'It must be very hard for him to, ah, contain himself,' he offered.

Adrienne put her index finger into her month and sucked on it. 'Who says he contains himself?' Nick joined in her laughter.

'I can't wait for you to meet Bobby. You'll just love him. He's so smart, and he says he'll make partner at his law firm next year. We may even be able to move to the New York or London office. That would be a blast. He'll be perfect for me.'

She changed subject. 'The podcasts are going just great. People out there can't get enough of true crime stories. We're getting upwards of five thousand more paying subscribers every month. We're currently doing an eight-part series on one of Korea's greatest murder mysteries, the Hwaseong murders of the 1980s. We're bringing them to light for a whole new generation. People just lap them up. We jazz it up a bit, with funky conversation and banter, and the odd bit of dramatic music or K-Pop. We've done a few that are a bit off-topic, but the fans have liked them.'

Nick had forgotten how intoxicating and amusing she was. The elderly waiter was equally captivated, giving her far more attention than any other diner. He tried to top up her wine glass on seven or eight occasions, and he appeared almost to die of pleasure when Adrienne put her fingers on his arm to indicate she didn't want any more.

Conversation moved to the sexual harassment complaint early the year before. 'I'm so glad that you didn't go through with it,' Nick said. 'It would've been a terrible ordeal for us both, and I probably would've had to leave the University. Perhaps now I'd be a junior relieving lecturer at a small college in Idaho. It doesn't bear thinking about.'

Adrienne smiled. 'You know why I stopped it, don't you?'

'Yes. You felt guilty about William's death, and the Korean guards on the Railway.'

'That's not the whole reason. I thought she might have told you.'

Nick was puzzled. He let her continue.

'Emily. Your daughter.' Nick leaned forward. 'She stopped me after one of Tobias's Law of War lectures, the day before I found out the awful news of how your grandfather died in the camps. I don't know how she knew my name or what I looked like, but as I came out of the lecture she came up to me in her school uniform and asked if she could have a coffee with me.'

'She never said a word to me. She asked me about you, but I had no idea she'd contact you. What did she say?'

Adrienne smiled affectionately. 'You can be very proud of her. She introduced herself. She apologised for your behaviour and expressed concern for my welfare and wanted to know that I was being supported by the University, and by family and friends. I told her that the whole thing was pretty yucky and stressful. She even took my hand, like my best friend or sister. She was so concerned for me, I almost cried.

'And then she said how upset you were, how you were a good man, how you had a history of telling jokes that didn't come out right, and that there was no way that you would ever have wanted to upset me or proposition me. She said you didn't have a bad bone in your broken body. Her words. She's a formidable advocate, Nick. She'll make a wonderful lawyer. I could see how sincere she was, and I felt even more terrible about the whole situation.' She paused. 'I realised that for every course of action there are consequences. Collateral damage, you might say. As you *did* say once in one of your lectures when you talked about the bombing of Cambodia. Poor Emily was part of the damage – your whole family too.' Her eyes glistened in the half-light of the restaurant. 'I didn't want to be responsible for all that hurt.'

Nick felt very tender towards Adrienne at that moment and said that they should go. She nodded. He settled the bill, leaving the old man a healthy tip. They strolled back through the Old Town in the evening chill. Diners ate and drank away in the plazas and in the bars and cafés, and the locals went about their night-time business. Adrienne held his arm and rested her head on his shoulder as they laboured up the stairs to their apartment.

Nick woke as the first light of the day seeped through the shutters of their bedroom window. He could hear Adrienne's breathing, gentle and regular on the far side of the bed. He could just make out her face in the dark. She was lying on her back, as peaceful as a sleeping child.

His head was a little fuzzy from the night before. Adrienne had been at her radiant best all evening, as attractive and hilarious as she had ever been in his company. When they reached the apartment she had said that she had to ring her mother. Nick couldn't hide his dismay, and when she saw his face she howled with laughter. 'Ha! Joking.'

She agreed with his suggestion that they leave their mobile phones charging in the kitchen overnight so their sleep would not be disturbed. His desire for her had increased by the hour during the evening, and he looked forward to sharing a bed with her again. He lay in bed on his back, watching Adrienne undress, her back to him as she slipped off her bra and pulled on a pink nightshirt over her white underwear.

She got in beside him and thanked him again for a lovely night. She slumped forward, her shoulders bunched and her hair falling in front of her face. 'Oh God, I'm so tired. Jet lag. I feel as though I haven't slept for three days. Your wonderful company and the lovely food and the super-attentive old waiter have kept me alive tonight, but I have to sleep now.'

She looked apologetically at Nick, who mumbled that he understood. She wrapped herself in her sheets, creating the cocoon around her body that Nick had first seen in San Sebastian, and put her head on her pillow. She faced away from him, and she seemed to be asleep within seconds. It did not take him long to yield to his own tiredness.

Nick crept out quietly for his morning pee and checked his emails and messages. He sent a text to Emily:

Thanks for everything. I'm so proud of you, and grateful. Love you always. Xxx

Sadie had texted at about ten the night before:

Hi handsome. Hope you're liking Alicante. Say hi to the former complainant for me. Missing you xx.

Nick smiled and decided he would reply later.

Adrienne was still fast asleep, now facing him, when he slipped back into the bed. He moved into the middle, just inches from her. He lightly stroked her hair, and then brushed his fingers over her forehead and her cheeks. Her breathing remained constant. He put his hand under the sheet and was pleased to find that her protective cocoon had unravelled during the night.

He gently started stroking her tummy over her nightshirt, feeling the soft warmth under his hands. Adrienne continued to breathe normally, apparently deep in sleep. He withdrew his hand, lay back and decided to get another hour's sleep.

He was just drifting off when he felt a soft palm alight on his stomach and move slowly like a feather up towards his chest. He opened his eyes. Adrienne was balanced on one elbow, looking at him with a half-smile as she caressed his torso. He reached out and pulled her to him, and in seconds she was lying in his arms and kissing him. Her lips were soft and her tongue firm. He enveloped her in his arms and stroked her hair and felt her breasts pushing against his chest. Adrienne freed an arm and slid her hand down inside his underwear, and he moaned with encouragement as she clasped his erect penis. He moved his right hand down her back to her bottom. She was no longer wearing underwear. Their passionate kissing continued, with heavy breathing, as their hands explored each other.

And so, at long last, and after many false starts, Nick and Adrienne consummated their relationship. Their bodies moved together with a frenzy borne – at least in Nick's case – of a year of anticipation and frustration. He delighted in her abandon and her youth and her softness, and even when they had finished he could not let her go. He kissed her and smoothed her hair as she lay back, catching her breath while looking at the ceiling with a contented expression.

'Wow,' said Nick, looking intently at Adrienne's flushed face. 'You're gorgeous and amazing and sexy and beautiful. Thank you, thank you, thank you.'

After a minute Adrienne composed herself. Her face was serious-looking, but Nick thought he saw affection and happiness too. 'That was lovely. We should've done that a long time ago. But it won't happen again. I'm engaged.'

Nick looked closely at her. Surely she was joking? He couldn't tell.

She looked at her watch. 'The ferry leaves in an hour. There's no time for lovey-dovey talk. Get your ass out of bed and into the shower. I'll go get some croissants for our *desayuno*, and then we have to rush out.'

29

The ferry to Tabarca sailed from a berth by the marina, no more than ten minutes' walk from their apartment. Adrienne wore her bikini under her clothes, and Nick had put his swimming trunks in a small backpack with their towels.

It was another gloriously sunny day. The morning air was still crisp, but they could feel the air heat up as they hurried down the narrow streets and through plazas to the waterfront. Alicante, like everywhere else in Spain, didn't seem to come alive until late in the morning.

The ferry was a substantial boat, probably about a hundred feet long. Nick and Adrienne sat at the back of the top deck to take in the views and get some sun. They spent most of the one-hour journey smiling at a voluble group of a dozen or so Spanish women on some kind of hen's outing. They were dressed all in white, with identical gaily-coloured ribbons in their hair. A few carried papier mâché masks which fitted completely over their heads. He guessed this was a local wedding or engagement ritual.

Adrienne's phone pinged a few times as the ferry motored out of the harbour. She texted back. He asked her who she was texting. 'One of my new friends. Emily. She says that she and I are babes now.' Nick didn't hide his surprise. He rather liked the idea that Adrienne and Emily were friends.

Tabarca was an unimpressive-looking island, little more than a flat, rock outcrop with a few small buildings and a handful of trees. It was just over a mile long. He later learned that it had a standing population of less than a hundred, although thousands of day-trippers visited during the summer months.

Nick and Adrienne did what nearly all of the ferry passengers always did: they walked around the island for half an hour, grateful for the breeze that took the edge off the heat, went for a swim and had a long lunch until the afternoon ferry came to take them back to Alicante.

After their swim they found a table on the forecourt of one of the larger restaurants on the island. They ordered *cervezas* and *aguas con gas*. Nick looked at Adrienne. 'That was wonderful this morning.'

Adrienne smiled back. 'Yes, it was. From now on, I'd like to take control of our activities. I think we should have a quiet and early dinner.' Nick nodded. 'In fact, I have a small surprise for you. Nothing major, so don't get too excited.'

A long lunch lay ahead of them. They ordered lots of local seafood and local wines. They laughed when the hen party from the ferry sat at a long table not far from them.

'You know, Nick, we've hardly talked about Hem since we met yesterday. Our mutual friend, without whom ...' She let the unfinished sentence hang in the air.

'You're right. Did you know that the great man spent a little time in Alicante? I didn't until last week when I looked through a few biographies. He visited in 1959, I believe and at least twice in the thirties, I think in 1937 and 1938. He was reporting the Civil War, as you know, and was what we now call embedded with the Republican forces. But Franco's Fascists overwhelmed them, and the Republicans had to beat a retreat to Valencia and surrounding areas, including Alicante.'

'I think you've become a bit of a Hem expert, Nick. A change of career for you? You do have some sensational base material to launch the "New Nick".'

'Ha, I'll stick to the law. And I still haven't decided what I should do with William's materials. It's tempting to let Andrew McGregor have them, all the publicity too. Or I could give them to a university. They represent a complication to my life – and my sister's – that I don't need. One option I haven't thought through is to publish and promote them myself. But I'd need to hire a literary or PR agent to do that. There'd be interviews, articles, documentaries. All a bit daunting.'

'You could always write a book about how you tracked down the 1941 monograph and then the 1927 memoir, and how you filled in a few other gaps in the story,' Adrienne said. 'That way you could give some credit to your resourceful and beautiful research assistant.'

Nick laughed as he eyed up the plateful of little battered octopi that the waiter had brought. 'I'd love to give credit to my fiancée, for sure. But if I did write the book I'd have to omit all the best bits about you. Your charm, your humour, your sexiness.'

'Not to mention allegations that the author sexually harassed his collaborator, and subsequently ravished her in a Spanish city.' Adrienne shrieked with laughter, and a few of the women at the hen's table gave her stern looks, as if she was having more fun than them.

'Tell you what,' Adrienne went on. 'I've had an idea. Why don't you write a book about your granddad and the search for his memoirs, but make it a novel? You can quote his stuff verbatim but pretend it's fiction. That has lots of benefits. You can spice it up with lots of sex and mystery. And the literary world, if ever you get it published, would be able to dismiss all the stuff about Don Ernesto as mere fantasy.'

Nick rather liked the idea. It was a bit like having his cake and eating it too. 'A little like *The Sun Also Rises* itself. There's a nice irony there, a circularity.'

'And what's more, you can portray yourself as the hero. You

can be the suave, good-looking lecturer, witty and intelligent, surrounded by beautiful women who throw themselves at you and beg you to sleep with them.' Adrienne's eyes were flashing. 'And you could portray me as intelligent and competent, sexy and incredibly attractive too. There may even be a movie in it. I'm sure you would settle for Daniel Craig playing your part, or perhaps a slightly older Benedict Cumberbatch. Lucy Liu's too old to play me. Perhaps Gemma Chan?' Nick didn't know who Gemma Chan was but said nothing.

She paused for thought. 'There is one Korean actress who would be perfect. Her name is Kim Tae-Ri. I'll show you a YouTube clip of her later. She's the most beautiful Korean woman you'll ever see. A bit young, possibly, and I don't know if she speaks English.'

Nick felt a wave of tenderness for Adrienne. In a little over twenty-four hours she would fly out of his life, back to her mother and then to a husband, and one day children, in a faraway country, lost to him forever.

He moved the plate of *jamon iberico* to one side and put his hand on hers. '*Ma chérie.*' Adrienne was looking at him affectionately, as if she had read his thoughts. 'No one could ever do you justice in a movie. You are truly one of a kind.'

She twined her fingers in his. '*Gracias, mon vieux.* You are kind as well as perceptive.'

Adrienne looked towards the boats in the bay, her face radiating contentment. After a while she turned back to Nick and fixed her gaze on his. 'And what will become of us, Nick? We're lovers now. That sounds grand, I know, but it means a lot. To me, anyway. I don't sleep with just anybody.' She left her hand in Nick's.

'Thank God for that. And for what it's worth, nor do I. And it's so exciting, thrilling even, to say that we're lovers. I, we, have waited so long for this day.'

'Yes, but what does it all mean? You have Sadie. I have Bobby.

I don't feel guilty – how could I, in such a beautiful part of the world? But I might feel terrible in a few days. And you know what, I might end up in love with you, and what good would that do me? I might be miserable, my marriage over before it begins, and you sailing on in your life. I'll be another piece of wreckage, like some of the other women you've told me about. Cast aside, like Hadley and Pauline were.'

'Steady on. You're getting a bit dramatic there. We have a lovely connection, which is mutual and long-lasting, and it's come to a wonderful new state. That's to be treasured. Quite apart from my attraction to you, I have the highest respect and admiration for you, and an overriding wish and desire for you to be happy and fulfilled. Things are very good for you at the moment – Bobby, your job, being back in Korea, and, last but not least, your special sugar daddy friend.'

Adrienne smiled, locking her eyes on to Nick's. 'Yes, you're right. You are my special friend. My extra special friend. And I am yours too. I think I'm overthinking things at the moment. We've come a long way in the last twenty-four hours, you and I. We have what we Koreans call *seukinsip*, or skinship, which is a special and loving relationship.'

She looked again to survey the tranquil yet busy view from their table.

The spell was broken by the sound of music and clapping behind them. Some of the women from the hen party were shuffling and swaying down the centre of the restaurant, wearing the outsized papier mâché masks. One was a caricature of a black man with outsized red lips and white teeth; another resembled Stan Laurel, complete with bow tie and a bowler hat. A woman in a skimpy T-shirt had on the mask of a Saracen with pointy beard, hooked nose and huge yellow turban.

Behind the dancers were the players in the band, half a dozen men in shorts and black T-shirts and white sun-hats. Some were bashing away at their kettle drums; one was playing a flute, another a trumpet. In the background Nick could see a cluster of expensive white motor launches bobbing on the light-blue waters of the bay. Diners stood and clapped as the band shuffled outside to the terraces.

Nick could sense that Adrienne too had been possessed by the moment. She raised her glass to him. 'Here's looking at you, Nick. My former fiancé.' She burst out laughing, and he was overwhelmed by the warmth and joy he saw in her eyes. He raised his glass too.

By eight, as the light diminished and they were showering and dressing for dinner, they were exhausted. The sun had shone without break all day, and it had taken its toll. All of the energy they had had in the morning and at lunch had gone.

'I'm pooped,' said Adrienne as she brushed her hair in front of the mirror in the bedroom. 'Shall we make it a quick dinner? Just one course each? I rather like the idea of an early night. Besides, there are a couple of things I told you I'd show you later.'

She gave no clue what those things might be, and Nick didn't ask. He liked surprises.

The restaurant Adrienne had chosen was a seafood one, famous for its paella with squid ink and other regional delicacies. Neither of them was hungry after their big lunch, and one glass of wine sufficed for each.

Their dinner conversation was stilted to begin with, but the quality of the food perked them up. Once their dinner plates had been removed, Adrienne looked at Nick. 'You and I have had the most amazing conversations, you know. Not just this weekend, but ever since we met. I don't think there's anyone in the whole world who knows more about me than you, and I know a fair bit about you too. But there's one subject you've kept very quiet about, Nick. You've hardly ever mentioned your marriage and why you got divorced.'

'Really? I suppose because it was such a long time ago. A lot has happened in the last ten years.'

'Tell me about it. Why did the marriage end? Your idea, or hers?'

'Do you want to know? It was hers. Laura's. She sat me down one day and told me that she was unhappy. With me, the marriage, and everything.'

'You surprise me. I thought you'd have been a very good husband.' She paused, and Nick looked at her to see if she was winding him up.

'Well, I thought I was, but Laura saw it differently. She said that I'd withdrawn from her, gone cold, and spent too much time either socialising with colleagues and friends or doing things by myself. In essence that I didn't work hard enough at the marriage.'

'And? Did she have a point?'

'Yes, I'm afraid she did. The romance and the adventure of the early days, they'd all faded bit by bit. I took my eye off the ball, as Hem might say, and I feel bad about that. And so you don't have to ask, no, there was no infidelity. She simply said that she'd be happier on her own unless I changed for the better straight away. Buck up or out the door was the choice.'

'But you must have seen the error of your ways and tried to patch things up. Weekends away, romantic dinners, gifts?'

Nick smiled at Adrienne. 'Well, I tried those things, but they didn't seem to work. After a month or two we had a long heart to heart, and I agreed to move out. I didn't want to, but she insisted, and that was that. It was tough on the kids, who ended up staying with Laura in the house. Not seeing them every day was hard. And I missed walking and playing with Fifi the family dog on a daily basis too. The separation and divorce were amicable, and I have nothing but praise and affection for Laura. She was, and still is, a warm, loving, intelligent and capable woman, and a terrific mother, and she was a devoted wife.'

It was Adrienne's turn to smile. 'She sounds like the perfect woman. What more could a man want?"

Nick toyed with his wine glass for a few seconds. 'Yes, you're right. I gave it a lot of thought at the time and have done ever since. I'm afraid my self-analysis concentrates wholly on my shortcomings. I just took her for granted, and while it's convenient to blame other things like my job and raising the children, the simple and obvious explanation is that I stuffed it up. I didn't make a proper effort, and I ended up getting what I deserved. Ten years of bachelorhood and counting.'

Adrienne appeared to be enjoying Nick's discomfort. 'Well, if you don't mind me saying, you do seem to be thriving on the single life.'

'Yes, I do like the freedom. And the, er, variety of bachelorhood. But you can't get away from the sense of failure, of not having had the right characteristics, the right stuff, to make the marriage work.'

'Don't give up yet, *mi viejo*. You're still young enough for a second attempt.'

Nick laughed. 'Very true, but I'm not on the lookout. If the right person came along then yes I'd be interested, but I'm not sure it would be fair to foist myself on any woman. I think I'd be a bit of a handful. I've got used to my own company, you know.'

'I know you're with Sadie now, and that appears to be going tickety-boo, but have you ever thought of going back to Laura? The perfect woman, after all. It's not such a far-fetched idea. People's priorities and wishes change, and she may even like having you around again. Can't imagine why, but she might.'

'Ha, you're in fine form today. I'm not sure she'd have me, as I don't think I've changed for the better in the years since we separated, but if I didn't have Sadie I think I might give it a bit of thought. Stranger things have happened, I dare say. My children would be shocked but pleased, too, I think.'

Outside the restaurant they looked for a grocery store so

Adrienne could buy a few things she needed. They found one quickly and made their way arm-in-arm through the narrow streets, past the diners on the pavements and up the steps back to their apartment.

As Nick fumbled in his pockets for the house key, Adrienne stood on the step in front of him and put her hands on his shoulders. She looked at him earnestly. 'Nick, you know you took charge this morning? Well, as I said, tonight I'm taking charge. Okay?'

Nick shrugged. '*Bien sûr. Tu es la chef de la nuit.*'

Inside Adrienne said that she first had to call her mother, to talk about arrangements for her flight to Paris. 'After that I'd like to show you some videos.'

While Adrienne harangued and shouted at her mother, Nick went to the small bedroom and called Sadie. She sounded pleased to hear from him and said she was having a quiet Saturday night at home, catching up on some work. He told her about Tabarca Island and the Old Town. 'You'd love Alicante, Sadie. It has beauty and charm, and what's more it has—' He paused, searching for the right word. 'It has integrity.'

She said she'd love to spend a weekend there with him in the future. 'And how is the young temptress? Has she wormed her way into your affections?'

'Well, sort of, I suppose. She's good company, despite the fact that we don't have a huge amount in common. She has much more energy than me. She dragged me out to a nearby island for the day, where we had a swim, and insisted that afterwards we hike up a steep hill to visit the castle that overlooks the city. So I'm quite tired.' He paused. 'I *am* looking forward to getting back to London tomorrow night, and to seeing you. Dinner on Monday?'

'Yes, I'd like that. I've been missing you. In a funny sort of way I'm a bit jealous, you holidaying with another woman. Thank God she's engaged to someone. Otherwise I'd be beside myself with worry. I'm not convinced you're good at saying no.'

'Don't you worry, my dear. She's spoken for, as you say, and she's constantly talking about her fiancé and about her wedding plans.' They bade each other good night. Nick stared out the window for a minute.

He brushed his teeth and sat in his boxers and T-shirt in the bed, waiting for Adrienne to finish her call. He checked out the *Guardian* online. The Brexit saga was lurching from crisis to crisis. He despaired at the lack of leadership from Theresa May, at her stubbornness, and was equally dismayed by the vindictiveness of different factions in the Tory party, constantly undermining the PM. And as for Corbyn and the Labour Party ... Nick had always voted Labour, to the surprise of many of his friends and colleagues, but he could see they were out of touch with ninety-five per cent of the population. British politics was the laughing stock of Europe, he thought.

Before Nick could work himself into a state about the prospect of a buffoon like Boris Johnson becoming prime minister, Adrienne emerged from the bedroom wearing her nightshirt. She got into bed beside him, their thighs touching. She had her laptop with her, and two purple lollipops.

'First up,' she said, 'let's have a lollipop. Suck it, don't crunch it, you'll see why soon.' Nick did as he was told.

She opened the laptop and clicked on the YouTube app. 'Have I ever mentioned the famous Korean film *The Handmaiden?* It's only three years old. It's a wonderful movie. Romantic. Suspenseful. Beautifully filmed. And the two lead actresses are mesmerising. It's sexy too. It's all about a young Korean woman who starts work as a handmaiden, a personal servant, to a rich young married Japanese woman in Korea during the Japanese occupation in the 1930s. She actually plans to kill the Japanese woman, but we needn't worry about that now.' Adrienne giggled. Her thigh felt warm and comforting against his.

'Here, this is the famous bath scene.' She clicked on a link.

In a bath in the middle of a dimly lit room sat the Japanese woman, probably in her late twenties, her hair up and her bare shoulders rising above the steamy foam and suds. She was sucking on a purple lollipop, while the handmaiden, dressed in servant clothes, was adding hot water to the bath and preparing to sponge down her mistress. Nick could not take his eyes off the beautiful women. They were like dolls, with flawless features.

Adrienne paused the video. 'You see the lollipop? It's an old Korean custom. Japanese too, I think. It's good manners to sweeten the breath before kissing.' Nick could feel himself beginning to get aroused.

'It looks like the mistress may want the handmaiden to kiss her,' said Nick, cursing himself for stating the obvious.

'You'll have to watch and see.'

She restarted the video. The mistress sucked on the lollipop, leaving a purple stain on her tongue. Nick fantasised about substituting his cock for the lollipop, as he was sure the film director intended him to. The mistress said she had a sharp tooth which was hurting, and the distressed servant girl rushed over to put her thumb into the older woman's mouth, to soothe it and possibly to dull the sharpness by rubbing the tooth. Back and forth she moved her thumb, the rest of her hand cradling her mistress's cheek. Their faces were only inches apart, and their eyes met. It was a genuinely erotic moment. The camera moved down to the mistress's breasts, resting in the soapy waves. The video ended.

'Now,' said Adrienne, turning to him and putting the laptop away. 'I have a sore tooth, right where the Japanese woman's one was. You know what to do.' Nick moved onto his knees, facing her, and put his left hand on her neck behind her head. With his right he eased his thumb, palm down, into her mouth, and slowly pushed it in. He found a couple of teeth at the back. He slowly started massaging them. Adrienne closed her eyes, and said – as best she could – how nice it felt. Nick felt her wet tongue against his thumb, and her lips began to open and close and suck on him as he moved his thumb forward and back. His pulse accelerated.

After half a minute, she took his hand away. 'Now I'm going to teach you the Korean kiss. You stay there, facing me. Close your eyes.'

Nick could feel the warmth of her face, inches from his. He could also smell the lollipop on her breath. He waited, then felt her lips touching his, light as a feather. They moved slowly to the left of his mouth and back again. It tickled, but in a sensuous way, the sensuousness heightened by her aroma, the warmth of her nearby face, and her shallow breathing.

He was entranced, as though he had been allowed into a new world, a world of mystery and eroticism. He pulled her to him and tried to push his tongue into her mouth. She pulled back. 'No. This is my time now.' She smiled at him. 'And now, for the *pièce de résistance*, the best sex scene you will see in a movie for a long time.'

'Bring it on,' said Nick, feeling as though he were Adrienne's handmaiden. Again they sat side by side, thigh to thigh, and Adrienne restarted the video. The two women were in bed, for the first time, it seemed, and clothed. They both looked surprised, as though superior forces were bringing them together. They started kissing – initially the Korean kiss, Nick noted with satisfaction – and soon their passions were leading them into nakedness and a frantic exploration of each other's body.

Adrienne, watching intently, slipped her hand inside Nick's boxers and started rubbing his erect penis. He let out a little sigh, of encouragement as much as of pleasure. At the same time he moved his hand between her legs. She wasn't wearing any underwear.

The clip finished after a few minutes of moaning and intertwining of bodies. Adrienne was right. It *was* a sexy scene.

He took off his T-shirt and moved to take off Adrienne's. She stopped him. 'Slow down. We have lots of time. Remember, I'm in charge. Now, lie down on your back.'

As he moved down the bed Adrienne turned out the lights then knelt beside his centre. She put both her hands on his penis. 'Do you know what this means, Nick?'

'Is it a sexy Korean ritual, like a tea ceremony?'

'No, it just means I like putting my hands on your *jot*, your *go-chu*.' No translation into English was needed this time.

Adrienne giggled, moved her head down and enveloped him in her mouth.

30

They were a few minutes late for their 10 a.m. rendezvous on the Promenade for their guided tour of Alicante. Nick was minded to skip it, but Adrienne, always with a thirst for knowledge of new places, insisted. When they woke they had time for some more lovemaking, and a little time to shower, pack and tidy the apartment. They left their bags with a neighbour. There was no time for breakfast.

Their group of tourists, perhaps a dozen of them, followed Javier, their young and enthusiastic guide, as they learned about Alicante's history. It seemed that all the great European invaders had held the city at some stage – the Greeks, Phoenicians, Romans and Moors, and in more modern times the Republicans and then the Falangists. Each left behind some vestige of influence in the form of churches and castles, walls and streets.

Adrienne appeared to absorb every informed word from the bearded and slightly built Javier. Nick, however, couldn't stop thinking of her soft lips, her breasts pushing against his chest, how she had cried when he told her he loved her as they made love that morning. She showed no sign that she might be thinking of similar things.

After the tour they walked back to one of the plazas in the Old Town, not far from their apartment, and sat out under an umbrella for lunch. They had about two hours before they needed to fetch their luggage and head to the airport. Nick ordered a *cerveza* and Adrienne *un agua minerale con gas*. There were faint beads of perspiration on her forehead and upper lip. Her face shone with colour and energy. They looked at each other, saying nothing, as they sipped their drinks, relieved to be sitting down after three hours of walking.

'I've had the most wonderful weekend, thank you, *ma chère amie*,' Nick said. 'You've been a revelation.' There was much more he wanted to say but Adrienne cut him short.

'Don't talk like that. Save it, if you feel you must say things, for the airport. Me, I don't feel I have to say anything like that. Let the memories carry all the sentiments. Let's enjoy our lunch. How about a paella to share, washed down with a bottle of *vinho blanco*? Besides, I've been thinking quite a bit over the last day or so and have made a few observations which I'll tell you about shortly. I've even jotted them down on my phone.'

Nick was intrigued. Adrienne was smiling, radiant as always.

The harsh midday sun filled the plaza, as locals and tourists alike sought refuge under the white-and-red umbrellas of the terrace restaurants.

'Any further thoughts on what you'll do with your Grandpa's papers?'

Nick shook his head. 'No, I've had my mind on other things the last day or two.' They both smiled. 'But I do need to make a decision soon. I got a text yesterday from my friend Andrew McGregor, pestering me to let him publish them.'

'I still like the idea of you writing a novel. Fact disguised as fiction. That way you can let your imagination run riot. Most importantly, you can make me a big part of the story. And you can add all sorts of embellishments. You can make me glamorous and seductive. You can change my age, my job, my dress style. My nationality or race, even. You can invent things about me. I won't mind at all, as long as you don't make me out to be mean or greedy or boring.'

Nick laughed. 'I would never in a million years think of you as mean or greedy. And you're not boring. Definitely not.'

Adrienne laughed too. 'And if you do write a book, there will be film rights and options to consider. I hope you'll let me have casting approval for my role. I want to be the *ssang-yeon*, the crazy bitch. You have to make sure that Kim Tae-Ri gets the part. She played the handmaiden in that movie.'

'Ah. The exquisite, sexy and innocent-but-not-so-innocent handmaiden. Yes, she'd be perfect. How will I be able to think of anyone else?'

Their paella arrived on a huge black plate. Pieces of prawn and calamari, and a few pink octopus tentacles, poked out of the saffron-coloured rice. The waiter poured out the wine.

'So, tell me, dear Adrienne. You say you've made a few observations this weekend.'

Adrienne swallowed her mouthful of rice. 'Yes. It's been fun for me getting to know you too, you know. It's not just one-way traffic. Believe it or not, I think you're quite an interesting man. I've been thinking about you, and about Hem, and I've noticed a number of similarities. Not to look at, obviously, but you *do* have a few things in common.'

'Really? I'm listening.' She was scrolling through her phone.

'Ha, here they are. My first observation, and I don't want you to take this the wrong way, but you're a bit of a chauvinist, sexist even. Just like Ernest.' Adrienne studied his face, perhaps worried that he'd be offended.

Nick was more surprised than offended. 'Oh? Sorry you think that. Hemingway was a classic macho type, cruel to women, a misogynist many would say. I can see why he's a sexist. Me? I much prefer women's company. I like to think I treat all women with respect and a sense of equality.'

'Yes, but all men think that. You often say things which indicate you judge women by their beauty or lack of it. You constantly comment about my looks, for example. I'm worth far more than my looks. They're irrelevant. What matters is my heart, my brain, my aspirations, my achievements, my humour even. These are the things that I want others to appreciate, and for men to be attracted to.'

'But I admire *all* those things, Adrienne. I'm possibly your greatest admirer. You're a very accomplished and successful woman.' He knew this sounded unconvincing.

'Yes, I believe you. But whenever you talk of other women, Kathy and Sadie, for instance, you present them as cardboard cut-outs, judged by their sex-appeal or bitchiness. Just like all of the heroines of Hem's novels: Catherine Barkley, Brett, Maria. It's almost as though you've taken a leaf out of his book. Unwittingly, I accept.'

She took another mouthful of rice. 'What's more, I've been observing you closely this weekend, spying on you when you think I'm not looking. I watch you eye up other women occasionally. When you do you always look at their faces, then their tits or crotch, or their bums if we're walking behind them. It's so superficial. It's a bit creepy, too.' She leaned forward to put her hand on his.

He was upset, and shocked because he knew she was right. He was about to defend himself by suggesting that all men and many women were like that, or that what she was describing was primal behaviour programmed into men by their DNA. Instead he said, 'Fair enough. I'll definitely think about what you've said. I'd hate to think anyone thought I was creepy.'

Adrienne laughed. 'No, you're not creepy. You're adorable and funny. Sweet, too. Especially this weekend.'

Nick felt a bit better now. 'And what else do I have in common with the greatest novelist of the twentieth century?'

Adrienne looked again at the notes on her phone. 'You and Hem are both fixated by sport. Hem used sports metaphors all the time and was consumed by boxing and American football, baseball, big-game hunting and bullfighting, if you can count them as sports. You, you spend so much time watching soccer on TV and reading thousands of newspaper articles about sport. Remember when we were in San Seb and then Burguete? It seemed that every evening our activities together were dictated by the schedule for the World Cup.'

'Hang on, the World Cup's only once every four years. People are allowed to watch it without being called obsessive.'

'Yes, yes, I know, but it's a daily thing for you. You follow Arsenal like a true believer, even though you told me they've been in decline for more than a decade. And you use sporting expressions quite often too, especially in your lectures. Here, I've jotted a few down.' She read from her phone. 'Kicking for touch, dropping the ball, offside, below the belt, curveball. Just like Hemingway, although less so in your case. It's just that the sports were not always the same: built like a line-backer, sucker punch, hitting a home run, getting to first base. Classic Hem metaphors.'

Nick felt himself on surer ground. 'Nearly all men, and quite a few women too, follow sport avidly. It's a normal thing to do. It makes us connect with our fellow humans, as a community.'

Adrienne smiled sweetly. 'I know. It's just that hardly any of my other friends are so into sport.'

'And what, pray, my former fiancée, is the next similarity?'

'Okay. Now, I don't want you to take this as a criticism at all, it's just my impression. You and Hemingway, both obsessed about your looks and appearance.' Nick snorted.

'I'll start with Hem. By all accounts he was fanatical about his looks. He exercised, so he remained muscly and fit, and was a snappy dresser. You can see it in the photos of him in Spain in the 1920s. Suits fitted him well, hats and berets at a dashing angle, tie always tight around his neck. His 'tache always looks carefully manicured. He was obviously proud of his strong jaw. Every photo seemed to show his jaw.'

'That's all very well, but I can't see where I fit into this.'

'It is a bit of a stretch, I suppose. But I did laugh last year when we were in Spain. You had bought all these flashy clothes, very on-trend and youthful, and they hadn't been worn before. And your grooming efforts were, er, unique.' She giggled. 'You'd shaved your pubes. Very cool and trendy. Left one or two grey hairs behind, admittedly, and it was hilarious to see a couple of nicks where your razor had dug in.'

Adrienne's face was red with laughter. 'But your effort in trying to shave your hairy back was a disaster. I presume you must have read somewhere that women are put off by hairy backs? Never worried me. But you must've stretched your hands over each shoulder and dragged the razor in a diagonal line through the tangled growth as if a lawn mower had zig-zagged across it.'

'Well, okay, fair enough. I just wanted to look presentable to you. Can't blame me too much for that. Having said that, I wasn't expecting you to ever see my naked body, but you never know how things might turn out. As my grandpa would no doubt have said, you should always be prepared.' He finished his wine. 'Sure, I admit to a bit of vanity, of minding how I appear to others, but I don't see a major comparison to our friend Hem. I think you're clutching at straws on that one.'

Adrienne didn't bother to push back. The waiter returned and took their plates. Nick had lost his appetite in the last few minutes, but Adrienne seemingly had a big lunch in mind. She ordered another bottle of wine and the dessert menu.

'And the next similarity? I hope there are some which put me in a good light?'

'Not many, I'm afraid.' Adrienne burst into laughter again. 'The next one is you're both moody. Hemingway was notorious for losing his temper, and also for withdrawing into sullen moods. I see that in you too, quite often. One minute you're animated and switched on, and then for no apparent reason you just clock out. Never bad-tempered, I admit, but it's a bit disconcerting for me, as I think I might have offended you.'

'Really? I've always seen myself as very even-tempered, but perhaps I'm not. Admittedly I will consciously say nothing rather than say something unpleasant, but I wouldn't say that I was moody.'

'Well, perhaps you just find my conversation boring from time to time,' said Adrienne.

Nick realised to his dismay that he was getting into a bad mood listening to all these criticisms, but he was determined not to prove Adrienne right. He smiled and said in an upbeat but still slightly acid manner, 'Perhaps that *is* the reason. And what other humiliations have you got for me on your list?'

'You and Hem are both heavy drinkers. Ernest was famous for his consumption of liquor. You can see that from *The Sun Also Rises* and from your granddad's account. And while you do not, at least to my knowledge, go on boozy benders like Hem, you do seem to be able to knock back a bottle or two of wine every day.'

Just then the waiter arrived with the bottle that Adrienne had ordered. Nick raised a quizzical eyebrow. Adrienne dissolved into giggles. 'I'm learning from you how to drink.'

Nick knew that drinking had always been an Achilles heel for him. He drank far more than all recommended levels, which gave him an inverted satisfaction of sorts at defying the spoilsports of the medical profession. A bottle of wine a night was a frequent occurrence, but the fact that he was able to give up alcohol for a month or two every year convinced him that he was not an alcoholic. Which was quite different from doing and saying risky and ill-considered things when he had had one or two glasses too many.

'I protest! Hemingway was a gargantuan boozer. Mary Welsh referred to it as over-drinking. Whisky, rum, beer, champagne, French wine, absinthe, Sauternes we've now learned. He'd have a few for lunch and start again at sundown. I do think I'm a bit more, ah, moderate?' Adrienne nodded and raised her glass to Nick.

The bells from the church at the other side of the plaza rang to announce that another hour had passed. The yellowy–pink sandstone walls of the church reflected the harsh sunlight, with faded blood-red lettering on the walls recalling some religious or historical events that Nick could not identify. A few tourists posed in front of the columns forming part of the church's imposing entrance. 'Let's move on from drinking,' Nick said genially. 'Do tell me more about these alleged similarities with Hemingway.'

Adrienne looked up from her phone. 'Only a few more to go. I've drawn a long bow here, but I've noticed that you and Hem both have, or had, this thing for younger women.'

Nick stared at her.

She was talking very quickly now. 'As Hemingway got older his preference for women seemed to be for younger ones. Agnes in Italy and both Hadley and Pauline were a few years older than him. By the time he took up with Pauline he was only in his mid-twenties.' Adrienne paused. 'I've just had a thought. Perhaps he had mother issues as a young man?'

'He most certainly did. His mother was a very domineering woman. When he came back from the war he was resentful and full of disdain for her. In fact, Hadley too had a very difficult and controlling mother.'

'That's fascinating, Nick. There's obviously a lot of it about, even now.' They both laughed. 'And perhaps you had mother issues once too? We could explore that another time.'

Nick wondered when that time might be, but Adrienne returned to her earlier comment. 'Martha Gellhorn and Mary Welsh were about eight or nine years younger than him, so you can see a trend there. And that trend followed through to his fiction. Maria was only about nineteen in *For Whom the Bell Tolls*. Nineteen! And in *Across the River and Into the Trees*, the hero was fifty or thereabouts and he was in love with an eighteen-year-old girl. That was apparently based on a real-life infatuation with an Italian girl. Talk about unhealthy and creepy. It borders on the criminal.'

Nick was unsure where he fitted into this.

'There are similarities, I'm afraid. You said your wife was about the same age as you. And here you are with me. I'm fifteen years younger, and at times it feels to me that you're twenty-five or even thirty years older. Not always, though.' She put her hand on his. 'At times you act younger than me. Like a little boy, and you're cute when you're like that. But the fact remains, here you are, on a romantic holiday, with a much younger woman.'

Nick was about to protest that this was not intended to be a romantic holiday, that things had happened by accident almost, but it would sound a bit unconvincing. She was right.

'Don't forget that Sadie, who is the closest to being my girlfriend, is the same age as me.'

'True, but perhaps she's the exception that proves the rule. That woman from Durham University, the law lecturer who would visit you last year for sexy weekends in London, isn't she more than ten years younger than you?'

Nick nodded.

'Plus, I've seen you interact with your female students. They all fawn over you. They sit at the front, making eyes at you, the famous, suave and witty lecturer; the handsome man who knows so much. And at faculty drinks functions you're always surrounded by a bevy of pretty girls.'

'Hardly. Sure, I like the company of attractive women. What man doesn't? And they're all intelligent too. But it's all very innocent. I never cross the boundaries, and none of them has ever propositioned me or anything like that.'

'Surely you can't be so blind? They stand there as you spout forth, with their tits half hanging out, laughing hysterically at every vaguely amusing word from you, playing with their hair or the stems of their wine glasses. Some of them are begging for it.'

Nick crossed then uncrossed his legs. 'Sorry, but you've got it all wrong. I'll make a point of being more observant, more aware, next term, but you mustn't forget the women students are my daughter's age. It's strictly hands off.'

'I *know* you fancy young women. When you were in the shower this morning I looked at your Instagram page. Nice pics of Alicante, I have to say. But I looked at who you're following. Quite a few young women. Movie stars, pop stars, models and unknowns. Plus, I had to smile when I saw that you're now following Kim Tae-Ri and Gemma Chan.'

Nick knew when he was defeated. 'Yes. Okay. I admit it. I do like looking at pretty women occasionally. It's not a crime, you know.'

'I know that. But just to round off this particular bit of our conversation, there is another similarity with the great Hemingway. A tiny one, admittedly. Here you are, telling me several times in the last twenty-four hours how much you love me and adore me – and no, I'm not objecting – and there's Hemingway who spent the last twelve years of his life infatuated with the Italian girl who was only eighteen when they met. Her name was Adriana. And mine is Adrienne. A cosmic coincidence, wouldn't you say?'

Nick laughed. 'Good for you for picking up on that. But there are two big differences. One, an age gap of thirty-one years is not the same as a fifteen-year one. And, more importantly, and this is where I feel that at least I've got one over the great man, his relationship with Adriana was never consummated, as far as we know.'

They both laughed. Nick looked at his watch. They still had half an hour before they had to retrieve their luggage and head for the airport. Adrienne beckoned the waiter over and ordered apple pie and dark chocolate gelato to share, and two glasses of the local bubbly.

'Well, Adriana, my teenage fiancée, what is the final similarity? I'm shattered; a broken man. You might as well put me to the sword, like a matador. Why don't you take that knife there, pretend it's a dagger, and then stab me in the back of my neck and put me out of my misery?'

'No, let's wait until our bubbles arrive.' Adrienne looked at her empty wine glass. 'You're such a terrible influence on me. I drink far more in your company than with anyone I've ever known. It's like being with Hem. It's fun, though. I'm not complaining.'

31

The heat of the day was making Nick's shirt sticky, and he drank a glass of water from their table. He looked at Adrienne as the waiter poured their drinks. She had colour in her cheeks.

She raised the flute of pink bubbles to him and looked him in the eye. 'And the final similarity, Don Nicolas, is that you are both incredibly exciting men.'

Nick laughed, startled.

'Let me explain. I'll start with Hem first. Virtually every biography, at least the two or three I've read, refers to his aura, his charisma. The word 'charisma' was virtually invented for him. So often we've read about his presence, his physicality. Women noticed it and were drawn to him. They couldn't help themselves. Men too wanted to be in his orbit, his inner circle. This was apparent even during the Paris years, when he was only in his twenties, and unknown. Very few people have that magnetism. But you do.'

Nick looked at her with disbelief. 'Do please explain.'

'You have charisma, too, but in a different way. Yours isn't a physical one, or a dangerous one, like Hemingway's was. No, yours is more intelligent, funny, a life-and-soul-of-the-party-type appeal. Everyone knows you can be hilarious and clever, and that is *so* attractive. And when you combine that with your success and your reputation, and your good looks, the combination is almost irresistible. You're a bit of a babe.'

'I think you've had a glass or two too many.'

'No. From the first day I met you in the flesh, at that Law of War lecture almost two years ago, I knew that you were someone very special. In fact—' Adrienne obviously thought better of saying what she had been about to.

'But when I got to know you, it was like your appeal just exploded. When you started supervising my thesis you showed such knowledge, and at the same time didn't belittle me or make me feel stupid. I *so* used to look forward to having coffees with you, and to your lectures. And then we went to see that French movie. I was half in love with you by then, and I wanted you to kiss me, or invite me back to your place. But you didn't.'

'Of course I didn't. I *couldn't*. You were a student of mine. And I had no idea you felt like that.'

'I felt let down, and confused. You were happy to spend time in my company, away from the university; you seemed to enjoy being with me and asking me personal questions and showing a real interest in me and my life. And then zippo. No effort to move things to the next stage. No explanation. It felt as though you were just toying with me. As though your jokes and stories, your interest in me, were for your benefit and not for mine.'

Adrienne was playing with her cutlery, and looking over Nick's shoulder at the church across the plaza.

'And then you said that silly thing to me at the cocktail party for the graduate students. I thought it was just another half-flirtatious line from you but with no follow-through, no indication that you actually liked me. So when Kathy Mulligan picked up on it I let her do it, and thought I'd punish you for rejecting me, or at least for not pursuing me.

'And in the days after the cocktail party I gave it heaps of thought. I realised that I knew very little about you, that I knew hardly anything about your personal life, your beliefs and values. You often deflected my questions about those things.

The overall impression I got was that it had all been one-way.'

Adrienne paused and wiped a tear from her left eye with her finger. Nick could see truth in what Adrienne was saying, and a pang of guilt and sadness swept through him. He felt naked, exposed, as he had been when Laura had asked him to leave their marriage.

'I'm so sorry you felt like that, Adrienne. To hurt you or confuse you, or to play with your emotions, was not part of any plan. Perhaps it all stemmed from the constraint that I felt with you being one of my students.'

Adrienne smiled at him, like a mother to her favourite child. 'Perhaps you're right.'

'And I hope you don't feel like that now? I'd be mortified if you do.'

'No, funnily enough, it's worked out fine in the end. Better than I could have hoped. Circumstances have worked in our favour. If you hadn't been stood down for a month, you wouldn't have researched William's war, and I wouldn't have been your research assistant, and I wouldn't have gone to Spain with you, twice, and you wouldn't have made love to me, and I wouldn't be sitting here now, having a wonderful lunch with the most interesting and exciting man I've ever known.' Adrienne emptied her glass with a flourish.

Nick smiled. 'I'm struggling to take it all in. For every two nice things you've said about me you've identified seven or eight things which are flaws in my character. It'll take me a while to process it all.' He paused for a second or two. 'But I certainly don't see any charisma in me. I like to think I have more to offer than most law lecturers, but I'm not all that different from all those men in cardigans with dandruff on their shoulders. And I can see no similarity with Hemingway. None at all.'

'But there is. You *do* have a presence. Students notice it when you walk into the lecture room or the student caféteria. Even in Spain the waiters and hotel staff treat you with respect. It's almost as if they sense your qualities.'

Nick thought Adrienne was talking rubbish, but said nothing.

'That's just your make-up. You have a huge vocabulary. You can talk knowledgeably on any subject under the sun, and I'm still trying to work out whether you know lots about a few things or just a little about everything, or even if you're full of bullshit.'

They both laughed. 'And you have a story for everything, usually based on experience and often at your own expense. You're a great listener too and, like Hemingway, you drill down to get answers and information on subjects you don't know much about. These are all wonderful character traits. It makes you exciting and attractive to others. To me.'

'I wonder,' said Nick. 'I may have okay social skills, but exciting? Don't think so. Hemingway was a brawling, hunting, boozing, shooting type of guy. So far from me.'

'You're wrong. Remember that night in Pamplona? I'd had such a wonderful time at the piano in the hotel bar, and yes, I'm sorry for standing you up that night. I felt very close to you. And then we were accosted by that American guy Carl. And you did just what Hem would've done. You whacked him. I was so proud of you. I had no idea you'd do that. Never has a man had a fist fight over me. It was one of the proudest moments of my life. I felt safe, loved, protected.'

'I surprised myself that night too. But I'm certainly no brawler or womaniser like Ernest.'

Adrienne gazed steadily at him. 'Let's not forget that you've slept with many, many women. Dozens, as you told me last year.'

Nick smiled. 'Different times. Besides, you can't believe everything I say.' He leaned over and put both his hands on hers. 'We must be off in a few minutes, but I want you to know I've had the most amazing and special time with you, and in this magical city and country. You're about to embark on a big adventure with your real fiancé, and I'm excited for you, but I hope you'll always have a soft spot for your sugar daddy billionaire, your much maligned and bruised one-time fiancé.'

Adrienne's face showed tenderness. He squeezed her hands. He wanted to tell her to break off her engagement to Bobby and marry him instead but he knew that he could never satisfy her spirit or her energy.

'I'll have a million soft spots for you. You've taught me so much, and you've been the best companion in every sense. If Bobby is half as good company as you I'll be a happy gal. And if we have a boy then we might just call him Nicolas, spelt the Spanish way. Or perhaps Ernesto.'

Nick looked at her, infatuated and flattered beyond measure. How he loved being with Adrienne. All the U-turns and surprises, the hidden depths, the honesty and directness, all parcelled up like a gift with gold wrapping paper and lace. But it was time to leave. He signalled to the waiter to bring the bill.

They found themselves short of time at the airport. Nick's plane was first to depart, and they didn't have much time for protracted goodbyes. He promised he'd attend her wedding. He could feel the tears on her cheeks as she gave him a Korean kiss.

After an eternity spent in the queue waiting to get through security, Nick looked back. Adrienne was still where he had left her. He waved. She waved back and mouthed 'I love you'. He turned away.

As a young man Nick had begun to appreciate the complexity of women and relationships. Now, thirty years later and as he sat in his easyJet seat at 35,000 feet, he knew that he was no closer to understanding the mystery of women. He would never understand the inner workings of his former fiancée, but he knew too that was always how it would be and how it should be. He closed his eyes in his cramped seat and turned his thoughts once more to Adrienne's soft lips and kisses.

32

'Oh no! Not again,' said Sadie as she let Nick into her apartment. The rain was crashing down outside. It had rained ever since the plane had landed the night before. He was carrying a bunch of white lilies which he had calculated was expensive and pretty enough to please her but not so extravagant as to cause alarm.

'You've been sleeping with her. How could you? I can see it in your face.'

'That's my tan you're seeing.'

'Don't be flippant. I can see you're in love with her, and I specifically warned you about that. Admit it.' Sadie glared at him.

He decided to tell the truth. In the brief moment since he saw her face after she had opened the door, he had done what he had learned at law school. He had performed what his lecturer had called a calculus of the risk, and decided that denial would be ultimately futile so it would be safer and easier to confess. Whatever that would mean for his relationship with Sadie.

'You're right. I'm sorry. Adrienne and I did, ah, sleep together, on our second night, but no I'm not in love. And nor is she, and she's heading back to Korea to get married and in all likelihood I'll never see her again. I'm sorry, Sadie. I can promise you I didn't intend it. The place in Alicante had two bedrooms. It just sort of happened, and I had trouble resisting. Simple as that.'

He proffered the flowers, embraced as they were in thick peach-coloured paper held together by a white satin bow. Sadie wouldn't take them, so he walked to the kitchen and put them in the sink. A meat casserole was sizzling in the oven.

'How *could* you? I trusted you. You're so weak. *Men* are so weak. You're all the same. You see a pretty young girl and whammo. Of course you couldn't resist. It was a set-up, don't you see? It was her idea to go to Spain with you. She got what she wanted, and you fell for it. You're so fucking pathetic.'

Nick was shaking his head.

'Where's the trust, Nick? Do I mean nothing to you?' Her face was red and tearful.

'That's unfair, Sadie. You know I think the world of you. I think you're amazing in a hundred ways. You're intelligent and successful.' He was about to acknowledge their sexual intimacy but caught himself in time. 'It was a one-off, physical thing. I'm not emotionally involved with her, and as I say I'll probably never see her again. You have nothing to worry about. It needn't have any impact on our relationship, on us.'

'You can't be bloody serious. It has everything to do with us. I now know that you're a cheat and a liar and untrustworthy. And disloyal to me. Every time I look at you in the future I'll be thinking who you're screwing on the side. You can't just put what happened into a little box and pretend there are no consequences. Sometimes I just don't understand you, Nick. All charm and wit, and yes ardour too, but now this.'

Sadie turned away, her head bowed. Nick moved towards her. He put an arm on her shoulder and pulled her to him. She didn't resist. She sobbed in his arms.

'I'm so sorry, Sadie. I can see how hurt you are.' He paused. 'Would you like me to leave? I completely understand if you want that.'

She turned towards him. Her expression was that of resignation. 'Yes, please go. I don't want to be near you.' She stepped back and went to the door, and was about to open it to let him out when she paused and looked at him.

'And one other thing. Do you remember our first meeting, eighteen months ago, when you first came to me after the harassment complaint was laid? I talked to you about crossing boundaries. Well, you haven't learned a thing since then, have you? Boundaries are there for a purpose, Nick. Stable relationships depend on them, as does the rule of law and the proper functioning of society. But you, you seem to think that the rules don't apply to you. But they do, and I hope for your sake you'll remember in the future. You think you go up to the line of acceptable behaviour, and don't cross it. But you do, time and time again. I just don't know if you're redeemable.'

Nick had nothing to offer in his defence. He gave a half-smile and shrugged his agreement. Sadie looked at him with what he later regarded as a look of angry incredulity, and opened the door without speaking again. He headed back out into the pouring rain and walked to Pimlico station.

He'd not seen her so angry before, nor so passionate. He felt terrible. He never liked causing distress or grief to others, but every so often he let people down. Occasionally by trying too hard to be funny or clever, or as a result of too much booze, but on other occasions wilfully and recklessly. He recalled the time that Kathy had found out, about four months after the debacle about her offer of a position in Edinburgh and a week before they were due to fly to Crete for a week of sun, sex and retsina, that Nick had been texting an old girlfriend from his days as a young lawyer in the City. The texts were mild and unflirtatious, but not to Kathy. Her rage and hurt were off any scale Nick had experienced before, even the newly minted Edinburgh one. She said she wouldn't let him travel with her. Instead she holidayed in Crete with a girlfriend. Their relationship ended soon after.

The westbound Circle Line train arrived, and Nick took a seat in a crowded carriage. Everyone was minding their own business, which suited him. He knew he'd been stupid, and hurtful, and Sadie was entirely within her rights to dump him. Yes, theirs was more than a friendship with benefits – they truly liked each other, without doubt, and he was sure that she looked forward to seeing him as much as he was keen to see her and spend time together, whether in the restaurant, the theatre or the bedroom.

Now he had jeopardised all that, for what? For a few romps with a woman he would never see again? For another notch, an ego-pleasing conquest?

He didn't want to lose his friendship – his rewarding, intimate relationship – with Sadie, but that looked highly likely now. His ingrained good manners required him to send her a message, to try to patch over the ghastly awkwardness of their brief encounter, but not for the first time in recent days he didn't know what to say. He tapped out a text as he alighted from the carriage: *I'm so sorry. I'll be in touch in a couple of weeks or so.* He decided against adding an 'x' at the end. He didn't want her to reply, nor did he expect her to. He hoped that things would have calmed down in two weeks. By then each would have a more measured take on the situation, and if that meant the end of their 'thing' then so be it.

Nick heard the ping of a text as he was looking for his door key. It was Sadie: *Don't bother.* He couldn't blame her.

He opened up WhatsApp on his phone. Adrienne had sent him three messages while he had been at Sadie's. He read them in the order they were received.

Hi there, got to our hotel by midnight last night. Told mom all about the weekend. She's dying to meet you at the wedding.

Merci bcp mille times for le weekend loved every minute of it must do it again next year haha this time mom wants to come with us xx.

This one was followed by a red heart emoji, and one of an aeroplane.

Let me know what you decide about williams papers please reserve all korean podcast rights for moi, and I want casting approval for the woman who plays me in le movie xxx.

Nick smiled. It had been little more than twenty-four hours since he'd seen her, and the intimacy, humour and – yes – vitality of her WhatsApps instantly transported him back to when they had been making love, holding hands as they toured Alicante, and to their last and memorable lunch in the courtyard across the plaza from the church. Perhaps Sadie was right: he *was* in love with her. He was definitely infatuated. Everything about Adrienne entranced him. How he wished that they could have had a few more days together. He closed his eyes and remembered the smoothness and fragrance of her skin.

Nick delighted in the moment, glad to free his mind after the difficult conversation with Sadie. He knew that the times with Adrienne were just frolics, albeit sensuous and stimulating ones, and it was right that she had already resumed her proper life trajectory. She would soon be back in her fiancé's arms – *lucky bastard* – and that was where she belonged.

Nick struggled to think of a suitable response to Adrienne's messages. He eventually came up with:

Muchas gracias senorita. Tu es absolument merveilleuse. I have Gemma pencilled in for you xx

It was a bit insipid but summarised his feelings accurately. Her reply came in in less than a minute:

De nada, mon vieux you are pas mal yourself. X

A minute later she sent a GIF of what appeared to be a Korean girl jumping up and down with her hand in the air, smiling broadly, and accompanied by three Korean characters he was unable to translate.

He felt tired now. He had a big day tomorrow, marking papers and writing reports, and lunch with the Dean.

Nick was glad to be back at his desk again. The academic year was almost over. No more lectures. Just marking exams and assignments, tidying up a few administrative and faculty matters, and doing a bit of planning for next term's lectures and subjects.

Peter Hargreaves had suggested it was time he and Nick had a good, long lunch. 'It's long overdue. Let's go to L'Escargot. I haven't been there for a year or more. Say one o'clock? We can get a taxi.'

Nick preferred brighter, more modern restaurants as a rule, but there was no denying L'Escargot's charm and old-world feel. The maître d' greeted Peter with a big grin and a *'Bienvenu, monsieur le professeur,'* to which Peter responded with noticeable delight. They were led to a corner table by the big red drapes. The red wall frames and the graceful, cascading chandeliers gave an impression of what Nick imagined Parisian café society would have been like in the 1920s. The large mirrors on two sides of the dining area amplified the sensation that they were in a different world and a different era. He could imagine Hem and Scottie sitting at their table, gossiping away about Ezra and Gertrude as they sipped on a glass of absinthe.

'I don't have anything planned for this afternoon, so I think we're entitled to indulge ourselves a bit.' Peter winked at Nick as he ordered a bottle of claret. 'It's been a long, arduous year. Two long years, in fact. It seems only yesterday that you and I had that difficult chat about the complaint from the Asian girl, but Lord, it must have been nearly eighteen months ago now. It's been all hands to the pump since. The summer holidays can't come soon enough.'

Nick smiled. Yes, it had been a 'difficult chat', and it had definitely been a busy few months recently. He too was looking forward to the break. The pleasure of the weekend in Alicante had been trampled on by his uncomfortable encounter with Sadie. Had they broken up? He didn't know for sure.

'Drink up, old boy.' Peter raised his glass. 'To another good year. To our men, as my old navy friends used to say on a Tuesday. Or should I say to our men and women?' They clinked glasses. 'Do you remember those staff surveys we had to fill in last month, as ordered by those faceless opportunists at the V-C's office? The 365-degree ones?' Peter snorted at the terminology now used throughout the University.

Nick did recall the surveys. Each member of the teaching faculty had to rate each other on topics such as collegiality, commitment to the University's values, adaptability, 'embracing differences', diversity, sustainability, research and publications.

Like most academics of his age and older, Nick thought the surveys were a joke, possibly part of a Trotskyist plot to obtain ammunition so that older lecturers might be put out to pasture. He had solved the problem of answering all the inane questions by giving everyone nine out of ten on every question. Everyone except Kathy. He gave her eight out of ten.

'Yes. Well, I've received the survey results. And also the results of the surveys the students were asked to fill out about their lecturers. It's been quite a revelation, I can tell you. Some of your colleagues have received dismal ratings, and it behoves me to talk to everyone individually to go through the results. I'm not looking forward to that. I'm afraid I can't tell you who those poor misfits are. But what I can tell you, Nick, is that *everyone* likes you. Across the board, men and women, young and old. There were one or two outliers, and we can guess who they might be, but you're undoubtedly our most highly esteemed faculty member. Or perhaps just the most popular. They even gave you high scores for publications and contribution to legal scholarship, even though I don't think you've published anything this year.'

Nick shook his head. Writing articles or text-books had never interested him.

'And I don't want you to get even more big-headed, but in the student survey you are miles ahead of the one in second position. Your average mark is 9.1 out of ten. The next best was 7.9. Well done, Nick. The old Crosser magic keeps on keeping on.'

Nick felt a bit embarrassed. He distrusted surveys, but was pleased nonetheless.

'So your job is safe for another year.' Peter took another swig of wine. 'I'm not sure I can say the same for mine. Apart from one kind person who gave me nine out of ten on all scores I got some terrible marks and some very hurtful comments. Especially on all these nebulous modern epithets like, God forbid, diversity, EQ, sustainability.' Peter rolled the words out with disdain. '"Past it", was one comment. "An old dinosaur". "Completely out of touch with the twenty-first century". "A sexist pig".' Peter's hand was shaking.

'I'm sorry to hear all that,' Nick said. 'It doesn't ring true to me. Perhaps a few of our more feminist colleagues have colluded to send you a message of sorts? I wouldn't worry about it.'

'But I'm afraid I do. It came as quite a shock. It certainly made me think. In fact, between you and me, I've decided to retire as Dean and leave the faculty before the next academic year starts. I'm sixty-five already, I've enough money saved up, and as it turns out I'm looking forward to retirement and spending more time in the vegetable garden and doing a bit more sailing.'

Nick was surprised. Peter had all the hallmarks of someone who would stay until his mid-seventies. 'Don't be too hasty, Peter. You still have a few good years left in you.'

'No, Nick, I don't think I do. I think now's the right time. What's more, you'll be perfectly placed to succeed me.'

'Seriously? You surprise me. I've never given much thought about wanting to be Dean. Lots of admin. Meetings, memos. Competition for funding with other faculties. Difficult chats with wayward staff members. I'm not sure I hanker after that. I prefer a less complicated life.'

'Well, think it over. The University Council will make the decision, and they'll need to do it in the next six weeks or so. Well before the start of the first semester. Do allow your name to go forward. I like to think that my recommendation will carry some sway. I'm confident the harassment complaint won't count against you. And the survey results, well, *res ipsa loquitur.* The thing speaks for itself. And you can't say that you'd not like having an extra twenty thousand a year.'

Nick smiled. 'Perhaps it's not such an awful job after all. I'll think about it and let you know in a couple of days.'

The waiter brought their first courses to the table. Nick had opted for the French onion soup, Peter the lobster bisque. 'There's one other thing I'd like to mention,' Peter said. 'You'll be aware how much London King's, all British universities, actually, depend on international students to fill up the coffers. A kind of reverse colonialism. Well, I was informed yesterday that only five per cent of the law faculty's students for the 2018/19 year were foreign, and the unpublicised target is twelve per cent. So, we need more Arab, Asian and African students. Simple as that. We've been asked to go forth and find them.'

Nick was beginning to sense where the conversation might be heading.

'This is where you come in. I'd like you to lead a delegation of two – we can discuss who the other will be, but it definitely won't be me – to Asia in the late summer or early autumn to publicise the faculty and the University with a view to drumming up some recruits. I envisage a two-week round trip. Beijing, Shanghai, Seoul, Tokyo, Hong Kong and Singapore. Taipei, too, if you can fit it in. Interesting places, and interesting people. And you'll be good at it, Nick. With your charm and manner you'll be a fine advocate for our faculty. In fact, I insist you do it, because believe it or not you already have a bit of a reputation in that part of the world.'

Nick gave him a bemused look.

'In the weekend I received an email from Charles Park. You'll remember him. He was the visiting lecturer five or six years ago, over from Korea. Anyway, he said he'd been listening recently to a Korean podcast about Koreans who had been conscripted to work as guards on the Death Railway in Burma and Thailand in the war. And, unbelievably, you get a couple of mentions as being a distinguished professor, and as possibly the leading scholar in the world – the world! – on the legal aspects of the war in South-east Asia. Remarkable coincidence. You simply can't buy publicity like that for the University. We might be able to arrange for you to give a couple of lectures over there. Crosser of the Far East. It has a nice ring to it.'

Nick thought of Adrienne, with her dancing eyes and Mona Lisa smile. She had kept very quiet about that podcast. He took a long swill, finishing his glass. 'I'd like that, Peter. It's not a part of the world I know well, but I do find Asian cultures fascinating.'

Peter laughed. 'By the way, what happened to Ms Kim? I know she finished her thesis, and got a high Merit for it too, I believe. As a graduate student she wouldn't have spent much time on campus, or at least in lectures. I can't even recall her first name. Andrea something?'

'Adrienne.' Nick instinctively wanted to tell the Dean that Adrienne was a fine student and a capable person of depth and sensitivity. 'I hear she went back to Korea, despite having lived in England for the last fifteen to twenty years. I'm sure she'll do well. She was very intelligent.'

'And hopefully she'll say nice things about London King's to her friends there. I do hope she wasn't jaundiced against us as a result of the alleged harassment and going through the complaints process. Presumably she dropped the complaint because wiser heads persuaded her your behaviour, your comment, was so innocuous.'

Nick said that he supposed Peter was right about that. As he tucked into his roast, Nick decided to seek his friend's advice about what he should do with William's writings about Hemingway. He spoke at length about the goblet, the monograph about the Hong Kong meeting, and the 1927 memoir and its contents. He didn't mention Adrienne's part in unearthing the materials. He spoke too about Andrew McGregor's keenness to publish.

Peter had the rare quality of being able to listen to long conversations and stories, even sensational one's like Nick's, without interruption. When Nick had finished, Peter, after a few seconds, said, 'Amazing.'

'Amazing?'

'Yes. I had no idea all of this was going on in your life. What a busy year and a half you've had. Successful too, I might add.'

Nick waited for him to continue, but nothing was forthcoming. Peter instead lifted a small carrot from his plate with his fingers and popped it into his mouth.

Nick had expected more from Peter without having to prise it out of him. 'And do you have a view on whether I should publish?' he asked at last.

Peter's gaze was cool. 'I'm surprised you even have to ask. I see it very clearly. You have to publish. You're in possession of new information, with authentic provenance, about one of the major literary figures of the last century. It will be of interest not just to Hemingway and American literature scholars, a large and noisy rabble if ever there were one, but to the reading public at large. Everyone knows of Hemingway. Millions around the world have read his books. In Spanish, German, Russian, probably even Mandarin and Swahili. There'll be a huge demand for what you have.'

Peter looked at the wine bottle, and then raised his eyebrows at Nick, who smiled. 'I think we need another bottle.' Peter gesticulated to the waiter.

'But there's a lot more to it, Nick. You owe it to your grandfather to set the record straight, to use his words. Sure, his memoirs will portray Ernest in a different light, but it will be a more honest one, don't you see? Hemingway's reputation will survive. He'll come through it all okay. His books are his legacy. Remember how law students are shocked to learn that law and justice are quite different things? That the application of the law and its processes often leads to injustices, innocent men being hanged and all that? Well, there's an analogy here. You have the opportunity, and I would say duty, to tell the world the truth about Hemingway the man and Hemingway the writer. It's serving justice to do that. Otherwise you'd be allowing a fraudulent and incorrect understanding to persist.' Peter raised his newly filled glass of St Emilion. 'No, the decision is not whether you publish or not. It's *how* you do it. Cheers.'

Nick felt a burden being lifted. 'Thank you, Peter. I admire your clarity of thought, your certainty. I've been troubled by self-doubt. But I now realise my reticence has been all about me. I mean, about what publication will mean for me. The distraction from my day job, my daily routine. The interviews and the publicity. The intrusions. Probably hostility from some quarters. Plus the negotiations about money. Not much of that appeals.'

'Yes, you'll have your time in the sun. But it'll pass. Anyway, I would've thought you'd rather relish the spotlight. You've never struck me as being backward about being forward. Quite the opposite, in fact. And you have to admit any money you earn will be useful. Neither of us has made a fortune out of academia.'

Nick nodded. Peter often grumbled about the low pay of lecturers. Nick reckoned that, as Dean, Peter would be earning just under a hundred thousand pounds, which Nick thought was more than decent. Peter often compared academic pay to the remuneration of the partners of law firms in the City, many of whom were earning over a million a year. 'And they were the less able ones at university, too,' he would note with a hint of bitterness.

Nick paused for a minute as he pondered the significance of Peter's reference to having a duty to publish the Hemingway memoirs. 'It's funny you should describe it as a duty, Peter, because only a month or two back I was reading a little memoir by A E Hotchner. It essentially consists of a recollection of various conversations Hemingway had with the young Hotchner during the great man's last decade or so of life. Some scholars say the recollections should be taken with a large pinch of salt. Anyway, in the introduction Hotchner mentioned a "fiduciary obligation" he felt he had to publish the recollections, as they added new information about Hemingway's marriages. It is interesting that he used a legal expression. He didn't specify whether the fiduciary duty was owed to Hemingway himself or to the reading public at large – probably a combination of the two. The situation isn't too different from my own predicament.'

'Yes, I can see the parallels there. I think you have no duty to Hemingway, but simply a moral one, to the literati and the readers of the world, to let the truth be out.'

Peter took a long drink from his wine, as though that was the end of that particular subject.

'Your Oxford friend Andrew seems to be sound, and I'm sure you would prefer that he rather than an American has the head start. I remember the fiasco of the Hitler Diaries in the early Eighties. What a disaster that was for the *Sunday Times*. I imagine they'll still be wary of forking out large sums for original materials dredged out of history without warning. Poor old Trevor-Roper's reputation never recovered. You'll need cast-iron affidavits of provenance from everyone involved. No one can risk publishing a forgery.'

Nick said he was confident that everything would stack up. He looked at his watch. It was 3.30 p.m. Peter settled the bill using his University credit card.

'And there's another benefit, too, Nick,' said Peter as they emerged into the remnants of the afternoon sun on Greek Street. 'Think of the additional recruiting pull you'll have in Asia, standing in front of dozens of potential students in China and Japan. Not just Dean of one of the UK's best law schools, but an international celebrity to boot. All of those pretty Asian girls will be swooning at your feet.'

Nick declined Peter's suggestion of a cleansing ale to finish the lunch. He had already resolved to write the afternoon off, but now he was in the fresh air he decided to try to shake off the alcohol by walking home. An hour or so of exercise would do him good, and there was much to think about.

33

Nick rang the bell at the top of the steps leading to Jo's house. He had told her the night before that he wouldn't be bringing Sadie for dinner this time.

'Why not, Nick? Is something wrong?'

'Well, it's a bit of a long story actually, but at the moment she and I aren't talking to each other.'

'Oh? Doesn't sound good.'

'No. It's all a bit unfortunate. I'll tell you all tomorrow.'

Jo opened the door. She had dyed her hair bright-red since he had last seen her, and he murmured 'Love the colour' as they hugged. Jo's house was roomy, double-storeyed and detached in a leafy street in Highbury. She led him into her sitting room, which doubled as a library, with thousands of books filling the shelves on three sides. The ceiling was high, seemingly designed to accommodate the bookcases.

Jo looked at him closely as he sat down holding the beer which she had brought him. 'Well? Do tell. Will I be seeing you and Sadie together again soon?'

Nick cleared his throat. Prevarication and dissembling would not work with Jo. She knew him too well, and he was aware that she and Sadie saw each other often. The thought flashed through his mind that they may even have spoken during the past few days.

'Well,' he began, looking at his beer and feeling embarrassed. 'I'm afraid I've mucked things up. Big time. You know how I spent the previous weekend in Spain, in Alicante?' Jo nodded.

'I spent the weekend there with Adrienne, the student who had accused me of harassment.' Jo's eyes narrowed. 'You'll remember she and I went on the fact-finding trip to Pamplona almost a year ago.' Jo nodded, barely. 'That was a completely platonic relationship, and she went back to live in Korea, where she's now engaged to be married.'

'I'm not liking the sound of this, Nick.'

'Nor am I, I'm afraid. Anyhow, she let me know that she was coming to Europe on a pre-wedding trip, as it were, and suggested a weekend with me, really to say goodbye. So we went to Alicante, as friends and certainly with no ulterior motive. I booked an Airbnb with separate bedrooms.'

'I think I know what's going to happen next. Did Sadie know about this rendezvous?'

'Yes, I told her, and she was pretty fair about it. Anyhow, one thing led to another, almost by accident' – Jo snorted – 'and we ended up sleeping together. Just a holiday fling, you could say. She's flown back to Korea. I'm back in England, and I'll probably never see her again.' Nick paused to take a swig on his beer, relieved to have now told Jo the story, or at least the spin on it which he had been rehearsing all day.

'And poor Sadie? Presumably you told her, or she found out about what you and that woman did?'

'Yes. I went to her place for dinner on Monday last week, the day after I returned from Alicante. She could see straightaway, women's intuition, that something was wrong, so I confessed. Yes, she was angry and hurt, and to cut a long story short she effectively hiffed me out the door. She's dumped me, at least I think she has. I'll contact her in a few days to see if there's a second chance, but I'm not sure there will be.' Nick looked up at Jo, his eyes wide and with a half-smile. 'And that's it.'

Jo had remained standing, her hands clasped together in front. She now moved a step or two closer to him. 'I can see how upset you are, little brother, so I won't give full vent to what I'm thinking at the moment. You've acted reprehensibly, and Sadie's perfectly justified in kicking you out. What a selfish, stupid thing to do. I told you Sadie was a treasure, a keeper.' Nick nodded. 'To put your relationship with her at risk because you were too weak to resist the charm of a pretty young woman. A former student, which is bad enough, but who is also engaged to someone else? Didn't you see all the ramifications?'

'I do now. I'm sorry, Jo. I'm one hundred per cent to blame. No doubt about that. And I know how much you like Sadie. Do you think you'll be able to stay friends?'

'I've no idea. I'll call her tomorrow, to give her my condolences, so to speak. She's an amazing woman, and I know how happy she was with you as her partner. And have you told Laura and your children? I think they all rather approved of you and Sadie as a long-term couple.'

'No, not yet. I'm catching up with Emily tomorrow. I'll let her know then.'

Eventually conversation moved to topics Nick found less excruciating to have to deal with. When he mentioned his agreement to allow his name to be considered for appointment as Dean of the law faculty Jo beamed and gave him a big hug. He saw no point in telling her that he was likely to make a recruiting trip to South-east Asia later in the year.

The silver goblet was on the mantelpiece. He got up from his armchair and walked over to it. Jo kept the goblet shiny and clean. 'To think it all started with this goblet,' he said. 'It's amazing to think that the great man himself held this very same goblet in his hands. You'll have to keep it polished for the cameras. I think it'll become quite famous.'

'So you've decided to publish? I thought you'd end up there eventually. I always thought hiding the papers away was a bone-headed idea. It's not as though you'd be protecting your own reputation, or our family's, by hiding Grandpa's work.'

'It was Peter Hargreaves, the current Dean, who persuaded me of that a few days ago. He said I had a *duty* to publish, a duty to the Hemingway scholars and to the readers of the world. They have a right to know the truth, Peter said. I think he's right.'

'I won't stand in your way. Make such arrangements as you see fit, but on the condition that you keep me out of it. No mention of my name, or address, or bookshop. You might as well take the goblet with you this evening when you go. I don't want cameramen and nosy journalists in my house.'

'I'll take it on loan and return it when the fifteen minutes are up. If I make any money then I'll account to you for half. Don't worry about that.'

'I know you will. Do you have a plan of action?'

'Not yet. First I need to speak to Andrew McGregor. He has some ideas of a series of articles in a prestige publication such as *Vanity Fair* or the *New Yorker*, or perhaps one of our broadsheets, with a TV tie-in, Netflix perhaps, or even the BBC. It's all very exciting. I'll tell you about his email about that shortly. I'll have to agree some kind of profit-sharing arrangement with him, and I have no feel on what that would look like. We'll need to appoint a literary agent to advise on how we should approach things and to negotiate contracts with magazine publishers and the like. They'll take their ten or fifteen per cent cut too. And possibly a PR agent to provide a buffer against press intrusions? Plus there will be expenses in getting things ready for publication. Come to think of it, there may not be any profit to hand out at all.'

Jo shrugged. 'It's not as though we've done anything to earn it.'

'I have had one idea, though. It's been quite an adventure tracking down Grandpa's papers. Starting with the goblet, then the prisoner-of-war diaries and letters, the visit to see Mary in Auckland, retracing Hemingway's steps in Pamplona, and tracking down old Beryl. I think there's quite a good story in there, and I'm minded to write it myself. I've always wanted to write something.'

'Good for you. But you've been writing law articles and reviews for yonks.'

'That's different. They're boring as hell. No, I have in mind something quite different. Either I do a straightforward narrative, which might be suitable for one of the Sunday colour supplements, or I might even make a little book out of it.'

'Go on.'

'Yes, I'm thinking of turning it into a novel, sticking to the facts, but sexing it up a bit, making it light-hearted, adding a bit of romance and mystery too. Introduce a few colourful characters, exotic locations, that sort of thing.'

Nick looked at Jo for some reassurance. None was forthcoming. 'Really?' she said. 'It does seem a bit odd, but in the right hands I suppose it could work. I could put you in touch with a couple of literary agents, friends of mine. They'll tell you whether you're bonkers or the new Antonia Byatt.'

Nick laughed. Jo had the knack of conveying criticism or scepticism in a manner which caused no offence.

He reached into his pocket for his phone and scrolled through it. 'Only this morning I got this email from Andrew. I think he sees it as the professional opportunity of his career. I'm afraid it's a bit long.' Jo smiled. He began to read.

'Welcome back, my learned friend. I trust the Alicante sun has bleached your dark views away and you are now back to reality. I have been thinking more about your grandfather's papers. I think a combined magazine/TV deal, 5 or 6 articles accompanied by the same number of 30–45 minute programmes (fronted by yours truly) should be worth about US$5 million. We'll split it down the middle, as I'll be doing most of the work. Plus, I've sketched out five article headings. That way we drip-feed all the revelations, to maintain momentum and maximise the moolah.'

By now Jo was laughing. Andrew, who Jo had met a few times over the years, was playing true to form.

Nick continued. 'Topic 1: The quest for the Papers. E.g. the goblet, the throwaway line in the POW diary, your visit to your Aunt Mary, the mystery of who Beryl was, the *tarjeta* photo. Topic 2: *The Sun Also Rises* revisited. Topic 3: 'Was Ernest Hemingway as original and creative as we have always thought?' Topic 4: 'EH's character re-examined.' A discussion of all of the new titbits about EH and his friends, his moods, his drinking, was he a wife-beater?, the Chinese prostitutes, his relationships with his wives, etc. Topic 5: Hadley Hemingway in a new light. Was she battered by EH? Did she have an affair with your grandfather? Why was she not included in TSAR? As you can see, there's a lot of meat in here. Each article will require a ton of research by me, interviews with scholars etc. I can't tell you how exciting this is for us, Nick. We'll be famous, and we'll be able to live well for the rest of our lives. Talk soon. Andrew.'

Jo looked impressed. 'Yes, it certainly does have major possibilities,' she said. 'I think you'd thrive on the publicity, and the money would certainly be nice.'

In the taxi back to Notting Hill he held the goblet tightly, wrapped in a tea towel inside a Waitrose bag. Jo had also put in there the contact details of her two agent friends. Nick felt good about where things were heading. Jo had been reasonably easy on him over Adrienne and Sadie when she could have excoriated him all night. And new adventures awaited in several directions. He had returned from Alicante ten days ago, but the sensations and memories remained vivid.

He wondered where Adrienne was now. By his reckoning she should have been back in Korea for several days, no doubt waking up every day in the arms of the sex-deprived Bobby.

While his mood continued to be upbeat about so many

things, the rupture of his relationship with Sadie nagged away at his conscience. He was acutely aware he'd treated her like shit. He had breached their unspoken understanding of exclusivity, and she was entirely within her rights to feel hurt and angry. It mattered nothing that he wished her no harm or unhappiness.

Several times he was on the brink of sending her a conciliatory text, a suggestion of a coffee on neutral ground, but each time he decided not to press Send. He was keen too to discuss with her the possibility that he might be promoted to Dean of the law faculty. Her take on it would be full of insight.

After a few more days he texted her:

I hope you're still talking to me. I've been asked to put my name forward for dean at the law faculty. Any advice?

The reply came the next morning:

I assume you are joking.

Nick was irritated. Her message was obtuse, which was not a good sign.

Joking about what? About you talking to me or about me being dean?

This time the reply was swift:

Both.

Dear old Sadie, he thought. Pithy and to the point, as ever. It would be futile now to try to patch up things. Perhaps in a matter of months she might be willing to be friendly again. Or perhaps not.

That evening, as he sat in his apartment cradling a glass of sauvignon blanc, he mulled over his feelings for Sadie. He couldn't think of a bad word to say about her. It didn't help his mood that that was the same as he felt about Laura. He thought of Oscar Wilde, wasting away in prison in Reading: 'Yet each man kills the thing he loves.' Nick had never appreciated the relevance of those words before. He began to examine his life and character in a broader sense. Two glasses of sauvignon could often make him maudlin and introspective, and this was one of those occasions. Was Sadie right in making all those accusations and critical comments?

He knew that these big questions would never receive any serious examination while his mind was muddled by the wine. He resolved to head to Hampstead Heath in a couple of days, to take in the fresh air and to appreciate the wide expanses. In the meantime he was looking forward to seeing Emily for lunch tomorrow.

34

Nick waved as Emily swept into the restaurant. She was in faded denim blue jeans and a white T-shirt, her satchel riding off her right shoulder. Her blonde hair was tied back in a pony-tail. She looked like any other first-year university student, impossibly young and a little bewildered.

Emily hugged her father. 'Sorry I'm a bit late. Legal System ran on a couple of minutes extra. We learned about promissory estoppel today. Hardly understood a word.'

Nick laughed. 'Yes, it's difficult stuff, that's for sure. Anyhow, how are you? Things going well?'

'Yes, everything's great, but I'm struggling a bit with all the assignments coming in thick and fast. But enough about me. How was the Costa Blanca? You're looking as though you've had an expensive tanning session.'

'It was terrific, thanks. We had a great time. Alicante's such a beautiful city. Two days wasn't enough.'

'Adrienne WhatsApped me some pics of you in your swimming togs. Hi-vis green eh, Dad? At least you won't get lost wearing them. She texted me later, from Paris. Said you guys had a real fun time.'

'I dare say that's one way of putting it. We certainly packed a lot in in a short time.' He described the touristic aspects of their visit.

'How did you get on with Adrienne? I'm dying to hear. I know she was a bit nervous of seeing you again, after such a long time. After everything. But definitely looking forward to seeing you.'

'Well, if you must know, we got on like a house on fire. She's a character and a half, as you know, and she's not short of energy when it comes to doing things.'

'Yes, I know that. But on a personal level, how was it? She says she gave you a bit of a hard time. Do tell me all about that.'

Nick shifted uncomfortably in his seat. 'A hard time? I wouldn't say that. We had a long D&M conversation at the end. You could say we cleared the air, after that difficult business last year. She's headed off back to Korea to get married, and that's very exciting for her. I can assure you we parted as the best of friends. Anyway, we should order our meals. The usual?'

Emily nodded, and Nick ordered lasagne and the quinoa salad.

'It's funny, but Adrienne and I are pretty close, despite the fact she's years older than me. We've been messaging for yonks, well over a year. I was dying to tell you that last year, but she asked me to keep it a secret. I'm relieved she told you in Alicante.'

'Really? Well, in a funny way I'm glad. I'm so grateful for your going to see her in the first place. Apparently you said nice things about me. Whatever you said it was enough to make her withdraw her support for the complaint.'

'Yes, so it seems. Can I tell you what I thought after meeting Adrienne?'

Nick nodded as the waiter placed their plates on the tables. 'I reckoned that Adrienne was emotionally involved, half in love with you. It was more than respect and admiration for you as her lecturer and supervisor, she spoke in awe of you as a person. She called you "amazing". It confused me.'

'I can imagine. But no, I don't think she was in love with me, then or subsequently.' Emily looked up from her salad. He continued: 'She's definitely one of a kind, a special person, and a good friend to both of us.' He smiled at the incongruity of the thought.

They paused while they ate. The restaurant was now full of London King's students and academics. 'Slight change of subject, Dad. How's Sadie? She must have found it a bit weird that you'd have a weekend together with another woman. If I were in her position ...'

Nick toyed with his fork for a second or two. 'I'm afraid she's reacted badly. Before the weekend she didn't seem to mind, or not too much anyway, but when I got back she was very upset and angry. The end result is that she's dumped me.'

'What? You can't be serious. Sadie thinks the world of you. On the few occasions we've met that's been obvious. Even Mum, after my eighteenth birthday dinner in April, said you and she made a great couple. Do you remember that Mum and Sadie spent over half an hour chatting to each other? Mum told me later that she was giving Sadie advice about all your foibles and bad habits.' Emily looked her father in the eyes. 'Something's missing, Dad. Are you telling the full story? Did something happen in Alicante? Between you and Adrienne?'

Nick hesitated and looked down at his lasagne. 'I wasn't planning on telling you, but yes, something did happen. Unintentionally, and almost by accident, something did happen. You can guess what.'

Emily nodded, her eyes wide. 'Unintentionally?'

'Well, after a fashion. And Sadie realised that something had happened, and that's that, I'm afraid. I was stupid, and yes, I know it was unfair on Adrienne, and Sadie was completely justified in giving me my marching orders.'

'God, Dad. What a disaster.' Nick braced himself for a lambasting, but it didn't come. 'Well I won't judge you. I'm devastated about you and Sadie, and it's awful for her, but I can't blame you for being attracted to Adrienne. She's one real cool lady. She always knows what she wants, and as far as I can tell she usually gets it.'

'Emily, are you suggesting that Ad—'

'Open your eyes, Dad. She set out to sleep with you. She even texted me a week before you went to Alicante, said you were a real babe and that you and she would have a great weekend together.'

'I had no idea. That does put a different complexion on things, that's for sure.' He scrunched up his forehead. 'Still, that doesn't help me with Sadie.'

'No, it doesn't. And it doesn't excuse your lack of self-control. As a friend of Adrienne's I won't give you a hard time about it. But she would no doubt say *c'est la vie*.'

'Thank you, Emily. I love you very much, you know.'

'Whatever.'

There were now only a few days until the formal end of the academic year. The University was almost empty of students. Removal men were clearing out the offices of leaving lecturers and taking away exam papers to a storage location on the outskirts of London. The days were longer and the air warmer. The summer beckoned.

Nick called his friend in Oxford. 'Andrew, I've got some good news for you. Yes, we'll publish and we'll be damned.'

Andrew whooped with delight down the phone. Nick could hear Andrew's wife Jane in the background asking what the fuss was about.

'We need to get together to talk it all through. Perhaps I could visit you in Oxford for the weekend.'

'Absolutely, maestro. Name the day. The red carpet awaits. I'm so excited.'

'Great. Let me lay out a few thoughts, ground rules as it were. First, confidentiality is essential until we're ready. Second, we need to appoint a literary agent to handle things for us.

Someone well connected, and tough too. My sister's offered me a couple of names. Third, you can handle all the contents of my grandfather's memoirs. Articles, TV programmes, lectures, whatever. You're the Hemingway expert, not me. But I want to reserve for myself the rights to the story of how the papers came to light. I think that may have legs of its own.'

'Not a problem, Nick. All yours. For whom the legs toil, and all that.'

'Quite. And we'll need to talk money too at some stage. The division of the spoils. I suggest we park that topic for a while. We can let our agent give us guidance on what we should do there. I know that you and I'll never fight over money.'

'Definitely not, boyo. We'll enjoy a farewell to alms.'

They made plans for Nick to travel to Oxford the following weekend.

It was now three weeks since Nick had returned from Alicante. Nick thought of giving Laura a call, to suggest a dinner together, just for old times' sakes, but in the end decided to wait a few months before doing that.

It was also three weeks since he had been messaging with Adrienne. During that time she had posted a few photos of Alicante (but not of her or Nick) on Instagram, and also a few of exotic-looking Korean restaurant dishes. He waited until he saw that she was online on WhatsApp and telephoned her.

'*Que pasa*, my former fiancée?' Adrienne laughed. 'It's great to hear your voice. I thought you'd given up on me, or at least ghosted me.'

'Sorry, I've been pretty busy, but there's lots to report. But first, how are you? You must be pleased to be back with Bobby.'

'Yes, I certainly am. He's so cute and adorable. He waits on me twenty-four seven. At times he's practically drooling over me. I think I should be able to hold him off until our wedding night. A little over four months to go now.' Nick and Adrienne both laughed. He had never been sure that Adrienne was telling

304

the truth about Bobby's passions being unrequited.

She talked about her podcasts, her wedding plans and her mother. She seemed to have settled straight back into her previous life. He was glad for her.

'Sadie and I have broken up, by the way.'

'What? Oh Nick, I'm so sorry to hear that. I know you were so into her. What was it you called her? One to grow old with, and you would never be bored?'

'Something like that.'

'I hope it wasn't because of me. Tell me it wasn't, Nick.' There was an urgency in her voice.

'No, it wasn't, my dear friend. It was one hundred per cent about me.' Rarely had he said truer words. 'So don't worry yourself.'

'Whew. Still, I'm very sad for you. I send you a kiss to soothe you. A Korean kiss.'

A Korean kiss. He changed the subject and told her about the decision to publish William's memoir and monograph, and also that he liked her idea of writing a novel about it all. She cackled with approval.

'I'm so glad you're going to publish. Your grandfather's papers will make a good story. I've been thinking about how I could help. Not sure there's much I can do from over here. Still, you never know.'

Nick laughed. 'Don't you worry, my dear Adrienne. Everything is well in hand.'

'Oh, and one other thing, Nick. Did you know that yesterday was the cut-off date for me filing a complaint over the harassment incident?'

Nick's heart seemed to miss a beat. 'The *alleged* harassment you mean. I didn't even know you knew about the eighteen-month period. Surely you haven't lodged a complaint? Please say you haven't.'

'Well, Kathy has been sending me a few texts over the past

year, encouraging me to do it. The last one came in only a week ago. But no, Nick, I've let it pass. You suffered enough at the time, and I feel bad about that. And now I think you're wonderful. You've redeemed yourself.' Nick could imagine Adrienne smiling at his discomfort.

'Well, thank God for that,' said Nick.

He didn't mention his candidacy to be appointed Dean. It wasn't such a big deal and meant little outside the academic world. 'But guess what? I'll be heading out your way in September. I'll be doing a whistle-stop tour of Asian capitals, trying to sell London King's and the law school to rich Asian students. I'll be visiting Seoul, too.'

Adrienne was enthusiastic. 'Could you postpone it to include my wedding, in early November?'

'No, sorry. Not possible with lecture timetabling. I'm afraid I'll have to miss the wedding.'

Adrienne sounded disappointed, but he sensed not too surprised.

'I'm thinking about taking a weekend off in Seoul. It would be lovely to see you. You can tell me all about your wedding plans and I'll tell you all about our publishing plans.'

Adrienne let out a shrill shriek, 'What a brilliant idea. I'd love to see you. I'll be able to travel up to Seoul. We can stay in a fancy five-star hotel, with a spa and room service, with wide views over the city, and I can show you around. No funny business, though. I *am* engaged after all, you know.'

Afterwards, when he had put the phone down, Nick couldn't stop smiling. The future was not so bleak after all.

35

Four weeks after Nick had spoken to Adrienne he was awakened by the persistent ring on his telephone.

'Andrew? Why are you calling at this godawful time?' Nick looked at his watch. It was 7 a.m.

'A disaster, my friend. The news is out. There's an item in the *Guardian* this morning. I assume you haven't seen it? It quotes a source in South Korea which is reporting that a major announcement about Hemingway is expected soon, which will transform the way the world sees him. It refers to the fact that some contemporary materials have surfaced and are in the hands of someone living in London. It has to be your materials they're referring to.'

Nick took some time to register his friend's news. 'Well, I'm gobsmacked.'

'Me too. God knows how your find got out, and God knows how the story has surfaced in Korea, of all places. Apparently there was a blind item on an obscure blog, dedicated to a Korean true crime series, which simply said that publication of the Hemingway materials would be forthcoming, but the people behind the blog would not be involved in the publication and wouldn't be giving any further information.'

'You mean, it's just a bit of attention-grabbing advance publicity for what you and I will be doing, without giving any details?'

'Yes, my learned friend, I think that's exactly what it is. So perhaps we shouldn't be concerned. Still, it's worrying that the story, or at least a precursor to it, is out there. We need to speed up our efforts to get publication underway.'

'I agree. I'll dig up the article myself to see if I take anything different from it. On the face of it we have now received some priceless PR.'

Later, after reading the *Guardian* article and a similar one in the *Telegraph*, Nick sent a WhatsApp message to Adrienne. It consisted of three big red heart emojis.

THE END

AUTHOR'S NOTE

I appreciate that I risk scorn and criticism from many quarters by aiming my sights at Ernest Miller Hemingway. The trouble with being Ernest is that he is such a huge target. Everything about his personality and life protrudes well above the highest of literary parapets. This is all the more so in the twenty-first century, when social attitudes and norms of acceptable behaviour have moved so far from those that prevailed almost a hundred years ago.

Readers should not think that I dislike Hemingway, nor that I think that his place in the literary pantheon is undeserved. Far from it. His novels were ground-breaking, and they remain readable and admirable to this day. I read *The Old Man and the Sea* and *For Whom the Bell Tolls* in my teens, and devoured Carlos Baker's classic biography at the age of nineteen. Hemingway's works made a mark on my young mind, and the details of his personality remain vivid.

Readers, especially those not familiar with *The Sun Also Rises*, will ask what is true and what is fabricated in Nick's grandfather's monograph and memoir. Hemingway was definitely in Burguete, Pamplona and Hong Kong at the times William encountered him. Hadley, Duff and the others were also there in Spain in 1925 with Ernest as indicated in my story. And so how much is true? The answer is that William is a fictional character, and every action and conversation involving him is the product of my imagination. My intention has been to allow the reader to think that it *could* be true, knowing what we do. Ernest is undoubtedly one of the most researched and best documented writers of all time.

The *tarjeta* photo exists, in the JFK Library in Boston. It is printed on heavy paper, like a postcard. However the exhibition in Pamplona where Nick and Adrienne first saw the photo is fictional, and the Guernica exhibition in San Sebastian was in 2019 and not, as the book suggests, in 2018. London King's University does not exist. All of the World War Two references to William are fictional.

I was led to this storyline when I read Lesley M.M. Blume's *Vanity Fair* May 2016 article about the visit of Ernest and Hadley and their friends to Pamplona in 1925. What a riot of intrigue and excess Ms Blume documented. I got hold of the hilariously informative *Everyone Behaves Badly*, from which the *Vanity Fair* article was excerpted. An idea for a book came to my mind, a coarser and more satirical one.

I read many other books during my research. These were particularly helpful:

The Hemingway Log by Brewster Chamberlin.
The Letters of Ernest Hemingway (vol 2 1923–1925) edited by Sandra Spanier, Albert J Defazio III and Robert W Trogdon.
Unbridled Dreamer: Hemingway and the Rise of Modern Literature, Volume 1 by Wylie Graham McLallen.
Hemingway in Love by A.E. Hotchner.
Reading Hemingway's The Sun Also Rises by H.R. Stoneback.

I learned much from Mary Gaitskill's acclaimed novella *This is Pleasure*, published in the 8 July 2019 edition of *The New Yorker*. Her insightful descriptions of a man of a certain type – outwardly charming and successful, but in reality a narcissist, manipulative and deceptive in his relationships with women – helped me shape Nick's character.

Every book depends on so many people giving their time, expertise or advice, and often all three at once. This one is no different. Stephen Stratford and Graeme Lay, both straight-faced, gave initial encouragement to an ill-formed and fanciful plotline. Heidi Wong generously gave me a guided tour of the suites and archive room of the Peninsula Hotel in Kowloon. James B Hill of the John F Kennedy Presidential Library and Museum in Boston gave me information about the *tarjeta* photo, and sent me a good copy of it too.

Shelley Truman and Mary McCallum read early drafts and gave me honest and valuable feedback which was in many ways distressing to absorb. Ginny Holgate, like me a lawyer writing a first novel, gave me helpful criticism and several ideas which I incorporated. Graeme Lay kindly offered me a number of pointers after reading a late draft. My long-suffering secretary Delwyn Diaz-Rodriguez patiently deciphered my scribblings to produce the manuscript, and several drafts too. Yuen Mon Kei gave me many insights into the culture and thinking of young Asians.

Above all, my patient wife Sheena allowed me the time to research and to write the book. She generously tolerated my absences on weekends and holiday mornings as I did my work. She contributed in a major way to various aspects of the plot.

Finally, I am grateful to my friend and editor Stephen Stratford, who was not too hard on me. The book is vastly better for his wise and sensitive input. Stephen died tragically young in November 2021, only a few months after completing the editing of this book. His loss was a tragedy for his family and friends and a sad blow for the New Zealand literary community. Since his death I have made a number of revisions to the manuscript, to take into account comments of others and more reflection on my part. Stephen has no responsibility for the finished product, but if the book receives any praise then much of it belongs to him. Nikki Crutchley gave the final manuscript a detailed and insightful copy edit, and made many helpful suggestions about the plot and characterisation.